RICHIE TANKERSLEY CUSICK

THE UNSEEN 2

BLOOD BROTHERS

·

SIN AND SALVATION

D0061604

speak

An Imprint of Penguin Group (USA) Inc.

Danger.

Lucy tried to pull free. *No more visions! Make them stop!*

But the stranger's hand squeezed tighter, sending a chaos of sensations to her very core.

Burning like the moon, red just like the moon, burning eyes, burning lips, burning souls—

"Is he?" she heard him ask again. "Is Byron *dead?*"

Lucy felt the walls sway around her, the stones shift beneath her feet. For one brief second the young man's eyes actually seemed to change color, black and amber fusing together in a liquid, luminous glow—yet she convinced herself it was only a trick of her own unshed tears. She tried to answer him—*wanted* to answer him—but her thoughts were all muddled, and she was so hot, and he was holding her so tight . . . *so tight . . .*

"Yes." *Don't make me say it—I can't bear to say it!* "Yes! He's dead!"

"You're sure?"

Memories stabbed through her head, pierced through her heart. "If you were really his brother, you wouldn't be asking me these questions! If you were really his brother, you'd already know—"

THE UNSEEN

THE
UNSEEN

PART THREE: BLOOD BROTHERS

SPEAK

Published by the Penguin Group

Penguin Group (USA) Inc., 345 Hudson Street, New York, New York 10014, U.S.A.

Penguin Group (Canada), 90 Eglinton Avenue East, Suite 700, Toronto, Ontario, Canada M4P 2Y3
(a division of Pearson Penguin Canada Inc.)

Penguin Books Ltd, 80 Strand, London WC2R 0RL, England

Penguin Ireland, 25 St Stephen's Green, Dublin 2, Ireland (a division of Penguin Books Ltd)

Penguin Group (Australia), 250 Camberwell Road, Camberwell, Victoria 3124, Australia
(a division of Pearson Australia Group Pty Ltd)

Penguin Books India Pvt Ltd, 11 Community Centre, Panchsheel Park, New Delhi - 110 017, India

Penguin Group (NZ), 67 Apollo Drive, Rosedale, Auckland 0632, New Zealand
(a division of Pearson New Zealand Ltd)

Penguin Books (South Africa) (Pty) Ltd, 24 Sturdee Avenue,
Rosebank, Johannesburg 2196, South Africa

Penguin Books Ltd, Registered Offices: 80 Strand, London WC2R 0RL, England

First published in the UK by Scholastic Ltd, 2005
First published in the United States of America by Speak, an imprint of Penguin Group (USA) Inc., 2006
This omnibus edition published by Speak, an imprint of Penguin Group (USA) Inc., 2012

1 3 5 7 9 10 8 6 4 2

LIBRARY OF CONGRESS CATALOGING-IN-PUBLICATION DATA
Cusick, Richie Tankersley.
Blood brothers / Richie Tankersley Cusick.
p. cm.—(The unseen ; pt. 3)
Summary: A stranger claiming to be Byron's brother appears, horribly wounded,
and throws Lucy's life into further turmoil.
ISBN 0-14-240583-3 (pbk.)
[1. Supernatural—Fiction. 2. Mistaken identity—Fiction.] I. Title.
PZ7.C9646Blo 2006 [Fic]—dc22 2005051630

Speak ISBN 978-0-14-242337-0

Set in Perpetua Regular

Printed in the United States of America

To Anne with love—for saving
me so many times
in so many different ways . . .

Thank you, my friend
You will always be my better half.

Prologue

He'd had to think quickly.

After this last kill he'd been so gorged, so utterly exhausted from frenzy and frustration, he'd been unable to return to his bed. He'd been forced to seek out another hiding place . . . and then he'd crept inside and he'd slept.

Slept far past his normal hour of waking . . .

Slept right through the day . . . into the night . . .

Slept the fathomless sleep of the dead.

He'd never seen the attack coming.

Never awakened fully, even, until the first hot spurt of blood, the first scream of ripping flesh, the whole world exploding in a thick, wet fountain of scarlet and black.

He had no idea which of them had struck the first blow. Or when instinct had taken ahold of him, every primal sense honed for survival, no matter what the pain, no matter what the cost . . .

He did not remember which had been the last to fall . . .

He was only and finally aware of the silence and the peace. The wind upon his face, the snow upon his lips. He was thirsty, yet could not seem to drink. He needed warmth and shelter, yet could not seem to move.

He was in desperate agony, yet could not help himself.

And so he lay there, stunned and weakened, too sick to lick his wounds. Until at last, and like a dream, the sound of quiet footsteps had floated through his mind . . .

He heard them from a distance, moving closer and closer, phantom footsteps of no real concern, no imminent danger. But as he struggled to comprehend them, he realized these footsteps were no dream at all.

They were real, and they were human.

They were coming toward the burial place, dangerously close to where he rested.

And so he'd had to think quickly.

Think quickly and act with haste.

Transform to a shadow? Mist? A guise of the living, a memory of the dead?

Or, in one swift, smooth motion, ready himself to strike again?

But then he paused, consumed by an ache so deep he had not even realized he moaned.

For now he saw this was no enemy.

Now he realized this was Lucy—*his Lucy*— approaching him unaware and unsuspecting, steeped in grief and sorrow as he had always known her.

And yet . . . different somehow.

Unsettlingly different, somehow.

He could feel it, as sharply as he could feel the rats cowering around him, their ears twitching in fear, their glowing eyes averted from his own, their teeth stained red from the remnants of his meal and the raw meat of his wound. And he could smell it, too—as surely as he smelled the slow and steady creeping of decay, the lingering despair of so many wasted lives rotting in the graves around him.

No, Lucy was not quite the same as before.

Something had changed since he'd last laid eyes upon her.

Despite her confusion, there was now resolve.

And amid her fear and helplessness burned a new strength—small yet, to be sure, but solid with determination.

How interesting, he thought . . . *and how curious.*

And also how very delightful.

So delightful, it made him smile, despite his anguish.

He couldn't help wondering what had happened—*one incident? or many?*—to touch her at such a profound level in so short a time.

But no matter.

This newfound strength of Lucy's would only serve to make the Game more interesting. More challenging. More worth winning.

So he'd narrowed his eyes and waited.

Waited until her footsteps were practically upon him.

Until, in one more second, Lucy would be at the gates of the mausoleum, peering into the shadows of the tomb, stepping across that crumbling threshold between life and death.

Could he take her? As this desperate need for her surged through every vein, filling him with brief and savage power?

Yes . . . yes! Take her now!

But he did not.

He thought quickly instead.

And felt that explosive rush of skin and muscles shifting, features rearranging, as quick as a heartbeat, as natural as breath.

So now he could listen.

Stay close and watch.

And like so many times before, Lucy would never even know.

1

She hadn't expected the cemetery to look so spooky at this hour of the morning.

Like wandering phantoms, tatters of soft white mist hovered among the graves, and an unnatural quiet smothered the sound of Lucy's footsteps as she made her way to the remote section of the burial grounds. The dead slept deep and undisturbed. Remembered and forgotten alike, they surrounded her on all sides, rotting peacefully to dust.

In the distance, the Wetherly mausoleum came darkly into view, silhouetted against the gloom. As Lucy got nearer, she could see the wrought-iron gates and stone angels that guarded it, and for one unsettling moment, she remembered her dream about Byron and his warning.

"Keep away . . . there's no one in this place."

An icy shudder worked its way up her spine. Hesitating, she dug her hands into her coat pockets and glanced back over her shoulder.

Come on, Lucy, get a grip.

It was easy to imagine eerie whispers and invisible watchers in a creepy place like this—what had she been thinking anyway, coming here so early?

Stop scaring yourself. Nobody here can hurt you.

Giving herself a stern mental shake, she walked over to the front of the tomb. To her surprise, the double gates weren't padlocked as she'd assumed they'd be—in fact, they were standing partway open, one of them creaking rustily as the breeze swung it back and forth.

Heart quickening, Lucy glanced around a second time.

If someone *were* here, they'd be impossible to see, she admitted to herself. Anyone could be hiding close by or far away.

Lucy suppressed another shiver.

Turning in a slow circle, she scanned the graves and headstones, the sepulchres and statues, the trees and shadows and mist. A taste of fear crept into her throat, and she tried to choke it down.

Cautiously, she turned back to the gates.

Taking one in each hand, she eased them open the rest of the way. Cracks had widened along the foundation, and leaves had sifted in over the broken, weathered stones of the floor.

Holding her breath, Lucy walked into the crypt.

She saw the muddy footprints and tufts of clotted hair, the dark, reddish-brown stains smeared along the walls . . .

But she didn't see the figure behind her.

Not till she turned and screamed and stumbled from his arms, trying wildly to fight her way free.

And then she stared up, shocked, into eyes as black and deep as midnight.

"Oh my God," she choked. "Who are you?"

The dark-haired young man gazed coolly back at her.

"Byron's brother," he answered. "Who the hell are *you*?"

2

He could almost have *been* Byron.

The likeness was so incredible that for one wild moment Lucy actually glanced around at the walls of the mausoleum, as though Byron himself might have stepped from his burial place to stand before her now.

And yet, in one swift moment of scrutiny, she could see that there were differences. Differences not only obvious, but subtle as well—differences she felt certain of but couldn't totally define. Even in that moment of shock, Lucy sensed a sadness even more complicated than Byron's, and a raw sensitivity far beyond any that Byron had ever shown.

She wanted to look away but was transfixed. At first glance, she'd mistaken his eyes for that same midnight black that Byron's had been, but now that she was closer, she could see they were actually a deep amber color, surrounding unusually large black pupils. The effect of this was a wide, unwavering stare that Lucy found both disturbing and fascinating, and as he held her gaze, she noted that his eyes never blinked.

Lucy guessed him to be about the same height and weight as Byron, with the same lean build. His face was less rugged, his cheekbones every bit as prominent, his nose more slender, his features slightly more delicate. He had a high forehead and low curved brows, the same faint beard shadow along his jaws and chin and upper lip. His perfectly shaped mouth looked both sensuous and seductive; his dark straight hair, parting naturally in the middle, fell to just below his ears.

Weary shadows rimmed his eyes. Shadows like bruises, hollowing his cheeks and accentuating the unnatural ghost-white pallor of his skin. And slashing downward from his left ear to the right side of his chin was a long, jagged scar that seemed very deep and very old.

In this quick instant of observation, two bizarre thoughts flashed unexpectedly into Lucy's mind.

That he was perhaps the most beautiful young man she'd ever seen in her entire life.

And that he and Byron could have been magically superimposed, like two photographs layered together, forming a familiar, yet brand-new face.

"Byron . . ."

Without even realizing it, she whispered the name. And though the stranger's gaze had seemed to stop time, Lucy jolted back to awareness, realizing that only seconds had passed.

Realizing he *wasn't* Byron.

This stranger, this bold trespasser standing before her now, *wasn't* Byron, could *never* be Byron. Byron was dead, Byron was out of her life forever, Byron had no brother or she would have *known*; he would have *told* her. It was all too much—too much to absorb, too much to process—and suddenly Lucy realized that she was having trouble breathing, that her throat was closing up.

"Who are you?" she heard the young man ask again, but his voice was like a dream, and Lucy couldn't answer.

She felt as if she was suffocating. The air in

the mausoleum was thick and heavy, settling over her like folds of velvet, crushing her with a sweetness that was almost sickening.

She knew that sweetness.

She'd smelled it before, that cloying fragrance of allure and elusion, but where was it coming from now? It hadn't been in the mausoleum when she'd gotten here—*had it?* Could she have somehow not realized?

Turning, she looked down at the dark red stains upon the stones, the clotted hair along the floor. Her mind reeled backward, back to the cave and back to her terror. *Dark splatters over the ground . . . dark smears trailing back into the tunnel where light couldn't reach . . .*

No, it's not the same, she tried to convince herself. *This grisly scene has nothing to do with the other: this was just some stray animal, this can be explained.*

But she was starting to feel light-headed and confused. Was this the scent of blood? The aftermath of fear? The lingering odor of death?

"What do you want?"

Had the stranger spoken aloud just now? Had *she?*

Lucy put her hands to her temples and tried

to concentrate. Bring herself back into focus. He was still staring at her, as though he didn't even notice the sweet, sultry odor enclosing them. What was wrong with him? Surely he could smell it—how could he not smell it?

Yet even as she started to mention it to him, the sweetness was already fading. And then a cold, raw breeze snaked through the tomb, and the fragrance vanished completely.

But the young man hadn't gone. The young man hadn't disappeared with the blast of the wind; he was still here, gazing down at her with a frown more curious than threatening.

Brother . . .

The word whispered softly through her head. Once again she wondered if one of them had spoken, or if the thought had simply crept unbidden into her subconscious.

"You didn't know?" His lips were moving now. His voice was deep like Byron's . . . soft like Byron's . . .

Brother . . . of course . . . that would explain the resemblance . . .

"You're not Byron's brother," Lucy said.

Her voice was strong with resolve, with a

defiance that surprised her. And then came the anger, fierce and possessive, rushing through her like fire. How dare this stranger encroach into Byron's resting place—how dare he claim Byron's name! Her insides were trembling, grief transformed to protective rage, as though she were facing down something evil that had crept onto hallowed ground.

She lifted her chin, fists clenched tightly at her sides. "Byron doesn't *have* a brother."

"Is that what he told you?" the young man countered. He sounded exhausted, too empty for any sort of emotion.

"Yes, he—"

Lucy stopped, suddenly unsure. What *had* Byron told her? He'd talked about Katherine and his grandmother, about himself when he was a child.

He'd never said anything about having a brother.

But then again, he'd never actually said that he didn't.

Flustered, Lucy gazed back at the stranger. He was leaning a little toward one wall, his left arm pressed close to his side. *He must be freezing*, she thought, and no wonder, dressed as he was in ragged jeans and T-shirt, scruffy denim jacket and dirty old boots. He'd looked pale before, but now he was even whiter. His skin seemed paperlike, almost translucent, and for the first time she noticed the slight trembling of his hands.

"I don't believe you." *Even though you look so much like Byron, even though you sound so much like Byron, even though I wish you were Byron because you've made my heart ache all over again.* "Matt would have told me if he'd found you."

"I don't know who you're talking about." He hesitated briefly. "And nobody knows I'm here."

"Then you'd better leave before I call the police."

"That wouldn't be a very smart thing to do."

Backing away, Lucy drew herself to full height. "Are you threatening me?"

"No, I'm just saying—" He broke off, breath catching sharply in his throat, and Lucy watched as he braced himself against the wall and clamped his arm tighter to his side.

"I'm just saying," he continued softly, "that I'm not particularly fond of authority figures, and I wish you wouldn't call them."

Lucy kept her eyes on him. "Why not? Are you in some kind of trouble?"

"That would be a very long story."

"Go ahead. I've got time."

"Not *that* much time, I'm afraid." One corner of his mouth twisted, though whether from bitterness or amusement, it was hard to tell. "You were close to Byron?"

The question caught Lucy off guard. As she fumbled for an answer, she saw those strange amber eyes of his glide smoothly down her body, then up again to her face, with an almost suggestive—and calculated—slowness.

"Close?" Cheeks flushing, Lucy did her best to recover. "I was . . . am . . . a friend."

"You must have known him well."

Again Lucy hesitated. "I didn't know him very long. Only a few days."

"That's more than just friendship I see in your eyes."

Startled, she glanced away. She remembered the secret Byron had shared with her—his ability to view people's souls through their eyes. Was this stranger referring to something that only Byron's brother could have known? Lucy forced herself to look back at him, but his expression revealed nothing.

"You don't know anything about me," she said angrily.

"You might be surprised."

It was a quiet answer, and matter-of-fact, but one that sent a chill through Lucy's heart. It was all she could do to keep her voice level. "What's that supposed to mean?"

His right hand lifted to fend off her question. With growing dismay, Lucy watched a violent shudder work through him, gnawing deep into his muscles. He bent lower, lips tightening, skin like chalk. His eyes squeezed shut, then opened again, seeking her out as though she'd suddenly gone invisible.

"Is Byron really dead?" he murmured.

He was still shivering but trying not to show it, easing himself onto his knees, left arm still clutched to his side. For a panicked moment she wondered if he might be on drugs or out of his mind—maybe even dying. Whatever was wrong with him, he was definitely in no shape to chase her, she decided. Now was her chance to run away, drive off, call for help. He even seemed a little disoriented; with any luck, he might not even notice she'd gone.

But he was between her and the doorway, and Lucy had to get past him. And even though there was enough space to slip by, something held her back. Something about the way he just knelt there, shoulders slumped, head bowed, his dark profile in sharp relief against the white marble of the crypt, seeming so alone . . .

She made a run for it.

With lightning speed he caught her, right arm flinging out, fingers clamping tight around her wrist.

Lucy gasped at the shock. Not just the iciness of his skin or the alarming strength of his grip, but the images that exploded through her brain.

Sweet night—leaves, stars, moonlight patterns— shadows swift on silent feet—dark desires deep as open wounds—wind flowing like blood, streaming like blood, hot wild fountains and rivers of blood— screams from secret places, screams that no one hears, pleasure pain and begging screams of terror and surrender . . .

No! Lucy tried to pull free. *No more visions! Make them stop!*

But the stranger's hand squeezed tighter, sending a chaos of sensations to her very core.

Burning . . .

"Please—"

Burning lungs, burning skin, burning eyes . . .

"Let go!"

Burning like the moon, red just like the moon, burning eyes, burning lips, burning souls—

"Is he?" she heard him ask again. "Is Byron *dead?*"

Lucy felt the walls sway around her, the stones shift beneath her feet. For one brief second the young man's eyes actually seemed to change color, black and amber fusing together in a liquid, luminous glow—yet she convinced herself it was only a trick of her own unshed tears. She tried to answer him—*wanted* to answer him—but her thoughts were all muddled, and she was so hot, and he was holding her so tight . . . *so tight . . .*

"Yes." *Don't make me say it—I can't bear to say it!* "Yes! He's dead!"

"You're sure?"

Memories stabbed through her head, pierced through her heart. "If you were really his brother, you wouldn't be asking me these questions! If you were really his brother, you'd already know—"

"How . . . long?"

He could barely gasp out the words. There was sweat along his brow and upper lip, though his breath hung like frost in the air. Lucy felt sick with both sympathy and dread.

"What is it?" she begged him. "What's wrong?"

"How long ago?"

Her mind raced feverishly, trying to find the answer. How long *had* it been since Byron died? Already much too long. Forever. A heart-breaking eternity.

"Days?" Strength was draining from his fingers; he fumbled for a tighter grasp. *"Weeks?"*

"Weeks. A couple of weeks—"

"Was there a funeral?"

"Yes."

"A service? A special service?"

"Some kind of service, yes—"

"A casket?"

As hard as she tried to prevent them, more unwanted memories flooded in. The gloomy day, the weeping crowd of mourners. The priest in black, the flowers and personal keepsakes arranged upon the coffin. She couldn't hold back tears any longer. They ran down her cheeks and dripped on the hand that held her.

"And there's no mistake?" he persisted. "There couldn't possibly be some mistake? You're absolutely sure he's dead?"

"I . . . " Sobs rose into her throat, though she stubbornly fought them down. "I was with him when he died."

His fingers slid from her arm. As Lucy stepped away and began rubbing circulation back into her wrist, she heard the hollow sound of his whisper.

"So . . . it's true, then."

Free to escape now, Lucy realized she couldn't. Something about the tonelessness of his voice, the defeated sag of his shoulders, held her there in a conflict of emotions. She watched in silence as he eased himself back against the wall, legs splayed in front of him, head bent to his chest. His right hand lifted in slow motion, fingers gliding back through his tangled mane of hair.

"Byron." Had he choked just then? Laughed? Sobbed? His voice was so faint, Lucy could barely hear. "Damn you, Byron . . ."

Her heart caught at the words. She didn't know what to do. What to say. What to think or even believe. Something inside her felt the need to comfort him; something inside her still sensed a threat. Finally, in spite of herself, she took a cautious step toward him and reached out for his shoulder.

"After all this time," he murmured.

Lucy stopped, hand poised in midair. "What?" she asked him gently.

He lifted his head and rested it back against the wall. He wasn't looking at her anymore. In truth, he didn't even seem to realize she was there.

"After all this time," he murmured again. "And now I'm too late."

3

Lucy was at a complete loss. One minute ago she'd been ready to turn him in; now she felt as if *she* were the intruder.

This can't be happening.

She glanced longingly toward the door of the mausoleum, judging her distance and her odds. The young man's eyes had closed; his body was very still. He didn't seem nearly as dangerous as he had before, only empty and sad and tired.

Stop feeling sorry for him—you don't know anything about this guy! You don't know what he's talking about, if he's even telling the truth. Haven't you gotten yourself in enough trouble already? Get out of here—now!—while you have the chance!

"I wouldn't, if I were you," he warned her.

Lucy froze. How had he known what she was thinking? His eyes were still shut, his face turned from her own. Once more an uneasy feeling grabbed hold of her, as though not only her body were vulnerable to him, but her thoughts as well.

"You're not very good at being quiet." The effort of conversation seemed to be becoming too much for him. "And I doubt you'd get very far."

He opened his eyes and tried to focus on her feet. As Lucy followed his gaze, she realized that she'd actually inched closer to the doorway, without even being aware. But obviously *he* had been aware—even without watching.

Simple explanation, Lucy. He can't read minds—he just has very good ears.

"So what are you saying?" Feeling braver, she took several more steps toward freedom. It was obvious he couldn't even stand now, much less pursue her. "Why wouldn't I get far? Are you going to stop me?"

"No. But something out there will."

Lucy stared at him. She could see that his eyes had shifted yet again, peering out through the shadows and tentacles of fog, far beyond the open gates of the mausoleum. Terror clutched at her heart. And when she finally spoke, her voice shook with anger as well as with fear.

"I'm going. I don't know who you are, but you're not Byron's brother. And I'm calling the police, whether you like it or not."

She made it as far as the door when she saw it—the slow, subtle movement beneath a nearby overhang of trees. It seemed to slink among the graves, a long lean silhouette, low to the ground, then silently disappeared behind a headstone. Lucy felt the hairs prickle at the back of her neck. She'd had that feeling earlier of being followed, and she'd managed to convince herself that it was only her imagination. But now . . .

"It's only a shadow," she said firmly. "There's nothing out there but shadows."

Yet glancing back, she saw the young man struggling up from the floor. His face contorted in pain, and with a feeble gesture that was almost protective, he motioned her to come closer.

Lucy stayed where she was. In a rush of indecision, she wondered which would be worse—to take her chances in here or in the cemetery. She couldn't see anything moving out there now . . . whatever she thought she'd seen was gone. If, in fact, it had ever really been there to begin with.

There was no time to make up her mind. She heard a groan behind her—scarcely louder than a sigh—and as she turned around, the stranger sank to his knees and collapsed. Only this time, as Lucy's eyes swept over him, she noticed the trail of dark liquid spreading out from his side, pooling across the floor.

"Oh my God."

She was beside him in an instant. She whispered to him, but sensed that he was far beyond answering. With growing horror she gazed down at the large wet stain on his jacket, then carefully lifted it away. His T-shirt was soaked, plastered to his side. His body and clothes reeked of blood. Taking a deep breath, Lucy began peeling the T-shirt from his skin, bracing herself for whatever she might find.

But nothing could have prepared her. Not even in her worst nightmares.

With a shocked cry, Lucy whirled away. Bile rose into the back of her throat, and she covered her mouth with trembling hands. And though his critical condition was instantly clear to her, it still seemed an eternity before she was able to compose herself and turn back to the gruesome sight.

At first she thought he'd been stabbed.

But then, as the true horror of it sank in, she realized that something had bitten him.

Bitten savagely into his side, leaving sharp, jagged teeth marks around a gaping hole of raw flesh and stringy muscle, gnawed bones, and dangling shreds of skin.

Dead leaves were mashed into the wound. Leaves and grass and dirt all mixed together into a bloody paste, as though some primal instinct had guided him in a desperate attempt at survival.

How he'd managed to survive even this long was past her understanding.

Lucy couldn't stop shaking. As she tilted her head back and drew in an enormous gulp of air, she willed herself not to throw up. What could have happened to him? What sort of creature could have done this? With an instinctive reflex of her own, she pulled off her wool scarf and coat and the sweater beneath it. Her undershirt was light, but she scarcely felt the cold. In fact, she didn't feel much of anything now except a strange sense of unreality.

She wadded her sweater into a ball. She lowered it to his side, then hesitated a moment, steeling her nerves. From some deep level of anguish he moaned again, as though subconsciously aware of what would come next. And as she pressed the sweater carefully against his wound, she felt a warm flow of blood, slick on her fingers.

"I'm sorry." Despite her resolve, Lucy's voice quivered. "I don't mean to hurt you . . . but you've got to stay very still."

She didn't expect him to answer. But when he did, his words chilled her.

"Nothing . . . nothing you can do . . ."

Lucy's heart sank. Was he telling her it was hopeless? Could he feel his life slipping away, even as she fought to save it?

"Shh . . . don't talk." As gently as she could, she worked the scarf under him and around him, using it as a makeshift tourniquet, tying the sweater firmly in place. Then she covered him with her coat and tried to think what to do.

Whoever this young man was, she didn't want to leave him. She couldn't bear the thought of his lying here cold and suffering and all alone, maybe even dying before she could get back. Yet there was no way she could manage him by herself. And even if she could, just moving him would probably do more harm than good.

Lucy made up her mind. "I'm going for help. I'll be back as quick as I can."

Had he heard her? He was lying so still, his eyes closed, and he didn't appear to be breathing. Terrified, she pressed her fingers to the side of his neck and searched for a pulse.

She jumped as his hand brushed hers. There were no visions this time—only a brief sense of fading light, like a candle burning low, or the moon slipping behind a cloud. The feeling was gone in an instant, and she wondered why she hadn't seen him move, why she hadn't felt even the slightest shifting of his body.

"Not . . . safe here . . ." he murmured. His eyes were still shut, and, to Lucy's horror, a trickle of blood oozed from one corner of his mouth. Bending closer, she smoothed the damp hair from his forehead and willed herself to stay calm.

"That's why you need a doctor. I've got a phone in my car, and I'll come right back, I promise. And then we can get you to the hospital—"

"No . . . please . . ." Even in his whisper, Lucy heard desperation. He tried to lift his head, but couldn't. His face was drenched with sweat, and the scar slicing his left cheek was like a jagged crack through ice.

"Listen to me," she said firmly. "You've *got* to go to the emergency room." Didn't he realize what was happening? Didn't he realize how seriously he was hurt? "I think you're going into shock—you're bleeding really badly—"

"No . . . no hospital."

"Don't you understand what I'm telling you? You could *die!*"

"Not . . . dying. Not . . . what it seems . . ."

He was rambling now, she was sure of it—out of his head with pain, making no sense whatsoever. But as she started to get up, his desperate whisper stopped her once again.

"Don't . . . leave me here. Please . . . *please.* I'm begging you. For Byron's sake."

All the argument went out of her. In stunned

silence she gazed down at his face, a face that could have been Byron's own death mask, a face growing blurry now beyond her quick swell of tears. Then at last she sat back on her heels, surrendering with a reluctant nod.

"What do you want me to do?"

His lips barely parted. "Somewhere . . . safe."

"But that's what I'm trying to tell you—I *am* trying to take you somewhere safe—"

"Close . . ."

"There's *nothing* close!" Frustrated, Lucy stood up and gestured futilely toward the gates of the mausoleum. "There's only *here*—and—and the *cemetery*! And my *car*! And—and—that old *church* over there!"

"Church?"

Perhaps it was only a trick of the shadows, but for a second she could almost have sworn that his eyes opened, fixing her with a wide, dark stare. And though he'd barely managed to utter that one word, it seemed to hang in the air between them now, like some strange and ominous echo.

"Church," he murmured again. "Yes . . . take me there . . ."

But she *must* have imagined that unnerving stare of his, because he was still sprawled there like a lifeless doll, and his head was turned away; he wasn't even looking at her.

"It's only used for storage now," she tried to explain. "I don't even know if we can get in."

He didn't answer. Suddenly fearing the worst, Lucy dropped down beside him again, her voice urgent.

"Please! Don't give up! You've got to hang on! *Stay* with me!"

Despite his wounds, she shook him violently. The smell of blood was stronger now, rusty at the back of her throat. She realized it was all over her—on her jeans and shoes and shirt, her hands, even strands of her hair. She wiped her palms across her thighs, but the red stains wouldn't come off. Terrified, she shook him again and was relieved to see a flicker of movement behind his eyelids.

Oh God . . . what am I going to do?

His breath was so shallow; she could hear a faint gurgling in his lungs. She pressed one hand to his chest, just to make sure his heart was still beating. Feeling more frantic by the second, she tucked her coat snugly around him, then got up and hurried to the door.

Soft gray light was spreading through the mausoleum. Outside the fog was beginning to lift. Yet despite the urgency of the situation, Lucy hesitated and peered off through the crooked headstones and fading shadows of the cemetery.

He said something was out there. He said it wasn't safe.

Lucy choked down a taste of fear. She wrapped her arms around herself and shivered violently.

Something real? Something stalking? Watching? Slinking between those graves?

"It's gone now," he whispered, and Lucy spun around, startled.

She was absolutely certain this time that he hadn't moved. Hadn't turned his body even a fraction of an inch, hadn't lifted up his head. He couldn't possibly have seen her watching the graveyard, couldn't possibly have heard her silent thoughts.

Which made it even more frightening when he whispered to her again.

"Hurry . . . before it comes back."

4

Déjà vu . . .

As Lucy ran through the cemetery, a bad-dream feeling ran with her, clawing with icy fingers, tearing at her mind.

A twisted reality all too familiar.

A trapped-in-a-nightmare feeling that had become her life.

Déjà vu over and over and over again . . .

Neither thoughts nor things made sense anymore.

There was only madness and evil. Darkness and danger.

And a hell she would never escape.

These were the ideas that mocked her as she ran—swift, sharp flashes of panic and hopelessness that numbed her long before she reached the old church. Her lungs burned with cold, but she swallowed the pain. She couldn't feel her legs, but her body kept going. She stumbled over neglected graves that pressed close to the side of the building; she wove through a maze of nameless headstones crowded together at the back. And as she finally reached the entrance, she couldn't help but glance in every direction, just to make sure she was alone.

"Hurry . . . before it comes back . . ."

How had he known, she wondered—how had the stranger known about that invisible presence back there in the shadows? That presence lurking so near, on the other side of the fog? And the way he'd spoken about it . . . warned her about it . . . almost as though it were something . . .

Familiar.

The word whispered through her head, and Lucy shuddered. Scrambling for a foothold on the icy stoop, she grabbed the door handle and pulled.

The church was locked.

She wrestled with the latch, but it held solid; she could hear no sounds at all from inside. Once more she glanced toward the sidewalk and the dead-end street beyond. *This is insane! That person you left back there is going to die! His life is in your hands, and you've let him talk you into something completely stupid! He needs to be in a hospital! You're wasting precious time!*

Furiously chiding herself, Lucy took off around the corner of the building. There had to be another way in—a back door, a window, something!

He's going to die, and it's your fault!

Broken stained-glass windows loomed high above her head. There were gaping holes in the eaves, and patches of rotted wood on the roof, but they were impossible to reach.

How would she ever get him here? There was no way she could carry him; she couldn't just drag him through the cemetery. *Like I dragged that headstone through the hall and onto the porch, that headstone with Angela's name on it . . .*

Her panic grew worse; her thoughts grew jumbled. What was she going to do about that headstone, anyway? She had to get home, make sure it was still hidden. What if Irene went out to get the morning paper and discovered the headstone instead?

Why are you thinking about that now? Why are you thinking about that while someone's dying?

Not someone. Byron's brother.

"No!" Lucy whispered angrily to herself. "He's not Byron's brother; Byron would have told me!"

Then why are you helping him? Why aren't you taking him to a doctor—why are you doing what he asked you to do?

"I don't know!"

She couldn't answer that—didn't *want* to answer that. She had to find shelter, but there were no doors along here, no way to get in, no place to be safe. *"Hurry,"* he'd said, *"hurry before it comes back."* Just a few months ago she'd have thought he was crazy; she'd have left him there and called the police, and her conscience would have been perfectly clear. Just a few months ago she wouldn't have listened, she wouldn't have believed him at all . . .

But that was months ago.

And that was before.

Before her world had turned upside down.

"Hurry . . . before it comes back . . ."

He'd known something was out there in the

cemetery, watching from the shadows, slipping through the fog.

And she'd known it, too.

In fact, she realized now that she'd known it all along, ever since that first cold chill of danger near Byron's grave. That sinister presence haunting her, as merciless as any recurring nightmare . . . that nameless specter she'd be forced to recognize one day . . .

Soon, Lucy.

She remembered the message in her notebook, the message that had so mysteriously disappeared—disappeared without the slightest trace, just like that phantom among the headstones . . .

Soon.

Lucy was half frozen. She sloshed through a mire of slush and snow, waded through dead, tangled shrubbery. Wind pierced the thin fabric of her shirt and gnawed her bare hands. And no matter how hard she tried to concentrate, her mind kept filling with thoughts she didn't want to think about and memories she wanted to forget.

Wanda Carver's death hung over her like a

pall—the visions she'd had of it weighed her down with guilt. She'd come here alone this morning for no other purpose than being close to Byron. She longed to feel the companionship of his spirit, a haven of peace and solitude where she wouldn't be blamed or judged. A refuge where she could sort out her thoughts, where she might understand what was happening and why.

And now this.

This mysterious stranger, bleeding to death in the Wetherly mausoleum. This stranger who claimed to be Byron's brother. She didn't even know his name.

First Katherine . . . then Byron . . .

Each encounter had led Lucy straight into tragedy and heartbreak.

Where would *this* one take her?

"Damnit!"

The ground was more slippery behind the church, and Lucy was forced to slow down. She noticed a door at the top of some steps, but it was boarded over with thick wooden beams. Frustrated, she turned and looked back at the cemetery. She'd felt so strong when she'd gotten here this morning, so capable and determined—and now, though that resolve hadn't entirely disappeared, it *had* taken a dramatic and unexpected shift. *Why are you so shocked?* Hadn't she told herself this was all she could ever expect from now on? An isolated world that became more surreal with every day? Bad surprises at every turn?

Lucy stared miserably at the old building. Where else could she go? She should never have come here in the first place—it might already be too late. As if there weren't enough deaths on her conscience already . . .

And then she spotted the cellar.

At least, she guessed it was a cellar. One of those old-fashioned ones, with double doors slanted up from the ground and opening from the middle. The door handles were looped together with a heavy chain, but there didn't appear to be a padlock. Lucy squatted down and began tugging. Apparently no one had used this entrance for a long time—the chain was heavily caked with dirt and rust, some of the links embedded into the rotting wood of the doors. After several minutes of intense struggling, she finally felt it give way, and it rattled to the ground.

Lucy hesitated, an ironic thought flitting through her mind. This was breaking and entering, wasn't it? Even though she didn't intend to take anything, wasn't she still breaking the law?

Yet trespassing into a church was far better than letting someone die, she told herself. And with that bitter reality hanging over her, she went to work on the doors.

They opened fairly easily. As a wave of dank air washed over her, Lucy peered down into a pitch-black hole, then steadied herself against the outer wall. The darkness . . . the musty smell . . . it was almost like being back in that cave again, and it took her several seconds to catch her breath. *Go on!* Yet she couldn't make herself move, and the pale morning light seemed to hesitate at the very threshold of those cellar doors. *Like an entrance to the underworld,* Lucy thought, then wondered why she had. It might be run-down, but it was still a church. *What a weird comparison to make.*

Very carefully, she inched forward. To her

relief there was a rickety flight of stairs, and as her eyes began adjusting to the gloom, more of the interior came into hazy focus. It wasn't as cold down here as she'd expected. Fresh air was already blowing in behind her, thinning out the stale, stagnant odor of neglect. She continued slowly to the bottom of the steps, wishing she had a flashlight. Silence lay thick around her, as thick as the spiderwebs crusting the walls and rafters. No footprints had disturbed the dust upon the concrete floor. Whatever parts of the cellar were being used for storage, it was obvious this tiny, cramped room hadn't been touched in quite a while.

Yet through the dim shadows, Lucy could definitely see clutter. Stacks of folding chairs and tables, cardboard boxes and wooden crates of every shape and size, a broken lectern, everything shrouded in layers and layers of dust. Stained-glass cutouts were piled on a desk; panes of glass were angled into a corner. Mysterious shapes lurked under drop cloths. An open carton held a jumble of crosses and crucifixes, while another was stuffed with candles. There were old clothes jammed into grocery bags.

From crooked picture frames along one wall saints gazed down at her, martyrs beheld her with wide and glassy stares, while Jesus himself in various poses seemed to follow her movements with a sad, forgiving smile.

In a matter of seconds, Lucy had scanned the entire area, her gaze finally coming to rest on a door in the opposite wall. It was hardly noticeable, camouflaged as it was between floor-to-ceiling shelves, and when she tried the knob, she found it locked from the other side. Backing away, she took one last inventory of the shelves and their contents—urns and incense burners, candlesticks, smashed bows and ribbons, vases, dirty altar cloths, and plastic flowers tangled into pathetic bouquets.

Definitely not the Hilton, she thought.

But a perfect room for hiding.

Warmer and drier than outside, at least. And out of the way, where nobody ever came.

And it wasn't exactly as if she was doing anything wrong, she told herself.

After all, the stranger was wounded and helpless.

What possible harm could he be?

5

He was lying just as she'd left him, sprawled there on the cold floor of the mausoleum.

Blood had thickened around his clothes and congealed beneath his arms.

When Lucy couldn't see him breathing, she thought he was dead.

It seemed an eternity that she stood there, paralyzed with fear, praying to be wrong, begging for a miracle. He looked *so much* like Byron—how could he possibly *not* be related? Just seeing him like this, suffering like this, ripped Lucy's heart in two. *You can't die! It's like losing Byron all over again!*

And suddenly, more than ever, it didn't matter to her what the truth turned out to be—who this stranger really was, or why he'd shown up here out of nowhere on this particular morning.

All that mattered to her now was that he *lived*.

She hadn't been able to save Katherine. She hadn't been able to save Byron. But she *would* save this stranger. This brother of Byron's, this nearly identical twin of Byron's—she would *not* allow him to die.

She gently placed her hand upon his back. There was an almost imperceptible rising and falling of his shoulders, and she breathed a sigh of relief.

"It's all right—it's me," she told him. "And I've found a place to take you. I just don't know how I'm going to get you there."

Had he understood her? Lucy couldn't be sure, so she gently stroked his forehead, smoothed his hair from his eyes. He was burning hot with fever. His hands were ice cold. Was his body still fighting, she wondered—or was it giving up?

"Please." She tried one more time. "Please let me bring someone. Please let me call a doctor—"

"Won't . . . help."

"Don't say that. Don't even think it."

"Can't . . . do anything . . ."

"Yes, he *could* do something for you, if you'd *let* him!"

"Already . . . already healing . . ."

Healing! Frustrated, Lucy pressed her hands to her temples and shook her head. "No, you're *not* healing! Don't you understand, you're very, very sick!"

But of course it wouldn't do any good to argue with him—he was still incoherent with shock; he didn't even know what he was saying.

"Let me . . . lean on you," he whispered, and once again Lucy placed a calming hand on his forehead.

"We can try. But it's dangerous for you to move."

"More . . . dangerous . . . here."

In spite of herself, Lucy glanced back over her shoulder, out through the gates of the mausoleum, out to the cemetery beyond. The fog had practically vanished, leaving cold, gray light in its wake. Snow clouds hung low over the trees. She could see the black silhouette of the old church looming against a sunless sky.

"If you won't let me call a doctor, then at

least let me call a friend," Lucy urged. "Some-one we can trust, who won't tell anyone—"

"Help me up."

Later she would wonder how the two of them ever made it to the cellar.

How she'd slipped her arms beneath him, oh so gently . . . coaxing him onto his good side . . . easing him up so that his head rested on her shoulder. Feeling his heart beat so faintly against her. Feeling the shallow whisper of his breath against her cheek.

She'd tied the sleeves of her coat around his neck to keep him warm. And she'd told him not to be afraid.

She didn't recall pulling him to his feet.

Suddenly he was just there, with one arm draped around her, and his body leaning un-steadily against hers. And yet he seemed curiously weightless . . . so very light to carry . . .

Later, when she tried to remember it, it would seem almost like a dream—how they'd managed that slow and tedious walk together through the cemetery.

As though time had magically suspended until the exact second she felt those wooden stairs beneath her feet and suddenly realized that the two of them were safe inside the hiding place.

She guided him to the farthest corner—a practically invisible spot behind some old trunks and suitcases—then eased him to the floor. To her relief the makeshift bandage seemed to be holding, so she decided to leave it for now. It was still inconceivable to her that he could even be alive. He must have superhuman strength to have lasted this long.

But he hasn't completely survived . . . not yet.

Quickly she began making a mental list. She'd have to bring food and water—no doubt he was badly dehydrated. And she'd have to bring clothes—his were soaked with blood. A pillow, blankets, first-aid kit, though she had no idea what difference any of that could possibly make in the shape he was in. Splints and stitches seemed useless—hopeless even—but she could at least clean him with antiseptics and bandage him, give him something for the pain. She had the medicine Dr. Fielding had prescribed for her after the accident—between that and all the drugs Irene took on a regular basis, there was sure to be something that would help.

It amazed her, really. How much calmer she was beginning to feel now, even though the situation was still so critical and so very surreal. She wouldn't let herself consider the probable outcome or how she'd be forced to deal with it. Better to believe that there would be time later for all the questions she needed to ask, all the answers she needed to know. Better to focus right now on making him feel comfortable and cared for and safe.

Gathering all the drop cloths she could find, Lucy took them outside and shook them. She used some soiled rags to wipe dust and cobwebs from the corner. Then she spread one of the drop cloths on the floor, emptied out the bags of old clothes, arranged them into a pallet, and topped them with another large cloth. The crude bed smelled of mildew, but at least it was thick and relatively soft. Until she could bring supplies, it would have to do.

As Lucy moved back to survey her work, she realized the young man was watching her. He was half lying, half sitting against the wall where she'd left him, but she'd been so involved in what she was doing, she hadn't been paying attention. His stare was fixed, his eyes glazed. She reached over and felt his brow.

"What's your name?" she asked gently.

His lips moved in a soundless response. As Lucy leaned in closer, he tried again.

Jared? Had he said Jared?

"Jared," she repeated softly.

His stare didn't waver. His eyes didn't blink.

"I want you to rest now," Lucy soothed him. "I want you to try to sleep while I go home for a while."

Could he even hear her? Was he past the point of understanding?

"You'll be okay here. I'll come back as soon as I can, and I won't tell anyone about you. I promise."

She thought he might have attempted a nod. Very carefully she lowered him onto the pallet, then piled more layers of drop cloths on top of him. She wouldn't bother with his clothes right now, not till she had fresh ones to replace them with. In the meantime, she prayed he'd be warm enough.

She started to reassure him again, but saw he was sleeping—either that or he was blessedly unconscious. She felt his forehead, then lifted his left hand to place it under the covers. The sleeve of his jacket had worked partway up his arm, revealing long, taut ridges of vein . . . sinewy cords of muscle . . . scars and calluses of hard work. And something else she hadn't noticed before.

It looked like a tattoo.

Or . . . what was left of one.

At some time there had been an intricate design, only now it was practically obliterated by the puckered remains of a burn. The scar was large—much wider than the slash on his face—and had seared into the tattoo, melting away both flesh and ink, leaving most of it illegible.

Puzzled, she bent down for a closer look.

The first thing she focused on was the snake. Or at least . . . it *appeared* to be a snake, some sort of reptilian creature, at any rate. Only half of its head was visible, and smoke seemed to be curling from its mouth. Most of the snake's body was seared away, but upon closer examination, Lucy thought it might be impaled on something—a spike, maybe, or a sword.

She ran her fingers lightly across the images, along Jared's arm. As if by touching those distorted figures, they might somehow speak to her and tell her what she longed to know.

My God . . . he could be Byron lying here . . .

Lucy checked his heartbeat one last time.

Then she climbed out of the cellar and chained the doors behind her.

6

What if he dies while you're gone?

Lucy broke all speed limits driving back to the house.

You left him there. You didn't call a doctor. You saw how bad that wound was, how dangerous, how deep. There's no way anybody could ever survive something like that. Are you out of your mind?

The Corvette squealed around a corner. Forcing herself to slow down, Lucy glanced in the rearview mirror, relieved that no other cars were behind her. The last thing she needed right now was to get stopped by the police. It was going to be hard enough sneaking into the house and gathering all the supplies she needed without Irene's knowing.

He's bound to die, and you know it. How could he not? Then what will you do with him? Leave him in the cellar? Make an anonymous phone call? Your fingerprints are all over the place. What have you gotten yourself into now?

She turned onto Lakeshore Drive, her mind spinning faster than her tires. Maybe she'd have to tell someone. Yes, she *should* tell someone. Maybe Matt. After all, he was a priest—priests *had* to keep secrets, didn't they? Wasn't that part of their job? No matter how bad those secrets might be, no matter how crazy?

You don't even know if that guy is really Byron's brother. You don't know where he's from or why he's here—he might not even know Byron at all!

Yet how could he *not* be related? With those eyes and that hair and that voice? With Byron's face gazing back at her, hovering just below the surface, like a displaced phantom?

What person in her right mind would do what you've just done? Think about it, Lucy—think about what you've done!

Lucy hit the brakes and leaned her forehead on the steering wheel. Her chest was tight; her stomach heaved in dread. She should do something. She should call for help right now. Her cell phone was right next to her, tucked inside her purse. All she had to do was dial. Jared would be taken care of—she'd never have to see him again. And if he survived, he probably wouldn't remember anything he'd said to her, anyway.

But *she* remembered.

"Please . . . for Byron's sake . . ."

That's why she was doing this.

Even though it made no sense, even though she wasn't sure she even believed him, she would do what Jared asked of her.

For Byron's sake.

Lifting her head, Lucy took a deep breath and started off again. Past all the homes of the rich and privileged. Past the sweeping lawns and tennis courts and four-car garages, until at last she reached Irene's street.

As she neared the house, Lucy's heart plunged to her toes. What looked like a police car was parked in front, and she could see her aunt and a bulky man in uniform talking together at the front door.

Oh no . . . now what?

For a moment, she couldn't even move.

Her first thought was that someone had

discovered Jared lying in the church cellar.

Her second thought was that Irene would glance down at any second and discover the headstone hidden in the shrubs beside the porch.

Lucy's hands were slick with sweat. She tightened her grip on the steering wheel and tried to stay calm. From the serious look on Irene's face, something was definitely wrong, and Lucy's mind struggled for an answer.

Angela? Had the search for Angela come to a tragic end? Or was it something else—some other bad surprise that would once again turn Lucy's world upside down?

But she couldn't escape now—she'd already been seen. She swung the car into the driveway. The man in uniform had turned to stare at her, and Irene was waving at her to get out of the car.

Lucy took a deep breath. Like a robot, she turned off the engine and opened the door. Even from here she could see how grave the man's expression was, how tightly Irene's hands were clasped together. Why wasn't anybody saying anything? What was going on?

Nervously, she shut the car door. She started around the front of the Corvette, then froze as she caught sight of her shoes.

With all she'd had to deal with this morning, there'd been no time to think about her appearance or the alarm it was sure to cause. She'd cleaned up a little before leaving the cellar, but now she stared in horror at her bloodstained clothes and hands, realizing there was probably blood on her face, as well. Her sweater and scarf were missing. Her coat was gone. She looked like she'd come from a slaughterhouse.

I can't let them see me like this. What am I going to say?

As her aunt's gestures grew more insistent, Lucy began walking again. By the time she reached the front door, she'd managed to come up with a few lame excuses that she quickly blurted out.

"I'm okay, but there was an accident."

Irene's spine slowly stiffened. "An accident? While you were driving?"

"No. Not a car accident."

"Then *what*? Where are you hurt?"

"I'm not, I'm fine." *Sound calm, Lucy. Sound*

convincing. "It was someone else who got hurt, and I . . . I just tried to help."

In her customary reaction to all things emotional, Irene looked supremely annoyed. "What on earth happened?"

"I went . . . jogging."

"Jogging? With the car?"

"I used the track at school. A lot of kids go over there early to run. One of the girls fell on some broken glass."

Lucy could feel two pairs of eyes raking her over. She managed an apologetic smile.

"Her cuts were pretty deep—a few of us finally got the bleeding stopped, but it took a while. And she was shivering so bad, I just gave her some of my clothes."

The brawny cop hadn't said a word. He stared at Lucy with a neutral expression and blocked her way inside. After a tense pause, Irene finally nodded.

"This is Sheriff Stark, Lucy. He wants to talk with you."

"With me?" Lucy's heart plummeted again. "Well, I really have to get ready for school—"

"This won't take long," the sheriff assured her.

Hugging herself, Lucy looked up at him with innocent concern. "Okay. Sure. What do you need?"

"It might be more comfortable if we all go inside."

Irene hadn't moved from the doorway. From the way she was regarding Sheriff Stark, it was clear she found the intrusion offensive. "As I said before, Presley, I fail to see the purpose of any of this."

Lucy glanced from her aunt to the officer. Her stomach was churning again, and she was starting to feel faint. Whatever this was, it couldn't possibly be good. Whatever this was, it could only mean delay and disaster for Jared.

"Well, you know how it is," Sheriff Stark said smoothly. "Just trying to do my job."

He stepped aside to let Lucy pass. Irene led the way to the living room and motioned them all to sit down.

"So, Lucy." The sheriff was smiling at her now. A forced, practiced smile that wasn't the least bit sincere. "First off, don't feel like you're being singled out. We'll be interviewing all the Pine Ridge students over the next few days."

Nodding, Lucy shifted uneasily in her chair. She knew she should understand what he was talking about, but her mind had gone totally blank.

"I just want to ask you a few questions," the sheriff continued.

Again she nodded, returning his smile for good measure.

"How well did you know Wanda Carver?"

The smile froze on her lips. What was this about? Why was he asking her about Wanda Carver?

Lucy thought a moment, then heard herself answer, "Not well. Just from school."

"So you weren't a close friend of hers?"

"No."

"Didn't hang out with her or anything like that?"

Lucy shook her head.

"But you did *know* her." A statement, not a question. The sheriff fixed her with a level stare.

"Well . . . I knew who she was."

"This is ridiculous," Irene fumed. "I don't see how any of this could possibly be beneficial—"

"Irene, please," Sheriff Stark cut in.

Silence filled the room. An uncomfortable silence that settled heavily on Lucy's shoulders. She watched the sheriff lean toward her and clasp his beefy hands between his knees. "Lucy, did you have any contact with Wanda Carver on Wednesday?"

Lucy gazed back at him. Contact with Wanda Carver? Her mind flashed a picture of the girl's face, then went vague and confused. She had to get back to the church, back to Jared in the cellar. From some far-off place she wondered if she looked as dazed as she felt.

"I . . ." She had to think a minute. She had to try to remember. "I saw her in the hall at school."

"And what happened?"

"Happened?" It was obvious Sheriff Stark was after something—dropping hints and expecting some sort of response. Lucy glanced over at her aunt, but she read nothing in those flint-gray eyes. "Nothing happened. She gave me a flyer."

"A flyer?"

"Information about the candlelight vigil. For Angela."

"And then what happened?"

"I went to class."

"And did you *say* anything to Wanda? *Before* you went to class?"

Lucy felt trapped. Why was the sheriff so interested in what she'd said to Wanda that day? How did he even know about it? And what made the event so important that he'd come here to the house to ask her about it?

"Do you remember, Lucy?"

But it was all getting clearer now. Running back to Wanda, warning the girl to be careful. Feeling so foolish about it, but still taking the chance. Feeling responsible somehow. *Wishing Wanda had listened . . .*

Wishing I'd never had that vision.

Lucy's mouth was dry. She ran her tongue slowly over her lips.

"Lucy," the sheriff said, "there are some stories going around. Now, I know how rumors get started and how they can get out of hand. But some kids are saying you threatened Wanda Carver that day before she died."

All the blood drained from Lucy's face. She held on tightly to the arms of her chair.

"Threatened her? What are you talking about?"

"This is outrageous," Irene said. "I think this interrogation has gone far enough."

But the sheriff lifted a restraining hand. "Irene, a young girl has been murdered, and—"

"Murdered!"

Had *she* gasped out the word, Lucy wondered, or had Aunt Irene? Or maybe they *both* had, Lucy decided, because Irene was looking every bit as shocked now as Lucy was feeling.

Murder?

The living room walls seemed to tilt and sway as her brain struggled desperately to compute. Even Irene's composure had temporarily faltered—Lucy could see her aunt staring at the floor and fingering her expensive pearls with quivering fingers.

"Murdered?" Lucy choked out at last. "But . . . but . . . no—she had an accident! That's what the police said last night—that Wanda had an *accident.*"

"Well, the thing is, I don't believe we ever *officially* called it an accident," the sheriff said.

Lucy's mind raced backward—back to the

candlelight vigil, to the unexpected arrival of the police, the shocked faces of the students, back to Dakota's stunned and sad announcement.

"She fell off the footbridge over that old drainage ditch in the park. She broke her neck on the concrete."

"But it *must* have been an accident," Lucy murmured. A chill traced up the length of her spine, and it was getting harder and harder to keep her voice steady. "Why would you think anything else? Why would you think it was murder?"

"I'm afraid that's confidential."

"But why are you asking *me* about it?"

"We're talking to everyone who knew Wanda. Just trying to gather as much information as we can."

At this Irene came to life again, planting herself between Lucy and their unwelcome visitor, fixing him with an icy stare.

"You're entirely mistaken about all this, Presley. You, of all people, should know that brutal crimes never happen in Pine Ridge."

"I know you'd like to believe that," the sheriff answered gently. "On account of Angela and all.

And you're right—we've never had those kinds of crimes here before." Pausing, he rubbed his forehead, then cast her a reluctant glance. "But we have now."

Lucy's throat was closing up. She tried to take a deep breath, but the air had gone thick and sour.

The stranger who was in the mausoleum, covered with blood . . .

"So what about these rumors, Lucy?" The sheriff's voice bullied its way into her brain. "*Did* you threaten Wanda Carver the day before she died?"

The stranger I tried to help . . . the stranger I hid in the church cellar . . .

"Oh, for heaven's sake!" Irene was furiously indignant. "Surely you don't think Lucy had anything to do with this! I've never heard anything so—"

"Why don't we just let Lucy tell us. I'm sure she has a reasonable explanation."

Reasonable? Oh, right, Sheriff, I bumped into Wanda Carver and got slammed with a supernatural vision.

For an instant, Lucy stifled a wild urge to

laugh. No matter what she said, it wouldn't sound reasonable. No matter how honest she was, he wouldn't believe her. Only Byron understood. And she doubted very much that Byron would suddenly appear to help her out.

"It was a dream," she said solemnly. "I had a dream about Wanda Carver. And it was so real, it scared me."

Sheriff Stark looked blank. "A dream."

"Yes."

"So . . . what happened in this dream?"

"I'm not sure. I mean . . . it was all mixed up, but in the dream, I knew Wanda was falling."

"Falling? How? From what?"

"I don't know. That part wasn't clear."

"You just said it was real to you."

"It *was* real. But not like whole scenes. More like images blinking on and off. Weird feelings and sensations." *And the fact that Wanda would die. And the* date *that Wanda would die . . .*

"And when did you have the dream?"

"Not then. I mean, it was days before that. But it just stayed with me—I couldn't forget about it. So I finally said something to her."

"And that's when you threatened her."

"No." Lucy was determined to hold his gaze. "I never threatened her. I just told her to be careful."

Another uneasy silence fell between them. The sheriff lowered his head and stroked his chin. Stared down at the floor for several moments. Looked at her again.

"So that's what Wanda's friends heard—you telling her to be careful?"

"I felt stupid about it. I mean, I didn't even know her, and I figured she'd think I was crazy, and then she'd tell the whole school. And it *didn't* make sense, not even to me. But . . . but I couldn't let it go. I had to tell her."

"And that's all you said?"

Lucy nodded.

"And nothing happened previously between you and Wanda? An argument, maybe? Problems with a boyfriend? Problems in class?"

"I told you. I hardly knew her."

"Presley." Irene's frosty tone demanded his attention. "You helped search for my niece recently when she went missing."

Sheriff Stark nodded.

"Then I'm sure you can appreciate the

severe trauma Lucy's suffered since her disappearance."

"I know she's been seeing Dr. Fielding, yes."

"And are you aware of the various ways that trauma can manifest? Depression? Amnesia? Severe nightmares . . . not to mention the possibility of hallucinations?"

The sheriff kept quiet.

"I'm sure Dr. Fielding will be more than happy to review Lucy's medical records with you. I'll willingly give my permission, and have my attorney sit in on your discussion."

Sheriff Stark obviously had sense enough to recognize Irene's limits. As a slow flush spread over his face, he shook his head politely and got up.

"No need for that, Irene. You've been more than cooperative. You, too, young lady. Thank you both for your time."

Miserably, Lucy watched Irene escort the sheriff to the door. She wished her aunt hadn't gone into quite so much detail about post-traumatic stress syndrome. Amnesia? Hallucinations? If anything else remotely suspicious *ever* happened in Pine Ridge, Lucy would be the first suspect on Sheriff Stark's list.

Still, she had to admire her aunt's protectiveness. In spite of the circumstances, it made Lucy feel good that Irene had rushed to defend her. She even smiled appreciatively as her aunt came back to the living room and regarded her with a long, appraising stare.

"What on earth were you thinking, Lucy?" Irene demanded.

Shocked, Lucy watched the stare harden into a cold frown of disapproval.

"Do you have any idea of the problems you've caused? Did you even *consider* how this was going to look?" Irene marched to the opposite wall and straightened an oil painting that didn't need straightening. "Is it because you want attention? Because you're new at school and feel a need to fit in?"

"I . . . I don't understand—"

"There are more *normal* ways of fitting in, you know. You don't need some bizarre identity in order to feel special."

"Aunt Irene—"

"No wonder Wanda Carver's friends thought you were threatening her. Walking up like that, telling her to be careful—and all because of some dream? I suppose the next thing you're going to tell me is that you read minds."

A knot of hurt and anger welled up inside Lucy, bringing tears to her eyes. "It was real," she said flatly.

"It was a dream. And dreams are *not* real. Dreams are simply bits and pieces of our subconscious—things we encounter during the ordinary course of a day. People we see, dialogue on television. Anti-anxiety pills and upset stomachs."

Lucy felt beaten down, too tired to answer. She lowered her eyes as the lecture continued.

"I'm sure the whole neighborhood saw the sheriff's car in my driveway. The whole *town* will know about it by this evening."

And then those final words as Irene turned to leave for work.

"Perhaps you came home from the hospital too soon, Lucy. It might be better for you to go somewhere else for a while. Somewhere peaceful . . . and private. For a nice long rest."

7

Irene wasn't serious, Lucy kept telling herself.

Those comments about peace and privacy and nice long rests—surely Lucy had misunderstood. Those comments that made her think of being sent away to another strange place and shoved out of sight in another strange room . . .

She didn't mean anything. She was just upset.

And Lucy didn't have time to agonize over it now.

As soon as Irene left, she washed her hands, changed her clothes, then began a mad sweep through the house, taking blankets and towels, gathering clothes from closets and what food she could find in the kitchen. There was a thermos in the pantry. A bottle of brandy in the dining room sideboard. Flashlights from her nightstand and the coat closet, a battery-operated lantern from the garage, sedatives and first-aid supplies from the medicine cabinet, and a nearly full carafe of French Roast in the automatic coffeemaker. She mixed the brandy with the coffee and made old-cheese-and-stale-croissant sandwiches. Once she had everything together, she stuffed as much as she could into her backpack and carried the rest. Then, grabbing a jacket on her way out, she threw everything into the trunk of the car and headed back to the church.

You'll never get away with this.

Lucy's eyes darted back and forth between the street ahead and her rearview mirror. She was breaking speed limits again, and she couldn't afford to get pulled over. She'd have to come up with some excuse for skipping school. Irene was sure to find out about it—as if Lucy wasn't treading on thin enough ice already.

You'll never get away with this, hiding that guy in the cellar, taking care of him all by yourself. If he dies—and he probably will—it'll be you who killed him. That is . . . if he doesn't end up killing you first . . .

"Oh God," Lucy whispered to herself. "I'm in so much trouble."

He *couldn't* be a killer, could he? Mysterious, yes . . . a little scary, even . . . but a *killer*?

Lucy wished she knew exactly what had happened to Wanda Carver. Knowing details about the so-called murder might help her figure out this crazy predicament she was in, who Jared really was.

And what if he is a killer? Would you just leave him there to die?

In spite of her better judgment, Lucy knew she wouldn't—she'd never willingly abandon anyone in need. Even if she ended up calling someone to help her. Turning the whole thing over to the authorities, letting somebody else handle all her weird, creepy problems for a change.

Byron's brother . . .

Leaning forward, Lucy stepped on the gas. She sped past a delivery van and was practically through an intersection before she even saw the stop sign.

"Damn!"

The whole car shuddered as she hit the

brakes. Several horns honked their annoyance, but she stared straight in front of her and tried to stay focused.

The truth is, I don't really know who *he is. He could be* anybody. *He could be an escaped lunatic. An escaped convict. He could be some homeless guy who got bitten by a very large, very mean dog while he was trying to break into somebody's house.*

Another horn blared, ordering her to go. Lucy floored the accelerator and took the next corner too sharply, hitting a patch of ice and sliding several feet before she finally got the car under control. Shaking badly, she swerved into the first parking lot she could find. Then she turned off the engine and lowered her head onto the steering wheel.

It was only eight-thirty, but the day—like so many others in her life lately—had already turned disastrous. She closed her eyes and thought back . . . to her vision of Wanda Carver . . . to the touch of Jared's hand. Surely she would have *glimpsed* something evil, *felt* something horrible, gotten some unmistakable sign if he'd been involved in Wanda's murder.

Blood . . . screams . . . burning . . .

But like all her other visions, no clear pictures, no definite meanings . . .

Pain . . . surrender . . . pleasure . . .

Why couldn't she see further? And why— despite some violent images—was she sensing somehow that Jared had no fatal connections to Wanda Carver?

Because that's what you want to believe?

Lucy's breathing slowed. For an instant she saw Jared again, piercingly vivid, almost as though he were sitting beside her now. The handsome stranger with the amber eyes and tousled hair, with that desperate expression as he'd begged her for help . . .

He *couldn't* be a murderer, Lucy told herself. *You don't* want *him to be a murderer.*

"Lucy!"

Eyes flying open, Lucy nearly jumped out of her skin. She hadn't heard anyone approaching the car, but now she saw a familiar face pressed against her window.

"Lucy, what are you doing here?"

As Dakota peered in at her, Lucy couldn't help feeling a twinge of guilt. She still remembered the way Dakota had looked at her last night, after Wanda Carver's body had been discovered. *"They're saying it happened sometime early this morning,"* Dakota had said. *"But then . . . you already knew that, didn't you?"*

And Lucy hadn't answered, hadn't said a word. She'd just turned and run away, leaving her friend behind and feeling like the worst kind of liar.

She felt ashamed of herself, even now.

She hesitated a second, then rolled down the window.

"I thought that was you," Dakota said matter-of-factly. "How come you're not at school?"

She was wearing camouflage pants, a white jacket made of curly fake fur, and a red plaid hunting cap with earflaps. Her multicolored scarf was twisted around her neck and hanging down her back, and at the moment, it appeared to be sparkling. Lucy realized it was covered with gold glitter.

"I . . ." Lucy stammered, "I . . . how come *you're* not?"

"Doughnuts." Dakota lifted a stack of large, flat boxes so Lucy could see. "I think they're supposed to lull us into a false sense of security." When Lucy didn't respond, she added, "Father

Matt sent me to get them. For the interviews. What's that on your face?"

Lucy's hand went immediately to her cheek. She scrunched down in her coat as Dakota leaned toward her.

"It looks like blood." Dakota frowned. "Are you hurt?"

"No, I . . . fell . . . someone—"

"You *fell* on someone?"

"No." What was it she'd told the sheriff earlier? Lucy couldn't remember now—all she could think about was getting away from here and getting back to the church. "I know about Wanda," she blurted out. "About it not being an accident."

She made herself meet Dakota's eyes. She thought once more about what Dakota had said to her after the discovery of Wanda's body— *"But then . . . you already knew that, didn't you?"*— and she braced herself for the questions and accusations she felt sure would come.

But there was no curiosity in Dakota's eyes, only that same open acceptance as before. And all Dakota said now was, "Is that why you ran away last night?"

"No." Lucy shook her head. For one quick moment she actually felt disappointed. For one quick moment she almost wished Dakota *would* confront her. "I didn't know anything about a murder then. Look, Dakota—"

"Well, I guess everyone knows by now. Small town. Front page of the paper."

"I haven't seen the paper." Reality was tugging her back again. She had to get back to the church—she had to hurry—*hurry!* But Dakota wasn't moving, so Lucy added, "Sheriff Stark was at the house this morning."

"Oh. He's a good friend of your aunt's, right?" Dakota didn't wait for Lucy to answer. "He's at school today, too. Everyone's scared and really upset—they can't believe another tragedy's happened. The police want to interview every single student. Behind closed doors, one at a time. So I guess you won't have to go through that."

"The visit wasn't about sparing me; it was a courtesy to Irene. Heaven forbid her glorious reputation should be smeared. They wouldn't dare arrest me in public."

"What do you mean, arrest you?"

"I mean . . ." Lucy's words trailed off help-lessly. She reached out and touched her friend's sleeve. "Oh, Dakota—"

"What's wrong?" The expression on Dakota's face softened, a knowing and genuine concern. It was all Lucy could do not to open her heart and spill everything out. "Lucy, what is it?"

Not now! There's no time! Hurry!

"It's . . ." But somehow Lucy held back. Somehow she collected herself and squeezed all her emotions into a guilty frown. "About last night, I know I owe you an explanation—"

"You don't owe me anything."

Dakota, I want to tell you, but I'm afraid! "Yes. Yes, I do." *I need to tell you, but I'm all confused about things, and I don't want you to get hurt!* "What you said to me—"

"I wasn't trying to put you on the spot. It was an observation."

"And why I went back to Wanda that day in the hall—" Lucy couldn't help it, she was starting to babble. If she didn't get out of here soon, she was going to explode.

"You don't owe me anything," Dakota assured her again. "But there's more blood here on your hand, and I just want to make sure you're okay."

Tears stung Lucy's eyes. "I don't know. For now, yes, I think I'm okay. But I need to talk to you. Later. Where no one can hear us."

Nodding, Dakota slowly drew back. "Are you coming to school?"

"I can't right now."

"Okay. I can call the office if you want. I'm pretty good at imitating your aunt's voice," Dakota mimicked, just to prove it. "I can say you're sick."

In spite of herself, Lucy almost laughed. "And if they catch you, you'll get suspended. I'll try to come in later. No use both of us being in trouble."

"Did you eat this morning? You look really pale; maybe you should eat." Dakota's voice returned to normal. "Father Matt thinks we'll all cooperate with the police more if we're eating. Thus"—once again she displayed her boxes—"doughnuts."

The mere suggestion of eating right now made Lucy feel sicker. She started up the engine again and managed a halfhearted wave.

But Dakota wasn't watching. The girl's head

was tilted back, her eyes sweeping over the cold dead sky. And Lucy was suddenly very much afraid.

"You sense it, too, don't you?" Dakota murmured. "Something in the air today. Something bad and dark, that's never been there before. Like the whole town's suddenly changed. And that bad thing is waiting. And nobody feels it but us."

Lucy followed the direction of her friend's gaze. Drawing a slow, shaky breath, she spoke with more conviction than she felt.

"It's just grief, I think. And also shock. Because . . . you know what people say . . . murders never happen in Pine Ridge."

"Well . . ." Dakota gave an odd little smile. "At least none they know about."

8

There *was* an eerie feeling in the air.

As Lucy made her way slowly through the graveyard, she couldn't help shivering—not only from the cold, but also from Dakota's unsettling prophecy. Her ears strained for each subtle sound; her eyes glanced keenly in every direction. But this section of Pine Ridge Cemetery seemed more silent and remote than ever.

The fog of early morning had been replaced by snow. Raw wind sliced between the headstones, and a pewter sky was darkening quickly to the north.

Unconsciously Lucy quickened her pace. She'd had to park the car behind the cemetery and away from prying eyes, which meant a longer, more difficult walk to the church. She felt fairly confident no one would be out here today, but she didn't dare take a chance on being seen. The weight of her backpack made her clumsy. She kept her head down, ducking for cover between lopsided markers and broken statues, using the blankets she carried to block the wind. And she wondered what she was going to do once she got to the hiding place.

What if Jared's dead? What if he's not there at all? What if someone passing on the street in front happens to notice me?

Lucy knew if she thought any more about it, she might lose her nerve completely. She checked her surroundings one last time, braced herself for the unknown, and made a beeline for the cellar.

It took several minutes to loosen the chain, another few minutes of struggling to pull open the heavy doors. Taking a flashlight from her pocket, she squatted on the top step and shone the light down, guiding it slowly from wall to wall.

Something moved.

Without warning, something dark and shapeless jerked back from the beam of her flashlight and vanished into the shadows.

A scream caught in Lucy's throat. Whatever had moved, had moved quickly; she hadn't been able to make out a single detail. In fact, as her brain struggled to compute, she wasn't entirely convinced that it *hadn't* been a shadow after all, just one among many, distorted by the sudden burst of her flashlight and the gray flitter of snow through the opening behind her.

"Hello?" she called softly.

Whatever she thought she'd seen, it wasn't moving now. The cellar was as quiet as a grave.

"Jared, are you here?"

She held her breath to listen.

She could hear the tripping of her heart, but nothing else. Her grip began to tighten on the flashlight.

"It's me. Lucy. I came alone, like I promised."

Was that a draft of wind she'd felt just now? Like an icy hand wrapping slowly around her ankle? She gasped and lost her footing, sliding down several steps and dropping the flashlight. As she flung out both arms to catch herself, a sliver of wood gouged deep into the palm of her right hand.

Lucy cried out, from surprise as well as pain. The blankets tumbled down the stairs, and the flashlight rolled across the floor, its single ray skipping over a pile of bloody clothes.

"Shut the doors," Jared said softly.

Despite the sudden chill up her spine, Lucy managed to keep her voice steady. "Where are you?"

"Please don't look at me."

She hesitated, unsure what to do. Then she reached up and drew down the doors, plunging the cellar into darkness.

It took several minutes for her eyes to adjust. The flashlight had finally come to a stop, angled directly into a corner, and as Lucy picked it up, she couldn't help but follow the direction of the light.

Jared was lying there, watching her.

Lying on the bed where she'd left him, except that the improvised bandages were gone, discarded with other blood-soaked belongings in that dirty heap on the floor. He wore only jeans now, low and tight around his hips, and still damp with his blood.

Something's not right.

Lucy gazed at him in confusion.

She could see the gauntness of his face, the tight clench of his jaws, the feverish glow in his eyes. Sweat shone on his bare chest and along his brow.

She shifted the beam of her flashlight.

The burned tattoo on his arm stood out in sharp relief against his skin—but not *pale* skin, Lucy realized with a shock—not that ghostly white pallor of death he'd had before.

"Don't do this," he whispered. "Turn away."

But she *couldn't* turn away, any more than she could keep herself from lowering the flashlight and redirecting its beam onto his wound.

His wound . . .

The light shook in Lucy's hand. It settled on the left side of Jared's body, and she stared in utter disbelief.

His wound had grown smaller.

Where a raw, bloody hole had gaped so hideously before, now small sections of flesh appeared to be shrinking and closing up. Protruding bones seemed to have pulled back toward the shattered rib cage. And the skin, hanging in hopelessly tattered shreds, actually looked as though it were starting to reattach.

"My God . . ."

The flashlight clattered to the floor. As if from some far and distant place, Jared's words reached out to her.

"It's not complete yet, Lucy. The pain won't stop till then."

"No. No . . . it's impossible . . ."

She wasn't conscious of backing up . . . of stumbling over her own feet as she tried to escape. But suddenly there were voices—voices coming from outside—and Lucy froze, halfway up the stairs.

"I *know* I saw someone!" a woman insisted.

Lucy recognized her voice at once. Mrs. Dempsey.

"Just as I got here for work—just as I parked my car! I'm telling you, I *didn't* imagine it! Someone was sneaking around behind the church!"

"Do you have any idea where they went?" a man asked.

Mrs. Dempsey sounded indignant. "How in heaven's name should I know that? But there's some crazy murderer running around Pine

Ridge, and I want you to check out *every inch* of this place!"

Lucy didn't see the swift movement behind her. She didn't even have time to react as the hand clamped over her mouth, as she felt herself being half lifted, half dragged back into the corner.

She tried to struggle, but only for a second.

Only till Jared's whispered warning in her ear.

"I don't want trouble. Stay still and keep down."

The flashlight snapped off. Jared pulled her to the floor as the cellar doors flung open.

"Someone must be in here!" Mrs. Dempsey exclaimed. "See? Just look at this chain!"

A brilliant beam of light swept around them, over walls and ceiling, arcing above their heads. *Help so close, and yet so far away*. Lucy wanted to yell, to break free, but she was pressed so close against him, and he was holding her so tight. She could feel his bare chest . . . his breath on her neck. His arms were surprisingly strong.

"Well if there *was* someone here, there's no one here now," the man announced. "Look, Mrs. Dempsey, you better get inside now—this snow's really coming down."

"As if I'll have any peace!" the woman fumed. "I've got my cleaning to do—I can't be worrying about some maniac breaking in and throwing me down the basement steps!"

"Well, lock yourself inside the church—*no* one could break through those doors. I'll put this chain on good and tight, but you'd better get a padlock, just to be sure."

No! Lucy's hopes sank. Once more she tried to pull away, but again found it impossible. She could hear the chain being secured on the outside doors; she could hear the voices arguing, then fading off.

Time hung suspended in the darkness. Thoughts of death and murder spun crazily through her brain. The air in the cellar was much too warm, squeezing her, suffocating her, Jared's skin so hot with fever, Jared's lips burning as they lowered to her hair . . .

It seemed an eternity that he held her. An eternity before he finally whispered to her again.

"When I let you go, you'll be very quiet. You won't scream. And you won't tell anyone I'm here. Understood?"

Lucy nodded. There was a razor-sharp edge

beneath his soft-spoken words. And a faint but unmistakable quiver that he was struggling hard to conceal.

"I didn't intend to scare you," he added, almost grudgingly.

At last Lucy was able to move. She pulled away and put distance between them as he retreated into the shadows.

There's another door in here.

She'd seen it earlier, camouflaged between some shelves, along one of these walls. She hadn't been able to open it before, but maybe— if she moved fast enough, if she could somehow break it down . . .

She dove headlong through the darkness. But instead of finding a way out, she found herself immediately trapped in Jared's arms.

"If you're looking for that door," he said, "you have a terrible sense of direction."

9

There was no force this time.

Lucy's captivity lasted only a moment before Jared released her.

It had nothing to do with courtesy or consideration, she was quick to realize—but because his strength was rapidly giving out. She could feel his exhaustion, the weakening of his grip. And in the silence of the cellar, his breathing was ragged with pain.

"It's not complete yet . . . The pain won't stop till then."

Jared's words sounded clearly in her head, though she knew he hadn't spoken aloud since letting her go. She began backing away from him again, then stopped abruptly, overcome with confusion and fear.

How had he known she would bolt for that

locked door? She hadn't even known it herself until the last possible second. How had he seen her in the dark? How had he caught her so fast?

Without warning the flashlight came on. The bright glare caught her full in the face, and she put up both hands, trying to shield her eyes. She felt like a deer trapped in headlights. And suddenly, the fact that he would put her at such a deliberate disadvantage made her furious.

"Turn that off!"

Lucy swung out blindly, sending the flashlight into a wall. With a weird sense of satisfaction, she heard plastic smashing apart.

"Why?" she demanded. "Why are you doing this?"

His answer was a long and guarded silence.

She couldn't see him, couldn't see *anything* except lingering pinpoints of light, but she stepped forward and threw out a challenge.

"I can wait just as long as you can. But we'll do it on equal ground."

Again the silence. A silence so lengthy that Lucy felt compelled to speak again.

"What is this anyway? Some kind of sick joke?"

Why wouldn't he answer her? Why wouldn't

he talk? Her head felt as if it was going to explode.

And then she sensed a stirring in the shadows. A calm presence . . . and curious . . . and much nearer than she'd expected.

"Why would you think it's a joke?" Jared asked softly.

"Why? Well, why *not*? I see the looks at school—I hear the rumors. It's not like I don't know what's going on."

"What *is* going on?"

"Things! Things that just happen to me!" The words burst out before Lucy even realized. She hesitated, unsure of what she'd just said, and unsure of why she'd said it.

His voice gave her a solemn prompting. "Tell me about those things."

"Things," Lucy said, evasive now as she stared through the dark at his question. *Crazy things like wounds healing all by themselves.* But out loud she added, "Things that nobody would ever believe. Unless those things really *were* jokes."

There was no response from Jared this time. Lucy forced a harsh and humorless laugh.

"So if this really *is* some kind of trick you're playing," she said bitterly, "let me set the record straight once and for all. I'm just as sad about Byron as you are—probably even more. I feel guilty every single day, because he died and I didn't. I wish I'd never come to this stupid town. I wish I'd never met Byron. I'd give *anything* if things could be different. I'd leave here in a second if I had some other place to go, but I don't. So please. You've had your fun. Just leave me alone."

She wouldn't give him the satisfaction of seeing her cry. She faced the shadows defiantly, but they seemed to be empty now.

Jared was standing right next to her.

His whisper caressed her like velvet.

"I'm not who you think I am, Lucy. And if you were mine . . . I'd never leave you alone."

A shiver went through her, languid and warm.

His fingers closed around hers.

"Let me see your hand," he said.

"What?" Lucy felt strangely disoriented. She was still angry, still determined—hadn't she made that clear? He was supposed to be letting her go now, but he wasn't. She was pushing him away, but he was getting closer.

"Your hand—it's still bleeding. Let me see it."

Still bleeding? She'd completely forgotten about falling on the stairs. But as Jared spread her fingers and pressed his lips against her palm, it wasn't the nasty scrape there that made her cry out.

Lucy clutched at her chest.

The pain was so intense, she couldn't bear it. It was as though her heart were being pierced—rendered in half—sliced straight through with a keen, swift blade. And then, just as quickly as it had struck, the anguish was gone again, leaving her breathless and shaken.

"It's a very deep splinter," Jared was saying. "It'll have to come out."

Lucy stared at him in amazement. Couldn't he see how she was trembling? Hadn't he seen what just happened? Wasn't he the least bit concerned?

It did really happen . . . didn't it?

"Jared—" she began, then broke off with a gasp.

His mouth was warm against her palm. She felt the splinter shift slightly beneath her skin . . . the effortless glide of it through her flesh, as Jared drew the splinter out.

"That's a very interesting scar," he whispered.

She wanted to give him an answer—something believable and acceptable that he would never recall again. But her mind had gone hazy, and her eyes had drifted shut. Darkness flowed over her, but she wasn't afraid. She knew she was awake, yet she seemed to be dreaming.

A trickle of blood on my hand . . .

Blood being kissed away . . .

"A girl was killed last night," Lucy whispered, and like before, she wasn't quite sure why she'd brought this up. It was such an effort to talk now. Her hand was throbbing, and her body felt flushed. Her pulse beat much too slow. "I can't stop thinking about it. I keep imagining how scared she must have been."

Silence stretched around her. When Jared finally spoke, his voice was low and emotionless.

"Maybe there wasn't time for her to be scared."

"But it was dark. And she was all alone."

"Yes," he murmured. "I know."

10

She dreamed she was in a storm.

A winter storm so fierce and cold that it was turning her into a solid block of ice. She could feel her limbs freezing, inch by inch . . . her hands . . . even her lips . . . until she couldn't struggle anymore, couldn't even scream for help. And yet there *was* help close by, searchers with dogs, trying to find her, calling her name, walking slowly past her and leaving her buried in the snow . . .

"I'm here!" Lucy screamed a silent scream. "Please don't let me die!"

She could hear their footsteps crunching over the frozen ground; she could smell the damp, musky fur of the dogs. Someone fired a gun— one single muffled shot—and then the whole world went white and still.

Lucy's eyes flew open.

There was no white world around her now, only black, murky shadows. She was gasping for breath, and her mind scrambled furiously, trying to make sense of where she was. Still trapped in a nightmare? The cave in the woods? Her bedroom at Aunt Irene's?

Every instinct warned her to escape. Yet at the same time, she began to realize that something was holding her down.

A fresh wave of panic engulfed her. She was too frightened to move, but her whole body trembled uncontrollably. It took several endless seconds for the truth to sink in. And even then, the truth seeemd unbelievable.

She was lying on her side, nestled in the curve of Jared's body. His left arm was draped across her shoulder, and her forehead rested lightly on his chest. She couldn't remember how she'd gotten here, couldn't remember even falling asleep. In fact, the last thing she remembered at all was Jared pulling a splinter from her hand.

Or was that just part of my nightmare?

Her right hand was pressed to Jared's heart.

His skin was warm, and she could feel the slow, even rhythm of his breathing. But there was a vague sense of discomfort, as well—as though her palm were swollen and tender. And a lingering throb of pain kept time to Jared's heartbeat.

Lucy heard him moan. As his body shifted against her, she was able to ease out from underneath his arm. The lantern she'd brought was glowing near the bed, and the initial terror she'd felt was finally beginning to subside. She propped herself on one elbow and watched him.

She wished this *were* a joke.

Because then, in the end, there would be answers, and everything would go away, and nothing would be real.

But Lucy had no answers. And nothing had gone away except people and things she loved.

And real was *here*; real was *now*.

Just like the change in Jared.

It was obvious that his wound had healed even more. Since the last time she'd checked it, it seemed to have shrunk to nearly half its original size. No matter the weakness she'd sensed in him before, or the quiver she'd heard in his voice—now the sharp hollows of his cheeks were beginning to fill in slightly, and the bruising had practically vanished around his eyes. Even his lips looked different, Lucy thought—fuller somehow, and no longer pale. The transformation was nothing short of miraculous. Yet even though he found respite in sleep, she could tell that the pain hadn't left him. Not all of it . . . not yet.

She placed her hand gently upon his brow.

Wind . . . earth . . . sweat . . . blood . . . They drifted from his skin and from his hair, though not unpleasantly. And with them came a sense of some deep, inner struggle. Something far more desperate—more dangerous even—than a struggle for self-survival.

Lucy's fingertips slid lower, tracing the jagged mark across his face. The shock she felt was immediate and unexpected—a bolt of rage, a hatred so intense that she nearly reeled from the impact.

Alarmed, she took a closer look.

It was even deeper than she'd thought, and much more gruesome. As though something had not merely stabbed the flesh, but twisted . . .

not only cut the flesh, but slashed with relentless force.

And yet . . . he's still so beautiful . . .

Lucy gazed at him with a kind of awe.

So beautiful and so handsome, in spite of the scars.

A dark, compelling beauty, full of secrets . . .

"Stop now," she whispered to herself. "Don't go any further."

But she was already touching his arm.

Trailing her fingers lightly over the puckered skin of his burn . . . the charred remains of his tattoo . . .

This time, she cried out when the shock wave hit. As the uncontrolled fury surged through her, searing every artery and vein.

She jerked backward, clutching her fingers, shaking violently, and becoming certain of two things:

At some past time, Jared had been tortured.

And both of his scars had come from the same merciless hand.

11

She'd never expected to see such cruelty.

Such brutal anger . . . such excruciating pain.

Was it even humanly possible, she wondered, for someone to inflict—or bear—that kind of suffering?

She'd only touched Jared's scars for a moment.

How many other scars ached deep within him, far beyond her reach?

Lucy sat on the bed and watched him sleep. It was colder down here now, and she could hear the wind outside, rattling the chain on the doors. An occasional burst of snow gusted through the cracks and settled on the stairs, as if the cellar were a giant coffin and she and Jared were being buried alive.

It reminded her of the dream she'd had earlier.

She'd forgotten about it till now.

Lucy slid quietly from the bed and stood up, flexing her cramped muscles. She had no idea what time it was, or how many of her classes she'd missed so far. The office had probably already called Irene to report Lucy missing from school. She shuddered to think about it. She'd have to come up with one more really convincing excuse. Except it was getting harder and harder to keep all her excuses straight.

She glanced anxiously over at Jared. He was still sleeping, but there was a flicker of pain across his face, and she noticed a small amount of blood seeping from his wound. She found her backpack and pulled everything out. After tending to Jared as best she could, Lucy piled the blankets on him and arranged the other items within arm's reach of the bed. Then she opened the thermos of brandy-laced coffee and dropped in several sleeping pills.

"Drink this," she whispered to him. "It'll help the pain."

He seemed to understand this at some level. With his eyes still closed, he allowed her to lift his head and tip the cup to his lips.

A wave of sympathy swept through her. And then resentment and frustration. She felt sorry for Jared, and she felt sorry for herself. How could another day of her life have turned out so badly, so quickly? And how had this stranger— who looked so much like Byron—slipped into her world with such heartbreaking familiarity?

It doesn't have to be like this.

Through her turmoil of emotions, Lucy suddenly realized that one thought was trying to break through.

You could use your cell phone. When you get back to the car, use your cell phone and call for help.

It would be so easy, she knew. Just the punch of a few buttons, and then Jared and all his mysterious secrets would be out of her life forever.

You have a choice.

Lucy gazed down at Jared. From his peaceful expression she could tell that the drugs and brandy were already working. He looked younger somehow. Innocent. And suddenly, helplessly vulnerable.

"Damnit."

She couldn't betray him.

Not just because she'd given her word. Or because of the torments he'd suffered. Not even because of all the time and lies and worry she'd invested in him, or the veiled threats he'd made, or the way his body felt, warm and protective beside her . . .

"My choice," Lucy whispered, though she knew Jared couldn't hear her. "For Byron's sake."

12

Lucy was still determined to find a way out of the cellar.

Jared would be sleeping for quite a while; he'd be safe here and undisturbed. She'd have time to go home and clean up and try to form some kind of plan. There'd been no time today for thinking ahead. She felt amazingly lucky that she'd made it through each bizarre moment and survived.

Her whole body ached with exhaustion. She was stiff and sore from dragging Jared through the cemetery, and lugging boxes and backpacks, and falling on the stairs. There was still a faint throb in her hand. She was cold, and she was hungry. And she dreaded facing Irene when she got back to the house.

Sighing heavily, Lucy bent to pick up the lantern.

And that's when she noticed the footprints.

It didn't sink in all at once, those muddled marks upon the floor. Outlines of large shoes, and impressions of large paws, overlapping and smearing together in the dust. The prints stopped at the edge of the bed, on the side where she'd been sleeping—then seemed to reverse and trail off again in the same direction from which they'd come.

From a wall of floor-to-ceiling shelves.

And a camouflaged door.

Lucy straightened slowly, chills racing up her spine.

And once more remembered the nightmare that had woken her.

Snow and a storm and being buried alive—people searching, calling my name—the musky smell of dogs—and a gunshot . . .

Lucy kept staring at the footprints.

She tried to tell herself that she and Jared had made them, as they'd moved about the cellar. She tried to tell herself she was just imagining shoe soles and animal feet etched there in the dust, just like people could interpret cloud formations in a million different ways. After all, if something really *had* been in here, how could she not have heard? No person or animal could have been *that* quiet.

Going more cautiously now, she followed the tracks all the way back to the row of shelves. She held the lantern close to the locked door, then lowered it toward the concrete.

She was right.

The footprints had definitely started here.

They went in both directions and vanished beneath the door.

She reached out for the doorknob. She pressed her ear against the door and listened.

And something listened back.

With a sudden, horrible certainty, Lucy *felt* it—a presence poised there on the other side of that door, something *listening* just like *she* was listening.

In one instant she stumbled back; in the next, she twisted the knob and pushed with all her strength, stifling a scream as the door burst open.

The threshold was empty.

There were no footprints on the other side.

Only a long, narrow passageway with a low

ceiling and walls of crumbling brick, and what looked like a staircase rising from the shadows at the opposite end. The floor was hard-packed earth, and the dust of many years blanketed its smooth, unbroken surface.

No footprints . . .

No presence . . .

Nothing.

Lucy shut her eyes and sagged against the wall.

Nothing . . . nothing at all.

And yet *someone* had opened this door.

And someone had walked to the bed in the corner.

And as she and Jared slept in each other's arms . . . *someone* had watched.

13

She had to see where the passageway would take her.

Leaving the lantern behind, Lucy armed herself with the backpack and extra flashlight and followed the dingy corridor to its end. She had a feeling this was only one small part of the cellar, and the last thing she wanted to do was lose her way. She convinced herself there was no one watching from the closed doors and heavily banked shadows on either side—that the faint whispering was only wind seeping through cracks in the foundation. When she finally reached the staircase, she was so shaky with relief, she could barely make it up the steps.

The door at the top was unlocked. As Lucy inched it open, she found herself at the back of a closet, surrounded by spiderwebs, mouse droppings, and dead roaches. She felt too grateful to be disgusted. Holding the flashlight toward the floor, she tiptoed out onto a narrow landing, then paused to listen. The building was dark and silent; Mrs. Dempsey had obviously finished her work. Lucy had no trouble sneaking through a series of rooms and hallways until she finally came to a threshold and saw the church altar a short distance beyond.

The church altar, with Matt right beside it.

Snapping off the flashlight, Lucy drew back against the wall. Thank God she'd kept the beam angled downward; she didn't think he'd seen it. But had he heard her? She counted off seconds while she waited, but he obviously wasn't coming to investigate. Her stomach tightened as she tried to think.

Surely Matt couldn't have been in the cellar just now. Sneaking and spying and listening at doors. He would have said something, he would have offered to help. And he certainly wouldn't have had a dog with him.

What a crazy idea . . .

She chanced another look through the doorway. Candles burned on the altar, casting

111

bizarre shapes along the walls and vaulted ceiling. Matt's face was lowered, angled slightly to the right. He seemed to be studying a small object in his hands, though Lucy couldn't tell what it was. After a while he placed it on the altar and, with detached slowness, began to unfasten his priest's collar. Then he wadded up the collar, tossed it onto the altar, and turned around.

Lucy ducked back behind the corner. She could hear his footsteps moving quickly, echoing through the emptiness of the church.

He was walking straight toward her.

Still as a statue, she held her breath and hid among the shadows of the hall. Matt was so close now, she could have touched him.

He stopped without warning.

His silhouette went rigid, except for the slow, wary turn of his head . . .

Away from her, in the opposite direction.

He listened. And waited. And finally passed her by.

She heard the sound of a door opening and closing. And then more brisk footsteps, fading at last into an eerie silence.

Lucy didn't stay to see if he'd come back.

As quietly as she could, she hurried to the main doors and slipped out into the snow.

The daylight she'd hoped to find was gone.

Dusk had already fallen, and deep drifts covered the street in front of the church.

Lucy wondered if the route to Irene's had been plowed. She hated the thought of being delayed on the roads—it was already going to take extra time just to wade around the block to the car. She didn't dare shortcut through the cemetery and run the risk of Matt seeing her.

What had Matt been doing in the old church anyway?

She couldn't help wondering what he'd been looking at so intently, why he'd seemed so upset. If she hadn't been such a coward, she could have examined the altar for herself. But she didn't have time to think about that now— there were more important things to worry about.

She felt frozen by the time she reached the car—even more frozen by the time she'd scraped all the ice off the back and side windows and windshield. A high snowbank had formed around the Corvette, and when Lucy realized she couldn't dig out, she climbed into the front seat, slammed the door, and let out a yell of frustration.

The clock on the dashboard read seven o'clock.

And the snow was still coming down.

I can't do this anymore.

Lucy leaned her head on the steering wheel.

I thought I could face everything alone. Fight everything . . . decide everything . . . solve everything. All on my own.

But I just can't.

She turned on the dome light in the ceiling. She pulled her purse from under the seat and found a crumpled business card in her wallet. After repeating the numbers printed there, she punched them in on her cell phone. And when the familiar voice finally answered, she breathed a deep sigh of relief.

"Dakota," Lucy said, "I need your help."

14

"Carbon monoxide," Dakota said solemnly.

Lucy stared at her, assuming an explanation would follow.

"Don't you know better than to sit in your car with the motor running?" Dakota frowned. "You could've died of carbon monoxide poisoning."

Lucy considered this. "Actually, that would have been the bright spot in my day."

"First, freezing. Now, carbon monoxide."

"I'm trying to be creative."

The two of them sat across from each other in the diner. The air was stuffy, thick with steam and old grease and cigarette smoke. After the dankness of the church cellar, Lucy breathed it in like perfume.

"I had my window cracked open," she defended herself.

"Not wide enough."

"Well . . . it's not exactly the best part of town to be stranded in."

"You fall asleep with some stranger whose entrails are hanging out, and you're worried about being mugged?"

"Ssh!"

"Sorry."

Their server arrived, setting plates of burgers and fries in front of them, sliding tall chocolate malteds across the tabletop. She slapped their bill down with an automatic smile, then walked back to a counter packed with customers.

Lucy took a bite of her extra-rare hamburger. A salad used to get her through the whole day, but lately she'd been craving more than just lettuce. In fact, she hadn't realized till now just how famished she was.

"I can't do this anymore," she announced, out loud this time, and around a huge mouthful of burger, pickle, and onion.

"Can't do what?" Dakota raised one eyebrow. "Eat?"

"No, not eat. I mean . . ."

"I know what you mean." Leaning forward, Dakota touched Lucy's hand. "I'm not making light of this. I'm just worried about you."

Lucy gave a vague nod. "Irene wants to put me away."

"Is that what she said?"

"Actually, I think she called it a 'nice long rest.' But she was serious, I could tell."

Dakota was philosophical. "It's a grown-up thing. My parents go through it about every three months—they threaten to lock us all up, and then they sort of forget about it."

"Dakota, what am I going to do?"

The two girls stared at each other.

"I don't know," Dakota said at last. "But thank you for telling me . . ."

Lucy *had* told her.

She'd waited in the car for Dakota to rescue her, and she'd argued with herself the whole time.

She'd given her word to Jared—just as she'd given her word to Katherine, just as she'd kept Byron's confidences. And maybe it *was* just coincidence that Katherine and Byron were both dead now—or maybe she really *was* bad luck—but if something happened to Dakota because of *her*, Lucy knew it would be the last straw. She'd never be able to forgive herself. She'd never be able to live with one more death on her conscience.

She'd heard the old truck wheezing around the corner, and even then she couldn't make up her mind. Dakota had brought shovels, and when the girls finally managed to excavate the Corvette, Lucy had suddenly thrown her arms around Dakota's neck.

"It's just a car," Dakota reminded her. "Not brain surgery."

"It's not about the car." Lucy was trying so hard to fight back tears, but she knew Dakota could hear her crying. "I've really got to talk to you."

"Is this the 'later where no one can hear us' thing you were trying to tell me this morning?"

"Yes. Where's a good place?"

Dakota thought a moment. "Your aunt's house. She's not there right now."

"How do you know?"

"Because I stopped by to see if you were okay. Come on—I'll follow you."

Dakota was right—Irene's house was deserted.

And when Lucy checked the answering machine, she heard Irene's voice announcing piles of paperwork to catch up on and very late hours at the office tonight. For once, Lucy was relieved to have the house all to herself. She fixed hot chocolate, then she and Dakota sat down at the kitchen table.

If you want to live . . . you mustn't tell anyone . . .

Katherine's warning still echoed in Lucy's ears. And though Lucy had kept that promise as best she could, even death seemed better now than carrying the burden alone.

"Dakota," Lucy announced, "this is going to take a while."

They'd spent the next three hours deep in conversation.

And Lucy had told her everything.

From that first night of fleeing into the cemetery, to Matt's strange behavior this evening at the church altar.

Everything.

At the beginning, Dakota kept quiet. A question here and there, a point that needed clarification—but generally, silence and a steady, solemn gaze. When Lucy finally exhausted herself and leaned back in the kitchen chair, only then did Dakota move, as though shaking off the spell of Lucy's narrative.

"Wow," she said quietly.

"Just 'wow'? That's it?"

"I don't know what else to say. I mean . . . you really expect me to believe all this?"

Lucy's heart sank. She gave a miserable nod.

"I do." Dakota nodded. "I *do* believe all this."

"You . . . do?"

"Lucy, I told you before. I believe in everything."

So simple. Just like that. Lucy hadn't known whether to laugh or to cry.

"But I'm cold inside," Dakota added. "I'll have to keep thinking about this. It's a lot to take in all at once."

"Imagine how I feel," Lucy replied glumly.

"I don't think I can. I think that part would be totally beyond my range of comprehension."

Lucy managed a smile. But one nagging question had kept at her, looming larger than all the others.

"Do you really think he's Byron's brother?" she asked.

"Well . . . why would he make up something like that?"

"I don't know, that's what bothers me so much. I mean . . . why would he suddenly show up now? Asking all those questions about Byron's funeral?"

"There could be a million reasons. Just because Byron never talked about him doesn't mean they're not brothers. And if he *looks* that much like Byron—"

"He does. So much, it's actually scary."

"And didn't you say Father Matt was trying to find some of Byron's relatives?"

"To help with his grandmother, yes."

"Then I'd say Jared is the least of your problems," Dakota concluded. "Considering everything you've told me, and putting it all in perspective."

Lost in their own thoughts, the girls sat for a while, neither of them speaking. It had been Lucy who finally broke the silence.

"Dakota . . . why *me?*"

"Why *not* you?" Dakota's answer was quick, but not unkind. "Remember that night in the bookstore when you saw Byron at the window?"

How could Lucy forget it? Uncomfortably, she lowered her eyes.

"Do you remember what I told you?" Dakota persisted. "About your being gifted? And brave?"

"Sort of."

"And how I knew you had an aura—a very special energy—like Byron's, only a whole lot stronger?"

"I remember."

"And how I told you to trust your instincts?"

Lucy nodded.

"So . . . what are your instincts telling you now?"

Lucy looked up into Dakota's calm stare. She wrapped her fingers tightly around her cup, but her hot chocolate had gone cold.

"I don't know," she admitted. "I don't feel like I know *anything* anymore. Nothing makes sense."

"But don't you see—that's just it. Things *never* make sense till they're *supposed* to. Answers don't come till we're able to understand them. And truths can't be revealed till we're ready to accept what they are."

A slight frown touched Dakota's brow. Her voice grew pensive as she reached over to squeeze Lucy's hand.

"This is one thing I believe. I believe we don't discover our purpose all at once. I believe we have to be eased into it, little by little . . . sort of like practicing. Till we're strong enough to handle it on our own."

"So . . . you're saying . . . what exactly are you saying?"

Lucy had wanted explanations. An end to all the madness. But what she'd gotten instead was Dakota's quiet prophecy.

"You've been chosen for something. Some destiny that's way beyond anything we could ever imagine."

"Don't tell me that, Dakota. Just tell me what to do!"

"I can't. But when it's time . . . you'll know."

So now they were sitting here eating at the run-down diner.

Because after their conversation, Lucy had needed noise and life and a sense of normalcy, no matter how false it might turn out to be.

She dragged one French fry through a thick pool of ketchup.

The red liquid reminded her of blood, and how she'd had to shower and change again before they'd come here, to wash away the stains and the smell and the shock of her day. From a distance she heard Dakota talking to her, and her mind snapped back into the present.

"What did you say?" Lucy asked.

"I said, you need to write everything down."

"Write what down?"

"Everything. Everything you told me. Everything that's happened to you since you came to Pine Ridge."

Lucy made a face. "What good would that do?"

"Well, just think about it. If you died mysteriously or disappeared again, you'd have documentation."

"That's a pleasant thought."

"You should keep a record of every experience. Like a diary."

"Are you planning to publish my memoirs after I die and make a lot of money?"

"No. I'm being practical." Dakota sucked

thoughtfully on her straw. "So . . . when are you going back?"

"To the church?" Lucy gave a weary shrug. "I can't just leave him there. But it'll be harder to get inside this time—and I *really* don't want to get arrested for breaking and entering."

"Maybe I can help."

"If you come with me, he'll know I told."

"But if he looks at my face, he'll know I'm very trustworthy."

Lucy couldn't help but smile. "You have a point."

"I just can't believe you didn't take toilet paper."

"What?"

"You brought all that other stuff for him, but you didn't bring toilet paper."

Lucy stared at Dakota. Dakota stared back.

"No toilet paper," Dakota sounded distressed. "And even worse . . . where's he supposed to go to the bathroom?"

"You know, I really don't think—" Lucy began, but before she could finish, a young man with spiked orange hair raced up to their booth and immediately plopped down beside Dakota.

Dakota just as immediately looked annoyed. "Lucy, this is my brother, Texas."

"Texas Montana?" The words were out before she could stop them, but Lucy managed a quick recovery. "The musician, right? Nice to meet you."

"Hey, how ya doin'?" The guy jerked his chin at her, though his attention was focused on Dakota. "You heard the latest?"

Dakota deliberately mulled this over. "The latest. Meaning . . . some earth-shattering event that actually broke up band practice tonight?"

"Couldn't practice without my bass guitarist, right?" he threw back at her. "Greg got called in."

"Greg works for the sheriff's department," Dakota explained.

Lucy nodded politely, but a prickle of apprehension was starting up her spine. Dakota's brother was so wound up, he was almost shaking.

"So he knows about that murder, right?" Texas went on. "That Wanda Carver girl?"

Lucy put her hands on the edge of the table. Her knuckles went white as she began to squeeze.

"You won't believe what happened to her." Texas's face was incredulous. "I mean—this is so, like, right out of the movies!"

"She fell," Lucy insisted firmly. "Someone pushed her."

"Yeah, well, maybe, but that's not all. And you can't say anything, 'cause the cops don't want anybody to know."

He motioned both girls closer. They leaned in over the table. He placed one arm over each of their shoulders and ducked his head down between them.

"That girl was drained, man," he whispered. "There was hardly any blood left in her whole body."

15

Lucy stared up at the bedroom ceiling.

She was holding the medallion Matt had given her, stroking it absently with her fingers. *"Someone gave me this a long time ago . . . an ancient holy symbol . . . helped through some pretty rough times . . . give it a try . . . special to you . . ."*

She'd almost forgotten about it through the drama of these last few days. She'd stashed it in her nightstand, where it had slipped to the back and gotten wedged behind the drawer. But tonight, after she'd washed Jared's clothes, and rounded up more towels and blankets, and fallen exhausted into bed, she'd found the medallion again, and she'd remembered Matt's words, and she'd longed to be comforted.

She still couldn't make out the medallion's design. Nor had she been able to discover what the carved symbol meant. The one time she'd tried to ask Matt about it, they'd been interrupted.

But now she squeezed it tightly with both hands. She'd been lying here for hours, unable to sleep and unable to turn off her thoughts.

"There was hardly any blood left in her whole body."

The death of Wanda Carver haunted her. The last moments of Wanda's life and what the poor girl must have gone through—the panic, the absolute terror and pain . . .

"The cops don't want anybody to know . . ."

And Lucy hadn't known either.

That day when she'd bumped into the cheerleaders, when she'd had that first inkling of Wanda's death . . .

How could she have known then that the death she'd seen in her vision would turn out to be a murder?

"I tried to warn her," Lucy whispered. "I tried to help."

And what was it Byron had told her? That day they'd been together, an eternity ago?

"You'll try to warn people, but they won't believe you . . . You'll try to save people, but you'll fail."

Lucy tossed restlessly beneath the covers.

It didn't surprise her that the police would be close-mouthed about Wanda's death. For a thorough investigation, they'd need to keep certain clues confidential. And they'd definitely want to prevent an outbreak of hysteria in the community. But who—*what*—could have done something this brutal to another human being? It *couldn't* be human itself, Lucy rationalized—it would have to be some sort of wild animal . . .

An animal that could blend into shadows . . .

That could stalk someone undetected . . .

That could rip a man's body to shreds with one bite . . .

A sinister chill crept through her. She huddled beneath the blankets, like a child afraid of the dark.

She was letting her imagination take over. Even an animal wouldn't be able to do what had been done to Wanda Carver. Even an animal couldn't drain a body of that much blood.

But what if it could?

What if there really *were* some animal that could do those things?

She was afraid to look at the curtains now, or

the sliding glass door . . . afraid to peer out on the balcony. Suddenly she was afraid to look anywhere, afraid even to move.

Because what if some horrible evil *had* come to Pine Ridge?

Hiding in cemeteries . . . roaming through woods . . . watching through windows in the night?

And what if I've seen it?

Her heart was pumping out of control, ice-cold terror coursing through her veins. The whole room was closing in.

And what if I've heard it?

For suddenly she sensed that she *had*. At some long-ago time, in some long-forgotten dream, she'd looked into its face and heard the sound of its voice . . .

And it touched me.

Like something was touching her now . . .

For one brief instant, the memory burned fierce and deep, and Lucy almost remembered.

Almost . . . but not quite.

Groggily, she sat up and reached for the blankets.

They were folded around her ankles, though

she didn't recall turning them down. The medallion had dropped to the floor.

I must have dozed off.

She tucked the covers under her chin.

Almost . . . she could almost remember . . .

That face, that voice, that touch . . .

So dear to her . . .

And so deadly.

16

The change in Lucy would be slow.

A transformation so subtle she would scarcely even recognize it in herself.

A delicate altering of the senses . . . a slight shifting of perceptions . . . so gradual . . . so very gradual . . .

Leaving emptiness in place of memories.

And realities where only disbelief had been before.

But most of all . . . most important of all . . . fixing *him* first and foremost in her mind.

It was *already* happening, in fact.

He had watched from the balcony tonight— watched her deep distress and restlessness—and he had suspected that she was trying to remember him.

Yes, Lucy, you need to remember. The one connected

to you now . . . the only one who can fill that ache inside you . . .

And when she fell asleep those few brief seconds, he had crept in to her. Gently turned down her blankets. Caressed her with a slow and tender touch.

Yes, Lucy, that's right. Remember . . .

Remember the way I lured you at the festival . . . blindfolded you behind the tent . . . when I first sucked the blood from your lip . . .

Such a sweet addiction that had been. Reeling him nearly senseless, with a craving he could scarcely control . . .

But now his own blood flowed through her veins.

His own blood, easing her through the transition.

Ah yes . . . the transition . . .

For a sudden moment he forgot about Lucy. Something like sadness swelled in his heart as his thoughts searched through the past.

He closed his eyes and tried, himself, to remember.

Tried to remember that first and wondrous change.

But his thoughts remained dark. Dark thoughts of pain and death and begging and tears.

For him it'd been a long, long time. *Too long.*

And that sacred memory he'd sworn never to forget had been washed away by an eternity of bloodshed.

No! He would *not* think of it—he would *never* think of it!

He would think of Lucy instead. He would think of how she'd come to him just a few nights ago, pulled by something she couldn't see, longing for something she couldn't understand and wasn't sure she'd find.

He would think of how he'd been waiting for her as she'd stepped from the house. How he'd watched as she'd opened herself to all the secrets of the night.

For one brief moment she'd come to him.

Come to him and surrendered.

Wearing moonlight like a bridal gown, hair shimmering over bare shoulders, reaching for him, reaching, so full of hope, of life, while he'd started toward her, closer and closer, ready to take her, in fact . . . when the woman had appeared.

The woman—the aunt.

The one who made Lucy so sad.

Soon, Lucy . . . soon. You won't be sad anymore . . .

Tonight he'd bent over her pillow.

Smoothed her brow, and gently stroked her hair.

His lips had found the pulse at her throat . . . he'd smiled as she moaned in her dreams.

He'd watched her first few drowsy moments of fading sleep . . .

He'd felt the warm surrender in her body as he'd kissed her.

Yes . . .

Her dependence on him was growing, just as he'd planned.

Touch by touch . . . and lie by cunning lie.

17

"I should have known this would happen." Lucy yanked open the door to her locker and jerked out a stack of books. "I mean, I *figured* it would happen; I just didn't think it would be this *bad*."

Her first clue had been in homeroom. The whole class fell silent the second she walked in, and the few students bold enough to look at her seemed either extremely nervous or downright hostile.

"It's like I'm a witch or something," Lucy grumbled. "Like I should wear a big red letter on my shirt. *D* for doom, maybe. Or *BL* for bad luck."

"Or *BO* for back off," Dakota added helpfully. "Except then people might just think you smell bad." She stood directly behind Lucy, as though to shield her friend from the rush of students through the hall. "Everyone's paranoid, Lucy. Just ignore them."

"Ignore them? If they thought they could get away with it, they'd stampede right now and pulverize me into the floor."

"But they *wouldn't* get away with it." Dakota made a subtle gesture toward the office, where several police officers stood talking to Principal Howser. "Not with all the uniforms around."

"Right. Like *they'd* protect me."

The two of them shouldered their way to the vending machines. Dakota opted for trail mix, while Lucy, after some hesitation, finally chose a packet of beef jerky.

"What's that about?" Dakota nodded at the strip of dried meat as Lucy unwrapped it. "You always get potato chips."

"I don't know. Maybe I'm just craving protein today."

Choosing a table just inside the cafeteria door, they unloaded their books and sat down.

"So what about Jared?" Dakota lowered her voice, glancing around as if spies might pop out of the trash cans.

Lucy's tone clearly conveyed her distress. "I

couldn't get over there this morning. Irene was in a terrible mood, and I thought she was going to give me the third degree about missing school yesterday. But she didn't. She never even mentioned it."

Dakota shrugged. "That's good."

"And at the last minute I couldn't get the car to start. So she had to give me a ride."

"No problem. We can go after school."

"*If* we can sneak in," Lucy reminded her. She hesitated, then said, "So you haven't changed your mind since last night?"

"About what?"

"About believing me. You said you still had to think about things."

"I *am* still thinking about things. I'm *always* thinking about things. That has nothing to do with believing you." Dakota carefully examined several raisins that she'd pulled from the bag. "Of course I believe you. These look like dead flies—you don't think they are, do you?"

After a cursory glance, Lucy shook her head. "Have you heard any more about the murder?"

"Not much. But I think that *thing* we're not supposed to tell anyone is starting to get around.

You can't keep news like that secret for very long. People are acting really, really nervous."

"Is that why we're having an assembly this afternoon?"

"Probably. The police and the sheriff's department are both going to be there. I'm sure they'll tell us to be careful and to travel in groups. Maybe even impose a curfew for a while. And I've heard the Holiday Treasure Hunt might be canceled."

Dakota finished her snack. She crumpled the cellophane and slowly licked the tip of each finger.

"It's weird, isn't it?" Her gaze shifted toward the noisy, crowded hallway. "I didn't even know Wanda that well—I didn't even *like* her that much—but now that she's dead . . ." Her voice trailed off. She looked at Lucy with a troubled frown.

"What is it?" Lucy asked softly.

"Can you feel her missing? Can you feel an empty spot where she used to be?"

Lucy thought a long moment. "I felt it with Byron."

"Me, too. Even though you know death isn't

an end to things . . . or an end to life . . . or whatever. Still, when someone leaves this dimension, there's this hole left in their place. And the world seems to shift a little off balance, till that hole fills up again."

The girls lapsed into silence. It was Lucy who finally spoke.

"Do you know when Wanda's funeral is?"

"They haven't released her body yet." Dakota sounded sad. "I think the police are making an attempt to avoid a major panic. Her family's just devastated. Mr. Carver had a heart attack last night and ended up in the emergency room."

"Is he okay?"

Dakota nodded, twirling a strand of red hair. "I hope so. They want to watch him for a few days."

"This is so awful," Lucy murmured. "I mean, what do the police think really happened? Do they have any clues? Any suspects?"

"Well, first they'll say it was someone just passing through town. That nobody in Pine Ridge could have done such a horrible thing. Then I'd be willing to bet they'll target the university—check out all the weirdos there."

"What do *you* think?"

Dakota fixed her with a level gaze. "What do *you* think?"

"I didn't see who killed her." Lucy sighed. "I didn't even see her actually dying, much less being murdered. God . . . I wish now that I had."

"Be careful what you wish for," Dakota said solemnly.

As the girls hurried to class, Lucy was struck by an oppressive air of mourning everywhere she looked. The shrines, the flowers and special presents, the whispers and tear-swollen eyes. It seemed that Pine Ridge High would never be allowed to recover from one tragedy before being hit by another.

Just like me, Lucy thought.

She and Dakota slipped into their seats just as roll was being taken. When Lucy heard her own name called, she answered but kept her eyes on her desk. It wasn't just wariness and anger she was sensing now from the other kids around her—it was fear.

The sudden realization surprised her. She could feel it in the air, sizzling like electricity—

suspicion and distrust coming at her from every direction. When the intercom came on, asking her to report to the office, she was almost relieved. She shrugged at Dakota, who threw her a questioning look. And as she neared the administration desk, she found someone unexpected waiting for her.

"Lucy." Matt greeted her with a smile. "Great. I wasn't sure you were even here today."

He thanked one of the secretaries, then ushered Lucy out into the hall.

"Come on," he joked. "Let's talk in my confessional."

"You mean I'm in some kind of trouble?"

"What possible kind of trouble could *you* be in?"

"Well, I didn't kill Wanda Carver, if that's what you're thinking."

Matt gave her that "get serious" look he was so good at. He seemed perfectly normal today, his usual self, not at all like he'd been at the church last night. Maybe he'd been dealing with a personal problem, Lucy decided. Even priests had problems, didn't they? She felt guilty now for spying on him.

Matt led her into his tiny office, shut the door, and motioned for her to sit down.

"Oh, I see you're wearing the medallion."

Lucy flushed. How could he tell? When she'd put it on this morning, she'd slid it down the front of her blouse. Only one small section of the chain showed—the part hanging just above her breasts—the rest of it was covered by her collar and long hair.

Self-consciously, she adjusted it around her throat. "I really like it. But you still haven't told me—"

"Where it's from? Hmmm . . . somewhere in Europe, I think. Now—anything you want to tell *me?*"

Lucy couldn't decide if he was kidding or not. "Should there be?" she asked cautiously.

"It's just that I covered for you yesterday when you skipped school."

"*You* did?"

"Yes. I committed a small sin on your behalf." Matt sighed. "I told Mr. Howser you were helping me out with a very important project. Important enough to keep you out of your classes the entire day."

"But . . . why?"

"Because Dakota said you had an important reason for being gone, and that was good enough for me." He lifted an eyebrow, his expression deadpan. "So . . . what? I *shouldn't* have believed her?"

"It's. . . it's not that . . ."

"Don't worry. She didn't tell me what the reason was, and I didn't ask."

"I . . . well . . . thanks."

"You're welcome. And I'm not trying to pry into your business. But if this reason of yours has anything to do with—"

"There's something I need you to see," Lucy said quickly. She wasn't exactly sure why she'd thought of the special-delivery headstone at that precise second. But since she'd planned on telling him anyway, now seemed as opportune a time as any. Besides, what better way to divert Matt's attention from the tricky matter at hand?

"You need *me* to see?" Matt echoed, surprised.

"Yes. It happened again."

"What did?"

"You remember the night you came over, and

I told you about that blanket and Byron's jacket in the car?"

Matt was beginning to look dubious. "Yes . . ."

"Well, something else happened. Something even worse this time. I got a delivery—"

"Delivery?" He picked up a mug from the desk and began stirring the contents with a spoon.

"A special delivery." Lucy explained. "In an unmarked truck. The box was addressed to me, and when I opened it, I found . . ."

She'd really thought she could recount the incident without emotion. Yet now the initial horror swept over her again, leaving her voice slightly unsteady.

"It was a headstone. And it had letters carved on it. R I P Angela Foster."

Matt didn't take his eyes off her. He set the mug back on the desk, his face pensive.

"You . . . you actually *saw* this headstone?" he asked.

"Of course I saw it. I opened the box. I totally panicked, and then I dumped it off the porch."

"You . . ."

"Dumped it off the porch. Into the bushes where no one could see it. I didn't want Irene finding it. That would have been too cruel."

Matt sat down. "And this happened . . . when?"

"Two nights ago," Lucy admitted reluctantly. "The night of Angela's vigil."

"And you're just mentioning it *now*?"

"I didn't know what else to do!"

"Well, if this is some kids' idea of a joke, maybe it's time for me to get involved."

"And what if it's not a joke?"

"Then the police should definitely be notified. For God's sake, why didn't you call them?"

"I wanted to. At first I thought if they saw it, then they'd finally have to believe me about all the other stuff I've told them. But . . . if you won't even believe me . . ."

"Hey, have I said anything about not believing you?"

"And now . . . with this murder . . . and Sheriff Stark asking me questions . . . and the way everyone's looking at me—"

"You were afraid," Matt concluded quietly. "Of course you were. No wonder you wanted to keep your distance from school."

"I still think someone's trying to send me a message. A warning."

"I don't know *what* to think about all this. If it's a prank, then Principal Howser should know about it. But if it turns out to be a real piece of evidence? You *have* to tell the police, Lucy—it could be crucial to finding Angela."

"Can't *you* just tell them you found it somewhere?"

"Wonderful. Now you want me to lie again."

"Matt, I'm confiding in you. If you tell, you'll be breaking your vows."

"Is there a name for this, besides blackmail?" Shaking his head in defeat, Matt began shuffling through some scattered papers on the desk. "Let me have a look at the headstone first. Then we can decide what to do."

Lucy didn't answer. Matt stopped arranging papers and focused on her dejected face.

"Lucy, like I said before, I don't mean to pry into your private life. But if you can't face coming to school . . . and especially now with the police hanging around . . ."

A long pause followed. Matt's face softened along with his voice.

"The thing is, I've heard all the rumors about what you told Wanda Carver. And of course, I think it's all bull—nonsense. And just so you know, I've had my *own* conversation with Sheriff Stark about your credibility. I think he and I are clear on the subject."

"You mean, you talked to him and took my side?"

"Great." A smile played at the corners of his mouth. "Now you're implying I'm not a good enough reference."

He got up and walked to the front of his desk, then casually leaned back against it. He seemed to be in deep thought, his eyes focused above her on the wall, his fingers running absentmindedly along his collar. The innocent gesture was almost seductive, and Lucy couldn't stop watching him. Embarrassed, she felt another hot flush creep over her cheeks.

What is wrong *with you?*

Dakota was right—no wonder the whole female population of Pine Ridge High was in love with Matt. While he, on the other hand, was completely clueless.

"The sheriff told me you'd had a dream." Matt shifted his gaze back to her. "And that you were trying to help."

Lucy wished they didn't have to talk about· this. She could feel guilt and depression tightening around her like a straitjacket.

"I did want to help," she agreed. "But I never thought it would turn into anything like this."

"And this dream," Matt continued quietly. "Do you have a lot of dreams like that?"

She hesitated a second. She chose her words with care. "You mean nightmares? I have them all the time."

"I meant dreams that tend to come true . . . in one way or another."

"I just . . . have dreams. They don't necessarily come true or mean anything at all. They're . . . you know . . . just dreams."

Matt's fingers slid from his collar to his face. Lightly he stroked his chin.

"Does Dr. Fielding still have you on medication?"

"Yes." Lucy shifted uncomfortably. Why was everyone so interested in her dreams all of a sudden? Why was *Matt*? "Sometimes the medicine gives me weird dreams. The doctor says that's normal."

Matt stared at her without speaking. Looked

into her eyes for several long moments, then finally nodded.

"Well." His shrug was philosophical. "Who can tell about dreams anyway? Sometimes they make sense; most of the time they don't."

"I did run into her once. Wanda Carver." *Now why did I say that?* "Literally. Going through a door."

"Well, there you are. Not so hard to figure out why she ended up in one of your dreams after all."

"I wish you'd convince the school of that."

Matt flashed that teasing smile. "Don't worry. I won't let them burn you at the stake." Reaching over, he ruffled her hair. "Now. Let's talk about another motive I had for bringing you here."

"What's that?"

"Don't sound so suspicious. It's good news."

"There *is* such a thing?"

He laughed at that. He folded his arms across his chest and stretched one long leg over the other.

"First," he announced dramatically, "I spoke with Mrs. Wetherly about your staying there."

This was definitely something Lucy hadn't expected. She sat up with a hopeful smile. "And?"

"She liked the idea very much. I told her about your aunt being away for a while. And that you needed a job and a place to stay. And that you could do light housework. And that you'd make a very good companion." Again that deadpan look. "Much better than a pet, in fact."

For the first time in days, Lucy brightened. "Really? She'll give me a chance?"

"By all means."

"That's so great! Now all I have to do is convince Aunt Irene."

"Piece of cake," Matt assured her. "How about I give her a call and see if she'll let me drop by this evening? I'm guessing you'd rather be gone when I ask her?"

"I'd be too nervous to hang around for that. But if you could get there before she comes home, then I can show you the headstone."

"Good idea."

"Do you think she'll say yes?"

"When it comes to the art of persuasion, being a priest has definite advantages."

"Thank you!" Before she even knew what she was doing, Lucy was on her feet, hugging him tightly. "Thank you so much—you don't know what this means to me—"

Abruptly she broke off.

Matt had already reached for her hands, to untangle himself from her hug. And now, as Lucy glanced up at him, she could see that his face was practically touching hers.

He was smiling, and his deep blue gaze seemed to draw her in. And for one instant, it was easy to imagine him stripped of his vows, with the tenderness of long-ago kisses still lingering upon his lips.

Flustered, Lucy tried to step back, but his arms were in the way.

"Thank you, Matt," she mumbled. "It seems like you're always there to rescue me."

Matt was the first to break eye contact. As the laughter slowly began to fade from his smile, something almost poignant took its place . . . and then was gone.

"Well, isn't that what priests are supposed to do?" He gave her a brief, brotherly pat on the shoulder. "At least, I think it mentions that somewhere in the Official How-to-Be-a-Priest Handbook."

And then he was behind his desk again, and Lucy was standing by the door, trying to look anywhere but at him.

"Now," Matt said brusquely. "I have more good news."

Curious, she watched him open the window blinds wider. Then he checked his appointment calendar and distractedly adjusted the collar at his neck.

"It's news I've been hoping for," he added.

"And what's that?"

"Byron Wetherly has a brother."

18

"A . . . brother?"

Lucy wondered if her voice sounded as stunned as she felt. She quickly sank down into the chair.

"I got a letter yesterday," Matt announced as he sat back down. "To tell you the truth, I didn't really expect to hear anything so fast. I thought it'd take months, at least."

"Byron's brother sent you a letter?"

"Well, you know how I was hoping there might be another relative somewhere—someone who could take care of Mrs. Wetherly?" Matt looked pleased with himself. "Sometimes this clergy connection can be a wonderful thing. It's amazing what the church can dig up."

"I don't understand."

"All I did was put the word out. I figured since the family's Catholic, that'd be an easy place to start. And it's not like their name's all that common."

Lucy shook her head. She sat stiff in her chair.

"My idea worked." Matt grinned. "Like a charm, in fact."

"So . . . what about this letter?"

"It's quite a story."

"I bet."

"Either one hell of a miracle, or one hell of a coincidence," he added. "Take your pick."

Before Lucy could answer, he leaned back in his chair, folded his arms behind his head, and began to explain.

"Apparently, Byron's father abandoned the family years ago, when the kids were small. But for some reason, he ended up taking this one son away with him. They moved out of the country, there was never any correspondence between the parents after that, so this boy never had a clue about his former life."

Matt paused. His eyes strayed to the window, to the snowy world beyond, and his expression grew troubled.

"It seems the father is—was—very wealthy. The boy spent most of his life in boarding schools."

"That's sad," Lucy murmured.

"I know. Taking a kid away from his own family, then never spending any time with him. What's the point?"

"So how old is he?"

"He didn't say. The tone of the letter sounds older though . . . you know, mature."

"Where did they live?"

"Different places. Europe, mostly."

"What's his name?"

"Jared. Jared Wetherly."

So it *was* true. The mysterious stranger she'd befriended *had* been telling the truth—even though he still had a lot of explaining to do.

Lucy felt almost dizzy with relief. She twisted her hands together in her lap and kept her gaze on Matt.

"But now," Matt went on solemnly, "it turns out the father's been sick for a long time. The son didn't know about it. *Nobody* knew about it. One day Jared called home, and his father's dying. And *that's* when his father finally told him the whole story."

"So . . . Jared didn't remember anything at all about his childhood?"

"No. But his father *did* mention Pine Ridge—that was the last place the family'd been together."

"Did he . . . say anything about a house fire?"

Matt winced. "I heard those stories, too, about Byron's mother."

"Do you think they're true? Do you think she's really in an institution somewhere?"

"I don't know. I'm not sure anybody really knows. But I'm not gonna be the one to bring it up."

Matt rose from his chair. Once more he stood beside the windowpane, his silhouette etched blackly against the pristine backdrop of snow.

"How would you feel?" he murmured. "Suddenly finding out you had a life . . . a past . . . a whole history you never even knew you had?"

Lucy's thoughts flashed wildly to the cellar. What awful thing could have happened to Jared before he'd even had a chance to phone Matt? And what if Jared had *died*? What if he'd had all those hopes . . . come all this way . . . and then died before reconnecting with his family?

With an effort, she picked up the conversation again.

"So . . . what else did he say in the letter?"

"He didn't know he had a grandmother, of course. He seemed really happy about it . . . but scared, too. He said he'd come here as soon as he could."

"Now?" Lucy asked quickly. "This week?"

Matt shrugged. "I don't know. I offered to meet him *when* he wanted, *where* he wanted—but he said there were things he needed to take care of now that his father was dead. He couldn't be exactly sure when he'd be here. So he said he'd just contact me once he got to town."

"That's . . . great. So he could actually be on his way here right now."

"Or not."

"Or he could already *be* here, maybe." Lucy tried her best to sound casual. "You know . . . working up his courage."

"Maybe . . . but I doubt it."

Clasping his hands behind his back, Matt began to pace. Slow, measured steps from the door to the window and back again.

"It's funny how things work out, though," he mused. "Jared finding all this out from his father right when we needed him to. I mean, when you look at situations like this, and how perfectly they fit together, you can't *doubt* there's a Power out there. Someone—some divine Force—whatever you choose to call it—in total control. Keeping things synchronized and running on time, just like clockwork. Just the way they're supposed to."

Lucy didn't comment. She was in no mood for divine philosophies at the moment.

"So," she asked him, "are you sure you still want me to stay with Mrs. Wetherly? Since she'll have her grandson here now?"

"Of course; you have to stay! They'll be strangers to each other."

"Well . . . I'm a stranger, too."

"No, you're not. Not like that." Matt spread his hands in appeal. "I think it's really important for you to be there when they meet. And besides—we don't want Mrs. Dempsey to be the first impression Jared has of Pine Ridge."

"Hmmm. Good point."

"Jared needs to get *acquainted* with his

grandmother first, not play nursemaid. And we don't even know how long he'll stay."

"You mean, you don't think he'll move here?"

"Would *you*, if you had all the money in the world?"

Lucy became instantly alarmed. "But he won't put her in a nursing home, will he?"

"I don't know why he would."

"Because of what you said—because he has money. Maybe he'll think she's a burden. Maybe he'll sell her house and stick her in one of those awful places. I thought we were trying to save her—not make things worse!"

"Wait—slow down—"

"Maybe he shouldn't come here at all! What if he totally ruins her life?"

"Whoa—*whoa!* Since when is everyone such a potential villain?" Looking amused now, Matt tried to calm her down. "Give him a chance, okay? I mean, if he *doesn't* want to take care of her, then he can use all that money to hire round-the-clock nurses."

"Matt, promise me—"

"Yes, yes, I *promise*. I *won't* let him put her in a nursing home."

But Lucy was only mildly pacified. "I don't want her hurt."

"I don't either. Which is why I'm glad you're gonna be there with her. To keep an eye on things."

Lucy pondered this a moment. Finally she gave a reluctant nod. "So when are you going to tell her?"

"I haven't quite figured that out yet."

"What do you mean? You have to tell her before Jared *gets* here." *Which means* now—*since he's hiding in the church cellar right this minute.*

Matt slid his hands into his pockets. He'd stopped pacing now, but his eyes were still angled toward the floor.

"The thing is," he said carefully, "Jared asked me to wait. I think he's still trying to get used to the idea himself. And since he's not exactly sure when he can get to town . . ."

"You can't just spring it on her."

"I know. But we shouldn't let her worry about it ahead of time either." Matt's voice went low and solemn. "With her stroke and all, and Byron's dying . . ."

And Katherine, too, Lucy thought sadly, *and so*

many other things that you and I will probably never even know about . . .

"Matt, what are you trying to say?"

"That we have to be careful. Because another big shock could kill her."

19

"I can guarantee you, Father Matt won't be at the old church anytime this afternoon," Dakota said.

Lucy held her hands out toward the vents. After making a quick pass through the grocery store, she and Dakota had been sitting in the parking lot for nearly fifteen minutes, waiting for the truck to warm up. The heater was straining, but spurting out only tepid air at best. Irritated, Dakota reached over, slammed the heels of both hands against the dashboard, then leaned back with a satisfied smile as a rush of hot air blasted over them.

"It's all in the touch," she said modestly when Lucy flashed her a grateful smile.

"So how do you know Matt—Father Matt— won't be there?"

"You heard what he said at our assembly

about being glad to stay after school if anyone still needed counseling. Didn't you see that stampede to the sign-up sheet? He might as well bring his pajamas and toothbrush, and camp out in his office indefinitely."

The two were silent a long moment.

Finally Dakota asked, "Do you think he *wears* pajamas?"

"Another esoteric mystery of the church," Lucy teased, trying not to blush. Just that brief, accidental encounter in Matt's office, and suddenly she could feel every detail of his body pressed to hers. *Well, that's one situation I might never tell Dakota about.*

Annoyed with herself, she turned to the window and leaned her cheek against the frosty glass.

"I bet he doesn't," Dakota reflected. "I bet he doesn't even wear underwear. I bet he sleeps naked."

"Dakota!"

"Well, I don't know, do you? But even if there's some rule priests have to follow—like, they *have* to sleep in black pajamas, or a black nightshirt, or black underwear—he just doesn't seem the type to go along with the crowd."

"Why don't you just ask him?"

"Maybe I will. He's helping out at the soup kitchen in the morning. Maybe I'll ask him then."

"Good idea. I'll come and help, too.

"And then when we're dishing out oatmeal together, and he wants to know if there's anything bothering me that I'd like to talk about, I'll just say, Father Matt, the thing that's bothering me most of all is wondering what you wear in bed."

"I bet Mrs. Dempsey would know." Amused, Lucy turned to face Dakota. "She's the housekeeper at the rectory, right?—she probably knows *all* their secrets."

"Especially Father Paul's."

"Why Father Paul's?"

"She's been in love with him for the last forty years. Everybody knows that."

"Mrs. Dempsey and Father Paul?"

"I know," Dakota made a face. "Not something you'd even *remotely* care to imagine."

Both girls burst out laughing. They laughed and laughed, from the grocery store till the truck finally rattled to a stop behind the cemetery.

"Oh, I hurt," Lucy moaned, holding her stomach.

Dakota slumped over the steering wheel and drew a deep breath. "Me, too."

"I can't remember when I've laughed this hard."

"Me neither."

"Especially when I shouldn't be laughing at all."

The laughter died. Dakota fixed Lucy with a sympathetic stare. "Life is extremely weird right now. *Your* life in particular. If this isn't the perfect time for you to laugh, I don't know what is."

But Lucy didn't answer right away. She stared down at the floor until Dakota reached over and took her hand.

"Thanks for telling me about your meeting with Father Matt," Dakota said. "Didn't his news about Jared make you feel a lot better?"

"Not particularly."

"The main thing is, you know now that Jared really *is* Byron's brother. And maybe if the two of you put your heads together, you can start figuring out some of this stuff."

"He didn't even know Byron." Lucy sighed. "What good is that going to do?"

"But he might have all these buried memories . . . things he hasn't thought about in years. Maybe by talking you'll find some new pieces of the puzzle. Whatever it is."

"I suppose," Lucy murmured.

"I mean . . . I've *heard* of people healing themselves." Releasing Lucy's hand, Dakota shifted and leaned against the door. "It might not be that common, but it's not impossible either. Some people have such powerful thoughts—such focused minds—they can actually make things move. They can bend objects and even levitate. Shamans . . . medicine men . . . some of those Bible guys . . . What you saw with Jared doesn't have to be a bad thing, you know. Sometimes what seems like magic can really be a gift."

"You mean . . . like *me*. Like the visions."

Dakota's shrug was noncomittal. "You know what's weird, though?"

"Besides everything?"

"When you touched Jared and had those visions, you didn't get really sick afterward."

"You're right." The car was almost *too* hot now, yet Lucy shivered. "I never thought of that."

"Remember that day you ran into Wanda? And then you had to go to the infirmary? And the other visions you told me about—it was almost like you had seizures?"

"So . . . what's your point?"

"I don't have a point. I just thought it was weird."

"Okay. That's one more mystery I'll add to my list."

"Maybe it's the quality time."

"Excuse me?"

"Quality time. Bonding time. You . . . you . . ." Dakota was searching for words. "You *helped* him . . . you *nurtured* him. You were kind. You made him feel safe. You gained his trust."

"You make him sound like a stray animal or something."

"Well," Dakota said seriously, "every living creature needs compassion, doesn't it?"

Lucy stared at her friend, at the depth of conviction in Dakota's eyes.

"Yes, Dakota, you're right. Even if we can't

always understand, we can at least show some compassion."

She pulled away, then glanced anxiously out the windshield. After yesterday's big snow, the cemetery looked like a vast white ocean, with softly curling waves where headstones used to be. The Wetherly mausoleum stood apart and alone, as if shunned by the rest of the dead.

"I wish you didn't have to sneak in the back way," Dakota said softly.

"Someone might see me at the front."

"They'll see your footprints anyway if they come around the side of the building. And you don't even know if you can get in like you did before. Then what?"

"Then I'll have to think of something else."

"I'll wait for you right here."

"But I don't know how long I'll be. Are you sure you don't want to leave for a while? Come back in an hour or so?"

"Okay, I'll get some coffee. And *then* I'll wait right here."

Stuffing her backpack full of groceries, Lucy started to open her door, then turned back to Dakota.

"What if Jared's not there? What if he turns out to be like the warning in my notebook? And like Byron outside the bookshop window?"

"He'll be there," Dakota insisted. "Things are all starting to make sense for a change, Lucy. He mailed that letter. He came here to Pine Ridge, but something happened to him before he had a chance to call Father Matt. The thing we don't know is . . . what attacked him?"

"The same thing that attacked Wanda Carver?"

"And maybe Katherine Wetherly, too? I don't know. Something bad, but . . . I don't know."

Lucy climbed out of the truck. She'd taken only a few steps when she turned back to look at her friend.

"Dakota, I don't think I could handle it if something happened to you."

"You could handle it. You could handle anything." Dakota regarded her with a pensive frown. She pulled her silly hat down to her eyes. She pulled her ridiculous scarf up over her nose. "And anyway, nothing's going to happen to me. I'm in disguise."

20

Lucy hadn't planned to stop at the mausoleum.

After everything that had happened yesterday, this was the last place on earth she should be.

And yet she couldn't help herself.

She paused a moment to look in the direction of the truck; she waved, just to let Dakota know she was okay. Hoisting the backpack over her other shoulder, she stepped inside the gates.

"Lucy . . ."

Gasping, Lucy whirled around. No one was there behind her, but she could have sworn she'd heard someone say her name. *Dakota?* She paused in the threshold and peered off across the cemetery. She couldn't see the truck, and she didn't hear a sound.

You're doing it again, letting this place get to you.

What was it that Jared had said to her just

yesterday? *"Hurry . . . before it comes back . . ."*

But there was nothing here now to be afraid of. No sense of danger like she'd felt before, no feeling of being watched . . .

Yet without warning, goose bumps crept over her arms. She could feel the hairs lifting at the back of her neck.

The enclosure was soft with shadows. Even on the sunniest of days, the narrow doorway and one grimy window afforded only a pale glow of light. Lucy hated to think of Byron here, in this dank and desolate tomb.

The mausoleum had space for nine bodies.

Every wall—except for the entrance— contained three individual crypts, each one large enough to accommodate a casket.

Byron's was to the right of the doorway, at the very bottom of the wall.

Once a coffin had been placed in its compartment, the opening was then sealed, and a name was engraved on the slab.

Byron had no epitaph.

His name—like those interred here long before him—revealed nothing about the life he had lived, or the person he had been.

Fighting tears, Lucy began walking toward his resting place.

Everything was just as it had been the day before—wind-strewn leaves, dark spatters across the walls, torn clumps of fur . . .

Only now the dark pool of Jared's blood seemed larger than Lucy remembered.

Frowning, she squatted down to examine it more closely.

It flowed in a wide, thick swath—spreading all the way to Byron's crypt. It had frozen there at the base of the slab and oozed down between the cracks in the foundation.

There was a bloody handprint beneath Byron's name.

The fingers were long and splayed, as though desperately reaching for something.

And on the floor beneath it lay a white rose.

Lucy gazed at it and shivered.

It had frozen in the perfection of early bloom, though its stem was wilted now, and its leaves hopelessly shriveled.

The soft creamy petals were stained with blood.

With a gesture that was almost reverent, she reached out her hand to touch it, then drew back again with a surprised cry as a thorn pricked her finger.

Her eyes went uneasily to the handprint.

Jared's hand, she told herself. While she'd left him alone yesterday to look for a hiding place, he'd tried to steady himself against the wall, tried to brace himself against his pain.

That's all it was.

That's all.

Lucy stood up again and sucked her finger. For one moment—and despite the thorns—she was halfway tempted to keep the rose for herself. But then, as an instant wave of guilt came over her, she knew she couldn't.

Someone had obviously left it here for Byron.

A simple gesture of love and remembrance.

An offering of beauty in an atmosphere of death.

She promised herself that when it got warmer, she'd come back here and clean everything up—wash the floor and window, bring fresh flowers, maybe even put a fresh coat of paint on the walls. She'd make it pretty, take some of the dinginess away, and—

"Lucy . . ."

Her heart froze. Her throat closed around a silent scream. She spun to face the doorway, but again, no one was there.

Lucy raced out into the graveyard. She looked frantically in every direction, but saw only Dakota, who was wading clumsily toward her through the snow.

"Did you call me?" Lucy demanded.

Dakota waved both arms in the air. "What?"

"I said, did you *call* me?"

Dakota's long scarf trailed behind her like a rainbow. She frowned, lifted the earflaps on her cap, and cupped one hand around an ear. *"What?"*

"Did you just call my name?" Lucy practically shouted.

The girl stopped and tried to catch her breath. "No. And I thought you were trying to sneak into the church."

"I was, but—"

"Well, you don't have to now." Taking the backpack, Dakota grabbed Lucy's hand and began pulling her back the way they'd come.

"Why not? What are you doing?"

Dakota looked pleased with herself. "I just found another way in."

21

"Here we go, Lucy—talk about luck."

Dakota pulled her truck up in front of the church. An old station wagon was angled against the curb, and as she turned off the motor, she gave Lucy a thumbs-up.

"And why is this lucky?" Lucy wanted to know.

"'Cause this is Mrs. Dempsey's car. I saw it on my way to get coffee."

"Are you insane?"

"While I distract her, you can pretend like you have to use the bathroom and sneak downstairs."

Lucy rolled her eyes. "And of course she won't suspect anything."

"I'll just get her to complain about something. She won't even notice you've left."

Unconvinced, Lucy followed Dakota into the church. Mrs. Dempsey was standing in one of the side aisles, clutching a mop and glaring at the floor.

"I thought I recognized your car outside." Dakota waved one end of her scarf. "How are you, Mrs. Dempsey?"

The cleaning woman squinted at them through the gloom. "Who's that?"

"Us," Dakota replied. She grabbed Lucy's hand and hauled her between some pews. "Can we use your bathroom, please?"

"Go home and use your own."

"It's an emergency."

"I'll show you an emergency. Just look at all the snow that blew in. Melting all over the floor. Ruining everything in sight."

Lucy glanced dubiously around the church, wondering what there was to ruin.

"It'll take me all winter to clean up this mess," Mrs. Dempsey went on, shaking her mop at them. "As if I had nothing better to do!"

Dakota stamped the snow from her shoes, only adding to the puddles. "Bathroom, please?"

"Oh, for heaven's sake. All you young people

ever think about is yourselves. Through that door there, and down the hall to your left. I don't know why you'd need a backpack though."

"She likes her own brand of toilet paper," Dakota explained in a conspiratorial whisper.

Throwing Dakota a grateful look, Lucy made her exit.

It took her a while to find her way back to the cellar.

With her usual poor sense of direction, she made several wrong turns before finally locating the closet with the door at the back.

She pulled out her flashlight and made her way carefully down the stairs, pausing at the bottom to get her bearings. The passageway was just as narrow and spooky as she remembered, and she forced herself not to run. When she reached the door, she'd knocked softly, then waited for a response.

"Jared?"

There was no answer.

"Jared? Are you okay?"

Suddenly apprehensive, she inched open the door. Almost as though she expected something bad to be waiting—and listening—on the other side.

"Jared? It's Lucy."

The first thing she noticed was the smell. Not the underground mustiness of a basement, but a smell like copper, flowing delicately through her nostrils and lingering at the back of her throat. She closed her eyes and tasted it. She swallowed it down, and then it was gone.

Feeling strangely light-headed, Lucy moved forward into the room. Jared was sleeping right where she'd left him, on his back beneath the covers, with his face turned toward the wall. She ran the flashlight beam over him and walked cautiously to the side of the bed. One of his arms lay outstretched on the floor, his hand clenched in a fist.

She realized at once that he was dreaming.

Quick, sharp spasms wracked his body, and wordless sounds mumbled from his lips. As Lucy gazed down at him, he tossed and struggled, locked in battle with some ferocious nightmare.

"Jared, it's all right," she soothed him. "It's just a bad dream."

She thought once more how much he looked like Byron.

And maybe it was because she'd just been to Byron's grave, or that she and Dakota had been talking about him so much lately—but in that moment, touching Jared, Lucy closed her eyes and pretended.

Pretended that things were different. That time had spun backward and fates had been altered. That Byron had managed to touch her hand in the last moment of his life, and broken the spell of what was to come.

"Byron," she whispered.

And that's when she heard the voice.

His voice. *Byron's voice.*

She heard it so clearly, knowing it *had* to be inside her own head, except it seemed so *real*, a real, living voice, coming from two places at once—from inside her head and from Jared's lips.

"Soon, Lucy . . . soon . . ."

Jumping back, she stared down with horrified eyes. Jared was still very much asleep. His body was quiet, his breathing calm.

I didn't hear Byron. It was only in my mind.

Thoroughly unnerved, she checked Jared's bandage. As the gauze fell away, she could see what little remained of his wound now—just a long, narrow swelling down the length of his rib cage.

I didn't hear Byron . . .

She ran her fingertips lightly over Jared's side. She felt the slow, smooth tensing of his muscles . . . she heard his breath catch softly in his throat.

For a split second she felt trapped there, trapped and helplessly paralyzed—trapped by eyes she couldn't see, by instincts she couldn't fathom.

I heard him because I wished it so much . . .

But it was only in my mind.

She left the clothes and food at Jared's bedside.

And recoiled from every shadow as she hurried back upstairs.

22

Maybe I do need a nice long rest.

Lucy stared down at the medicine bottle in her hand.

And maybe hearing Byron's voice was just a side effect of post-traumatic stress.

But she hadn't taken her pills today—hadn't, in fact, for *several* days, though Irene certainly didn't know that. Still . . . it took a while for the medication to get out of your system, didn't it? A few days? *Great. Maybe Jared's part of my syndrome, too.*

Sighing heavily, Lucy set down the bottle and checked the clock on her nightstand. She began pacing back and forth in the bedroom, like a caged animal.

There'd been a message from Matt on the answering machine when she got back home, confirming his appointment with Irene at eight o'clock tonight.

Nothing to be nervous about. It's only my future.

Her stomach was in knots just thinking about it. To be away from Irene would be great enough—to be out of this horrible house, and in a place that actually had some warmth and emotion in it, would seem like heaven.

The doorbell rang, and she let out a yelp.

She'd never get used to being alone in this stupid house —she'd never feel secure, no matter how many locks or alarms.

Matt. Thank goodness.

She'd almost forgotten he was coming early. As she ran down the stairs, she fought a sudden wave of nervousness and tried to convince herself that this time everything would be okay. This time she had real proof to show Matt—not just some wild story she couldn't back up. In fact, she'd checked the bushes as soon as she got home tonight—just to make sure the headstone was still there, hidden beside the porch.

If someone was intent on stealing it—just to make her look crazy—they'd have to be awfully strong and work awfully fast.

Squinting through the peephole, Lucy smiled and opened the door. He looked very much the priest tonight in his official clothes and collar. If *he* couldn't sway Irene, Lucy thought, no one could.

"Am I early enough?" Matt grinned. "Am I intimidating enough?"

"Yes to both. And look down to your left. There in those bushes. That's where I hid it."

She watched the humor fade slowly from his face. He dropped lightly to the ground and parted the evergreens with both hands. Then he stood for several moments without speaking.

"See?" Lucy said quietly. "I didn't make it up."

His glance was immediate—and regretful. "Lucy, I—"

"It doesn't matter about the other time. It was real, and I saw it—but when *you* went to the car, and the stuff was gone—*that* was real, too. I'm just glad you're seeing *this*."

Matt's expression was clearly troubled. "And the delivery truck was unmarked?"

"It was a van. A black van. It didn't have a sign or a name—and the driver was dressed in black, too."

"Nothing on the uniform?"

"No"

"Did you get a good look at his face?"

Just remembering it made her shudder. "He was pale. Angular face . . . his features were bony and sort of sharp. He had deep-set eyes."

"And you're sure you never saw him before?"

"I'm sure."

"Even on the sidewalk, maybe? In a store? Someone you might have passed in a car?"

"I think I would have remembered that face."

"So you'd remember it if you saw it again?"

Lucy nodded. "It was . . . creepy."

"Not someone around school?"

"No. Much older."

"Lucy." As Matt sighed and shook his head, Lucy knew he was scolding her again. "I just wish you'd called the police right away."

"But I told you why I didn't. If I can't get *you* to believe me, why would *they*?"

She hadn't meant to sound so sarcastic, but Matt gave an audible wince. He covered the headstone with the bushes again, then boosted himself back onto the porch.

"I'm considering options," he said.

"What options? The police are treating me like a criminal—the kids at school are treating me like a leper. If I show this to anybody, it's just one more reason to suspect me of . . . whatever everybody suspects me of."

"Lucy, nobody's gonna think you did anything to Angela. That's ridiculous."

"But they'll wonder why the headstone was delivered to me. And why I didn't report it that night." Folding her arms across her chest, Lucy shrank back against the wall. "Nothing I say will make sense to them. And why should it? It doesn't make sense to me either."

"Hey. Stop."

"And with everything else happening, I think part of me really *wanted* to believe it was a joke, except now I don't think it's a joke at all, I don't think it was *ever* supposed to be a joke—"

"Stop. It's okay."

"It's not okay. Somebody sent that to me, and I think they did it because they wanted me to know Angela's dead."

Matt's hands settled firmly on her shoulders. He leaned down until his face was even with her own.

"That's why you *have* to tell the police. For all you know, it could even be connected to Wanda Carver's murder. At the very least——"

Matt broke off, his expression grim. He let go of Lucy's shoulders and gestured adamantly toward the bushes.

"At the very least," he continued, "someone knows who you are and where you live and how to scare you. And maybe it *isn't* anything more than just some perverted joke. But . . . are you willing to take that chance?"

Lucy hesitated. "But what if——"

"I'm not. I'm not willing to take that chance."

He held her in a silent stare. As Lucy gazed back at him, he lifted one hand slowly toward her face.

"I'm not, Lucy."

A glare of headlights suddenly swung into the driveway and raked across them on the porch. Without missing a beat, Matt hastily made the sign of the cross in front of Lucy's nose.

"Bless you, my child." He winked, but without a smile. "And don't worry, I'll take care of it."

23

The world seemed almost beautiful tonight, Lucy thought.

Matt had reassured her that he could talk Irene into anything. And he'd promised to take care of the headstone. And as Lucy drove through the quiet streets toward Pine Corners, she realized that the snow had stopped falling and that stars were scattered brilliantly across the sky.

She'd told Irene she was meeting Dakota at the bookstore to study. Not exactly a lie, Lucy rationalized—Dakota *would* be showing up later, after she went shopping with her mom. And it wasn't as if Irene paid much attention, anyway—the only thing Irene had been concerned about was Angela's car.

"But it started right up," Lucy had reassured

her. "It seems to be running perfectly fine."

"Which doesn't necessarily mean it will start right up and run perfectly fine the next time you try it," Irene had reminded her crisply. "This is a very expensive car, Lucy, and a very good one. You must be abusing it in some way. It never gave Angela one bit of trouble."

Lucy had bit back an angry reply. But only because Matt had made a mimicking face at her over Irene's shoulder.

Now she didn't want to think about Aunt Irene anymore. Or Jared. Or Byron. Or Wanda Carver's murder, or the sheriff's interrogation, or the possibility of some lunatic running loose around Pine Ridge.

She just wanted to go somewhere comforting.

She just wanted to believe that her life might finally be getting better.

The Candlewick Shop was crowded when Lucy got there. Those same wonderful smells of musty books and strong coffee and aged wood greeted her the second she came through the door. Mr. Montana wasn't at his usual spot behind the counter; Lucy could hear him talking and laughing with someone in the adjacent room. She was actually glad to slip in unnoticed. As much as she liked Dakota's father, she didn't really feel like having a conversation tonight.

She wove her way around the store, taking her time. She strolled slowly through each section, up and down each narrow aisle, checking out titles from time to time, taking down a book to browse through it. But as the small rooms began to grow more and more packed with customers, Lucy finally headed upstairs.

Disappointingly, she found the second floor nearly as busy as the first. After squeezing herself in and out of several more cramped rooms, she escaped to the the last and tiniest one.

Supernatural section, she realized. *Dakota's favorite.*

To her surprise—and relief—there weren't as many people in here. Probably because it was so claustrophobic, she reasoned, with its impossible maze of tall shelves, nooks and crannies, and dead ends.

Dakota's favorite. Dakota's passion.

Pausing inside the doorway, Lucy scanned the overflowing collection of books. She could still remember when Dakota had shown her all these, and the conversation they'd had at the time.

"Some people call it supernatural," Dakota had told her. "Some call it real. There are just so many things out there that can't be explained or understood—not by our limited human perceptions, anyway. But those things still exist. They still happen. People are still affected by them . . . destinies are still controlled by them."

"Is that what you believe?" Lucy had been both curious and fascinated with the discussion. "That our destinies are predetermined?"

"I believe in everything," Dakota had answered. "But the question is . . . what do *you* believe in? Just because you can't see what's in front of you doesn't mean it's not there."

Lucy sidestepped a reader and moved slowly down the first row of shelves. She'd been right to confide in Dakota, she told herself—it had been absolutely the right thing to do. Dakota hadn't flinched at Lucy's confessions—Dakota hadn't seemed shocked or scared or even all that surprised.

Dakota believed in everything.

And Dakota would keep Lucy grounded.

With a sudden rush of gratitude, Lucy wished her friend would hurry and get here. She felt better with Dakota around. She felt almost like a sane, normal person.

"Is that her?"

The voice spoke softly and at a distance. In fact, Lucy didn't even pay attention to it until she heard the question repeated, and then the muffled laughter that followed.

"Don't touch any books in here. You might get the Lucy Curse."

Startled, Lucy spun toward the door and saw two girls huddled together, whispering. Instantly she recognized them from school and assumed they were whispering about her.

Her face flushed with embarrassment. Realizing they'd been caught, the girls ducked their heads, giggled again, and quickly disappeared.

Lucy felt sick. Just what she'd feared would happen was actually happening. Were the whispered insults and superstitions outside of school now? All over town? How could she keep going, day after day, knowing how everyone felt about her and trying to act as if it didn't hurt?

Slipping to the end of the aisle, she busied herself skimming through books. Top to bottom, left to right, pretending to read every title. Perhaps at one time they'd been categorized, but now there was just a messy and double-shelved hodgepodge of subjects that were mostly alien to her.

Witchcraft. The occult. Time travel. Ghosts and spiritualism, vampires and werewolves. Death, near-death, and how to talk with the dead. More myths and legends than she'd ever known existed. Satanism. Magic. Dreams and astrology and Tarot cards.

From time to time Lucy glanced around, alert for more whispers. The customers were dwindling now, and the upstairs area was quiet, except for an occasional sniffle and shuffling of feet. *Isolated incident,* she told herself, *no need to get all paranoid.* But in her heart she knew better. In her heart, she knew that facing the kids at school was only going to get worse.

Making her way down yet another aisle, Lucy

continued exploring. Symbols and talismans. Zombies. Rituals and secret societies. Haunted houses. Unexplained disappearances. Mysterious ships and lighthouses. Human sacrifice. The history of Evil.

Lucy nervously checked over her shoulder and peeked around the end of the aisle. A scholarly looking gentleman was still in here, and a woman in a purple velvet cape, and three college guys who were taking notes. One of them lifted his head and leered at her, and she moved farther back into the labyrinth of shelves.

She wondered what time it was. It must be almost closing time, she figured, and Dakota still hadn't shown up. Well, she'd wait just a little while longer. Pull out some homework and try to get something done. As she rounded the last row, she spotted a brick-manteled niche in the wall—what might once have been a large fireplace—but was now empty and perfect for studying. She opened her backpack and took out her history assignment. Then she spread out some papers to sit on, wedged herself into the opening, and began to read.

It was warm in here, and she hadn't bothered

to take off her jacket. As she flipped back and forth through her textbook, her head began to nod. She was so sleepy all of a sudden, she could hardly keep her eyes open. *Just for a minute*, she thought . . . *I'll finish this page, then I'll close my eyes just for a minute*. Dakota would be here anytime now. Even if she happened to doze off, Dakota would find her and wake her up . . .

Lucy was asleep almost at once.

Before she'd even read another word.

Asleep and blissfully unaware of anything else around her . . . oblivious to the minutes creeping by.

It was the silence, she decided later.

The vast, crushing silence that finally woke her—penetrating her subconscious with a troubled sense of something not quite right.

The room was pitch-dark. For one terrifying second, she didn't know where she was. Starting up in panic, she smacked her head against something sharp, and stars burst softly behind her eyes.

The bookstore! Calm down—you're in the bookstore—you fell asleep . . .

Moaning, Lucy felt her head. Her hair was

wet and sticky, her scalp already beginning to swell. A trickle of blood oozed over her forehead and into one eye, and she angrily wiped it away.

She remembered now—sitting down, studying, nodding off. This time she was more careful straightening up. She reached for the top of the opening, to the border of bricks where she'd hit her head. She hesitated, and she listened.

No one was in the room with her now.

And it didn't sound as though anyone was in the entire building.

What happened to Dakota?

Still feeling slightly dizzy, Lucy braced one hand against the bricks and shoved herself out. She stood for a moment on wobbly knees, then began searching for the door. If she could just get to the light switch, she'd feel a whole lot better. Even though she was pretty sure now that she was locked in here all alone.

"Mr. Montana?" she yelled.

Why hadn't he woken her up and sent her home? Why hadn't *anybody* woken her up and sent her home?

"Mr. Montana? Is anybody there?"

Lucy was determined to stay calm. As she made her way painstakingly through the maze of aisles and shelves, she reminded herself that this was no big deal, that all she had to do was use her cell phone and call Dakota to come and rescue her. It had probably happened lots of times, people being overlooked and locked in. With the crazy way this place was laid out, how could it *not* have happened before? She'd even managed to find the humor in her situation until she reached the door.

Reached the door and found it locked.

It didn't make sense. She knew the door had been wide open when she'd first come in and sat down—why would anyone close and lock it after hours?

Lucy fought down a fresh wave of fear. She ran her hand along the wall, feeling for the light switch.

She flipped it on, but nothing happened.

The dark seemed to swallow her whole.

"Mr. Montana!" Lucy banged on the door as hard as she could and shouted even louder. "Mr. Montana—*somebody*—*please* let me out!"

Her heart was pounding in her throat, filling her ears with panic. She flattened herself against the wall and tried desperately to think.

You have your cell phone. And a flashlight is still in your backpack. Turn on the flashlight, make the call, pull yourself together, and wait.

Fumbling blindly, she groped her way back to the corner. She forgot where she'd left her backpack, so when she tripped over it without warning, she fell sideways against the fireplace opening. She heard the painful crash of her shoulder, her feet scrambling for balance, and then something else.

A flat, heavy thud of something falling.

As though a book—or something like a book—had dropped onto the floor.

Lucy felt an immediate upsweep of dust, and backed away from it, coughing. She dug through her backpack, found the flashlight at the bottom, and quickly turned it on.

It *was* a book.

And even at first glance, Lucy could sense that it was unique.

It was of medium size—five inches wide, perhaps, and no more than eight inches in length—but it was extremely thick. The leather binding was brittle and cracked with age, ragged around the edges. The book was caked in dust and mold. A shroud of spiderwebs held it shut, and dampness had disfigured the front and back covers, leaving black sores of decay along the spine.

Even to Lucy's unpracticed eye, it was obvious that this book had been long abandoned and utterly forgotten.

Approaching cautiously, Lucy shone her flashlight over the opening in the wall. She could see now where several bricks had come loose where she'd fallen against them, leaving a deep gap in the mantel.

A hiding place. A secret hiding place.

In spite of the circumstances, Lucy's heart quickened with excitement. What else *could* it be but a hiding place? Someone had taken great pains to conceal this book inside that mantel, no telling how many years ago. But who? And why?

She wondered if Mr. Montana or Dakota knew about it. If *anyone* in Pine Ridge knew about it. Probably not, or else it would be in somebody's personal library right now. Or on one of these cluttered bookshelves, waiting to be sold.

Still, Lucy hesitated to pick it up. She stood over it for several more moments, illuminating it with the flashlight, peering down at its cover. Was that a title, barely visible beneath all that dust? Or some sort of design?

She didn't even realize she was holding her breath.

She knew there was something extraordinary about this book. Something different . . . something . . .

Lucy chewed doubtfully on her lip. *What?* What was it about this tattered old book that made her feel such a sense of . . .

Reverence.

It came to her, like a gentle whisper.

Reverence. Power.

Very slowly, Lucy knelt down. She held the flashlight in one hand and reached for the book with the other.

She was trembling.

Reverence . . . power . . .

Destiny.

24

She completely forgot about making the phone call.

About being alone, about being frightened, about being locked in.

In fact, once Lucy had gathered enough courage to pick up the book, she made herself comfortable on the floor and slowly began to examine her treasure.

At first the book wouldn't open.

As though after all this time, it still resisted being discovered and revealed.

It had taken both time and patience, working her fingers beneath the cover, prying oh so carefully, until at last, and with an almost audible sigh, the book parted itself in her hands.

Using her sleeve, Lucy wiped most of the dust away. She was able to see the cover more clearly now, but she still couldn't make it out. The title had practically disappeared, and the few engraved letters remaining were a language that was foreign to her. She touched the letters with one fingertip, delicately tracing each shape. They seemed almost regal—as if connected to some grand and glorious past.

The text, however, was different. No words had been boldly engraved here—instead, these lines and lines of writing had been done by hand, most probably with a quill. The ink was badly faded—in some spots, hopelessly invisible. Many of the pages had crumbled at their edges, or been carelessly torn, or even completely ripped out. Some bore the marks of fingerprints, or water spots, or candlewax, or burns. And here and there along the margins, a tiny sketch had been added, or an odd design, a sequence of numbers, or what might have been a spontaneous note.

A journal? A manual? Some sort of logbook?

Thoroughly intrigued, Lucy searched on.

There was far more than just writing here, she soon realized. She found maps of places she couldn't identify, drawings of plants she'd never seen. Long-pressed flowers and leaves, now turned to dust. And an occasional spattering of brownish drops that reminded her of blood . . .

What is *this?*

The more pages Lucy turned, the more eager she was for answers. Whose book had this been, and what had become of the owner? How had the book ended up here, and why had it been hidden away? How many years ago had it been written? What secrets did it hold? Lucy felt as though she were strangely and suddenly obsessed with it—she couldn't rest until its mysteries were solved.

She held the flashlight closer. She'd totally forgotten her fear, how frantic she'd been to get out of the bookstore. And she had no intentions of leaving now—not when she wasn't even halfway through the book. Turning another page, Lucy stared down at the sharp, slanted writing. Like swift slashes upon the page. *Male*, she thought, though she wasn't sure why. She liked his penmanship. She tried to imagine his hand moving over the paper, and she moved her hand over it, too.

A strong hand, this writer of words—a strong and gentle and merciless hand . . .

Her cell phone rang, shattering the silence.

Lucy screamed and jumped, and fumbled into her pocket.

"Hello?"

"Lucy! Where are you?"

"Dakota?" Darkness engulfed her as she dropped the flashlight. She lunged for it across the floor.

"Lucy, what are you *doing*? And where *are* you? My dad just called, and said Irene just called *him*, and—"

"Wait a minute. Where are *you*?"

"Out in the middle of nowhere. Picking up my brother from my aunt and uncle's house. Because my brother and my cousin are both idiots, and they drove my brother's car onto a frozen pond. Which turned out not to be as frozen as it looked."

"Are they okay?" The flashlight stopped rolling. It flickered once, went out, then glowed again dimly.

"For now. However, my brother's fate is subject to change the minute my dad gets ahold of him.

We're on our way back to town, even as I speak."

"What did your dad tell Irene?"

"To call me."

"So what did *you* tell her?"

"That you were with me, but you were in the bathroom and couldn't come to the phone."

"I owe you one. I owe you many."

"You owe me nothing. It's my absolute pleasure to protect you from Irene."

"Thanks," Lucy smiled. "What time is it?"

"Almost midnight."

"Midnight!" Retrieving her flashlight, Lucy plopped back down. She couldn't find the book. It must have fallen when she'd gone after the flashlight, but now she couldn't see it anywhere.

"Lucy, how come you didn't meet me?"

"I *did* meet you. In fact, that's where I am right now. Locked in your store."

Dakota's reply was a long, confused silence.

"I said, I'm locked in your store." Where was the book? It had to be here somewhere—it couldn't have fallen that far.

"But I looked for you. And Dad said you hadn't come in."

"He didn't see me. I fell asleep studying, and when I woke up, everyone was gone."

"So where are you now?"

"In your favorite room . . . sort of in the fireplace."

"Oh, yeah? I like that spot, too. No wonder nobody found you." Dakota gave a tolerant sigh. "Look, it might take me a while to get there—it is supposed to start sleeting tonight."

Lucy made an uninterested sound into the phone. She was trying to shine the flashlight, hold on to the phone, and feel around the floor at the same time.

"Look, you should probably just come home with me," Dakota went on. "Since you don't really know how to drive on ice. But these roads are really bad out here, so if I don't think I can make it within the next hour, I'll call my dad and just have him pick you up, okay? Oh, and he always turns the shop thermostat down at night—so if you're cold, feel free to make coffee."

"I would, but I'm locked in," Lucy mumbled.

"So what does that have to do with making coffee?"

"No, I mean I'm locked in this room. And the lights don't work."

Dakota paused. Lucy aimed the flashlight toward the empty fireplace.

"What do you mean?" Dakota asked. "None of those doors have locks on them."

25

Lucy didn't realize that her phone had gone dead.

That her hand was trembling, that the flashlight beam was wavering off through the shadows.

"None of those rooms have locks . . ."

Suddenly she felt the cold. She'd been so warm and comfortable before, so engrossed in the book, but now she was absolutely freezing.

She was afraid to go near the door.

Afraid to go near that door that held her prisoner . . .

"None of those rooms have locks."

But she'd tried the door, and it hadn't opened; she'd tried the knob, and it hadn't turned. *It must have been me then . . . the door must be stuck . . . I should have pushed it harder.*

Swallowing a taste of fear, Lucy listened again through the silence.

She listened to the old building creak and settle around her, to the drafts seeping up through the floor.

It sounded almost like footsteps.

Footsteps out in the hallway. Footsteps coming closer.

Lucy's grip tightened around the flashlight. She shut it off and sat there trembling in the dark.

Please, Dakota, please hurry . . .

She told herself that the footsteps weren't real, that the bookstore was safe, that nobody was in here except her. She told herself to quit being so ridiculous, to get up, to move. Go downstairs. Wait for Dakota.

But she *couldn't* move. She couldn't stop shaking.

And something was breathing now . . .

Short puffs of air, on the other side of that door.

A snuffling sound moving back and forth along the door, a gutteral sound creeping low across the floor.

She could hear it pause to sniff the air . . .

She could hear it trying to get in.

Oh God . . . oh my God . . .

She squeezed herself tight into the corner. She hugged her knees to her chest and pressed her head back against the wall.

The doorknob rattled softly.

No . . . please no . . .

There was a sharp clicking sound along the floorboards . . . a long scraping sound across the door . . .

Then something thumped hard against it.

Something strong enough to shake it in its frame and cause the room to shiver all around her.

Go away . . . go away!

The door began to open. Inch by torturous inch.

Teasing her . . . taking its time.

She would use the flashlight, she told herself. Use it as a weapon—strike first, think later. She had the advantage of darkness on her side—she was well hidden—she could use the element of surprise.

But now she realized the thing was coming toward her.

211

Step by muffled step, up and down the narrow aisles, between the crooked shelves, it was coming *toward* her, directly and stealthily toward the exact spot where she hid.

It knows I'm here, she realized.

It's known all along.

Reason deserted her. In that instant, self-preservation kicked in with such force that Lucy was on her feet before she even realized. She let out a shout of fear and rage. And she threw herself so hard, so fast, against the closest bookshelf that she didn't have time to feel the pain.

The bookshelf went over.

With a deafening crash, the rickety bookshelf toppled forward, spilling its entire contents and crashing down to the floor.

Then . . . silence.

Silence and blessed emptiness.

Because whatever had come for her was gone now.

And Lucy knew it would not come back tonight.

26

She should still be terrified.

Lucy sat on the overstuffed couch by the front window of the bookshop. Sleet scratched against the glass and whirled through the courtyard in a silvery frenzy.

Of *course* she should still be terrified, she kept telling herself. After what had just happened upstairs . . .

But I'm not.

Shocked, yes. Bewildered, yes. Badly shaken, yes.

But not terrified.

She curled up on the cushions and watched the weather. A few of the wind chimes—those not yet frozen—were bouncing on the clothesline, clanging merrily away. Lucy felt a smile tug at the corners of her mouth.

She could still hear the crash of the bookshelf hitting the floor.

She could still hear the explosion of books going in all directions.

And whatever had been skulking there in the dark had probably been caught right in the middle of everything.

But now it was gone.

Lucy still wasn't sure how she knew this. How she could tell from the very feel of the air around her that she was alone now, and safe. That there was no longer a threat in the shadows, or a reason to panic and hide.

She just *knew*.

And right now she didn't want to think beyond that or understand it or try to figure it out.

Right now, just the knowing was enough.

Pleasing, somehow. And liberating.

A part of me. It's becoming a normal part of me. It's who I am.

The realization surprised her a little, but she found it comforting, too. And curiously intriguing, just like the book she held in her arms.

Lucy turned her attention from the courtyard. Dakota had warned her it would take a while to get here, but Lucy didn't mind anymore. She didn't even mind that the electricity seemed to be off in the whole shop. Winter shone in through the windowpane, bathing her in a pale glow. She didn't bother with the flashlight now—somehow the reading seemed better without it.

If only I knew what it said—if only I could figure it out!

Cradling the book against her chest, she rested her chin against it. It was maddening not being able to decipher these words, these maps, these cryptic symbols she felt herself so totally drawn to. She couldn't shake the feeling that there were great and wondrous secrets hidden between the pages, and a world of revelations beyond any imagining.

Like an enchanted fairy tale, she concluded.

So maybe I've been bewitched.

The idea amused her. She put the book in her lap, opened the cover, and resumed her search.

Page after page of the unknown language. Page after page of the sketches and notes. Maybe there was someone who could actually translate it, Lucy thought. Maybe someone at the university. Maybe she could ask Irene. Or maybe Matt or Father Paul would know.

But I won't tell them much. I won't give anything away. This is my book.

Frowning, Lucy paused. Of course, it wasn't her book—she'd found it upstairs, it belonged to Mr. Montana.

Didn't it?

But after all, *she* was the one who'd discovered it. If it hadn't been for her, who knew how many more years or centuries would pass before anyone ever found it? In fact, the book had probably been here long before Mr. Montana even owned the shop. And to be even more precise, it had been hidden in the fireplace mantel—who knew *where* that mantel had originally come from?

Yes . . . the mantel . . .

Lucy hadn't considered this before, but it opened up a whole new range of possibilities. Scarcely able to contain her excitement, she tried to get back to her reading.

Strong, beautiful letters . . . and . . . sensitivity . . . but fear . . . resignation . . . time is running out . . . and someone must know the truth . . .

She wasn't sure exactly when it happened—or when she fully became aware of it. Her fingertip gliding beneath each sentence on the page . . . her lips reading the foreign words aloud . . . her mind seeing them in English.

It was almost like the slow lifting of a curtain, the gradual letting in of light, the shadows melting away. For suddenly, Lucy realized that the words in front of her were making sense, and that she could understand what some of them meant.

Her eyes began to widen. Her finger moved from word to word, pointing, going faster—sentence to sentence, paragraph to paragraph, page after page. As in her visions, there was no complete, unbroken narrative—but rather bits and pieces, a comment here, a phrase there, and through it all, the slow emergence of a dark, disturbing theme . . .

. . . *during daylight* . . .

. . . *handsome young man* . . .

. . . *transform* . . .

. . . *wolf or large black dog* . . .

Lucy couldn't stop. Her fingers fairly flew across the pages.

She could read it, though the words made no real sense to her. And with every brief touch, something seemed to stir within her heart. Sorrow? Familiarity? Longing? Lucy couldn't tell, though at some deeper, more instinctive level, she felt that some connection had been made.

But she was growing tired. Her hands were beginning to shake; her head was aching. Whatever had happened just now had taken far more out of her than she'd realized. Despite her fascination, she knew she had to rest.

One more . . . just one.

And so she turned just one page farther.

And felt the shock go through her like a knife.

There before her was a sketch of an angel.

An angel with no face.

An angel that cradled a rotting skull beneath its great, soft wings . . .

No . . . it can't be . . .

She'd seen that angel before.

Seen four of them, in fact.

Guarding each corner of Byron's mausoleum.

Lucy's strength drained out of her in a rush.

She wanted to look away, but she couldn't.

Her eyes went over every detail of the featureless face, the mighty wings, the macabre skull. Something had been written just beneath them—sharp, slanted letters much larger, much bolder, than all the others. And even though her stamina was spent, Lucy knew she had no choice—she *had* to know the meaning of these words.

She pressed her trembling fingers to the page.

And in her mind, the mystery fell away.

MY SON . . .

MOST POWERFUL OF THE UNDEAD.

27

He would have to feed, and feed soon.

It was the only way he could heal completely, gain back his strength.

His physical wounds had mended, as they always did. And though he had managed to exist for a while on what was convenient and readily available, it was not the nourishment his soul demanded.

He had never lacked for prey before, never known starvation.

Bus stops had proved to be natural, never-ending sources. Homeless shelters, soup kitchens, and abandoned buildings. Filthy street corners and flophouses, subways and subterranean tunnels—all havens for the hopeless and indigent, the ones never missed or mourned.

Blood banks were a little trickier, of course. And hospitals always required that extra bit of caution, though he had certainly foraged enough of them through the years with no mishaps whatsoever.

Nursing homes were no challenge at all.

And grave robbing was a delicate art he had long ago honed to sheer perfection. That consummate mixture of skill and timing and speed—the undetected rearranging of soil and spoiling flowers. With or without blood, the flesh was still tasty. All worth the risk taking, all worth the thrill.

Just thinking of it now made him ravenous.

His pace lengthened, and his body flowed.

He prowled a quiet neighborhood, past house after house of locked doors that could never keep him out. He briefly considered returning to the park, then decided against it. Not wise to strike in the same location again so soon—better to keep a low profile, at least for a few more nights.

Breathing deeply of the raw, cold air, he detected the scent of . . .

Child.

Small child . . . boy child . . .

He frowned and tested the air again.

He'd never been keen on children—only when there was no other possible way, only when his hand was forced, only in the most dire and desperate of circumstances. And even then, he was always left with a half-empty feeling, a sense of discontent.

This child was still three blocks away; he had two young parents with him, and an old grandfather, and a dog.

No, he decided impatiently, even as hunger pains ripped through his belly. No . . . even as he started to salivate . . .

No. *Too much trouble for too little satisfaction.*

Swiftly he ran in the opposite direction, his thoughts on survival, his thoughts on Lucy.

His body quivered, and his hunger grew.

She had drawn him there tonight, to the old bookshop, to the old part of town. With the first oozing of blood from that cut on her scalp, his body had craved, and his appetite surged. She had not known, of course, and the wound was inconsequential at worst. But still, he had needed to see for himself that she was safe and relatively unharmed.

Once reassured, it had amused him to stand against the door and shut her in. To make the creaking sounds upon the floor. To hear the growing panic in her voice, until every crack and crevice of the building was filled with Lucy's fear.

He had breathed it in like a prisoner too long without air.

But tonight he had tired very quickly of sport. Even before that bookcase had come crashing down while he'd watched from the safety of the hall.

You'll have to be much quicker than that, Lucy.

Her defiance had excited him and made him restless. His hunger was too great, and the scent of her blood too much a torment. When she was his at last, then he would toy with her as long, and as slowly, as he pleased.

And she would love him for it all the more.

But now he must feed, and feed soon.

Perhaps in the wilderness tonight, outside the confines of the town.

He never forgot how much he missed it, or how good it felt to come back. The silent woods, deep and dark with secrets . . . the hills flowing endlessly toward the stars. Snow unspoiled by plows, and roads that stretched unwalked for miles and miles.

His woods—*his* stars—*his* moonswept sky.

Only now, his moon was hidden by the clouds, and sleet ripped down in razors, slicing his face like scars. He embraced the cold; it stung, and it was bitter. His silky hair, his sinuous shadow, ethereal as smoke . . .

But what was this?

From a distance he saw it, abandoned in a snowbank. It was coated thickly in ice. Old and rusty and undependable, and conveniently unlocked.

He recognized it at once, for he knew this truck well.

Polluting the streets of Pine Ridge, chauffeuring family and friends, parked at the festival, the cemetery, the church. At the soup kitchen and at Lucy's . . .

He opened the door, eyes narrowing.

Ah, yes . . . I see we're out of gas.

And it's quite a long walk back for help.

A *very* long walk, in fact, down these snow-sunken country roads. Where the night lured and confused. Where the sounds of unearthly howling were not always made by the wind. And where uncertain detours led almost certainly to dead ends.

He reached one hand toward the passenger seat.

His lips curled into a smile.

The annoying brother had been here most recently, but Lucy had been here before that. Those moments of laughter were still here—he could sense them. Those rare moments of happiness he so marveled at.

Those moments of happiness he was so seldom a part of . . .

Lifting his head, he sniffed the frozen air, then groaned with an all-consuming hunger.

They were coming back to the truck now, and they were cold and tired.

He slipped inside and crouched low on the seat.

He rested.

And waited

And planned.

28

"So, I hear you're spending this afternoon with Mrs. Wetherly."

"A couple hours, I think."

Lucy tucked the receiver under her chin and tried to pull on her socks.

"Am I good, or what?" Matt teased.

"You're perfect." What was it Dakota always liked to say? *Just because he's a priest doesn't mean he's dead?*

"Then why the glum voice? I thought you'd be bouncing off the walls with joy."

"I . . ." Lucy made a valiant effort to show some enthusiasm. "I'm really happy."

"I've heard happy, and believe me, that's not it." There was a shuffling sound as though he were sifting through papers. "What's going on?"

Tell him about the book. Tell him.

But instead of giving her a chance to answer, Matt asked, "Have you seen Dakota?"

"You mean, today?"

"We were supposed to meet at the soup kitchen this morning, but she never showed up."

Lucy winced. She'd promised to meet Dakota there, too, and she'd completely forgotten about it.

"She might not be home yet. She was at her aunt and uncle's last night, and her dad told her to stay over if the roads were too bad."

"That makes sense."

"I'll have her call you, if I hear from her," Lucy promised. "And thanks, Matt. For setting this up with Gran."

"I'm just glad things worked out so well. So here's the plan. You're supposed to be at her house at noon to have lunch. Mrs. Dempsey's cooking up a feast. And I'm going with you."

"For me? Or for the feast?"

"Hmmm. It's a toss-up."

As another telephone rang in the background, Matt sounded annoyed.

"Lucy, can you hang on for just a second? I

hate to put you on hold, but I need to take this for Father Paul."

"It's okay."

Obligingly, Lucy sat down on her bed and finished pulling up her socks. Matt was right— she *should* be overjoyed about staying with Gran. Yet suddenly, what had been so important to her before didn't seem like such a priority.

Not with that book to think about.

Not with Jared to take care of.

Because of the bad weather, she hadn't been able to see him this morning. She wondered if he was cold and hungry or if his wound had somehow gotten worse. Or if someone had found him. She felt responsible for him; she needed to be there.

She needed to know he was okay.

She needed to know if a *lot* of things were okay.

Come on, Dakota, call me.

She'd already tried Dakota's house five times this morning, but no one had answered.

Call me . . . we have to talk!

Lucy had so much to tell her.

Especially about the book . . .

She'd taken the book with her last night.

And it wasn't as though she'd planned it, either—it had just sort of happened.

She'd been sitting there on the couch in the bookstore, still stunned from the last thing she'd read. She'd seen Mr. Montana hurrying into the courtyard, then bursting through the door on a blast of icy wind. And she'd simply slipped the book into her backpack. Slipped it right in without a second thought.

"Taxi at your service," Mr. Montana had greeted her. "I think I'm supposed to take you home."

"Where's Dakota?"

"Well, she got stuck out at her aunt and uncle's house. Those country roads are impossible in this kind of weather."

"Is she okay?"

"Oh, sure. I told her to just spend the night there. You'd better leave your car, too, Lucy. And keep the doors unlocked so they won't freeze. You girls can come back and pick it up later."

He'd flicked the light switch several times, then frowned.

"Looks like the power's out again. Oh, well. Every single time we have sleet like this."

"I'm really sorry about getting locked in, Mr. Montana."

"Oh, it's happened before. And it'll probably happen again. The worst thing would be if you didn't like books." He'd smiled and ushered her out the door. "Come on, let's get you home."

So she'd taken the book, but she still felt guilty afterward. A little. She told herself it was just a loan; that as soon as she finished with it, she'd return it and hide it back behind the bricks, and no one would ever have to know.

But in her heart, she had no intention of giving it back.

She didn't understand why, exactly.

She just *had* to have that book.

She'd felt so conspicuous in Mr. Montana's car, as though she had "thief" written all over her face. She couldn't wait to get inside and up to her room, but Irene was waiting for her in the living room.

"Lucy, where on earth have you been? I thought you were studying tonight."

Lucy waved good-bye to Mr. Montana. She

shut the front door, shook the sleet off her coat, and stomped her shoes on the mat. "We *were* studying."

"Where's the car? How did you get home?"

"Mr. Montana brought me—he didn't want me driving on the ice. He told me to leave the car and pick it up tomorrow."

She wished Irene would stop talking. She could hardly keep herself from pulling out the book and reading it on the spot.

"Lucy?"

"What?" She'd been so anxious about tonight, about Matt and Irene talking. Discussing her future and a new place to live. But as Lucy stood there holding her backpack, she hadn't been able to concentrate on anything else but the book.

"Lucy, sit down. I want to talk to you."

That's when she'd gotten that sudden, sinking feeling that Matt's visit had all been for nothing. She'd lowered herself onto the couch and braced herself for bad news. She'd thought about the book. Her heart sank to her toes.

"As I'm sure you know," Irene began, "Father Matt and I had quite an interesting talk tonight."

Uh-oh, here it comes . . .

She was used to bad news by now. But the book was in her backpack, and she had to finish reading it. She could hardly keep from fidgeting. She watched Irene's face, but it told her nothing.

"Lucy, I don't want you to think that I'm staying away indefinitely. This job in Paris isn't permanent, you know."

Hesitantly, Lucy nodded.

"I just don't want you to think that . . ." Irene plucked nervously at the sterling silver chain around her throat. "I don't want you to feel that I'm abandoning you."

Wow. Matt must have laid a huge *load of guilt on her tonight.*

This time Lucy shook her head.

"Father Matt thinks this is a wonderful idea, your living with Mrs. Wetherly. A marvelous opportunity for you. And I agree with him."

"You . . . do?"

Lucy had been totally shocked. She'd stared at her aunt with suspicious disbelief.

"And," Irene went on, "it seems to resolve many of my concerns for you. You'll have a safe place to stay, and I'm sure you'll be an enormous help to Mrs. Wetherly. You'll be earning money of your own. And it will certainly give me peace of mind while I'm gone."

Right. Like that was ever an issue.

But Lucy felt too preoccupied to hold a grudge. Relieved about staying with Gran, and stunned by her discoveries in the book, her mind had continued spinning in a dozen different directions.

"Well, it's late," Irene announced. "We both should be getting to bed."

Hardly able to contain herself, Lucy waited while Irene turned off the first-floor lights. Then she followed her aunt up the stairs.

On the landing, Irene paused. She'd looked at Lucy with a frown that was almost defensive. "I'm glad you're home safe," she'd said.

But Lucy scarcely heard. All she could think about was the book.

She locked her bedroom door, got undressed, and put the medallion back in her nightstand. Then she showered in record time, threw on pajamas, and jumped into bed.

She'd been pondering the book all night. Ever since she'd deciphered that last mysterious message.

She'd decided it was a hoax, of course.

It had to be.

The whole idea of "undead" was just too fantastic, too unbelievable.

Someone had made it up, like a ghost story.

Someone had made it up and written it all down to look like a journal. But it wasn't a journal at all—it was a work of pure fiction, just the renderings of a brilliant imagination.

She told herself this as she propped herself up in bed, holding the book open on her lap. She told herself this while at the same time she wondered how she could possibly have read and understood the unknown language it was written in.

And the way I discovered it, hidden away in that mantel . . .

How weird was *that*?

She told herself it was just another prank; she told herself a lot of things.

But the truth was . . . the book was *real*.

The book was *genuine*.

And Lucy had no clue how she knew this.

She just *did*.

She'd found it. And understood it.

And as she sat there flipping slowly through the pages, she summoned all her concentration and touched the letters once more with her fingertips.

Nothing happened.

That's weird . . .

She tried again. She pressed her fingers to the words and held them there, but absolutely nothing came into her head.

No! I didn't imagine it!

She was absolutely certain this time.

In fact, here was the sketch of the faceless angel, and the bold writing beneath it.

Once more she'd focused. Once more she'd touched her fingers to the letters.

Nothing.

What's going on here?

She told herself all she needed was rest.

A good night's sleep to replenish herself by morning.

Yes, that's all it is. A good night's sleep.

Frustrated, she'd closed the book and laid it on her nightstand.

She'd promised herself to wake up refreshed, and then she'd try again.

And this time she would understand every word . . .

"The news is," Matt said, "that Father Paul might be leaving us."

Engrossed in her own thoughts, Lucy said nothing.

"Hey, are you there?"

"Sorry. Yes, I'm here. He's moving?"

"Retiring, I think is how they're putting it."

"So . . . you'll be the only priest now?"

"Looks that way. And don't sound so disappointed. Oh, there goes that phone again. Look, how about I pick you up? Quarter till?"

"Quarter till. And Matt?"

"Hmmm?"

"I really am happy about living with Gran."

"Good. I want that in writing."

She heard the click on Matt's end of the line. She sat there and clutched the receiver.

Writing . . .

What was it Dakota had told her? That she should write everything down? So if she mysteriously died or disappeared, there'd be documentation?

Well, it was time.

Lucy took out a clean notebook and a pen. She sat cross-legged on her bed, and she thought.

At first, she didn't quite know how to start.

"Everything that's happened to you . . . a record of every experience . . ."

And then, finally, she wrote.

Everything.

Just like she'd told Dakota.

29

Lucy wrote all morning—racking her brain, trying to recall every detail.

She wasn't sure why she felt such a sudden need to do this. Maybe it had something to do with finding the book in the mantel. Maybe *that* had inspired her to write her own unbelievable story. Maybe someday someone would read her own personal journal and want to believe it as much as she wanted to *be* believed.

But then again . . . maybe her words would be doubted.

Just as she doubted the words of that strange and magical book. Those words she'd been able to translate.

Those words that hinted of truth.

She didn't realize how much time had passed. Checking the clock, she hid her notebook and hurried downstairs just as Matt rang the bell.

She didn't even have a chance to say hello before he reached out and grabbed her by the shoulders.

"Great news, Lucy."

"What?"

"Jared Wetherly called me this morning. Right after I hung up with you."

Lucy stared at him. "Called you? From where?"

"I assume from the place he's staying. Although he sounded like he was in a cave or something—it had a funny echo."

Was there a phone in the church cellar? She didn't remember one.

"He's ready to meet his grandmother." Matt sounded pleased.

"He is?" Lucy told herself she shouldn't really be surprised. She'd seen how Jared's wound had miraculously healed. And he couldn't hide forever. Sooner or later he'd have to face what was left of his family and reconnect at some level. She knew she should feel glad about it, but for some strange reason it depressed her.

Matt helped her into the Jeep, then sat down

behind the wheel. "I'll drop you off at Mrs. Wetherly's. You and she can have a nice chat while I go pick up Jared—and then we'll all sit down to Mrs. Dempsey's pot roast and homemade apple pie."

"Sounds good," Lucy agreed without enthusiasm. "Where are you picking him up?"

"You know that bed-and-breakfast on the north edge of town?"

"You mean Stratton House?"

Matt looked dubious. "I . . . think that's it. All I know is that it backs right up to the woods."

The woods. Was that where Jared had been attacked, she wondered? But there were lots and lots of woods around here . . . it could have happened any place. *Like the woods behind Irene's house . . . like the woods around the park . . .*

"Are you okay?" Matt eased up on the accelerator and gave her an anxious glance.

"Sure."

"You seem a million miles away."

"Just thinking."

He slowed at a railroad crossing and glanced at her again. "It's gonna be fine, you know. She'll love you."

"Thanks. But that's not what I was thinking about."

Before he could respond, Lucy turned and fixed him with a solemn frown.

"Do you remember when Byron died, and you went to Gran's house to tell her?"

Matt looked puzzled. "Yes."

"You said the front door was unlocked, and she was sitting up in bed, just like she was waiting for you."

Matt nodded, but didn't speak.

"So here we are, not saying anything to her so she won't worry. But what if she already knows? What if she knew before we did?"

Matt considered this. They were on Gran's street now, and Lucy could see the Victorian house at the end of the cul-de-sac. The two of them sat there while the Jeep idled at the curb.

"How could she know about Jared?" Matt asked reasonably. "She *lived* with Byron—she *raised* Byron. They were close."

"How did she seem when you told her Jared was here?"

"I haven't told her yet."

"Matt!"

"I know, I know, but he asked me not to. He said he wanted to tell her himself, in private. He said he wanted it to be personal and . . . and special."

"You're the one who said another shock might kill her!"

"Well, I thought maybe if you were there with her, it wouldn't."

"You're the priest. You're the one who's supposed to be good at handling things like this."

"Who told you that?" But at Lucy's sigh of exasperation, Matt rushed on. "Look, all I'm saying is, there's no possible way she could know that Jared's coming here. There's no . . . connection like she had with Byron. She wouldn't necessarily have any memories of Jared if his father took him away that young. Maybe she wasn't even living here when it happened. Maybe she never even knew about Jared at all."

"How could she know about Byron and not Jared?" Lucy insisted. "How could she not—"

"I'm late," Matt broke in. "Sorry, but I've got to go across town . . ."

"That should take a good five minutes."

"Funny. I'll be back in a little while."

Lucy got out of the Jeep, but Matt added one last thing.

"Lucy—about that headstone. I think you're right about Irene. I don't want her to be there when I take it."

Lucy gave a distracted nod. She couldn't think about the headstone now—not with Jared and Gran to deal with. She could see Mrs. Dempsey waiting for her in the front doorway, yet she stood there on the curb, watching Matt drive away.

She didn't know why this was bothering her so much—this link between Jared and his grandmother. She supposed it was because Byron had told her about Gran's ability to "see" things before they happened. But maybe Matt was right. Maybe Gran never even knew about Jared. Maybe Jared had been a well-kept secret.

Lucy walked up the sidewalk to the porch. Mrs. Dempsey was glaring at her.

"She wants to see you right away. I got the house fixed up just the way she likes it. Special occasion and all."

"It looks beautiful," Lucy agreed, noting the

thoughtful touches Mrs. Dempsey had added. As on Lucy's previous visit, everything gleamed and shone; there wasn't a speck of dust to be found. Vases of fresh flowers filled the house with fragrance, wafting together with the comforting smell of roast beef and fresh-baked bread. The same large cat was here as well— only this time it watched Lucy from behind an umbrella stand in the hall.

Yes, Lucy thought suddenly, and with some surprise. *Yes, this is where I belong.*

It seemed so right somehow.

Almost as if she were coming home.

"Well, go on now." Mrs. Dempsey broke into Lucy's reverie. "She's waiting."

Lucy remembered her way to the bedroom. She walked down the hallway, then paused a moment right outside the door.

Gran motioned her in before Lucy even knocked.

Still lying in the old-fashioned bed, surrounded by fluffy white covers and soft stacked pillows trimmed in delicate lace. Her nightgown was still the color of cream, and her long braid of silvery hair still fell across one tiny, thin shoulder. It was obvious that she'd been beautiful when she was young. She still was.

"Big day," Lucy said, almost shyly. She walked toward the bed, then began to notice that Gran wasn't smiling. That those huge dark eyes, so much like Byron's, were pinned intently on Lucy's face.

Lucy faltered. "I . . . I don't know how to thank you, Mrs. Wetherly. Byron loved you so much. I just feel . . . honored."

Finally . . . a feeble attempt at a smile. Gran moved her left hand again and gestured Lucy to come closer.

"What is it?" Lucy asked softly. "Is there something you want me to do?"

She could see the slate and the piece of chalk.

The painstaking movement of Gran's palsied hand as it scratched childlike letters across the surface of the slate.

DANGER.

Lucy reached out in slow motion. Trembling, she closed her fingers around Gran's.

"What is it?" she murmured. "What's wrong?"

"We're here!" Matt called from the porch.

And Gran was looking at her with such emotion—such profound emotion in those midnight eyes—but Lucy couldn't read it, didn't know what Gran was trying to tell her. Unsure what else to do, she turned the slate over and tucked it beneath the covers, talking gently to Gran the whole time.

"Mrs. Dempsey is going to show me everything I need to learn—the way you like the house kept, and what you like to eat, and—"

Footsteps came striding down the hall.

"—your favorite books and flowers . . ."

Matt stepped across the threshold and gave Gran his warmest smile.

"Mrs. Wetherly," he said softly, "there's someone I'd like you to meet."

Jared was standing behind Matt, and now Lucy saw him come forward. She heard her own breath catching in her throat—she felt herself clutching Gran's shoulder.

"Grandmother?" Jared's voice quivered, and his eyes shone with tears. "I . . . after all this time . . . I don't know what to say."

Lucy didn't either.

For this wasn't the Jared she'd rescued.

The Jared she'd hidden in the church cellar . . .
the one she'd tried to save . . .

This tall young man standing before her now
was someone else.

Someone she'd never seen before in her life.

THE
UNSEEN
PART FOUR: SIN AND SALVATION

SPEAK

Published by the Penguin Group

Penguin Group (USA) Inc., 345 Hudson Street, New York, New York 10014, U.S.A.

Penguin Group (Canada), 90 Eglinton Avenue East, Suite 700, Toronto, Ontario, Canada M4P 2Y3
(a division of Pearson Penguin Canada Inc.)

Penguin Books Ltd, 80 Strand, London WC2R 0RL, England

Penguin Ireland, 25 St Stephen's Green, Dublin 2, Ireland (a division of Penguin Books Ltd)

Penguin Group (Australia), 250 Camberwell Road, Camberwell, Victoria 3124, Australia
(a division of Pearson Australia Group Pty Ltd)

Penguin Books India Pvt Ltd, 11 Community Centre, Panchsheel Park, New Delhi - 110 017, India

Penguin Group (NZ), 67 Apollo Drive, Rosedale, Auckland 0632, New Zealand
(a division of Pearson New Zealand Ltd)

Penguin Books (South Africa) (Pty) Ltd, 24 Sturdee Avenue,
Rosebank, Johannesburg 2196, South Africa

Penguin Books Ltd, Registered Offices: 80 Strand, London WC2R 0RL, England

First published in the UK by Scholastic Ltd, 2005
First published in the United States of America by Speak, an imprint of Penguin Group (USA) Inc., 2006
This omnibus edition published by Speak, an imprint of Penguin Group (USA) Inc., 2012

1 3 5 7 9 10 8 6 4 2

Copyright © Richie Tankersley Cusick, 2005
All rights reserved

LIBRARY OF CONGRESS CATALOGING-IN-PUBLICATION DATA
Cusick, Richie Tankersley.
Sin and salvation / Richie Tankersley Cusick.
p. cm.—(The unseen ; pt. 4)
First published in the UK by Scholastic Ltd., 2005.
Summary: The deadly force returns to haunt Lucy as she confronts the violence surrounding her, not knowing
whether those closest to her are friend or enemy.
ISBN 0-14-240584-1 (pbk.)
[1. Supernatural—Fiction. 2. Psychic abilities—Fiction. 3. Horror stories.] I. Title.
PZ7.C9646Sin 2006 [Fic]—dc22 2005051631

Speak ISBN 978-0-14-242337-0

Set in Perpetua Regular

Printed in the United States of America

For you, Holly—
Who faced the unseen with me
every step of the way,
with your wisdom, grace, and inspiration.
I will always cherish our journey together.

PROLOGUE

The Game, at last, was drawing to a close.

The Game he could well have played out indefinitely, stalking Lucy into final and desperate submission.

But now that his hand had been unexpectedly forced, he would stand and claim what was rightfully his.

Stand and *fight* for what was rightfully his.

Yes, it is best this way.

Even for a master of deceit such as himself, lies could grow tiresome after so long. Flowing and fluent lies, cloaked in tragedies. Sad and seductive lies, veiled in sorrows.

Lies that slipped so easily into Lucy's tender heart, begging pity and compassion.

Lies that brought her closer.

Lies that made her trust.

Your weaknesses are my strengths, Lucy.

And now he would be stronger than ever.

No matter that the attack in the cemetery had taken him completely by surprise. Or that the ensuing battle, though brief, had been savagely brutal.

Lucy was to blame for all of it.

Lucy, the cause of his inattention, the source of his carelessness.

A distraction he could no longer afford.

So now the Game must end.

He closed his eyes, wincing slightly, touching the bruised and bloodied skin along his side.

The last of his wounds had practically disappeared.

The pain had faded into a bitter memory.

But the *old* wounds, the *ancient* wounds, had festered for hundreds of years, and the old scars still burned deep.

And though there had been many other battles in the past, none had ever been so important as the one he would soon be facing.

For his birthright . . .

His bloodline . . .

And for all eternity . . .

For you, my Lucy.

1

If only she'd known what was about to happen.

If only she'd been able to see how much worse, how much darker, the tragedies were that lay just ahead of her.

But it was Sunday, and she and Matt were going to Gran's, and for a few brief moments, she actually allowed herself a flicker of optimism.

So Lucy didn't know, and Lucy didn't see all those horrors yet to come.

And even if she had . . . it was already too late.

She'd been so excited when Matt picked her up that morning.

Excited about having dinner at Gran's house, but even more thrilled that Gran had invited her to live there while Irene was away in Paris.

And then Matt had given her the unexpected news: "Jared Wetherly called me this morning. Right after I hung up with you."

"Called you? From where?"

"I assume from the place he's staying. Although he sounded like he was in a cave or something—it had a funny echo."

Her mind had instantly switched to Jared. He'd been asleep when she'd last checked on him. He'd been asleep in the hiding place, and she hadn't woken him up. And now Matt was saying that Jared had *called*? Was there a phone in the church cellar? She couldn't remember one.

"He's ready to meet his grandmother," Matt announced then.

He'd sounded so pleased about it. And though Lucy hadn't exactly anticipated this turn of events, she'd told herself she shouldn't *really* be surprised. She'd seen how Jared's wound had miraculously healed. And Jared couldn't hide forever. Sooner or later he'd have to face what was left of his family and reconnect at some level. In her heart, she'd known she should feel glad about it, but for some strange reason it had only depressed her.

"I'll drop you off at Mrs. Wetherly's," Matt told her. "You and she can have a nice chat while I go pick up Jared—and then we'll all sit down to Mrs. Dempsey's pot roast and homemade apple pie."

But Lucy hadn't felt much enthusiasm. "Where are you picking him up?"

"You know that bed-and-breakfast on the north edge of town?"

"You mean Stratton House?"

"I . . . think that's it. All I know is that it backs right up to the woods."

The woods. Was that where Jared had been attacked? she wondered. But there were lots and lots of woods around here . . . it could have happened any place. *Like the woods behind Irene's house . . . like the woods around the park . . .*

"Are you okay?" Easing up on the accelerator, Matt had given her an anxious glance.

"Sure."

"You seem a million miles away."

"Just thinking."

He slowed at a railroad crossing and glanced

at her again. "It's gonna be fine, you know. She'll love you."

"Thanks. But that's not what I was thinking about."

Before he could respond, Lucy turned and fixed him with a solemn frown.

"Do you remember when Byron died, and you went to Gran's house to tell her?"

Matt looked puzzled. "Yes."

"You said the front door was unlocked, and she was sitting up in bed, just like she was waiting for you."

Matt nodded, but didn't speak.

"So here we are, not saying anything to her so she won't worry. But what if she already knows? What if she knew before we did?"

Matt had considered this. They'd turned onto Gran's street, and Lucy could see the Victorian house at the end of the cul-de-sac. The two of them sat there while the Jeep idled at the curb.

"How *could* she know about Jared?" Matt asked reasonably. "She *lived* with Byron—she *raised* Byron. They were close."

"How did she seem when you told her Jared was here?"

"I haven't told her yet."

"Matt!"

"I know, I know, but he asked me not to. He said he wanted to tell her himself. He said he wanted it to be personal and . . . and special."

"You're the one who said another shock might kill her!"

"Well, I thought maybe if you were there with her, it wouldn't."

"You're the priest. You're the one who's supposed to be so good at handling things like this."

"Who told you that?" But at Lucy's sigh of exasperation, Matt had rushed on. "Look, all I'm saying is, there's no possible way she could know that Jared's coming here. There's no . . . connection, like she had with Byron. She wouldn't necessarily have any memories of Jared, if his father took him away that young. Maybe she wasn't even living here when it happened. Maybe she never even knew about Jared at all."

"How could she know about Byron and not Jared?" Lucy insisted. "How could she not—"

"I'm late," Matt broke in. "Sorry, but I've got to go across town."

"That should take a good five minutes."

"Funny. I'll be back in a little while."

Lucy had gotten out of the Jeep, but Matt added one last thing.

"Lucy—about that headstone. I think you're right about Irene. I don't want her to be there when I take it."

Lucy had given a distracted nod. She couldn't think about the headstone now—not with Jared and Gran to deal with. She could see Mrs. Dempsey waiting for her in the front doorway, yet she stood there on the curb, watching Matt drive away.

She didn't know why this was bothering her so much—this link between Jared and his grandmother. She supposed it was because Byron had told her about Gran's ability to "see" things before they happened. But maybe Matt was right. Maybe Gran never even knew about Jared. Maybe Jared had been a well-kept secret.

She'd walked up the sidewalk to the porch. Mrs. Dempsey had been glaring at her.

"She wants to see you right away. I got the house fixed up, just the way she likes it. Special occasion and all."

"It looks beautiful," Lucy agreed, noting the thoughtful touches Mrs. Dempsey had added. As on Lucy's previous visit, everything gleamed and shone; there wasn't a speck of dust to be found. Vases of fresh flowers filled the house with fragrance, wafting together with the comforting smell of roast beef and fresh-baked bread. The same large cat was here, as well— only this time it watched Lucy from behind an umbrella stand in the hall.

Yes, Lucy had thought suddenly, and with some surprise. *Yes, this is where I belong.*

It had seemed so right somehow.

Almost as if she were coming home.

"Well, go on now." Mrs. Dempsey broke into Lucy's reverie. "She's waiting."

Lucy remembered her way to the bedroom. She walked down the hallway, then paused a moment right outside the door.

Gran motioned her in before Lucy even knocked.

Still lying in the old-fashioned bed, surrounded by fluffy white covers and soft stacked pillows trimmed in delicate lace. Her nightgown was still the color of cream, and her long braid of silvery hair still fell across one tiny, thin shoulder. It was obvious that she'd been beautiful when she was young. She still was.

"Big day," Lucy said, almost shyly. She walked toward the bed, then began to notice that Gran wasn't smiling. That those huge dark eyes, so much like Byron's, were pinned intently on Lucy's face.

Lucy faltered. "I . . . I don't know how to thank you, Mrs. Wetherly. Byron loved you so much. I just feel . . . honored."

Finally . . . a feeble attempt at a smile. Gran moved her left hand again and gestured for Lucy to come closer.

"What is it?" Lucy asked softly. "Is there something you want me to do?"

She could see the slate and the piece of chalk.

The painstaking movement of Gran's palsied hand as it scratched childlike letters across the surface of the slate: DANGER.

Lucy reached out in slow motion. Trembling, she closed her fingers around Gran's.

"What is it?" she murmured. "What's wrong?"

"We're here!" Matt called from the porch.

And Gran had been looking at her with such emotion—such profound emotion in those midnight eyes—but Lucy couldn't read it, didn't know what Gran was trying to tell her. Unsure what else to do, she turned the slate over and tucked it beneath the covers, talking gently to Gran the whole time.

"Mrs. Dempsey's going to show me everything I need to learn: the way you like the house kept, and what you like to eat, and—"

Footsteps came striding down the hall.

"Your favorite books and flowers—"

Matt stepped across the threshold and gave Gran his warmest smile. "Mrs. Wetherly," he said softly, "there's someone I'd like you to meet."

Jared was standing behind Matt, but now Lucy saw him come forward. She heard her own breath catching in her throat . . . she felt herself clutching Gran's shoulder.

"Mrs. Wetherly?" Jared had sounded slightly uncomfortable. After one quick glance, he'd gazed at the floor. "I . . . after all this time . . . I don't know what to say."

Lucy hadn't known either.

For this wasn't the Jared she'd rescued.

The Jared she'd hidden in the church cellar . . . the one she'd tried to save . . .

This tall young man standing beside her now was someone else.

Someone she'd never seen before in her life.

2

"Lucy?"

Had someone spoken? Had someone said her name?

"Lucy, I want you to meet Jared."

Or was she just imagining it?

The voice seemed oddly familiar, yet, at the same time, distant and disconnected—the same way *she* was feeling disconnected from this silent tableau around her: Matt in the doorway with a puzzled frown; Mrs. Dempsey behind him in the hall, wiping her eyes with a balled-up handkerchief; Gran lying so small and still in the bed, with Lucy's hand still clutching her shoulder. And all of them staring at the young man who'd suddenly walked into their midst.

The young man Lucy had never seen before.

"Lucy?"

Who *was* that? Lucy was sure she knew the voice but was at a loss to identify it. She was sure she knew the room, and the house, but, for that same inexplicable reason, sensed that everything had suddenly changed.

Am I the only one who's noticed?

The faces around her certainly didn't seem concerned. Except for Matt, who appeared to be saying something and trying to make eye contact with her.

Something's *different.*

With concentrated effort, Lucy tried to pinpoint the answer. *Good something? Bad something?* But she couldn't decide; her thoughts told her nothing.

"Lucy!"

Matt's voice broke through at last, scattering those thoughts in all directions. Startled, Lucy saw his face come into sharp focus and realized that no one was watching the young man anymore; they were all looking at her.

"I'm . . ." She glanced around, flushing in embarrassment. "I'm sorry . . . what?"

"I said, this is Jared Wetherly. Jared, this is Lucy."

She realized then that she hadn't taken her gaze off Jared Wetherly since he'd first come through the door. That her perceptions of everyone and everything else had come from other senses, but that her sight and attention had been firmly fixed on this long-lost grandson who had so recently—and conveniently—shown up out of nowhere.

My God, he could be a prince.

This was the first impression that came to her, as her eyes drifted over his hair, his face, down the length of his body.

A prince with night-black eyes.

Those Wetherly eyes, so much like Byron's, deep and dark and fathomless, unsettlingly intense. Eyes that could hold an interminable stare; eyes unhindered by shadows.

Eyes that can see into souls . . .

Eyes that reminded her all too well of that *other* stranger, that *other* Jared she'd rescued and cared for, that *other* Jared who'd claimed to be Byron's brother . . .

Lucy gave herself a firm mental shake and continued her silent inspection.

This Jared was taller than Byron, but it was

more than height or posture or angular frame that afforded him such regal bearing. It was his poise and aloofness, the way he held himself back, watching Gran with an expression of utmost courtesy and composure. And there was an underlying strength in him, as well—one that casual observers might not detect at first meeting.

His hair was the color of twilight—a dozen shades of darkness and shadows and fog. It fell in loose waves to his shoulders, framing his high forehead, his perfect cheekbones, and every elegantly defined feature of his face. A noble face, Lucy decided—an intriguing balance of striking and handsome, yet definitely not beautiful, as the other Jared's was.

Still . . . it was riveting. Compelling, somehow.

And vaguely disturbing to her, because of it.

So similar to the other Jared . . . yet so different. Even their clothes . . .

The realization startled her into one more quick assessment. Jeans and dark T-shirt, well-worn hiking boots with frayed laces, though instead of a denim jacket, this Jared wore a black coat, unbuttoned, that flowed smoothly to his ankles.

"Actually," Lucy heard him say, "Jared's my given name—an old family name. Only my father called me Jared." And then, before anyone could ask, he added, "I've always preferred my middle name. Nicholas."

"Nice to meet you," Lucy mumbled, without the least hint of sincerity. Had Nicholas even noticed? If he had, he certainly didn't seem offended. In fact, the look he was leveling at her right now held no emotion whatsoever.

Uncomfortably, Lucy glanced down at Gran. Gran's eyes were immeasurably sad—so sad that tears began to brim and spill over, coursing down the deep wrinkles of her face.

"Gran," Lucy whispered, but before she could say any more, Nicholas Wetherly stepped forward and withdrew a handkerchief from the pocket of his coat.

"Forgive me, Grandmother," he said softly. "I wanted to wait for the perfect moment . . . but perhaps this is it. I . . . I know explanations are in order." He reached toward her, then stopped abruptly, the handkerchief he held out to her still dangling in midair. "Please don't cry."

It was all Lucy could do not to push between them. A feeling of protectiveness surged through her, followed by an instant wave of shame. She had no right to interfere with this home-coming—this long-overdue meeting between grandmother and grandson. She had no right to pass judgment or to doubt this young man's character, no right to question Matt's careful and caring decision. And yet, her heart was beating frantically; she felt sick. She could feel Gran's shoulder trembling beneath her hand. And all she could think about was that *other* Jared—that other Jared she'd trusted and taken in, the one she'd helped and believed in and left alone in the cellar, and *what's he doing now while this stranger's standing here claiming to be a Wetherly? I've got to get back, I've got to go right away*—

"I shouldn't have come."

Nicholas's voice snapped her back to the present. As Lucy shot him a startled glance, she sensed a sudden awkwardness beneath his cool exterior, though his face gave nothing away.

"No," he reaffirmed quietly. "This was a very bad idea."

It took several moments for his words to sink in. By then, he'd already reached the front door, leaving Matt to hurry after him and block his way outside.

"Nicholas, wait. I know this can't be easy for you, but you're here now, and Gran needs . . ."

Lucy couldn't hear the rest. Mumbling apologies, she headed straight for the bathroom and locked herself inside.

Why don't you just let him leave, Matt? He doesn't belong here.

He doesn't belong here with Gran.

She leaned heavily against the sink, studying her reflection in the mirror. The glass was old; the person staring back at her seemed even older. Not the same person who'd once thought the world was safe and friendly, that tomorrows could only get brighter, that life made some kind of sense.

What happened to that person? I wouldn't even know where to look for her now.

Breathing deeply, Lucy splashed cold water over her face. Her thoughts wouldn't quiet; her nerves were as taut as stretched wire. She dried her face with a towel, then lowered herself slowly and sat on the edge of the tub.

"Danger," Lucy whispered to herself.

DANGER!

That's what Gran had written on her slate, and that's what Lucy was feeling now.

An icy shudder worked up her spine. She dropped the towel to the floor, then hugged herself tightly to keep the chill away.

Who are *you, Nicholas Wetherly?*

And why are you really here?

3

"Lucy, answer me. Are you okay?"

Through the fog in her brain, Lucy heard Matt's loud whisper from the hallway.

"Look, I'm not sure I can break this door down, so please don't make me humiliate myself."

Any other time she would have laughed. But now she just sat there on the tub, staring at the bathroom door and wondering how much time had passed since she'd locked herself in.

"Is Nicholas still here?" she finally asked him.

"Of course he's still here. Dinner's ready. We're all waiting on you."

"Will you take me back to Irene's?"

Now it was Matt who hesitated. "What's going on, Lucy?"

"I just want to go back, that's all."

"Don't give me that. You never want to go back to Irene's."

"Look, I'm just . . . really tired."

"Open the door."

She could picture him hovering out there, mumbling at her and trying to be inconspicuous, acting as if her sudden retreat to the bathroom was the most normal behavior in the world. But what could she say to him that would make any sense? That she'd already found *another* Jared Wetherly in the graveyard who claimed to be Byron's brother? That maybe—just maybe—Gran *had* received a premonition after all, because she'd written a warning on a slate?

That Mr. Jared Nicholas Wetherly's appearance here today couldn't have been more timely and convenient?

Or that I have such a dark, dark feeling that something's wrong . . .

Lucy got up from the edge of the tub. She rinsed her face and hands one more time, dried off, and hung the towel on the rack.

What good will it do to tell Matt? Levelheadedness hasn't exactly been my strong point lately.

Matt was leaning against the door. As Lucy

jerked it open, he scrambled to keep his balance and nearly fell on top of her.

"Where's Nicholas?" she demanded.

Matt motioned toward Gran's bedroom. "In there. With his grandmother."

"Why didn't he leave?" Alarmed, Lucy tried to peer around him into Gran's room, but the door had been pushed nearly shut. "I thought he was going to leave!"

"No, he's not leaving. He was just . . . overwhelmed. I mean, what did you expect? Meeting her after all these years? Why *wouldn't* he be overwhelmed?"

"And I suppose you're the one who talked him into staying?"

"Excuse me, but isn't that why he came all this way in the first place?"

"And what if he's not who he says he is?" Lucy blurted out.

Matt stared at her in complete bewilderment. Then he took her arm and began steering her toward the dining room. "What are you talking about? And for God's sake, keep your voice down."

"Does Gran know yet? Did he tell her?"

"Yes, he told her."

"I thought you wanted me to be there. Why didn't you wait for me?"

"Well, I couldn't very well plan a family reunion around your time in the bathroom, could I?"

Lucy ignored his poor attempt at humor. "So were you there when he told her?"

"He asked me to be. I think he really needed the support."

"What did Gran do?"

"She listened."

"Did she seem surprised? Or upset?"

"She held his hand."

"She held *his* hand? Or he held *her* hand?"

Matt's grip on her arm tightened, making Lucy wince. "What difference does it make? You saw her face when Nicholas came in. She had tears in her eyes; she seemed very emotional. In fact, I even found myself wondering if she *did* recognize him. Or some-thing *about* him, anyway. Like you said in the car—maybe she *did* feel some connection."

"Or not."

"Okay, that's it." Without breaking stride,

Matt led her into the parlor, glanced around to make sure they couldn't be overheard, then sat her down in a chair. "What's going on? I thought today was supposed to be a happy occasion. I thought—"

"What if everything you thought is wrong?"

Lucy gazed earnestly into his face. She saw the brief flicker of surprise, and the tiny bit of doubt that followed, but those weren't enough to stop her.

"Matt . . . what if Nicholas isn't who he says he is?"

"Well, who else *would* he be?"

"I don't know. I just think it's awfully convenient, him showing up right now—"

"Because I was *looking* for him. Because I *found* him—"

"You said yourself, it could be one hell of a coincidence."

"That was a *joke*, Lucy. Of *course* I don't think it's a coincidence. How could something like this possibly be a coincidence?"

"And what if he's a fraud?"

"A fraud. Right. That makes perfect sense." Groaning softly, Matt began his habit of pacing the room. "He intercepted my e-mails to his parish priest. He wiretapped the rectory phones. He faked his passport, his birth certificate, and all his other ID papers—"

"It's easy to fake IDs. People do it all the time."

"—and then he traveled *all* this way to another country, just so he could pretend to be a Wetherly. And now, after all his intricate scheming, he can finally claim his inheritance as the sole surviving heir."

"I'm serious, Matt."

"Oh, and while he's at it, he'll probably empty Gran's bank account. And swindle all her million-dollar investments. Not to mention stealing the family silver."

The loud whisper he'd been trying to maintain had steadily escalated. Now he stopped in front of Lucy's chair, planted one hand on each armrest, and leaned toward her.

"What aren't you telling me?"

"Nothing. And *you* be quiet; they'll hear you."

"What . . . aren't . . . you . . . telling . . . me . . . Lucy?"

"I just want to be sure, that's all."

"How could you be any more sure? And why would Nicholas pretend to be someone he's not, when there's absolutely nothing he can gain from it?"

I don't know! Lucy wanted to scream back at him. *I don't know why, but this* isn't *Jared Wetherly! This isn't Byron's brother, but now he's here in Byron's house, and we* let *him come in, we* asked *him to come in, and something's very wrong now, Gran can feel it, and I can feel it, too——*

"Why can't you just be happy for them?"

Matt's tone was mildly accusing. Lucy realized that he'd squatted down on his heels, so his eyes were level with her own.

"I am," Lucy managed to choke out. "I *am* happy for them. I just . . . want it to be real."

"Lucy, this *is* real. That the two of them finally found each other—after all this time—it's a miracle. And the thing is, if Byron hadn't . . ."

Matt lowered his eyes. He seemed to be choosing his words carefully.

"If Byron hadn't been in that accident, then probably none of this would ever have happened."

The irony of Matt's statement tore at her

heart. For one second, she could hear the faint echo of Jared's voice again, begging her as he bled out on the floor of Byron's mausoleum . . .

"Please . . . for Byron's sake . . ."

"So maybe," Matt went on, "if you could just look at it that way. Something good coming out of something tragic. A final gift from Byron to his grandmother, because he knew he couldn't be here for her anymore."

Lucy stared hard at the floor. What good would it do to argue, to even continue this discussion? Matt didn't know what she knew, hadn't seen what she'd seen. Matt hadn't met Jared Wetherly face-to-face, hadn't touched him or talked to him, nursed him or spent time with him. Hadn't heard the distress in his voice as he'd asked her over and over about Byron's death. As though he hadn't been able—or willing—to believe it. As though the reality of it was simply too unbearable to accept.

"All this time . . . and now I'm too late . . ."

Jared's words still haunted her.

The *real* Jared, the *true* Jared.

Not this stranger here now in Gran's house, in Gran's room, deceiving Gran's friends . . .

How am I going to protect you, Gran? And what am I protecting you from?

"Come on, Lucy, dinner's ready." Matt's voice coaxed her back again. "They're waiting for us."

He'd already started for the doorway before either of them realized someone was standing there.

"Nicholas." Matt's smile was slightly guilty. "Did Mrs. Dempsey send you to threaten us? Sorry, we were just coming."

But Nicholas didn't return the smile. He was holding something small and rectangular in his hands, and his solemn expression was still unreadable.

"She . . . wrote this," he said at last.

Lucy watched suspiciously as he passed the object to Matt. "That's Gran's slate. What are you doing with Gran's slate?"

"Nicholas, this is just what I hoped for." As Matt's smile widened, he offered the young man a quick, warm handshake. "This is great. Really. And you *should*. In fact, I can help you move in tonight."

"Move in?" Lucy whispered. "Let me see that."

29

Without waiting for a response, she jerked the slate from Matt and quickly read the crude letters scratched across its surface.

STAY.

"Matt—" Lucy began desperately, but neither he nor Nicholas was paying the least bit of attention to her now.

She watched the two of them head off toward the dining room. She heard Matt call her name, telling her to hurry. Then she turned around, walked slowly over to an end table, and held Gran's slate close to the lamp.

One simple word.

STAY.

But not the *only* word that had been written there.

Frowning, Lucy examined it more carefully. She could *swear* that something else had been scrawled directly above Gran's message. Four more painstaking letters. Letters that had been practically—but not entirely—erased.

WANT?

"Want stay." It seemed pretty clear what Gran had been trying to tell Nicholas. "I want you to stay."

Then why had the word "want" been erased?

And why are you making such a big deal out of this?

She almost felt guilty about it. And yet she couldn't stop herself from scrutinizing the message one last time, tracing each nearly invisible letter with the tip of her finger.

WANT?

Or . . .

Lucy drew a quick intake of breath.

Her fingertip froze over the word, and she felt the slate trembling in her hand.

"Oh no . . ."

Because she couldn't *really* be sure, could she? Couldn't really be certain at all—not with the letters so unreadable, as though someone had very quickly and very determinedly tried to wipe them out completely—

"Oh, Gran," Lucy whispered.

DON'T.

DON'T STAY.

4

She didn't know how she ever made it through dinner.

Later, she couldn't remember anything about it, what she'd eaten or how anything had tasted, or even what people had talked about, fragments of conversation going on around her as though she were invisible.

A few times she'd been vaguely aware of Matt sitting next to her, kicking her gently under the table. And once, realizing someone had spoken her name, she'd glanced up from her plate to see Nicholas watching her, and Mrs. Dempsey scowling at her, though she was never really clear about what their reasons were.

As usual, Matt had saved her.

"Too much studying, Lucy." He winked at her as he stood and began gathering dirty dishes. "I keep telling her she needs to get more sleep. Good grades aren't worth ruining your health—or appetite."

The explanation seemed to satisfy Mrs. Dempsey. Lucy realized the woman was looking particularly offended at the amount of uneaten food left on Lucy's plate.

"She needs apple pie," Matt added, tapping the side of Lucy's head. "Stimulates the brain cells."

Nicholas, not looking particularly amused, managed a polite smile and excused himself from the table. Lucy heard him walk down the hall toward Gran's room, and a minute later, Mrs. Dempsey followed.

"He's not really going to move in, is he?" Lucy blurted out.

Matt was trying to balance a huge platter in one hand, a stack of serving bowls in the other. At Lucy's sudden outburst, he nearly dropped everything on the floor.

"Is this still about Nicholas?" His glance went sharply toward the hall, then back again to her. "What's happened now? Is this a conversation we should be having in private?"

"You can't let him stay, Matt. Gran doesn't want him here!"

Matt rolled his eyes heavenward. "God? Give me strength."

"You've got to listen to me. He changed her message—"

"What in the hell are you talking about?"

But before Lucy could answer, Mrs. Dempsey reappeared in the dining room. After giving Matt a perfunctory nod of approval, the woman aimed a scowl in Lucy's direction.

"Can't eat dessert till the coffee's ready," she announced.

Matt actually sounded grateful. "I'll make it. Aren't there some things you wanted to show Lucy?"

"Lots of things. Important things. Things she needs to remember. Things she'll need to do every day, if she's going to be living here."

"You two go ahead, then. Please. I insist."

"Well, now's as good a time as any, I expect." Mrs. Dempsey regarded Lucy with undisguised misgivings. "Just be sure you pay attention to everything I say. I can't be running over here all hours of the day and night just because you can't remember what you're supposed to be doing."

Lucy had no choice but to comply. As Matt escaped to the kitchen, she trailed Mrs. Dempsey through every part of the house and tried her best to retain each lecture and detailed instruction.

"I've fixed lots of food and put it in the freezer," the cleaning woman told her. "At least you'll have leftovers for a while. Can't give Mrs. Wetherly pizza and those nacho things, you know. Not healthy."

"I don't eat pizza and nacho things." Lucy couldn't help sounding indignant. "And I *know* how to cook, Mrs. Dempsey. I've been cooking since I was five years old."

"Hmmph. Gas stove. Tricky pilot light."

"I can manage."

Mrs. Dempsey's expression suggested otherwise. Grudgingly she continued the tour, rattling off information as they went.

"The cat's name is Cinder. She likes to slip outside every chance she gets, so you'll have to make sure she's in at night before you go to bed. And leave the basement door cracked—her litter box is down there."

"What about a vet?"

"What *about* a vet?"

"If Cinder gets sick or—"

"Cinder doesn't get sick. But there's a list of important telephone numbers if you need them. I put them on the refrigerator door."

Mrs. Dempsey was nothing if not thorough. From the washing machine and temperamental furnace in the basement to the piles of dusty clutter in the attic and every room in between, by the time she and Lucy finished with their inspection, Lucy felt she knew the Wetherly house almost as well as if she'd grown up in it herself. Mrs. Dempsey had even shown her the bedrooms that had once belonged to Katherine and Byron.

"It's a real shame," the cleaning woman told her matter-of-factly. "All this space, and no one to fill it."

The rooms made Lucy feel intrusive. *Too recent . . . too personal.* She pretended to glance in, but she shut her eyes instead. It was bad enough trying to shut out her memories.

I was probably the last one, she thought miserably.

The very last one to see Katherine and Byron alive.

"Guess if this grandson decides to stay, I'll make up the bed in here." Mrs. Dempsey paused on the second-floor landing, indicating the room at the top of the stairs. "Can't say as I approve of you two young people living here without supervision, though. Too much temptation, if you ask me."

"Believe me, Mrs. Dempsey. There's absolutely nothing for you to worry about."

"Hmmph. I know all about good intentions, and I can tell you this. Once you break them—and it only takes one raging hormone—you'll have all the worry you can handle."

Lucy bit back a scathing reply as the two of them returned to the kitchen.

"Now, I'm not sure what Father Matt told you about what things you'll be expected to do." Mrs. Dempsey pulled a carton of ice cream from the freezer and began slicing thick wedges of apple pie.

Lucy sank into a chair. Her head was throbbing, and the thought of faking her way through dessert made the pain even worse.

"There's a nurse who comes regular," Mrs.

Dempsey went on. "Has for years—her name's Thelma. Soon as you move in, she'll be over to talk with you. She has her own key—oh, which reminds me. I asked Father Matt to make you one, too. And there's always an extra key in the garden shed out back. On a nail, just inside the door."

"What if Gran has an emergency?"

"That's why she wears that little alarm contraption around her neck. All she has to do is push that button, and help's on the way."

"I have a cell phone. I'll be sure to keep it on when I'm not here so Thelma can call if she needs me."

"You'll need to keep the place neat and clean. Do the laundry . . . take care of meals. Help out Mrs. Wetherly as much as you can. She's used to being by herself a lot of the time, but that's no excuse for you to go off socializing. At least when Byron was here, she knew he'd be coming home every day and . . . "

The woman's voice trailed off. As Lucy felt her own eyes fill with tears, Mrs. Dempsey jerked open a drawer and pulled out the ice cream scoop.

"Well, don't just sit there like a bump on a log," she snapped. "Make yourself useful."

Matt and Nicholas were both back at the table when Lucy brought out dessert. After Mrs. Dempsey poured coffee all around and sat down to eat, Lucy saw her chance.

"Did you hear that?" she asked anxiously.

Everyone paused, forks midair, to listen.

"Was that the cat?" Lucy sat up straighter, eyes darting around the room. "Has anyone seen Cinder?"

Mrs. Dempsey looked immediately perturbed. "Oh, for heaven's sake, I just got through telling you—"

"I'll go check. Be right back."

Before anyone else could say anything, Lucy hurried to the kitchen, let herself out the back door, and shut it softly behind her.

The cold struck her full force. She recoiled from it, yet welcomed it at the same time. Already the afternoon light was fading, casting long gray shadows across the snow, wrapping her in a soft cloak of dusk.

It made her feel safe somehow.

Free.

Free from fear and fretting, free from un-solved problems. If she closed her eyes tight enough, breathed deep enough, she could almost—almost, but not quite—make her mind dark and calm and blessedly empty.

Nicholas changed Gran's message. He's going to move in; he's going to live here with us. And I don't know how to stop him.

Despite her best efforts, the troublesome thoughts crept in. She tried to make sense of the last few days, but everything blurred together. She wondered about Dakota. She remembered the white rose in the mausoleum. She thought of Jared and wished she could talk to him now.

She realized she'd been thinking of him a lot.

That she could still feel his lips upon her hand.

Unconsciously, she pressed her palm to her mouth, testing the center with her tongue, imagining a lingering taste of . . .

"Blood," said a voice behind her.

Lucy whirled around with a cry.

She hadn't heard the back door open, hadn't even noticed the tall figure who was now leaning against the wall. His head was lowered, one hand cupped around a match as he tried to light the cigarette dangling from his lips.

"What did you say?" Lucy whispered.

The match caught; the tip of the cigarette glowed. Nicholas gave the match a careless shake and flicked it into the snow.

"The wind." His chin lifted. "Cold enough to chill your blood."

Lucy's stomach gave a queasy lurch. She wanted to look away from him, but his movements were strangely fascinating.

"Didn't mean to scare you," Nicholas added.

"You didn't."

His dark eyes narrowed. A thin stream of smoke curled from one corner of his mouth.

"You like the cold," he murmured. "So do I."

"Actually, I just like being out here by myself."

"And, my guess is, you don't like *me* much."

"I just think it's pretty amazing the way you suddenly show up here after all these years. And you better not try to stick Gran in some nursing home."

"And why would I do that?"

"You tell me."

"I'm afraid I'm not much good at riddles."

Lucy paused, suddenly tongue-tied. She knew she was acting like a complete idiot, but she couldn't seem to stop herself.

"So," Nicholas went on calmly, "I understand that you and I are going to be housemates."

Oh great, Matt, thanks a lot. Lucy felt herself bristle. Of course Matt would have told Nicholas about her plans to move in here. She only wondered what *else* Matt might have said about her.

"For Gran," she answered sharply. "I'm coming to help Gran."

Nicholas took another long drag on his cigarette. "I've been to Paris many times. Maybe your aunt will decide to stay."

A hot flush crept over Lucy's cheeks. Had Matt made her sound like some pathetic charity case? But before she could get defensive, Nicholas continued smoothly.

"Some might call it a coincidence—Matt finding me halfway around the world. And my grandmother . . . and you and I . . . all here together at this place. At this particular point in time." Nicholas raised an eyebrow. "I've never believed in coincidence myself. But I'm curious, Lucy . . . what would *you* call it?"

The cigarette seemed to drift in slow motion. He crushed the last spark beneath his heel and left her there alone.

5

I have to see Jared.

I have to go back tonight.

It was the only thing Lucy could think of as she tried to get through the rest of the evening. No matter what story she'd have to invent for Irene, no matter how icy the streets, even if she had to sneak from the house after Irene went to bed, Lucy was determined to get back to the church. The uneasiness building inside her was becoming unbearable. As though dangers and warnings and dire premonitions were clawing at the edges of her consciousness, yet all of them too vague to identify.

I have to make sure Jared's okay . . . that he's safe.

I have to tell him about Nicholas.

It was only after Matt dropped her off later that she suddenly remembered that she didn't have a car. That she'd left the Corvette parked at Pine Corners last night, and that by now it was probably one solid block of ice.

She didn't want to call Matt for help again. She knew there wasn't a chance in hell of borrowing Irene's car. And she still hadn't been able to get ahold of Dakota, though she'd tried repeatedly throughout the day.

Thoroughly frustrated, she went straight to her room, changed into sweats, then sat cross legged on the bed with the telephone in her lap.

Come on, Dakota, where are *you?*

It wasn't like Dakota not to call. Even if she were still snowed in at her aunt and uncle's house, she would at least have left Lucy a message by now.

Maybe the phone lines are down, Lucy tried to tell herself. *And maybe, even if her aunt and uncle have cell phones, they're out of range.*

Nothing's wrong. She's fine.

But in spite of her rationalizations, Lucy couldn't help growing more and more worried.

Please, Dakota. Please call.

"Lucy, I need to speak with you."

Surprised, Lucy saw that the bedroom door

had opened. Irene was leaning in, looking even more stiff and strained than usual, and plucking nervously at the diamond pendant around her neck.

"Lucy, I know this is sudden . . ."

Uh-oh. Not a good sign . . .

"But the truth is, I had absolutely no warning myself . . ."

Definitely *not a good sign.*

Lucy could feel her heart starting to pound. She stared at the tight lines around Irene's mouth.

"I received the news while you were out," Irene went on. "And I didn't want to call and ruin your afternoon."

An image of Angela whirled through Lucy's brain—even though she realized Irene was far too calm for that.

"There seem to be some very urgent matters in Paris. Unexpected problems having to do with my new position. In fact, the office needs me to leave much earlier than I'd expected."

"How much earlier?" Lucy murmured.

"In exactly"—Irene's arm lifted, showing her dainty gold watch— "two and a half hours."

The impact of the situation was slowly sinking

in. Lucy had a distant awareness of her world once again collapsing around her.

"Unfortunately, this is the only flight they could book me on with such short notice." Irene sounded annoyed. "And as you know, it's quite a lengthy drive to the airport."

Lucy did know. She could still remember riding in the car with her aunt when she'd first come to Pine Ridge. The trip had seemed endless, and endlessly sad.

"So . . ." Lucy struggled to get the words out. "You're leaving right now?"

"As quickly as possible."

Much to her dismay, Lucy felt tears prick behind her eyelids. This woman who'd shown her neither love nor understanding was now abandoning her, and yet for one crazy second, she actually considered throwing her arms around her aunt and begging her not to go. Even though she knew it was useless. Even though she knew Irene would never respond or reciprocate.

"And if . . ." Irene's voice trembled faintly, though her tone remained passionless. "And if you should hear anything—anything at all about Angela—"

"I'll call you. Of course I'll call you."

"Good. I've written down several numbers where I can be reached. And there's always my cell phone."

As though concluding a professional interview, Irene clasped her hands together and gave Lucy a dismissive nod. Then she glanced once more at her wristwatch, as though the passing of time had become one more thing of great inconvenience to her.

"Lucy, I'm afraid I won't have time to take you to Mrs. Wetherly's. I barely have time to finish packing."

"But I can't just go over there tonight and move in. Not without giving her any warning."

"I *am* sorry. But you're a big girl, and until you're able to stay with Byron's grandmother, you and I both know that you'll be perfectly safe here in the house by yourself."

"Aunt Irene—"

"Please, Lucy. I'm running late as it is."

With that, Irene hurried back to her travel preparations, leaving Lucy to stare forlornly at the doorway.

Just when you think things can't get any worse . . .

The few bites of pot roast and vegetables she had managed to choke down earlier threatened to come back up. In slow motion, she stacked pillows against the headboard, then leaned back into them, staring wide-eyed at the ceiling.

I can't stay here. I won't stay here.

She could hear muffled sounds of hangers clanging, of drawers opening and closing. The thud of suitcases hitting the floor. Then Irene's voice, crisp and matter-of-fact, out in the hall again, saying good-bye.

"I'll be leaving my car at the airport, Lucy. I've made arrangements for one of my coworkers to pick it up and use it while I'm away."

Lucy nodded.

"And I've contacted Sheriff Stark. You're to call *immediately* if you feel the least bit frightened about anything. He assures me that someone will be patrolling regularly and keeping an eye on the house."

"Have a good time." Lucy made a feeble effort at sincerity.

"And I left word with Father Paul. Just in case."

"In case of what?"

For a brief second, Irene seemed to falter. "In case . . . you might need anything. It's just good for . . . someone to know."

"Oh. Sure. Have a safe trip."

Lucy hadn't expected any show of emotion, so she wasn't surprised or disappointed when Irene turned abruptly and went downstairs. The front door slammed, and the house was still. A car pulled out of the driveway, and Lucy was alone.

The emptiness was crushing.

She hugged herself tightly as the silence echoed around her, as the rooms closed in, as fear crept along every hall.

"You're a big girl."

That's what Irene had told her, and that's what Lucy told herself now. It was ridiculous to be scared in a house with locks and deadbolts and alarms. Ridiculous to be frightened of being alone. Ridiculous to feel unloved and left behind . . .

And ridiculous to feel sorry for yourself!

She was angry at her own self-pity. She'd been through worse crises and endured them, faced bigger dangers and survived them. She should be glad Irene was gone; she should be taking advantage of her freedom, enjoying herself and doing exactly as she pleased.

But instead she was curled up here like a child, her heart thudding so fast it was making her dizzy. Her eyes so full of tears that the whole room swam out of focus.

The chill started at the base of her spine.

It rippled through every bone and muscle and lifted the hairs along the back of her neck.

As her vision cleared, her eyes moved slowly, reluctantly, toward the sliding glass door and the black night beyond.

And Lucy suddenly realized the truth.

That if she stayed here alone in this house tonight . . .

I'll die.

In a reckless panic, she grabbed for the phone, then screamed as it began to ring just when she'd reached it. She dropped it back on the bed, but it was too late, the voice was already there, saying her name, over and over again, on the other end of the line—

"Lucy . . . Lucy . . . I'm coming to get you—"

"*No!*" she shrieked, but the voice wouldn't

stop, wouldn't stop saying her name, and she *knew* that voice, she was *sure* of it, had heard that voice many times before, and the voice knew *her*, and the voice knew she was *here*, and the voice knew exactly where she *lived*—

"Lucy!" Matt sounded fuzzy and foreign and faraway as his words crackled out at her through the static. "Can you hear me?"

Her hands were shaking so badly, she could hardly grip the receiver.

"Matt?" she finally managed to choke.

"Lucy," Matt said, "It's Dakota. She's been hurt."

"Wh-what?"

"She's in the hospital." Matt sounded grim. "Did you hear what I said? I'm on my way there now. And I'm coming to get you."

6

"What happened to her, Matt?"

"I don't know."

"How bad is it?"

"I don't know that either."

Huddled in the front seat of the Jeep, Lucy fixed him with a frustrated stare.

"All I *do* know," Matt sighed, "is that her mom called and left a message with Father Paul early this afternoon. Something about Dakota being in an accident."

"You mean, Dakota's been in the hospital all day, and Father Paul didn't even tell you?"

"Look, I don't think it's any great secret how forgetful he is. It's probably one of the main reasons I was sent here."

"But this is important! What if—"

"I'm sure if it were . . . critical," Matt chose

the words carefully, "he'd have notified me right away. Or gone to the hospital himself."

Yet Lucy was all too aware of how fast Matt was driving. How quickly he was taking corners and sliding through stop signs, in spite of the icy roads. And that he was definitely *Father* Matt tonight, solemn in his official black, every bit the priest from head to toe.

"I should have known something was wrong," Lucy said miserably. "I mean, I *felt* like something was wrong, but I didn't do anything about it."

"Lucy, how could you possibly have known? And even if you had, what could you have done about it?"

"I could have gone to the hospital sooner. I could have been there with her." Lucy frowned. "They *will* let me be with her, won't they?"

"I'm not sure. She might not be allowed visitors yet. We'll just have to see."

"Then if I can't see her . . . why am I going with you?"

Even in the shadowed interior of the car, she could see Matt's face darken.

"Because," he said tightly, "Father Paul *also*

told me about the message from your aunt."

"Oh. That."

What could she say, really? This was the way it was, and no matter how much she hated it, no matter how much she dreaded it, the situation wasn't going to change. Irene was never going to cancel the trip; Irene was never going to love her.

"Oh, well." Feigning indifference, Lucy shrugged. "Just think of all the wild parties I'll be able to have while she's gone."

But Matt obviously didn't find it amusing. "And just what'd she expect you to do? Stay alone in that house tonight?"

"I think that was the general idea."

"Over my dead body."

"Look, Matt, it's too late to spring me on Gran tonight. With Nicholas showing up and all, she's had enough trauma for one day. And I certainly don't expect—"

"Unbelievable." A muscle clenched in Matt's jaw, and his eyes stayed glued to the windshield. "I mean, wouldn't you think with Angela missing, and some maniac running loose, Irene would have some sense of responsibility? Or show just one tiny bit of concern?"

Lucy didn't answer. From the clipped tone of Matt's voice, she could tell he was trying very hard to control his temper.

"I'm sorry, Lucy. I have no right to say that. And you know that Irene taking this trip doesn't have anything to do with you, right? That you shouldn't take it personally?"

"I . . ." Lucy's voice trailed off. She swallowed the lump in her throat. "Actually . . . it does seem *pretty* personal."

"Well, it's not. Really. I promise."

Matt had managed to calm down a little. Lucy could see his shoulders relaxing, his grip loosening on the steering wheel. And when he spoke again, he sounded both sad and resolved.

"Look . . . it's *not* about you. It's about her. Like *everything* is in Irene's world. *Always*, all about *her*." He paused a moment, then added, "And she's doing what she always does when she can't control what happens around her. She's trying to escape."

It wasn't what Lucy wanted to hear. Even though the words made sense, even though they struck a note of truth in her heart. Right now she wanted to be *angry*—as angry as Matt had been only seconds before—because anger took away the hurt.

"I don't care," she said, surprised at her own response. Surprised even more when she saw Matt smile.

"You don't have to care. Or be generous. Or even understand it. But you can't deny your own strength. That's what *you* have that Irene doesn't." His tone softened. "That's why you've stayed. And that's why she's run away."

They'd reached the hospital parking lot. As Lucy considered Matt's theories, he helped her out and locked up the Jeep. "Come on. If they won't let you see Dakota, you can hang out in the waiting room. I'll find out what I can."

"And then what?"

The look he gave her was stern. "And then I run you by the house, and you pack an overnight bag, and I drop you off at Gran's."

"But—"

"Never argue with a priest. It could endanger your soul."

Taking her arm, he hurried her through the main doors to the reception desk. Then, after a brief conversation with the volunteer on duty, he and Lucy rode the elevator to the third floor and went straight to the nurses' station.

"Down this hall, Father, but you just missed the family. They've been here all day; we finally talked them into getting something to eat."

Lucy hung back, her dread mounting. She could see several nurses talking with Matt, nodding toward the opposite end of the corridor, their eyes lowered, their faces grim, as they glanced at Lucy and shook their heads. The sick feeling spread out from her stomach and crawled up the back of her throat. *Oh God, it must be bad.*

"Lucy." Matt's hand touched her lightly on the shoulder, making her jump. She hadn't even noticed him coming back. "Dakota's sleeping—they've got her pretty sedated—"

"I have to see her."

"Not now. The doctors want her to rest tonight. But she's gonna be fine."

"Please, Matt."

"I want you to stay here." Matt guided her into a small waiting room directly across from where they stood. "I'm just gonna look in on her, and I'll be right back."

"Then at least tell me what happened to her. About the accident."

But he was backing away, giving her a thumbs-up, as he finally turned and disappeared from view.

He knows, but he doesn't want to tell me. He knows, and it's even worse than I imagined.

Lucy had no choice but to sit. Sit and stare at the potted plants and stained chairs and dingy carpet. Sit and watch an elderly man dozing in a corner, four teary-eyed women holding tissues, a husband and wife in deep conversation while the wife rocked a baby in her arms.

Dakota, you have to be okay. You have to.

The distinctive hospital smells were making her nauseated. Burned coffee and antiseptics and sick people lying in stuffy rooms. She crammed her gloves in the pocket of her coat, then turned and tossed her coat over the back of her chair. Heavy footsteps plodded by the open doorway, and when she saw who it was, she felt an instant stab of fear.

Sheriff Stark and a deputy were stopped at the nurses' station. For the moment, their backs were to Lucy, but it was obvious from the set of their bulky shoulders that they weren't here for a social call. Lucy immediately moved to another seat and pretended to read the newspaper. She wished she could hear exactly what the two men were saying, but they were too far away.

They're here because of Dakota. I just know it.

Her heart began to race. Somehow, the sheriff's presence made Dakota's situation even more real, even more terrifying. As a thousand horrible images burst through Lucy's brain, she forced herself to peek around the edge of the newspaper, just in time to catch a glimpse of the sheriff's angry face. He seemed to be arguing with one of the nurses, and the nurse seemed to be winning. After several more minutes, both men marched off, looking extremely irritated.

They wanted to see Dakota. And the nurse wouldn't let them.

The fears inside her were escalating to panic. Grabbing her purse, she made a beeline for the restroom, soaked a paper towel with cold water, and pressed it to her face. Her reflection was chalky in the mirror, and worry lines furrowed her brow. *Why hasn't Matt come back yet? What's taking him so long?*

It took a while to calm herself down. When she finally went back to the waiting room, it was depressingly empty. Even the nurses had disappeared from their station, and Lucy fought down a fresh wave of apprehension as she took her coat from the chair.

That's weird . . .

Frowning, she stopped. She distinctly remembered putting her coat over the *back* of the chair, not on the seat.

Hadn't she?

It probably just slipped off. Or maybe I just thought I put it on the back of the chair, and I'm obsessing, and what difference does it make anyway, where my stupid coat ends up?

Except now, as she lifted it, a tiny piece of paper fell out—a piece of torn, smudged paper with some numbers scribbled on it.

It meant nothing to Lucy. She tossed it onto a table of magazines, then suddenly noticed something sticking out from her jacket pocket. Something too large to fit, something soft and bulky and wrapped in plain brown paper.

Definitely not her gloves.

Cautiously, Lucy reached in and pulled the thing out. It was tied with string, and her name had been printed across the top in small, straight letters.

Once more she scanned the empty room.

She could feel that coppery taste of fear rising into the back of her throat, that painful quickening of her heartbeat.

Matt? Had Matt put it there? She couldn't think of a single reason why he *would* have—but who *else* could it have been?

Working her fingers beneath the string, Lucy slid it free. Then she paused, took a deep breath, and slowly opened the package.

The note was lying right on top.

A crumpled scrap of paper. A message of just four words:

MY GIFT TO YOU.

But then she saw what was underneath— *realized* what was underneath . . .

The long wool scarf folded so neatly . . . the rainbow colors and silly sparkles soaked through with blood . . .

Lucy was scarcely even aware of running.

Or taking the elevator down, or stumbling out into the night . . .

All she knew was that she had to get away.

Get to a place where no one could see her or hear her screams.

7

It was the retching sound that brought her back again. The pain in her stomach and the gagging in her throat as she dropped to her knees behind a Dumpster in the hospital parking lot.

Exactly what she expected to find out here, she didn't know.

She was shaking all over. She'd left her coat and purse, but Dakota's scarf was still clutched tightly in her hands and against her heart.

Dakota! Who did this to you? And why?

Kneeling there in the snow, Lucy felt helpless and outraged. The darkness seemed to shift and deepen, so consuming that it frightened her.

She realized then that she wasn't alone.

That perhaps she hadn't been alone since she'd first fled out to the night.

With a slow intake of breath, she clung to

Dakota's scarf and peered hard into the murky blackness.

He's close . . . so close . . .

Though she couldn't hear his breathing, though she couldn't see his face—

His eyes!

Those hidden eyes she'd felt so many times before. Invisible eyes, stealthy and oh so cunning. Eyes full of knowing . . . and hunger . . . and lust.

"I know you're here!" Lucy shouted.

The parking lot was deserted. She saw no cars except for Matt's, no movement whatsoever, not a single sign of life.

"Who are you? What do you want?"

But the breeze was calm, and the silence settled around her, deep as death.

"Leave Dakota alone!"

Lucy knew the eyes were still watching. That they'd witnessed her sudden fury as she'd struggled to her feet. She could feel their calm intensity and curious sort of wonder. They were waiting to see what she'd do next.

So she started walking.

She walked, faster and faster, toward the place where she could feel the eyes hiding.

Toward the dim streetlight at the farthest edge of the parking spaces. Toward the trees beyond that, and the vacant lot beyond that, where the sputtery glow of the streetlight couldn't reach.

"Yes, Lucy, that's right."

Startled by a voice, Lucy gasped and spun around. Had she only imagined it? Or had *he* spoken to her from the dark?

There was no one behind her. No one going in or out of the hospital. A fresh surge of anger spurred her on, and she began to run.

"Yes . . . yes . . . that's right. Come to me."

This time her feet froze, halting her midstride. She willed herself to keep moving, but some overwhelming instinct seemed to be holding her in place, begging her to remember.

Her mind raced backward as she struggled to think.

Night . . . shadows . . . eyes . . .

Keen eyes glowing feral, clever eyes waiting their chance.

"And not just his," Lucy whispered.

Wild flames against the sky . . . terror and pain . . . whispers from the darkness . . . black phantoms closing in . . .

"There were others that night."

Just like there were others here *now*, Lucy realized.

Many others.

And they were all around her.

"Oh God."

Half frozen with terror, she cautiously began to retreat, all too aware that even one reckless move could prove deadly.

That one careless move would be fatal.

Keep going. Walk slow. Don't stop.

And yet she sensed that these watchers weren't following—at least not for the moment. Their stares were focused, their muscles taut; they were poised and wary but seemed to be holding back. Preparing themselves. Waiting for . . .

What?

Some signal? Some command?

She wondered how she could possibly know any of this. Her whole body was numb. Her knees threatened to buckle and spill her to the ground. Some deep impulse told her not to let this happen, not to turn her back on those eyes, and most definitely not to run.

She kept her head lowered. Small, steady steps. Unhurried. Unthreatening.

A hand came out of nowhere.

It encircled her throat as a body pressed hers from behind.

"You should know by now, Lucy," the voice murmured. "Escape is just an illusion."

8

The night sucked her in.

Swift and silent, it closed around her and swallowed her whole.

She floated there, lost in never-ending darkness, till something coaxed her back again, pulling her gently toward warmth and a familiar touch.

"Lucy? Lucy, are you okay?"

"Where is he?" she whispered. "Are they gone?" She was struggling, but couldn't get away. She recognized Matt leaning over her, but the guttering streetlight had grown brighter, and the world seemed upside down.

"Who?" Matt sounded alarmed. "What happened? Did someone try to hurt you?"

Yes, but he didn't; he let me go. You must have scared him away. As her mind slowly began to clear, Lucy realized she was leaning against Matt's chest. That one of his arms was around her and his other hand was carefully smoothing her hair back from her eyes.

"What am I doing?" she mumbled.

"That's exactly what I'd like to know. What the hell *are* you doing out here?"

"No . . . I mean . . ." Frowning, Lucy tried to survey her surroundings. "Why am I on the ground?"

"It's where people usually end up when they faint."

"No, I didn't faint."

"Hey, I think I know a faint when I see it. Come on. We're making a trip to the emergency room."

"I'm not an emergency. And I didn't faint."

"Lucy."

"It was something else." She suppressed a shudder. "Like all the strength just suddenly drained out of me."

She could see the worry in his eyes—*and* the doubt. Now it was Matt who took a nervous appraisal of the parking lot and the shadows beyond it.

"Really, I'm not hurt," she tried to reassure him and change the subject at the same time. "How's Dakota? Did you see her?"

But Matt was pulling Lucy to her feet, steadying her with his hands, supporting her with his shoulder. "We need to tell security about this. They can check it out and file a report."

"But I'm telling you, there's nothing to report."

"Look. You said someone was here. You asked me where they'd gone."

"I did? Well . . ." Lucy glanced away from him, her mind racing. "Well, I guess I was just confused."

But she wasn't confused now. She knew with absolute certainty that the ones who had watched her and closed in around her had completely disappeared.

"When I found your stuff in the waiting room and you weren't there, I didn't know what to think." Matt's grumbling drew her back again. He shrugged out of his coat and wrapped it tightly around her, leading her back toward the hospital. "You scared the hell out of me."

"I . . ." *Tell him! Tell him about those invisible eyes! That hand on your throat! Dakota's bloody scarf!* "I felt sick. I thought if I got some fresh air—"

"This air isn't fresh. This air is frozen. This air is twenty degrees, and so are you."

"I'm sorry, Matt."

"What were you thinking, coming out here alone? I mean, isn't the whole point of you staying at Gran's tonight to keep you safe?"

"Please, let's drop it. What about Dakota?" Lucy's voice was tight with dread. *It's bad, isn't it? That's why you're not telling me. Is she . . . dying?"*

The glance he gave her was both swift and tender. "No. Of course she's not dying—"

"That's why the sheriff was here. That's why—"

"Lucy, what are you talking about?"

"Dakota! All the blood and—"

"Yes, she needed *some* blood, but not that much." Matt seemed genuinely confused. "Of course, if you'd like to donate, they always need—"

"Don't lie to me, Matt! Tell me the truth!"

"I *am* telling you the truth." As they came to an abrupt halt, Matt stared solemnly into her eyes. "She probably would've lost a lot more blood if it hadn't been so cold out. And if that snowplow hadn't stopped to help."

"Wait. I don't understand."

"The driver spotted her in his headlights. He thinks it must've been a hit-and-run. That some car probably skidded into her and kept on going."

It took several moments for the news to sink in. Without even realizing, Lucy clutched at her heart, at the spot to which she'd been holding Dakota's scarf.

"Someone was obviously going way too fast on that icy road." Matt scowled. "But how they could've just driven off and left her there is beyond me. They didn't even check to see if she was hurt."

"So . . . she wasn't attacked?"

Matt immediately looked shocked. "Like Wanda Carver in the park? Is *that* what you thought? Oh, Lucy, I'm so sorry. I should've made it clear. No. *No.* Nothing like that."

"And you're absolutely sure it was a car that

hit her? That she wasn't chased or stalked or—"

"She was out on a country road, for God's sake. Somewhere near her aunt and uncle's farm. In subzero temperatures! I can't imagine any stalker being *that* desperate—*or* stupid."

"It's not funny."

"You're right, it's not. And I didn't mean it that way." Taking a breath, he offered Lucy a compassionate smile. "Dakota's got some deep cuts that needed stitches . . . a few bad bruises . . . a sprained ankle and a broken arm. The nurse said she's been awake off and on, but mostly off. She's heavily sedated, and she's pretty beat up, but she's gonna be okay."

"You promise?"

"Of course I promise. And anyway, didn't you talk to her brother?"

"Her brother? When?"

"Her family stopped by to check on her while I was there—they only stayed a minute. Texas said he had something Dakota wanted him to give you. I told him you were in the waiting room."

Lucy felt blindsided. She put a hand to her forehead and tried to think. "No, I didn't see

him. I didn't see anyone. But I was in the bathroom for a while."

"Then I guess that explains it."

"What was it? What Dakota wanted him to
give me?"

"I don't know." Matt shrugged. "But he said
you'd understand."

The queasiness was back again. The watery
feeling in her knees, the dizziness in her brain.
Again she pressed a hand to her chest and
squeezed Dakota's scarf—

Dakota's scarf!

Gasping, Lucy looked down at the front of
her sweatshirt, at the clump of fleecy fabric she
held in her fist.

Dakota's bloody scarf! Where is it?

She knew she'd had it when she'd first come
outside. When she'd gotten sick behind the
Dumpster, before she'd realized she was being
watched . . .

Oh God . . . what happened to it?

Her gaze went frantically around the parking
lot. The scarf *had* to be here somewhere,
somewhere close by. *I must have dropped it and
not noticed. Maybe when I got up and started*

running—or maybe when those fingers slid around
my throat.

"Lucy, what's wrong?"

But Lucy's thoughts were going in all directions, and she scarcely heard him. *If Dakota sent
me the scarf, then she must have had a good reason—
she was trying to tell me something—something
important, something she didn't want anyone else to
know because . . .*

Because she knew no one else would believe it.

She knew no one would believe it but me.

Without warning, two memories exploded
in her brain. Flashbacks so sudden, so vivid,
that Lucy gasped and grabbed her head with
both hands. *Katherine Wetherly lying in an open
grave . . . Byron holding a green necklace . . .*

"Don't faint on me again." Matt was pushing
her through the hospital doors; Lucy was
pushing him away.

*Eyes glowing through shadows . . . night smells,
night sounds, damp and cold . . . fog so thick . . .
woods so black . . . blood flowing . . . life flowing—*

A strangled cry caught in her throat.

Eyes glowing through shadows . . .

Eyes . . .

"The scarf," Lucy mumbled. "I've got to find it."

The scarf Dakota never took off. The scarf Dakota was surely wearing when the car had run her down.

The scarf that just might show Lucy what had really happened.

And who had tried to kill her best friend.

9

Matt helped her search the parking lot.

While his back was turned, Lucy had un-fastened one of her earrings and slid it into the pocket of her sweatpants. A *favorite* earring, she'd managed to convince him—it must have come loose and fallen off when she'd been outside.

Matt hadn't been thrilled about it, but he'd helped her all the same. Together they retraced her route the best she could remember—Matt muttering that they'd never find something so tiny out here tonight, and Lucy keeping a sharp lookout for Dakota's scarf.

It had to be somewhere.

It couldn't have just disappeared.

But though they combed the whole area, the scarf wasn't there. And when Lucy gathered her purse and coat again in the waiting room, she found that two more things had vanished as well: the plain brown wrapping paper and the note with its cryptic message.

A nurse informed her that the cleaning crew had been there only fifteen minutes before. And that anything resembling trash had most likely been picked up and disposed of.

Lucy was despondent on the drive back to Irene's. How could she have lost that scarf—especially when Dakota had trusted her with it? Mentally she went over her steps again, wondering if there was something she'd forgotten or miscalculated. The streetlight had been dim, after all—and she'd been sick. Sick and shocked and frightened.

And watched by shadowy figures the whole time.

Shadowy figures not only terrifying to her, but terrifyingly *familiar*, as well . . .

Could *they* have taken Dakota's scarf? But for what purpose?

"I'm sorry about your earring," Matt tried to console her. "You'll probably find it when some of that snow melts."

It took Lucy a second to realize what he was

talking about. "Oh, forget about the earring. I've got lots of earrings."

She ignored Matt's look of bewilderment. It was all she could do to think clearly right now—all she could do to even think at all.

Should she ask him to go by the old church? Just so she could check on Jared? But what excuse could she give? And how would she get away from Matt once they got there?

"I told Dakota you send your love," Matt continued, trying to fill the awkward silence. "And that they wouldn't let you visit, but you came anyway."

"I thought you said she was sleeping."

"I'm sure she heard me in her dreams."

Dreams, Lucy thought? *Or nightmares?*

"Gran only lives about four blocks from the hospital, you know." Matt pointed vaguely toward several neighboring streets. "Once Dakota's better, you can be over there in just a couple minutes."

"Really? I still have trouble finding my way around this town."

"Too many one ways and dead ends. Oh! And I almost forgot—no school tomorrow."

"How do you know that?"

"Message from Principal Howser. Seems the furnace went out, so it's too cold to have classes." Pausing, he threw her a sidelong glance. "Doesn't that at least merit a smile?"

But Lucy's head was still spinning, rapidly clicking off plans. With school canceled, she'd have time to do all the things she needed to do. Pack up the rest of her things to take to Gran's. Check on Jared. Think of some way to see Dakota.

And do some detective work on Nicholas Wetherly.

Because that nagging feeling of unease still hadn't left her. And as much as she wished she could believe in this miraculous, long-lost grandson, something still warned her to be on guard.

"I left the car at Pine Corners last night," she mumbled. "Can you take me to get it?"

Matt checked the rearview mirror and immediately eased into a turn lane. "Is there a particular reason you decided to commute from Pine Corners last night?" he asked, puzzled.

"The storm. Mr. Montana gave me a ride home."

Matt nodded. Lucy's mind continued to whirl.

What would Jared's reaction be when she told him about Nicholas? About Nicholas claiming to be Byron's brother? About Nicholas moving in with Gran? Ever since she'd laid eyes on Nicholas Wetherly this morning, a continuous storm of questions had been raging through her head, and she couldn't ignore those questions any longer. Especially not if Nicholas was going to be moving in with Gran. And especially if Lucy was going to be living with both of them.

"I don't see the car, Lucy. Where exactly did you park?"

Matt's voice startled her back again. She hadn't realized they'd reached Pine Corners already, or that Matt was circling the area for the third time.

"Over there." Frowning, Lucy rolled down her window and stared out at the deserted curbs, the rows and rows of empty parking spaces.

"Are you sure?"

"Yes. The streets were so icy, Mr. Montana told me to leave it."

"And I bet you left it unlocked, too."

"Of course I did. That way the locks won't freeze."

"Yeah, well." Matt's expression was carefully deadpan. "That way someone can break in and steal your car, too."

"Oh no, please don't tell me that—"

"Okay, here's what I *will* tell you. First, we'll go by your aunt's house so you can grab a few things. Then I'll drop you off at Gran's. And then I'll call Sheriff Stark about Angela's car."

"I don't believe this. I mean, who would steal—"

"An unlocked and very expensive Corvette?" Matt thoughtfully stroked his chin. "Hmmm. That's a tough one."

Lucy felt even more depressed by the time they got to Irene's. While Matt retreated to the kitchen to check his pager, she hurried upstairs and gathered just what she needed for one night. She could always come back tomorrow and pack everything else—*if* she could get transportation. *Damnit! Of all times to be without a car! How will I ever get back to Jared now?*

Sinking down on the bed, she nearly let

despair overwhelm her. The fear over Dakota's accident, the panic over the scarf. The guilt about leaving Jared for so long, and the doubts about Nicholas . . .

But you were suspicious of Jared, too, when you first met him, Lucy reminded herself. *So why not now? Why Nicholas instead?*

Leaning forward, she propped her elbows on her knees. She stared at one blank wall. She rested her chin in her palms.

What *was* it about Jared and Nicholas that spoke so differently to her intuition? Both bore an uncanny resemblance to Byron; both claimed to be his brother. Both even stirred confusing and unsettling feelings deep within her—just as Byron had—burning at the level of her soul.

But the account of why Nicholas had shown up here in Pine Ridge was almost too incredible to believe. Too incredible and far too convenient.

And Jared?

Frowning, she thought back.

The truth was, Jared hadn't actually given her any account at all. He'd been much too ill, much too weak. All he'd really done was to ask her over and over again about Byron—strange, intense questions about Byron's death.

Lucy glanced longingly at the telephone.

Of course she couldn't call Dakota now; of course she'd have to wait till her friend was feeling better. But what was it Dakota had said to her before?

"What are your instincts telling you?"

"They're telling me they're exhausted," Lucy muttered. "And that they're not going to say one more word to me tonight."

Rousing herself, she reached over to get her alarm clock and immediately saw the old leather journal lying beside it.

It was just where she'd left it this morning. After one more futile attempt to translate its secret pages, she'd finally given up and tried to concentrate on remembering her own personal experiences instead. All the strange and frightening experiences Dakota had insisted she write down, so that every incident would be accurately documented for God only knew what purpose.

My life. Lucy gave a mocking smile. *The Painstakingly Documented Account of Lucy Dennison's Descent into Madness.*

And yes, it probably *was* a good idea to write these things down, she conceded, but the ancient book she'd discovered and stolen was still foremost in her mind. The brittle bindings stained with mold. Page after crumbling page of unknown words in a long-lost language. Macabre drawings, pressed flowers, maps of nonexistent places. And through it all, those overwhelming sensations of urgency, passion, and resignation . . .

And just last night she'd been able to read it. After discovering it inside that mantel at the bookshop, she'd skimmed the fragile pages with her hands, touched the quill-penned words with her fingertips—and somehow, magically, been able to translate some of the text.

Disturbing and frightening text . . .

But not since then.

Not after Mr. Montana had brought her back to the house, or even when she'd awoken this morning.

It just doesn't make sense. I must be doing something wrong, something different from what I did before.

But what?

Holding her breath, Lucy placed a tentative finger on the fragile cover. She held it there for several minutes and tried to clear her mind.

Nothing.

No feelings . . . no meanings . . . no images . . . nothing.

Maybe I'm just too tired. Disappointed, she stroked the journal, then held it against her breast. The day's events had taken everything out of her. She was just too drained to pick up anything of value, psychic or otherwise. She didn't have time for this now, anyway. She'd take it with her to Gran's and try it again later, when she was calmer and more rested.

"Hey!" Matt yelled from the foot of the staircase. "You need some help?"

"No thanks!" Very carefully Lucy slipped the book into her overnight bag, tucking it at the very bottom, beneath some clothes. "I'm almost done!"

"Take your time! I'm not trying to rush you!"

She grabbed her alarm clock, her medications, her headphones. She pulled open the nightstand drawer and took out her notebook and pen. Then she spotted the medallion Matt had given her and, almost as an afterthought, scooped it into her hand and slammed the drawer shut.

"Ouch!"

Stepping backward, Lucy stumbled over the bag sitting directly behind her on the floor. She managed to catch herself on the edge of the dresser, wincing as the medallion dug into her palm.

"What's going on up there?" Matt shouted again. "You okay?"

"I'm fine!"

And yet . . . not *quite* fine, Lucy began to realize.

Straightening up, she pried the medallion from her hand, then leaned in for a closer look. The nerves in her palm were tingling—a rapid succession of ice cold and fire hot—*pain desire power life*—and for one brief instant—*eternal life!*—it was almost as though she could see an imprint there—*immortal life!*—an impression etched sharply into the very palm of her hand.

Arrows and . . . circles and . . . familiar—familiar somehow. I should know this! Why don't I know this?

Even as the violent emotions were already beginning to fade, the images melting away, her heartbeat slowing to its natural rhythm once more . . .

Dazed, Lucy lifted the chain a little higher. The medallion hung there at eye level, and she gave it one more cautious touch. It looked and felt just as it had when Matt first gave it to her, the design unclear and worn away.

Unrecognizable.

And meaning nothing to her at all.

10

"I should have known better," Lucy muttered to herself. "Whenever I start feeling hopeful, it ends up being a bad thing."

She'd been so excited yesterday about moving in with Gran. So thrilled about getting away from Irene and Irene's house, so happy about being in a real home.

And not just for herself.

"For Byron's sake . . ."

How many times had those words of Jared's come back to haunt her? Words so right, so *true*, Lucy thought—of course *for Byron's sake.* Surely it would give Byron peace to know that she was here looking after his beloved grandmother, that Gran wouldn't be abandoned or alone or with strangers.

Or alone with long-lost relatives like let-me-just-

make-myself-right-at-home Nicholas Wetherly.

Lucy's expression soured. Nicholas hadn't been here when Matt dropped her off. It was Mrs. Dempsey who'd met her at the door, in a foul temper and in a hurry to leave.

"He called and rented himself a car," she'd informed Lucy. "Went back to the inn to get his things."

"Why don't you go on home then?" Lucy had tried to coax her. "I'll sit up with Gran."

But the cleaning woman had been ornery to the last. "She's asleep, and she doesn't *need* you to sit up with her! It's not like she's some helpless infant, you know. Don't be going overboard with all kinds of fussing. She *doesn't like* being hovered over. She's independent."

"I know that. I promise I won't hover."

Lucy wasn't in the mood for more confrontations tonight, and she'd practically shoved Mrs. Dempsey out of the house. But that had been well over an hour ago, and as she tossed her nightgown onto the bed, she actually found herself wondering what could be taking Nicholas so long. She'd already looked in on Gran at least ten times. She'd rechecked the baby monitor Byron had always kept near his grandmother's pillow, and she'd placed the other monitor on her own nightstand so any little noise would be sure to wake her. *Not like I'm that far away.* Lucy's bedroom was the one closest to Gran's, just a few short steps from threshold to threshold.

Checking the clock again, Lucy restlessly folded up the last of her clothes and stuffed them in a bureau. Unlike her room at Irene's, this one had a personality both cozy and charming, and she'd fallen in love with it at first sight: the ivy-and-yellow-rose wallpaper, the antique bed and matching furniture, even the window seat with its hand-embroidered cushions. And there were shades on the windows. Heavy ones that no one could look through from outside. With dainty yellow curtains over those.

I belong here.

For a brief instant Lucy was completely overcome with emotion. The shocks of today versus the sanctuary of this room. *If only this place really could be all I want it to be. If only I really could be safe here.*

Lucy yawned and turned down the covers. It seemed silly to wait up for Nicholas any longer, and Mrs. Dempsey had probably given him a house key, anyway. Still, she couldn't help feeling nervous as she undressed and put on her gown. She slipped Matt's medallion into the drawer of the bedside table, then stood gazing at it, lost in her own thoughts.

She hadn't told Matt about her startling experience with the medallion. But on their drive over from Irene's afterward, she'd casually mentioned bringing the medallion with her, and being curious again about its design. Matt's response had been one of genuine surprise— and puzzlement.

"An ancient holy symbol," he'd explained again. "I'm sorry . . . I thought I'd told you."

Lucy had dropped the subject. *Eternal life . . . pain, desire and power . . . well, you can't get much holier than that.*

Frustrated, she shut the nightstand drawer, then checked the bottom of her overnight bag. The journal was still there, and she decided to leave it where it was. She hid the bag at the back of her closet.

Oh God, please let me sleep tonight . . . please keep the nightmares away.

Lucy sank deep into the feather mattress. The handmade quilts enveloped her like warm hugs. Somewhere in slumber, she dreamed a familiar smile—*Byron? Jared?*—but as the smile finally melted away, something eerie and disturbing took its place.

Crying?

The sound was muffled and faraway. Helpless and heartbroken, ragged and deep . . . *the way a man or a boy might cry.*

"Who's there!" With a frightened cry of her own, Lucy bolted upright, eyes going wide. The room was dark and strange to her. The only light came from the small, round clock on her nightstand—a pale glow of suspended time.

Her breath came out in a rush. She remembered now where she was, and that the sound of weeping had woken her.

She hadn't heard Nicholas come home.

And I'm sure I didn't close my door.

In fact, she distinctly recalled leaving the door open, so she could see the night-light in the corridor, so she could listen for Gran.

There was no sound at all from the baby monitor. Slipping from bed, Lucy padded cautiously down the hall.

"Gran?"

She tiptoed into Gran's room. Leaning down over the pillow, she could hear the peaceful rhythm of Gran's breathing.

Did I only imagine that crying? Or was Gran having a sad dream?

Despite her relief, Lucy couldn't shake off a lingering sense of uneasiness. The dim night-light shadows smoothed Gran's face, yet as Lucy continued to gaze at her, both of Gran's cheeks suddenly and violently flinched.

"Gran?"

Lucy put a cautious hand to Gran's brow. There was an instant hissing of air—an audible gasp—as Gran's eyelids began to tremble, to strain, to bulge wildly, as though the eyes behind them were rolling in fear.

"Wake up, Gran. You're having a nightmare!"

But wherever Gran was, she was trapped.

Her frail body began to shake, one fist kneading the covers in a feeble attempt to hang on. What little color remained of her skin immediately drained away. And while Lucy tried desperately to calm and reassure her, Gran's mouth split in a soundless scream.

"Can you hear me, Gran? It's not real!" *But what are you seeing? What black place are you in, and what is it that's terrifying you?* "Please wake up!"

Without warning, a shadow fell across the doorway. In the next instant Lucy felt herself being pushed aside as Nicholas crowded in close to the bed.

"What's wrong with her?" Nicholas demanded. He still wore that same stony expression, but Lucy sensed true fear just beneath the surface.

And you're very good at hiding fear, Nicholas. You've had to do it for so long.

Startled, Lucy stepped back to give him more room. She had no idea where her sudden thought had come from, but now she watched anxiously while he tended to his grandmother.

His hair was shoved carelessly back from his forehead, tousled softly about his face. He wore no shirt or shoes, and the low-slung jeans on his narrow hips had been hastily zipped but not buttoned. It was as though he'd been startled from sleep, yet he didn't appear to be groggy or the least bit tired. On the contrary, his skin had a sort of flush to it—a fevered sort of glow that usually came from raw wind and bitter cold. And there was a smell, Lucy realized—a faint scent that clung to him, something fresh and . . .

Pure. The word flashed through her mind, and a rush of sensations followed. *Pure, like night, like winter breezes, snow and freedom, earthy, woodsy, miles of moonless sky.*

Lucy refocused on his face. What was taking him so long? Why wasn't Gran coming out of her bad dream? Nicholas's hands were on either side of her pillow; his mouth was close to her ear. For a brief second, Lucy wondered if she'd seen his lips move, but it was hard to tell. *A whisper? A secret? A smile?*

"Wake her up," Lucy said. And then, when Nicholas didn't answer, she began moving toward him. "Wake her up *now!*"

A cry pierced the silence.

A cry so shrill, so plaintive, it nearly stopped Lucy's heart.

As Nicholas shifted position, she finally managed a shocking glimpse of Gran's face— the round, wide-open eyes; the mouth gaping desperately to one side, even as the piteous sounds, the gibberish sounds, spilled helplessly from Gran's thin, pale lips.

"My God, what'd you do?" Lucy cried, but Nicholas immediately took hold of her and held her where Gran could see.

"Didn't I tell you, Grandmother?" His voice was soft velvet. "Lucy's perfectly safe. And she's not going anywhere."

11

Lucy felt no sense of peace when she awoke the next morning.

She'd stayed up with Nicholas till Gran finally went back to sleep—and then her own slumber had been plagued by fears the rest of the night. She'd dozed in fits and starts, jolting up in terror without knowing why, checking the baby monitor or listening through the dark, expecting to hear Gran calling for help.

What did you dream about last night, Gran?

What frightened you so much, and why was I a part of it?

She remembered how uneasy she'd felt when Nicholas tried to comfort his grandmother. Almost as if he'd *known* what Gran had been dreaming about.

Because he truly is her grandson? Because he truly

is *Byron's brother, with that same psychic connection?*

Lucy stretched one arm across her forehead and closed her eyes.

Why is that so hard for you to believe? To accept?

Why is something inside you still so resistant to that possibility?

An image of Jared popped into her mind.

Somehow she'd have to get back to the church today, make sure he was safe. By now, he might have decided she'd abandoned him. By now he might have assumed she'd broken her word, or gone to the police.

It made her sick just thinking about it.

And then even sicker to think of Dakota.

You have to get well, Dakota—you have *to!*

Maybe Dakota would be able to have visitors today, Lucy hoped. Maybe Matt would take her over there and...

Groaning out loud, Lucy turned on her side.

But should I leave Gran? Leave her alone with Nicholas?

"I hate this," Lucy muttered to herself. "All I want is a nice, normal, boring life. Is that too much to ask?"

Irritated, she sat up in bed and tried to think. If

she could manage to sneak out this morning, she might be able to walk to the hospital and find Dakota's scarf, and then be back again before anybody missed her. After all, it wasn't like Gran would be here alone. She hadn't heard Nicholas moving around yet, which probably meant he was still asleep upstairs—and he *had* been really sweet to Gran last night, she had to admit grudgingly. It had impressed her, how quickly he'd appeared in Gran's bedroom—especially with his own room being out of earshot on the second floor.

"I heard you on the baby monitor," he'd explained, not missing a beat when she'd questioned him. "There's one by my bed—I could hear you talking, and you sounded upset."

Mrs. Dempsey, Lucy had immediately concluded. Of course Mrs. Dempsey—and Thelma, too, probably—had insisted both she *and* Nicholas have intercoms to Gran's room.

Nothing weird about that, Lucy told herself now. *It makes perfect sense.* If she was going to live here, she'd have to get over these suspicions of hers, right? After all, she should be *thankful* to have Nicholas for backup. *Right, Lucy, keep telling yourself that.*

She hated feeling trapped in one more dilemma; she could already feel a guilty headache coming on. Trying to clear her mind, she got up and dressed in warm clothes, checked on Gran one last time, then let herself noiselessly out the front door.

It was still very early, very cold. Freshly fallen snow whitewashed the darkness, and drifts had piled up against the house like giant mounds of whipped cream. As the wind hit her hard, slicing through her jacket, Lucy slid both hands into her pockets and hunched her shoulders against the blast.

The few blocks to the hospital felt more like miles. When she finally reached the parking lot, she tramped through poorly plowed snow and again tried to recall the exact route she'd taken before. She reminded herself that Dakota's gaudy scarf wouldn't necessarily be visible after last night's snowfall, but after a painstaking search of the area, she finally stopped, overcome with frustration.

The scarf simply wasn't there.

So how am I going to help Dakota now?

Leaning back against a lamppost, she

squeezed her arms over her chest and huddled deeper into her jacket. Tears stung her eyes and forced them shut. For several long minutes she stood there, gathering her composure, then let her eyelids slowly drift open.

Byron was watching her from a window.

A window on the second floor of the hospital.

Staring straight at her—straight *through* her— with a solemn and sorrowful gaze.

Lucy went rigid. Her cry shattered the morning quiet as a raw chill pierced her soul.

Byron! Oh God!

And she was practically to the building now, though she wasn't aware of running. Stumbling through the snow, though reason screamed at her to stop—*you* know *better—you* know *it's just like last time—last time at the bookstore—you know it's* impossible*!*

But she ignored that screaming, that wild burst of reason, as she kept on going, as she kept looking up at that heartbreaking profile, the haunting power of his eyes . . .

"Byron!"

His face was against the glass now. His eyes were wrenchingly sad.

Then, all at once, he was gone.

"Byron, wait! Please stay!"

She was struggling with the main door, trying to get it open, but someone was on the other side, coming out and blocking her way. With one last heave, Lucy pushed past him, not even seeing him, not even realizing who it was, until he grabbed her arm and forced her to stop.

"Whoa!" Matt grinned. "Where's the fire?"

"Let go! I don't have time—"

"Time for what? Hey, there's no way you're gonna sneak in to see Dakota. She's still not allowed to have visitors, and the nurse on duty this morning's a real—"

"It's not Dakota!"

"Then what is it? Don't tell me you came back at this ungodly hour to look for that earring?"

"Matt, please! It's an emergency!"

But at that, his grip only tightened. "What is it, Lucy? What's going on? Are you sick? Is it Gran? What—"

"It's Byron!"

"Byron?" Matt looked as though she'd punched him. "What are you *talking* about?"

"He's *up* there, Matt! Standing at the window! I saw him from the parking lot—I know it's *him*!"

The words just kept tumbling out, wild ravings of someone she scarcely even recognized. *What are you doing? What are you saying?* As crazy as she sounded to herself, Lucy could only imagine how much crazier she sounded to Matt.

Byron at the window? Byron watching me?

"Lucy," Matt began, even as she managed to pull away from him.

You're not crazy, Lucy Dennison. Byron was alive. *He was* there. *You* saw *him.*

But of course Byron couldn't have been there. Because Byron was dead. And she had to keep telling herself that, over and over and over again, no matter how long it took, no matter how much she wished it weren't so.

"Byron's dead, Lucy," Matt said softly, sadly. Lucy could only stare at him.

Byron is dead, Lucy.

Dead.

You've got to stop seeing him through windows . . . and the windows of people's eyes.

Her body went limp. She bowed her head and gazed miserably at the floor as Matt lay a comforting hand on her shoulder.

"I'm sure," he ventured carefully, "that you really thought you saw Byron. That's not an unusual experience for people who've lost a loved one."

Lucy managed a halfhearted nod. "Well . . . but that's what I meant." And then, at Matt's obvious confusion, she added, "I meant, I *thought* I saw Byron in the window—or someone who *looked* like Byron. And I was . . . going to check for myself. To *convince* myself I imagined it."

"I see." As Matt raised an eyebrow, she knew she hadn't fooled him for a second. "I'm taking you home now." He sighed and immediately escorted her out.

Lucy had no choice but to go. No amount of arguing, persuasion, or bribery was going to sway Matt at this point—it would only make things worse.

The two of them were quiet on the drive to Gran's. It was only when Matt pulled up in front of the house that he turned toward her with full attention.

"Nicholas wants to see where Byron died," Matt said.

The announcement was unexpected, to say the least. And even shocking, Lucy felt, after what she'd just seen at the hospital.

"I think it's a good idea," Matt went on reasonably. "That's why I told him you'd take him."

"You . . . you what? Are you crazy?"

"No, and neither are you." Matt focused his eyes on the windshield. "I think you need closure. You need to face what happened and forgive yourself. And then you need to get on with your life."

Silence settled between them. Lucy's hands twisted nervously in her lap.

"I can't believe you're doing this to me," she whispered.

For a brief moment, a look of anguish seemed to flicker across his face. "I'm not doing this *to* you," he said softly. "I'm doing this *for* you."

"I don't even know where it happened."

"It's not too far outside of town. I can give you directions."

"Well . . . can't you come *with* us?"

She felt his smile before she saw it. He faced her again and slowly shook his head.

"I think this is something that's both private and sacred. And I think you and Nicholas are the perfect ones to share it."

You and Nicholas.

Just hearing Matt link their names together made Lucy uneasy all over again. And as private and sacred as Matt considered this experience to be, she had no desire to go anywhere, do anything, or share any more with Nicholas Wetherly.

"I don't want to go there, Matt. I don't want to see it. I *never* want to see it."

"I understand."

Matt felt through his pockets, pulled out a pad and pen, and hastily covered a piece of paper with lines, arrows, and scribbles.

"Here," he said, handing her a crudely drawn map. "You shouldn't have any trouble finding it. Just follow the south road straight out of town."

"I don't have a car."

"Nicholas has a rental. He can drive."

Lucy got out of the Jeep. She went up the

walkway and into the house without so much as a good-bye.

The day's already bad. And it's only going to get worse.

Yet despite Lucy's misgivings, her mood began to lift when she saw Gran. That gentle face, that sweet glow of welcome and warmth. Lucy figured it was probably just because she wished it so much, but she felt as if Gran truly wanted her there.

Thelma was already busy with Gran's morning routine, so Lucy forced a cheerful wave and went to her room. Maybe, by some miracle, Nicholas had decided to leave town. She hadn't noticed any other cars outside— maybe he'd left while she was gone and would never come back.

Closing her door, she threw off her jacket and flopped down on the bed. Even with everything else going on, she still couldn't get Dakota or Jared out of her mind. Dakota's accident . . . Jared's survival . . . and both of them tangled up in a complicated web of Lucy's own guilt and feelings of failure.

And now she'd have to face the accident site.

She'd have to see the place where Byron died.

Where Byron died, and I lived.

Exhausted, Lucy reached for the extra blanket at the foot of the bed. She pulled it around herself and turned onto her stomach, stretching both arms underneath one of her pillows.

Her fingers touched something cold.

Something cold and waxy and pleasantly smooth, hidden out of sight.

Puzzled, Lucy sat up. She lifted the pillow and squinted down, trying to figure out what was there.

Flowers? Flower petals?

No . . . only *one* flower, she suddenly realized, her heartbeat quickening.

One flower.

One white rose.

Its stem was split and broken. Its creamy petals were wilted and crushed and stained with drops of blood.

Just like another rose she remembered.

The one she'd seen in Byron's tomb.

12

It's not the same rose.

It can't *be the same rose.*

She'd tried so hard not to think about it.

She'd shoved it out of sight into a drawer, and then changed her mind and hidden it in her bag with the journal.

She'd told herself to get rid of it—to throw it away—but she couldn't do it. As though it held some weird and compelling connection she simply wasn't able to break.

How long was it there under my pillow? All night? Just this morning?

But now it was afternoon, and Lucy was staring out a car window, seeing nothing. Not the scenery flowing past in a blur of snow and shadows . . . not the swollen gray clouds hanging low over the hills.

Not even Nicholas, as he reached over to pull the map from her hands.

Neither of them had spoken a word since climbing into the Land Rover and heading out of town. For nearly twenty minutes now, Lucy had sat rigidly against the back of her seat, while Nicholas clenched the steering wheel and kept his eyes on the road ahead.

Someone put that rose in my bed. But who? And why?

Despite the car's warm interior, Lucy shuddered.

I thought I was safe at Gran's . . . I wanted to be safe at Gran's . . .

But it was still happening. Still following her. The fear . . . the danger.

"We must be almost there by now," Nicholas said.

As the car picked up speed, Lucy realized she had shifted positions and angled herself against the passenger door. Her hands were gripping the edge of the seat, and there was a growing tightness in her chest. *Oh God, I don't want to be here.* She felt the tires skid briefly on the slick road—she felt jarring images skid out of control through her brain . . .

That night—that last awful night—bloodred moon—dark shape—tires squealing, brakes screaming, falling falling falling into nothingness . . .

"It's all coming back to you, Lucy."

She started at the sound of Nicholas's voice. He was watching her now, but his only sign of emotion was the faint crease along his brow.

"Please don't go so fast," was all she could say.

It had been dark the last time she'd traveled this particular road; she'd been worried, she'd been distracted, she'd been lost in a thousand thoughts. Yet the farther Nicholas drove, the more familiar certain things began to feel. Sharp bends . . . sheer drops . . . miles and miles of never-ending curves.

"What was it like?" Nicholas asked, but Lucy turned her face to the window.

The dark shape—the dark, blurry, frightening shape darting in front of the van.

"It was dark," she murmured.

"But you remember."

Tears scalded the back of her throat, burned behind her eyes. "Only some things."

The Land Rover sped up again. Lucy could see where snowplows had been through, leveling the drifts down to two narrow lanes, but there were still plenty of snowbanks and slippery patches of ice.

"What happened that night with you and Byron?"

Fiercely, she shook her head. Memories pounded in her head, threatening to break through. It hurt to hold them back.

"Tell me, Lucy. I need to know."

"It happened too fast."

"How fast? A minute? A second?" Nicholas pressed the accelerator. The car skidded around a hairpin turn, bringing Lucy up with a cry.

"What are you doing! Trying to get us killed?"

"Was he driving too fast?" Nicholas persisted, speeding up a little more. "Was he being too reckless? Did he lose control of the van?"

"It wasn't Byron's fault!"

"Then whose fault was it?"

Lucy's eyes were glued to the speedometer. At the needle creeping upward: fifty miles per hour . . .sixty . . .

"Whose *fault*?" Nicholas demanded.

"It ran out in front of us!"

"*What* did?"

"It . . . it was dark, and I couldn't see! Something big and dark, and it was just *there*. Byron tried to stop—"

"Why wasn't he watching the road? Why couldn't he stop in time?"

"I—it just—it just came out of nowhere."

"Was he looking at something else?"

"It—he tried not to hit it."

"What was he looking at?"

I saw Byron turn toward me . . . saw his hand slide across the seat to reach for me . . . I looked into his eyes . . . deep and black as midnight . . .

"Did he say anything?"

He opened his mouth . . . he started to say my name . . . but he never got the chance . . .

"What was the last thing he said?"

Nicholas didn't seem to notice as Lucy bent forward in her seat. As she buried her face in her hands . . . as she struggled to breathe and not to scream.

"Please! I—I don't remember—"

"What was Byron doing when he ran off the road?"

"He swerved!" Lucy cried desperately. "He swerved the van so he wouldn't hurt anyone!"

"He died."

Lucy's head came up. She stared at Nicholas in mute horror, not even realizing that the Land Rover had come to a stop.

"This must be it," Nicholas muttered. With one quick motion he got out of the car, slammed the door, and walked away.

They were parked on a narrow strip of roadside, at the top of a snow-covered hill. A large wooden cross had been staked into the ground, with flowers and greenery twined around it; piled around its base were flowers of plastic and silk, flowers now frozen in cellophane wrappers. As Lucy stared, sick and trembling from her place in the car, a vague thought came to her. No one had left white roses.

"Are you coming?" Nicholas had stopped and was looking back at her, over his shoulder. His long wavy hair whipped wildly about his face, and his narrowed eyes were wary, giving him a strangely feral look.

"No," Lucy whispered, though she knew he couldn't hear her.

No, she would never set foot on this site,

never go near that memorial, never come back here again. The pain was unbearable. She felt as if she were suffocating under the weight of her own guilt. She hated Nicholas for what he'd said to her—for what he knew about her. It had been a trick coercing her to come out here with him today. A cruel deception and an even crueler punishment.

He blamed her for Byron's death.

Just like everyone else does.

Without warning, her door jerked open, causing her to scream. Nicholas immediately reached in and took hold of her arm.

"Come on. I want to see where Byron died."

"You've seen it!" Lucy snapped back at him. With one angry swipe, she knocked his hand loose and tried to wrestle the door shut. Nicholas blocked it with his shoulder and unceremoniously hauled her out.

"This isn't where the van ended up. Down this hill—that's the spot I need to see."

"How would you know where the van ended up?" she threw back at him, fighting tears. "And how do you know he wasn't already dead when the van hit the ground?"

Shocked at her own outburst, Lucy grabbed for the open door, but Nicholas quickly shut it.

"Matt told me the van landed down there." His arm made a general sweep toward the bottom of the incline. "I'm sure you remember."

"Well, I *don't*! So why can't we just go?"

"Because I've come a long way. Because this is important to me."

"Well, it's not important to me!" Her voice was quivering, her whole body shaking. "You've made your point, okay? Now I'm *leaving*! Even if I have to hitchhike! Even if I have to walk all the way home!"

"You don't have a home. That's why you're living with my grandmother."

Lucy felt as if she'd been kicked. Her lips parted, but no sound came out. For a brief second, the world went hazy, drowned beneath a sudden swell of tears.

"You bastard." It was scarcely more than a whisper. The tears brimmed and spilled over, and a sob choked out before she could stop it. And then, to her amazement, she finally saw emotion in Nicholas Wetherly's eyes.

It was there for only an instant, hiding itself in

his cold, impassive stare. But Lucy saw it—and recognized it—at once.

Shame.

One brief glimpse . . . then it was gone.

And Nicholas was starting down the side of the hill.

"You're cruel!" Lucy shouted.

The words were out before she could stop them. She watched him hesitate just long enough for her to shout again.

"Does it make you feel good to hurt people?"

Nicholas's shoulders stiffened; his hands clenched into fists at his sides. He whipped around with a dangerous stare.

"That's the nature of people, Lucy. To hurt."

But Lucy shook her head. "Not *my* nature." Frowning at him, she lowered her voice. "I'm sorry I said that to you. Even though you deserved it."

The dark eyes actually seemed to smolder. As though this was a response he'd never anticipated and wasn't quite sure how to deal with—except, perhaps, with anger.

"And those questions you were asking me?" Lucy added, almost as an afterthought. "Those things you said? Well, you're right about me living with Gran. I *don't* have a home."

Nicholas didn't answer.

Taking a deep breath, Lucy felt her way carefully down the slope, dreading each and every step she took. And when she finally caught up with him, she kept her eyes on the ground below and not on his face.

She would never have recognized this place again by sight. Etched in her mind forever were shadows and flames; gnarled, dead branches against an endless black sky; that bloodred moon overhead. But today, the landscape looked entirely different. An undulating field of pure white snow, broken here and there by thick stands of pine. Mist from a pewter-gray sky. Hushed. Peaceful.

"Byron didn't say anything when we ran off the road," Lucy spoke at last, quietly. "He didn't have time. Like I said, everything happppened so fast. He hit the brakes . . . the van started sliding. And then it was over."

She paused. Drew a deep, ragged breath. But her voice was calm now, and resigned.

"He was looking at me. That's all I remember."

Nicholas was gazing down across the field. The wind had almost stopped, but snowflakes still drifted through his hair. There was only silence. Sharp and brittle, like the cold.

After what seemed like forever, Lucy saw him slowly shake his head.

"I didn't know," he murmured.

"Of course you knew." The laugh she forced was flat and humorless. "That's exactly why you went off on me back there. But I guess . . . I guess I can understand why you're so angry."

"I am angry. But it doesn't have anything to do with you. And I *didn't* know about . . . about you and Byron at the end. What you just said."

To Lucy's surprise, he suddenly seemed uncomfortable. He turned away and started off again down the hill.

"Wait!" Lucy yelled. "I'm coming with you!"

She didn't know why she decided to join him—or how she'd handle things once she got there. Only that it seemed very crucial for some reason that Nicholas not go alone. When they finally reached the bottom, he stood there uncertainly till Lucy pointed off across the field.

"Over there, I think. When I came to, I'd

been thrown pretty far. But I remember there were trees around me . . . like those." She indicated a stretch of woods off to one side. "And I could see the van over my left shoulder."

"Anything else you remember?"

Her shudder was instantaneous. Just like the unwelcome image that flashed through her mind.

Shadows slinking along the ground—through the trees—slivers of black and pale, pale gray—sparks of—

"—light," Nicholas was saying, and Lucy's mind snapped back again. "Was there any other light except for the fire?"

"No." Abruptly she turned away, her glance going straight to the trees.

"Something wrong?"

"No. I just . . . " *Haunted. This place feels haunted.*

"What?"

Lucy was annoyed with herself. "Nothing. Bad memories."

The shadows came; that's the last thing I remember. Till I woke up again in that cave . . .

"Hard to believe anything bad ever happened

here." Nicholas let his gaze travel slowly from one end of the clearing to the other. "Or that anything bad *could* ever happen here."

He's right, Lucy thought uneasily. No wreckage. Nothing burned. A picture-perfect winter scene where no one could ever die.

"This place is haunted," Nicholas murmured.

Startled, Lucy followed his gaze off through the trees. Branches hung heavy to the ground, layered thickly with ice and snow. Beyond that stretched a deceptive labyrinth of drifts and banks and broken limbs, hollows and fallen trees, all swathed in snow and shadows.

Where something else is hiding.

Something Lucy recognized, even though she couldn't see it—something that had been here once before, on the night of the accident.

I was right. I was right . . .

Something she'd tried to forget every single day since then, but knew she never would.

Something that watched me last night in the parking lot . . . wanted to take *me last night in the parking lot . . .*

"What is it?" she whispered, unable to move, unable to take her eyes from that deep, dangerous place in the woods. *"What is it?"*

Because it *was* real.

Just as real as the last look on Byron's face, as the flames against the sky, as the evil bloodred moon. Just as real as lying there in the grass, in the cold, in the dark, bleeding and helpless and terrified . . .

Feeling them close in around her . . . feeling their breath on her face.

"Lucy . . . there's no name for what we are . . ."

Oh yes . . . they'd been here then, those nightmare things.

And they were here now.

13

"But not now," Nicholas was saying.

His chest was against her back, and Lucy realized she'd stumbled into him. Her eyes were wide, glued to the trees. Blood pounded in her ears. All she could think about was running back to the car and getting as far away from here as she could.

"Do *you?*" Nicholas asked her.

Lucy glanced up in confusion, oblivious to his hands steadying her shoulders.

"I said," Nicholas began again, "that I had a strange feeling a second ago. But not now."

Lucy's heart stuttered, then began to slow. Her fearful gaze shifted reluctantly from the woods.

Nicholas was right.

That haunted feeling . . . that hunted feeling . . . was gone.

"Hmmm . . . I must have imagined it." A slight frown creased his brow. "Though I certainly wouldn't want to be here after dark."

Lucy shifted away from him, watching as he slowly scanned the perimeters of the field. "But . . . you felt *something*?" she asked.

"I thought I did. But I guess that's not unusual where there's been a bad accident."

Was that remark meant for her, Lucy wondered? She studied his face, but it told her nothing.

"They say when someone dies suddenly—or tragically—their spirit stays behind," Nicholas added. "It doesn't realize it's dead."

Once again, Lucy's eyes shot to the trees. *No lurking shadows low to the ground . . . no gleaming eyes . . .* Nothing, in fact, to suggest that anything threatening had ever been there at all. The shadows lay still. The wind was calm.

Unnaturally calm . . .

Lucy retreated several steps. "I'll wait for you in the car."

"It's locked."

Irritated, she held out her hand for the keys, but Nicholas was heading off in another direction.

"There's nothing else to see here!" Lucy insisted. "Why can't we just go?"

"Because I'm not finished. When I'm finished, *then* we'll go."

"Well, I think you're doing this on purpose. I think you're doing this out of—of spite!"

"I don't have any reason to do anything to you." Nicholas didn't break stride. "I don't even know you."

"You're doing this because you're so upset about Byron!"

"I am upset about Byron."

"And you want me to suffer for it!"

This time he stopped. He stood for several long moments before finally turning around.

"Look," Nicholas said, his voice low and even. "I'm sure you feel guilty about the accident. Because Byron died and you didn't. But don't put all your paranoia on me."

Speechless, Lucy watched him continue across the field. The hurt she'd felt before now gave way to anger—an anger so hot and suffocating that her mind went black like smoke.

"You don't know what I'm feeling!" she heard

herself shout. "Don't you *dare* presume to know what I'm feeling!"

Her outburst didn't slow him down. But she could hear his comment, loud and clear, tossed back over his shoulder.

"I'm not presuming anything. *You* know it—and *I* know it."

Lucy didn't even realize she'd run after him. Not till she saw him looking down at her with calm dispassion, and she saw his arm gripped mercilessly in both of her hands.

"Who the hell do you think you are!" she exploded. "Who the hell are you to tell me—"

"It doesn't take a mind reader to see it, Lucy," he interrupted. "You've suffered every single day since Byron died; you've gone over and over the accident a thousand times. You wish you could go back and do everything different. You wish you'd never met him because it hurts too much, now that he's gone. You wish you'd said things you never said, let him know things you never told him. You wish it could have been you instead of him. And now you're on this desperate journey, trying to find some way to forgive yourself, trying to find some way to atone for the fact that *you're* still here and he's *not*."

As Lucy stared at him open-mouthed, he pried her fingers from his arm and pulled slowly out of reach. And for the briefest instant, she could almost swear she saw another emotion—pity—in the dark night of his eyes.

"Who the hell do you think *you* are?" he went on tonelessly. "As if *you* have any control over death? You're not immortal; you're not some god. You have no powers against time or fate; you don't get to answer prayers, or choose who lives or who dies. You're only human. Weak and insignificant, like every other human. Just stumbling through life, and waiting to die."

Without warning, he grabbed her shoulders and pulled her close. He was amazingly strong—much stronger than he looked—and though Lucy was too shocked in that second to struggle, she could feel his whole body trembling with restraint.

"Guilt is your *enemy*, Lucy," he murmured. "Guilt and regret both. They make you weak and unhappy and vulnerable. They're sly and insidious. They steal your whole life away from you before you've even begun to live it. And then the years are gone . . . and you're left with nothing."

He released her so roughly that she almost fell. And though she quickly caught her balance, he was way ahead of her again, moving even more purposefully across the clearing.

His words cut straight through her. Trying not to cry, she glanced longingly toward the top of the hill, wondering if she might be able to wrestle the car keys away from him. If she could get the keys, she might be able to reach the car before he did and just drive off. Just leave him here.

And then what?

Tell Matt that Nicholas had gone crazy and frightened her? Threatened her? Hurt her? *See, Matt, just like I told you—he's* not *Byron's brother—please,* please, *send him away!*

Yet today, for the first time, she'd actually sensed some sort of emotional battle in Nicholas.

Emotions aching in his eyes and struggling in his body.

Emotions he'd never intended—or *wanted—* her to see.

Frowning, Lucy glanced up the hillside once more.

She'd never get those keys away from Nicholas. And even if she could, he had the map.

Damnit!

She *hated* being here—hated being here with *him*! She hated everything he'd just said to her and accused her of, hated the way every single observation of his had hit home. He was mean. He was insensitive.

And he was right.

Lucy swallowed the lump in her throat. And then, knowing she'd be stuck here till Nicholas decided otherwise, she lowered her head and followed his footprints through the snow.

When she walked up behind him, he wasn't moving. Just standing with his shoulders slumped, hands in the pockets of his long black coat.

"So you think it was this general area?" he asked flatly, without looking at her.

Lucy hesitated. Nodded.

"It feels like it," Nicholas agreed, as though somehow he'd seen her gesture of confirmation.

"Please let's go. There's nothing left to see."

"I don't have to see him to feel him here."

The statement caught her completely off guard. Her heart squeezed painfully in her chest.

"You . . . feel Byron here?" she finally managed to whisper.

"Can't you?"

Lucy's head came up. Was he doing it again—throwing veiled questions at her, trying to confuse her? Or were her guilt and imagination taking over as they had before—reading negative comments into innocent remarks?

"What is it about me that offends you, Lucy?"

Again he caught her by surprise. Lucy responded with a suspicious stare.

"Have I done something to you?" Nicholas went on, his tone vaguely curious.

"You mean, other than being rude and hurtful?"

"On the contrary, I thought I was being truthful."

Lucy did her best not to sound flustered. "You just don't seem like you should be Byron's brother, that's all."

"Because of me? Or because of Byron?"

Lucy's mind shifted immediately to Jared. When she'd first discovered Jared in the mausoleum—and in spite of his own personal suffering—his distress over Byron had been clearly evident, his concern over Byron genuine, his questions about Byron openly emotional.

But Nicholas . . .

The only thing Nicholas had expressed so far was a casual interest to see where Byron had died. To wander around where Byron had bled and burned. And to interrogate Lucy in the most arrogant and malicious way possible.

"You're not at all like Byron," she answered him now.

"No?" Nicholas threw her a sidelong glance. He looked amused as he withdrew a pack of cigarettes from his pocket and pulled one out. "Well . . . we did have different upbringings, after all."

"So why did your father take you and not Byron?"

"Byron was fortunate, and I never discuss my father. As far as I'm concerned, he should have died years ago."

Lucy watched him light a cigarette and exhale a sinuous coil of smoke. She chose her words carefully before asking them aloud.

"Matt said you hardly ever saw your father. So . . . I mean . . . didn't you at least have some regrets? Or feel cheated?"

Nicholas's expression remained impassive, his tone empty. "You can only feel things like that for someone you love."

Love . . .

Without warning, Lucy felt an ache in her heart. It struck her in that instant how terribly sad Nicholas was . . . how sad he'd *always* been. She could hear it in the cold hardening of his voice; she could read it in the bitter resignation on his face.

But there was something else, as well. Something deep and unreachable in the way he'd uttered that one word.

Love.

And though dislike and distrust still cautioned Lucy against him, this sudden revelation moved her in a way she never expected.

Quickly, she looked away. She didn't *want* to be moved by Nicholas Wetherly. Terrible sadness or not, she had no desire whatsoever to listen to him or sympathize with him or close the distance she'd deliberately placed between them. And yet she could hear herself starting to talk again, fumbling for those right words, feeling utterly foolish, and wondering why this need for explanations seemed suddenly so important.

"But your father . . . your family . . . you may not think you love them, but there's something between you. You share the same blood; it's a bond. It's an *identity*. It's who you are. It's . . . where you've come from, and where you'll be, years and years and years from now."

Shrugging his shoulders, Nicholas gave a harsh laugh. "You make it sound like forever. Do you really believe in forever?"

"Well . . . yes, in a way." Lucy's voice went soft and sad. "A little part of eternity. A little part of yourself that might never have to die."

As she gazed off across the snow, her cheeks began to sting, her eyes squinting against needle-sharp slivers of cold.

When had the wind sprung up again? she

wondered. Only seconds ago, everything had been so peaceful . . . so still.

She jumped as she felt a hand on her arm.

Nicholas was looking down at her with his dark, brooding stare.

"Thank you for sharing that, Lucy," he whispered. "You explain it all so well."

14

If only I could explain this journal, Lucy thought impatiently. *If only I could figure it out.*

She glanced at her clock on the nightstand, surprised at how late it was. A little past midnight, and the house lay quiet around her. She hadn't seen Nicholas all evening, not since they'd gotten back from the accident site, in fact—and Gran had fallen asleep hours ago. But Lucy didn't feel like sleeping. Didn't even feel tired. Just frustrated.

Frowning, she placed her hand on one brittle page of the book. She closed her eyes and tried to empty her mind. Then she lightly traced her fingertips over the faded, old-fashioned penmanship.

Nothing.

No images, no feelings, not a single translation.

This doesn't make sense! I did it before in the bookshop—why can't I do it now?

She sighed and opened her eyes again, her glance going at once to her cell phone. For at least the hundredth time, she willed it to ring; for the hundredth time, it stayed silent. Since getting back to Gran's this morning, she'd made every call she could think of, but with absolutely no luck. No one at the hospital would tell her anything about Dakota. She hadn't been able to get ahold of Matt. Nobody answered at Dakota's house. Mr. Montana hadn't been at the bookstore and wouldn't be in all day.

And Lucy's emotions had been in a constant turmoil.

She couldn't stop herself from worrying, from feeling that something was very wrong and out of sync. Her mind was ready to burst with all the things she needed to tell Dakota. And she still hadn't been able to check on Jared.

Not that she hadn't tried.

On the way back from the accident site, she'd made up a story about having to pick up something for Matt. She'd convinced Nicholas to stop by the old church and wait for her in the car. And she'd prayed Mrs. Dempsey would be there to let her in.

But the doors had been locked.

And while she was tugging on them, hoping for a miracle, Nicholas had grudgingly decided to get out and help her.

He hadn't understood her distress and frustration. Or the reason she'd kept glancing toward the side of the building, babbling about a window she might be able to crawl through, and why didn't he just get back in the car because it would take her only a minute. But since he *hadn't* taken the hint, she'd been forced to give up and leave with him, which had made her even more anxious about Jared than she'd been before.

Why are you so worried about Jared, anyway? He can take care of himself. After being with him, and after what you saw, how can you doubt it?

But it wasn't merely Jared's safety and well-being, Lucy had to admit. She needed to tell him about Nicholas. And she needed him to know . . .

That you didn't abandon him.

That you haven't forgotten him.

Feeling more restless by the minute, Lucy got up and walked to Gran's room. The night-light glowed softly beside the bed, illuminating Gran's face on the pillow.

It was a mask of pure terror.

Just like last night—the bulging eyelids and twisted mouth, the frantic gasps for air, as though Gran were choking, as though Gran were dying.

"Gran, wake up!"

In her panic to lift Gran's head, Lucy bumped hard against the nightstand, sending the baby monitor crashing to the floor. She could see Gran's fingers plucking helplessly at the covers, clawing back and forth, as though holding a piece of chalk, as though writing on a slate.

"Wake up!"

Lucy wasn't being careful anymore. She gave Gran's shoulders a fierce shake, and tried to raise her higher against the pillows. Where was Nicholas anyway? Last night when Gran had gotten so bad, he'd shown up in a second. Surely he could hear what was going on—wasn't that why Mrs. Dempsey had put that other baby monitor by his bed?

As Lucy gazed anxiously down at Gran's face, she saw the dark eyes open at last. Gran's labored breathing calmed, and her lips began to close.

"A bad dream, Gran." Lucy sighed in relief. "Just like last night. Just a bad . . ."

The words died in her throat.

Yes. Exactly *like last night.*

Very slowly she stroked Gran's hair. She smoothed it from the bony cheeks and the feverish, wrinkled brow.

What's going on with you, Gran? How come you've had such awful dreams since Nicholas came?

"Gran?" Lucy whispered.

But even as Lucy said her name, Gran was already drifting back to sleep.

For a long time Lucy stayed at the side of the bed, wrestling with these new and nagging doubts. Maybe she was making too much of this. Maybe this was just a coincidence, Gran having bad dreams two nights in a row. After all, Lucy wasn't familiar with Gran's sleeping habits—for all she knew, this could be a regular occurrence. For all she knew, Gran could have suffered bad dreams every single night of her life.

But wouldn't Mrs. Dempsey have said something? Or Thelma? Or even Byron?

Satisfied that Gran was sleeping peacefully, Lucy tucked the blankets around her and stepped back from the bed. She stumbled over the baby monitor and leaned down to pick it up.

That's weird.

She could see at once that the little light wasn't on. Which meant the monitor probably wasn't working.

Great. I must have broken it.

She'd just have to try to fix it for Gran, Lucy decided. And to be safe, maybe even wake up Nicholas to let him know what had happened.

Going back to her room, Lucy sat down on the edge of her bed and fiddled with the monitor. Maybe she hadn't really broken it, after all— maybe she'd simply jarred the batteries loose.

She turned it over and opened the battery compartment.

It was empty.

There weren't any batteries inside.

Staring in disbelief, Lucy actually wondered if her eyes were playing tricks on her. It even took her a few seconds to realize her cell phone was ringing, and that it might finally be Dakota.

"Hello? Dakota, is that you?"

"No." The voice on the other end was just a whisper. "But she wants to see you."

Lucy's heart fluttered uneasily. "Who is this?"

"Dakota's brother."

"Texas?" Dropping the monitor on the bed, Lucy tried to focus. "Thank God. Is Dakota all right? I got your package! What happened?"

"Can you come to the hospital?"

"I can hardly hear you. Can you talk a little louder?"

"I don't want the nurses listening. Dakota's not supposed to have visitors—you'll have to sneak in."

"Sneak in? When? You mean *now*?"

"She says it's really important. Can you come?"

Lucy's eyes went instantly to the clock. It was almost one in the morning.

"Of course I'll come. But how—"

"There's a door on the south side of the building, by the doctors' parking lot. It says 'No Entry.' You can't miss it."

"Are you sure? What if someone catches me?

What if they call security?"

"They won't. It's a fire exit. There won't be anybody using it. The stairs go straight to the end of the hall on the third floor. Right by Dakota's room."

Again Lucy glanced at the time. "My car got stolen two nights ago, so I'll have to walk."

"That sucks. My folks dropped me off here, or I'd drive by and get you."

"It's no problem. I'm staying with Mrs. Wetherly right now, and the hospital's not far. I'll come as quick as I can."

She heard the smile in Texas's voice. "I'll be waiting," he said.

15

*You'll have to dress warm—you'll have to hurry—
you'll have to tell Nicholas you're going out.*

Lucy threw on some clothes, her mind
spinning in all directions.

Despite her responsibility to Gran, the last
thing she wanted to do was bring Nicholas into
this. There were enough strained feelings
between the two of them already—she didn't
need any questions about why she was taking off
alone in the wee hours of the morning.

But Dakota was asking for her—that's what
mattered most right now. Which must mean
Dakota was feeling better, that Dakota must have
something to tell her about the hit-and-run,
something no one else was supposed to hear . . .

*"She wants to see you . . . she says it's really
important."*

Fumbling with her boots, Lucy mulled over the brief conversation she'd just had with Texas. He hadn't actually *said* Dakota was better. And if Dakota *was* better, he hadn't actually explained *why* he was at the hospital this late.

Lucy shook the distractions from her mind. What did it matter, anyway? Dakota needed her, or Texas wouldn't have called. Dakota needed her, and she would go.

After adding batteries to the monitor, Lucy placed it at Gran's bedside and crept upstairs to Nicholas's room. No light showed beneath his closed door, and she hesitated a moment, unsure what to do. Finally she gave a quiet knock and a cautious whisper.

"Nicholas? Are you there?"

No one answered. But as Lucy pressed closer to listen, she could swear she heard a faint movement on the other side of the door.

"Nicholas?"

Again no answer; again that muffled sound. Not a footstep, exactly, but something softer . . . lighter . . . gently stirring the air.

Lucy forced herself to try the doorknob.

It was locked, and it was cold. As though a

window in the room had been left open. On a hunch, she crouched down and felt along the floor. Yes, there was definitely a draft.

He must be home, then. He's just sleeping.

She'd probably heard him turning over in bed, she told herself—but would he be alert enough to hear his monitor if Gran needed help?

Recalling the missing batteries, she felt unnerved all over again. It had to be an innocent mistake—someone must have started to change the batteries, become distracted somehow, then simply forgotten to replace them.

Just forget about Nicholas and leave. You'll be there and back before anyone realizes it. There's a baby monitor in his room . . . Gran's asleep. What could possibly happen in the short time you're gone?

Having convinced herself, Lucy slipped out of the house before she could change her mind. *Four blocks—isn't that what Matt said?* But it seemed an awfully long and awfully scary four blocks, Lucy quickly decided. There wasn't a sign of life anywhere, and she kept to the main street, with every sense alert.

What am I doing out here at night? Out here

freezing to death, with some maniac on the loose?

She began to walk faster, and was running by the time she reached the hospital. The doctors' parking lot was well lit, and she found the side door without any trouble.

No Entry.

After a nervous glance around, Lucy went inside.

She found herself in a cramped space, at the bottom of a concrete stairwell. A dingy bulb hung from the ceiling, and an interior door had been propped open with a rusty trash can. Lucy couldn't see anything but darkness beyond that. And it was obvious Texas wasn't here to meet her.

He must have been sidetracked, Lucy told herself. *Or maybe I'm late, and he got tired of waiting.*

She thought back to what he'd said on the phone. She realized he hadn't actually been specific about where he'd be when she got here.

Maybe he's upstairs. Maybe he just assumed I'd know.

Nervously, she peered up the stairwell, but the feeble light seemed to die out completely at the first landing. A cold breeze crept through her hair, as though someone had breathed down the back of her neck.

Lucy whirled around, her eyes darting into every corner. "Texas?"

"Shhh . . . this way."

"But I thought we were going upstairs."

Texas didn't answer. As Lucy followed him through the inner door, she heard it close behind her.

"Texas?" Instantly, Lucy froze, trying to adjust to the gloom. She seemed to be in a narrow corridor with doors on either side—none of them marked and none of them open. As in the stairwell, the light here was weak at best, and she began to walk slowly, fear building steadily inside her.

"Texas! Come on, where are you? Where's Dakota?"

She couldn't hear or see anyone. Surely Texas had noticed by now that she wasn't right behind him—why wasn't he coming back to look for her?

"In here, Lucy."

Stifling a cry, she saw the pale sliver of light about fifty feet ahead of her, spilling out from one wall and slanting across the floor of the hallway.

No . . . not from a wall, she realized then. From an open door.

And she knew she should have stopped, but she couldn't. Should have turned and run for her life, yet all she could do was watch helplessly as her feet kept moving, as that doorway got closer. As though she had to look and see for herself. Had to know . . .

Lucy stood on the threshold and stared. It was a large room, filled with shadows and stale, cool air. There were desks and books, meticulously arranged; file cabinets and lab tables; and computer screens glowing eerily like giant malformed eyes.

But it wasn't just the computers that were glowing.

As her gaze swept incredulously from one end of the room to the other, she could feel her pulse beginning to race—hard, sickening throbs.

The back wall was completely lined with illuminated glass doors. At first glance, it reminded Lucy of the refrigerated sections in grocery stores, until it suddenly dawned on her what she was really seeing.

Blood.

Shelf after shelf, row upon row, of blood. Bags of it, stored and locked away like rare and precious treasures . . .

Dark red, life-giving blood, chilling at perfect temperatures like the finest of wines.

Sweet wines . . . irresistible wines . . .

Wines that someone would sip with the greatest pleasure . . .

Like someone was doing now.

Someone tall and regal, silhouetted against those glass doors. Someone bathed in the soft, gray light that clung to him like an aura.

Someone standing there with his head tilted slightly back . . .

And a bag of blood poised delicately above his lips.

16

"Ah, Lucy—there you are. May I offer you an hors d'oeuvre?"

The room receded around her.

The night, the world, her broken life spun away and vanished instantly into oblivion.

Like a distant observer, she could see herself frozen there beside the door—a phantom Lucy, without form or substance—trying to make sense of what was happening, too overwhelmed to comprehend.

Yet she could hear his voice—that rich, deep, velvety voice—and she recognized it at once.

She could see his elegant profile, and she was certain she'd seen it before.

In my dreams. In my nightmares.

His was a face too handsome, too beautiful, too dangerous and seductive for the normal light of day. A face far too perfect for reality.

And yet . . . *the strangest thing* . . . this face she knew so well hovered just beyond her consciousness, hiding itself behind her shock and confusion, elusive as a fantasy.

Lucy struggled to clear her mind. To move, to breathe, to think.

"I am familiar to you," the voice murmured, and Lucy, with the greatest of efforts, was finally able to nod.

"Yes."

"We have met on numerous occasions, you and I. But never in a place so . . . shall we say . . . suited to my personal tastes?"

She watched the silhouette of his arm. The sinuous glide of it, withdrawing another container of blood. He gave it a silent puncture. He gave a satisfied sigh.

"I can't see your face," Lucy said.

"You've seen many of my faces. Choose whichever suits you at this moment."

His head was erect now; he ran one hand slowly across his mouth. The empty bag dropped to the floor at his feet.

"Come in," he told her. "Close the door."

Lucy's own movements were surreal. She seemed to be floating weightless, strangely detached from herself, trapped in a daze beyond fear.

She pulled the door shut and waited there, watching him.

And in a serene kind of horror, she knew she'd been expecting this exact moment, this very encounter, though she didn't know how or why.

"You've locked us in." He sounded pleased. "I like that. It conveys a certain amount of trust."

"And why should I trust you?"

"I've saved your life. I've done you many favors."

"Lucy . . . there's no name for what we are . . ."

"Tell me your name, then."

"Don't you know? It flows so easily from your tongue. It stirs your blood to say it."

A shudder started at the base of her spine and slithered up her neck. She didn't want to hear any more, yet she had to listen—didn't want to stay, yet she needed the truth.

"You're acting very courageous, Lucy—in spite of your fear. It's filling the room, that fear scent of yours. I find it quite exciting."

"What do you want from me?" she asked, trying to hide the trembling in her voice, knowing full well she couldn't deceive him.

And it was horrible—*unnatural*—the way he slid through the shadows toward her, closer and closer, without even making a sound.

"I want all of you," he murmured. "But then, you already knew that. You've known it since the beginning."

She felt the air stir faintly against her cheek. She drew a shallow breath and held her ground.

"I remember the first time I saw you," he whispered. "You stood at that upstairs window, more sorrowful and alone than you'd ever been in your life. No one could have even sensed me there, hiding in the night, and yet your eyes found mine. And at that second, you wished you could come to me."

"I don't know what you're talking about."

"You pressed yourself against the glass, and I could feel your desire and desperation. And every time I've looked upon you since that very first night, your need for me has grown."

"Stop it."

"You've longed for me each time I've stood

beside your bed . . . each time I've knelt beside your pillow to calm your nightmares—"

"*You're* my nightmare!"

"I'm your *salvation*." His tone grew hard. "I've lured you, and you've followed. I've lied and pretended, even as you've taken me in and befriended me. I've stroked your hair, and I've tasted your skin, and I've kissed you where no one's ever kissed you before."

The heat! Where was it coming from? The terrible, scalding heat, closing in and suffocating her and searing all the way through? Her entire body was shaking. She could hardly stand . . . could scarcely even breathe . . .

"You feel it, don't you, Lucy? That part of me flowing through your veins?"

"No."

"Don't you see—I've given you life. Without me, you would have died that night along with your precious Byron. I've given you *life*, and I could take it back from you in a second."

"How do you know Byron?" The world was burning around her, dissolving into smoke, sucking the air from her lungs. "What are you talking about?"

"Do you deny it? The connection we have?"

To Lucy's shock, she felt his lips move slowly, deliberately, down the length of her neck. She gasped and tried to pull away, but he wasn't even there—only shadows were there, shadows like silk, shadows embracing her, and a whisper caressing her cheek, and the coppery smell of blood . . .

"You know the ache I speak of," he said, even as she felt herself melting, melting from the merciless, ravaging heat. "The ache so deep inside you that no one can fill but me. Not your most secret dreams—not your most forbidden fantasies. It's not just your body that aches for me, Lucy. It's your soul."

She couldn't struggle anymore. His lips burned everywhere they touched her . . . he kissed the pulse at her throat. Tender and urgent. Teasing . . . demanding. Taking his time.

"I am your death, Lucy. And your life. And you are my destiny."

"No!" But her words were no more than a whisper, drowned in the frantic beating of her heart. "I'm my own destiny—no one else's. And you're *nothing* to me. And *nothing* will ever happen—"

"Happen? But it's already happening." His voice held the hint of a smile. "You're already feeling the changes—you know you can't deny it. Subtle at first, barely noticeable. Small things, so gradual, so natural . . . until one day you realize nothing's the same. Not you . . . not your world. You've become something else entirely. Something only your own kind can ever accept and understand."

What's wrong with me! Why can't I move? Why can't I scream and push him away? "I don't know what you're talking about!"

"Of course you do. And very soon, you'll be *begging* to be at my side."

"I'll never beg you for anything. And I'll *never* be *with* you."

"But I know so much about you, Lucy. Where you live now, where your bedroom is in the Wetherly house. Who you see, and who you spend time with. And poor Gran . . . it would be such a shame if anything happened to her. She's so . . . defenseless."

"I swear, if you ever go near—"

"I *have* been near her, and what would you do anyway? Enlist the help of that handsome young man in the upstairs room? Byron's brother, isn't he?"

Her head was pounding, her thoughts going dim. Her strength was rapidly draining away, drifting in a warm, crimson fog.

"Nicholas . . . Wetherly." He pronounced each word with great care. "Perhaps you could ask *him* to be your protector."

"Who . . . are you?"

"But surely you realize he has no power against me. And by trying to protect you, he could very easily get himself killed."

His lips traced the curve of her neck. They spoke softly into her ear.

"Hmmm . . . sort of like Byron, don't you think?"

17

Only the darkness held her up.

As her knees began to buckle, Lucy felt herself falling . . . falling . . . yet never reaching the ground. She tried to call for help, but it was useless. Suspended there in a web of terror, her only awareness was that voice—*his* voice—still whispering in her ear.

"I know where Angela is." Another hint of a smile. "How important is that to you?"

Lucy's cry echoed desperately through the void. "What have you done with her?"

"I don't think those details would please you at all."

"Where is she? Why won't you let her go?"

"Lucy, I'm surprised at you. Do you actually think I'd keep Angela against her will? The truth is . . . I've never heard her complain. Not once."

"Then let her come home!"

"But she's not happy at home. Don't you remember? That's why she left with me in the first place."

"Just bring her back! I'm begging you!"

For an endless moment there was silence. Then at last he said, "I'll make you a bargain."

"Wh-what kind of bargain?"

"Come to the mausoleum, tomorrow at midnight. Come in secret, and come alone."

"But—"

"Do as I say, and I'll let you see Angela."

She wanted to believe him—*needed* with all her heart to believe him. Yet even before she could answer, she knew he was gone. The dark was simply darkness now—the shadows, only shadows.

There was no presence.

No danger.

And now she was completely alone, out in the corridor, sagging against the wall as though she'd just woken from a dream.

Oh God . . . Angela . . .

Moaning at the effort, Lucy tried to rouse herself. Her head was heavy, her muscles weak, her thoughts numb.

Oh, Angela . . . what has he done to you?

Could he *possibly* be telling the truth? Lucy's instincts warned her against it, but what else could she do? If there was even the slightest chance Angela might still be alive, Lucy knew she had to take it. She had to do whatever she could to bring Angela home.

The sound of a door opening brought her upright. As something moved at the opposite end of the hall, she stifled a cry and began to back away.

"Hey!" a voice called sharply. "What are you doing in here?"

Lucy turned, staggering clumsily as she tried to escape. She could hear heavy footsteps in hot pursuit, and they seemed to be gaining on her.

"You there, stop!" There was a loud burst of static as a radio crackled to life. "Quick! I need security!"

Lucy panicked. She felt as if she were trudging through cold, thick molasses, getting absolutely nowhere. She heard a dull echo as she hit the exit door, felt a raw blast of wind pierce all the way through her, and then she was half running, half skidding across the frozen parking lot.

Running without stopping.

Running wildly and frantically where she didn't want to go . . .

Into the deep, black night.

18

Byron!

He knew about Byron!

But how? How!

Lucy was sobbing now. Gut-wrenching sobs that ripped her whole body, yet still she kept on running.

Was the guard still after her? She was too frightened to stop or look back, but she half expected sirens behind her at any second. Instinctively, she ducked between two buildings where she couldn't be seen from the street.

Oh God! She felt sick with terror, sick with shock. She'd practically forgotten why she'd rushed to the hospital in the first place—and even though Dakota obviously wasn't the least bit involved, Lucy was too distraught to feel relieved. She didn't even notice where she was headed, didn't even care—just as long as she could escape.

Escape?

You can't escape—you'll never escape!

Her lungs burned from the cold, but Lucy welcomed the pain. *Anything* to block out what had just happened—*anything* to wake her from this nightmare! The shadowy presence . . . the whispery voice . . . the painful pleasure of fire down her neck and through her veins *and deep, deep . . . so very deep.*

Lucy tried to go faster. She wove her way through backyards and side streets and alleys, praying that somehow she'd eventually end up at Gran's.

But he could be out here right now! He could be anywhere—how would I know?

And how had he known so much about her, she wondered? *Everything* about her!

"You've seen many of my faces . . ."

His voice echoed mockingly in her ears. She could still feel his lips at her throat.

"You are my destiny . . . my destiny . . ."

A memory flashed through her mind: she and Dakota sharing a heart-to-heart talk, and the wise, calm look in Dakota's eyes. "You've been chosen for something," Dakota had told her, "some destiny that's way beyond anything we could ever imagine."

But I don't want it! Lucy wiped angrily at her tears. *Whatever it is,* I don't want this destiny!

With a start, she realized she was going up steps to a porch. She froze in confusion and looked around.

Gran's. I'm at Gran's house.

She didn't remember getting here, and she didn't feel as relieved as she'd thought she would.

This house isn't safe anymore.

No place is safe anymore.

Still trembling, she went directly to Gran's room. She stood beside the bed for a while, then gently rearranged the covers around Gran's chin.

Sleep tight, Gran. I promise I won't let anything happen to you.

But Lucy found no comfort in that promise, and her thoughts were scattered. She knew something nagged at the back of her mind— something *he'd* said, as he'd mocked her in the darkness. Something she hadn't been able to acknowledge then, and didn't want to accept now. So instead, she went systematically around the house, checking windows and doors, finally pausing right outside Nicholas's bedroom. She felt guilty and shameful for the way she'd behaved. She should never have treated him so badly.

"That handsome young man in the upstairs room? Byron's brother—Nicholas Wetherly—perhaps you could ask him *to be your protector."* And she could hear *his* voice again—his amusement, his disdain—just as clearly as if he were speaking to her now. *"Surely you realize he has no power against me. And by trying to protect you, he could very easily get himself killed."*

"What have I done?" Lucy whispered. Tearfully, she went back downstairs to her room. She put on her nightgown and burrowed deep beneath the covers. Her trembling grew worse, and though she'd piled on more blankets, they were useless against her chill. Her head felt as if it were splitting. And in a rush of pain, those nagging thoughts she'd tried so desperately to deny burst free at last.

"I've lured you, and you've followed."

"No," Lucy pleaded. "No . . ."

"I've lied and pretended, even as you've taken me in and befriended me . . ."

Oh God, what have I done!

But Lucy knew all too well what she'd done. She knew if she went back to the old church right this instant, the cellar would be empty, and Jared would be gone.

I helped the wrong one.

As the brutal truth struck her full force, Lucy buried her head in her pillows and gave in to despair.

It was Jared.

It was Jared all along.

19

"Is Father Matt there?"

"What is it you want?" Father Paul's voice was thick with sleep. "Can you talk a little louder?"

Lucy hesitated, then drew a slow intake of breath. "Please—may I speak to Father Matt?"

"A dire emergency, I hope," the old priest grumbled. "Just a minute."

Rocking back and forth on her bed, Lucy chewed on a thumbnail and stared miserably at the clock. Another hour had passed since she'd climbed into bed—another hour of sleeplessness and growing panic. She'd reached for the phone at least a dozen times since then, but had managed to stop herself.

Until now.

Now she convinced herself that just hearing the sound of Matt's voice was all she needed. It would reassure her, calm her down, put things in perspective. It would make her feel safe.

She wouldn't have to explain anything; she'd simply tell him she'd had a panic attack, or a nightmare that seemed much too real. She'd think of something. *Anything*, just to talk to Matt.

"Is there something I can do?" Father Paul's voice jolted her from her excuses. "Father Matt doesn't seem to be here at the moment."

"Not there?" Lucy's mind raced. "Well . . . do you know where he is?"

Another grumble, this time under his breath. At last Father Paul said, "If you leave your name, I'll have him call when he gets back. Or—if this really can't wait—I'll page him."

Lucy hesitated. She remembered now that Matt had given her his cell phone number. Matt had said to call anytime. Matt had promised he'd be available twenty-four-seven.

"No," she answered, "but could you tell him that Lucy called? And I'm sorry I woke you."

"Me, too," he sighed, and Lucy clicked off.

Reluctantly she put down her phone. Whatever Matt was doing, it must be critical for him to be out at this hour. Maybe someone was very sick; maybe someone was dying. How could she in good conscience interrupt him from someone's time of need? *I just want to hear your voice, Matt. I just want to hold on to your strength. I just want you to tell me everything's going to be okay.*

I want you to tell me that Angela's *going to be okay.*

But, of course, she couldn't confide in Matt about Angela. Even though she was desperate to believe in Angela's safe return . . . and even though she had a horrible feeling it might not really happen. No matter what, she was resolved to meet secretly at the mausoleum. She hadn't been able to help Angela before, but maybe—*somehow*—she could help Angela now.

Lucy couldn't cry anymore. She felt utterly exhausted, yet she still couldn't fall asleep. She stared nervously at her window, at the door opening out to the hall. She kept her lamp turned on, to keep the darkness away.

I'm so scared, Matt. I really need you right now. I really need your faith.

Opening the nightstand drawer, she pulled out the medallion he'd given her. In spite of his teasing, Lucy knew how sincere he was. And despite his concerns about her state of mind, he *must* believe her a little, right? Otherwise, why would he have wanted her to have the medallion in the first place? *"Someone gave me this a long time ago."* She remembered what he'd told her that night, and the look on his face when he'd said it. *"It's helped me through some pretty rough times. It's an ancient holy symbol . . . I hope it'll be special to you."*

The chain slipped easily over her head. She tucked the medallion down the front of her nightgown and pressed it against her heart. Then she lay there, staring wide-eyed again at her window, as if the curtains might flutter at any moment, and open, and reveal a dark, dangerous, deadly face gazing in at her . . .

He could be out there right now.

He could be *anywhere* right now, with fresh blood on his lips.

Nowhere and everywhere, watching and waiting.

Waiting to hurt her and the people she loved.

Waiting to make her his.

20

She dreamed of forests.

Pine trees, tall and fragrant and dusted with snow. Cushion-soft needles underfoot, prisms of ice on branches, frozen crystal streams. It was night, and the world was beautiful. She could see every detail in the dark, and the air was fresh and sweet . . .

Sweet with a scent she'd smelled before . . .

Delicate and addictive . . .

The scent was coming from her. As she ran among the trees, it flowed from her hair and the pores of her skin. It lingered on her lips and on her tongue. So sweet—so intoxicating—and though it filled her with contentment, she longed to embrace it and taste it again.

"Then come," the voice whispered to her. *His* voice, touching her heart, possessing her soul.

"The night is pure enchantment, Lucy. Come . . . share it with me."

And they were the air, the wind, the swiftest of shadows, free and wild and unafraid . . .

And I'm happy, Lucy thought. *I've never been so happy.*

"This is where you belong, Lucy. Here in this world. Where no one can hurt you again."

"Yes . . . I don't want to be alone."

"Then stay, my beloved. Stay."

"Lucy?" But not *his* voice . . . another voice, pulling her back—

"I want to stay," Lucy mumbled, but the night was fading, his face was fading—

"Lucy. Telephone."

"I want to stay!"

Gasping, Lucy opened her eyes. Nicholas was standing in her doorway, gesturing toward the hall.

"Okay." He shrugged. "I'll take a message."

For a brief second, she hovered precariously between sleep and waking. And then she remembered where she was.

"What time is it?" she asked him.

"Six o'clock."

"Are you serious? Okay, I'm coming."

As Nicholas disappeared, Lucy struggled to get out of bed. Every muscle ached. Her throat hurt, and her skin felt chapped. Even her bones were sore.

"Great," she muttered. "I must be coming down with the flu."

She made her way painfully to the telephone. There was an unfamiliar smell in the house this morning—a faint smell of sickness and medicine and old age—and as Lucy heard a plaintive meow, Cinder slunk out from beneath a chair to rub fretfully against her legs.

"What is it, girl? You seem almost as nervous as me."

For Lucy suddenly realized she was *afraid* to answer the phone. Suppose it was *him* again? Another trick to lure her alone somewhere? So when she heard the familiar voice on the other end of the line, she let out a cry of relief.

"Dakota! Are you okay?" But then, before Dakota could answer, Lucy added solemnly, "Say something so I know it's really you."

There followed a moment of silence. "One

cannot have a spiritual experience on a bedpan."

"Oh thank God. I've been so worried."

"Me, too. About you."

"Me?" That uneasy feeling was beginning to creep over her again. Lucy braced herself and held tight to the receiver. "What about me?"

"I heard you were staying at Gran's now. But let's not talk over the phone. Can you come over here? Can you come now?"

"But you're not supposed to have visitors."

"They've moved me to another room. It's far from the nurses' station, and my parents won't be here till noon. I've *got* to see you."

"I'll be there," Lucy promised.

"Just . . . be careful."

Something in Dakota's voice, Lucy thought. *Something like fear . . . and more than just a warning . . .*

She turned as Nicholas came out of Gran's room. Should she mention the empty baby monitor? Should she say anything about their visit to the accident site yesterday? Should she apologize for treating him so suspiciously? But Lucy didn't have to make any decisions, because Nicholas stopped beside her with a dark frown on his face.

"The back door was open," he said.

Lucy stared at him, not quite sure where this was going.

"The back door," he repeated. "When I got up this morning, it was unlocked. It was standing wide open."

A ripple worked its way up Lucy's spine. She glanced in the direction of the kitchen.

"What are you talking about? I checked every single lock before I went to bed."

Nicholas's eyes grazed her calmly. "And when was that?"

"Late."

"There was water on the floor. Like someone had tracked in snow."

"Well then . . . it must have been Cinder." Unconsciously she put a hand to her temple. *The air, the wind, the swiftest of shadows, free and wild and unafraid . . .*

"What's wrong?"

"Nothing. I was just saying, it must have been the cat."

"The cat." That tone again, that not-so-subtle mockery. "Right. A cat who unlocks deadbolts and forgets to close the door when she goes in and out."

"I have to get dressed," Lucy mumbled, but again his voice stopped her.

"That's not all. My grandmother doesn't look very well this morning. I'm not sure what to do about it."

Immediately, Lucy headed for Gran's room. But when she leaned down over the bed, she couldn't believe what she was seeing.

Gran looked like a different person. A completely different person from the one Lucy had tucked in last night. Her eyes were enormous, fixed in a wide, shocked gaze, showing no sparks of light. Her wrinkles seemed to have collapsed into her face; her skin was like yellowed parchment; her chest was almost concave, scarcely even moving as she breathed.

"Gran?" Lucy placed a hand on Gran's forehead, only to find it startlingly cold. "Gran, what's wrong?"

She waited for a flicker of eyelids, or sounds from her throat, or the slightest tremble of gnarled fingers—but Gran simply lay there, motionless.

"Tell me, Gran," Lucy urged her on. "Write it

for me—can you write it down for me?"

Even as she spoke, Lucy was searching for the slate. Shaking out the covers, glancing around at the furniture, hunting along the floor where the slate might have fallen. Where was it? Gran always kept it close by—it was her lifeline, the only way she could communicate.

"Where's your slate, Gran?"

Lucy grew more anxious. Feeling under the bed, groping beneath the pillows. Surely no one would have taken it—everyone knew how important that slate and chalk were to Gran's peace of mind and health.

Unless . . .

The deadbolt was unlocked, Nicholas had said. The kitchen door was open; there were tracks on the floor . . .

Was he *here? That nameless, faceless shadow— creeping through the house while everyone slept? Standing over me, watching? Giving me a warning? Showing me what he'll do if I don't cooperate?*

A bone-chilling shudder went through her. With renewed effort, Lucy kept on with her search, while Gran lay there staring with dull, dark eyes.

"Where is it?" Lucy muttered, growing more panicky by the second. "Where is it, Gran? Do you know who took it? Did you *see* who took it?"

But Gran was unresponsive. And as Lucy tried to stretch one arm beneath the mattress, she heard Nicholas behind her in the doorway.

"What's going on?"

"Her slate." Lucy didn't even glance his way. "I can't find her slate."

"You mean, the—"

"Yes, yes, the one she writes on. The one she *talks* on."

"Well, it has to be here someplace."

"Well, it's not," she argued, more harshly than she intended. "I've looked everywhere. It's not here."

"Someone just misplaced it, then."

"Misplaced it? Like the missing batteries from the monitor?" Lucy froze, instantly regretting her outburst right where Gran could hear. Taking Nicholas's arm, she pulled him down the hall and out of earshot.

"That was very tactful of you," Nicholas mumbled, though he seemed genuinely confused. "*What* are you talking about?"

Lucy faced him squarely, hands on hips. "The batteries. When I checked her monitor last night, there weren't any batteries in it."

"You're joking."

"Why would I joke about a thing like that? If something had happened to her, *no* one would have known about it!"

"So what are you saying, exactly?" His eyes narrowed. "Would you like to search my room? Maybe you'll find *all* the missing things up there."

As their gazes locked, Lucy felt her temper flaring out of control. With a huge effort, she took a step back and put up her hands, trying to ward off a confrontation.

"Look, I'm sorry. I didn't mean it the way it sounded. It's just that I'm so worried—"

"And you don't think I am?" His voice softened, though the defensive edge hadn't quite disappeared. "How do you think I feel? After all this time, I discover I have a family. A brother who is dead, a sister who is missing, and a grandmother who seems to be the only one left. And there's so much I want to know—

so much I need to ask her—and she can't tell me."

Lucy watched in guilty silence. Watched the way his black eyes smoldered, the way he raked one hand back through his hair. For one brief second he glanced wildly at his surroundings, as though the walls were suddenly too much for him, too close and confining, before his eyes finally shifted to the floor.

He seemed to be composing himself now. When he looked at Lucy again, a muscle clenched tightly in his jaw.

"I have absolutely no reason to hurt my grandmother. Absolutely nothing to gain. And I can't imagine why anyone else would want to hurt her either."

"I think," Lucy said quietly, avoiding his glare, "I think maybe you'd better call the doctor. And . . . and Father Matt. Their numbers are in that book by the phone."

Nicholas started to leave. He took several steps, then stopped again, turning back to her with a tight frown.

"Do you think she's had another stroke?" he murmured.

Lucy felt sick at the thought. Slowly she shook her head. "I don't know."

"The door was open," he reminded her, his voice solemn. "And there were tracks across the kitchen floor. And . . . you saw her eyes."

Again Lucy shook her head, not wanting to confirm what he was suggesting, not wanting to admit she'd seen it, too.

"That look of fear," Nicholas said. "Horrible fear. Like something nearly scared her to death."

21

"Uh-oh." Dakota sighed. "Am I that scary?"

Lucy stood by the hospital bed, fighting back tears. She'd told herself over and over again that she wouldn't show any negative emotions, no matter how bad her friend might look. But seeing Dakota now was like viewing a haphazard collage of cuts and bruises, slings and swellings, stitches and bandages—and Lucy could feel all her best intentions crumbling away.

Dakota attempted a smile. "Stop trying to be so noble—I've already seen myself in the mirror. It's an interesting look, but I'm not sure I'd have chosen it on my own."

"It's a great look. Sort of . . . eclectic."

"Sit." Dakota patted the covers, though her voice and her movements were weak. "We have serious things to discuss."

"I think we should wait till you feel better. I mean, you're lucky to be alive. That car could have killed you."

"It wasn't a car," Dakota said solemnly. "And that's what we have to discuss."

Lucy stared. She slipped out of her jacket, tossed it on a chair, and perched on the edge of the bed.

"Dakota—"

"I just *told* everyone it was a car, so they wouldn't ask me questions. And you and I both know they wouldn't have believed me anyway."

Lucy's heart crept into her throat. She tried to swallow it back down as Dakota took ahold of her hand.

"Something was in my truck," Dakota said. "It was waiting for me."

Lucy wanted to answer but couldn't. The air seemed to be getting colder. The room seemed to be growing smaller. Her heart was squeezing, and all she could do was nod.

"We were trying to get home, but I ran out of gas and slid into a snowbank." Dakota might just as well have been reading from a book, she was so matter-of-fact. "Texas and I had to walk all the way back to my aunt and uncle's house to get a gas can, so we were both in a terrible mood. We ended up having this huge argument—he wouldn't even keep up with me when we went back to the truck."

Again Lucy nodded. She could feel the steady grip of Dakota's hand; she could feel her own hand trembling.

"That's why he didn't really see what happened." Dakota said. "I opened the door, and it—it was in the front seat."

"Oh God, Dakota."

"Everything happened so fast, I just . . . I just can't remember all the details. There was this sound—sort of like growling. And I felt pain, and I hit the ground. I could hear Texas yelling, but he sounded far away. And I knew something was on top of me, but I couldn't see what."

Lucy didn't think she could listen anymore—didn't *want* to listen anymore—but Dakota kept stoically on.

"It had me pinned down, and it was so strong. And the pain . . . I've never felt pain like that. Like my throat was being torn. Like my shoulder was being ripped off."

"Please, Dakota. I don't think you should be talking about this now—"

"I *have* to talk about it. *We* have to talk about it." Dakota's eyes gazed straight into hers, filled with that wisdom Lucy always found so unsettling. "You told me things—private things—because you knew I'd believe you, right?"

"Yes . . ."

"Well, now I'm telling *you* things because I know *you'll* believe *me*."

For a long moment, neither of them spoke.

"You're right," Lucy whispered finally. "I believe you."

"I thought I was going to die."

Releasing Lucy's hand, Dakota settled back upon the pillows. Her long red hair was tangled, and her freckles stood out against the ghostly pallor of her skin.

"I thought I was going to die," she said again, and as her voice broke at last, tears ran slowly down her cheeks. "We rolled off the road into a ditch. It was holding me so tight, and it wouldn't let go, and it wouldn't stop biting me. I could feel teeth and spit all over my face. And blood, too—I could smell blood."

187

Dakota took a long, deep breath. Gesturing impatiently, she struggled to get her emotions under control.

"It had fur," she choked out. "And it smelled dirty and damp. Sweaty. But . . . kind of sweet, too. Does that even make sense?"

The hairs lifted on Lucy's arms. She leaned toward Dakota, her voice urgent.

"What do you mean, sweet?"

"I don't know . . . almost *too* sweet, *sickening* sweet. But like a *leftover* sweet, too. Like the way it smells when someone goes away, but her perfume's still there." Dakota hesitated. "Is that the same thing you smelled? The same smell you told me about?"

Lucy managed a nod. Dakota nodded back, then closed her eyes to finish the rest of her story.

"And then it was gone—just like that. I was lying there, and I knew I was bleeding, and I knew I was really hurt. But everything was so quiet . . . so peaceful. Like everything was normal. Like nothing had ever happened."

"And Texas didn't see any of this? He didn't even hear you being attacked?"

"Like I said, it happened so fast—it was over in a second. By the time Texas got there, he couldn't even see me in the ditch. I tried to yell at him to help me. I could hear the snowplow coming . . . and that's when I thought up the story about the hit-and-run driver. I mean, we were at the junction anyway, so it was perfect. I just told everyone that some car ran me down, and that it must have taken off down one of the other roads."

Lucy was silent. Just thinking of what Dakota had been through—and what worse things *could* have happened—so completely overwhelmed her now that she gripped the bedrail and looked off toward the window.

"Hey." Dakota's voice drew her firmly back again. "It's okay. I'm still here."

"But—"

"Don't start catastrophizing on me. We have more serious things to worry about."

"For God's sake, Dakota. What could be more serious than you almost getting killed?"

"The fact that this thing—whatever it is—is really and seriously after *you*."

The two girls stared at each other. Lucy had

gone so numb that for one endless moment she felt completely and helplessly paralyzed.

"Are you listening to me?" Reaching over, Dakota plucked at Lucy's sleeve. "I think whatever attacked me is the same thing that attacked Wanda in the park. I think it's the same thing that chased you and Angela that night when you were driving home from the festival. And I think . . ." Dakota paused in a split-second decision.

Lucy, watching her friend's expression, already knew what Dakota was going to say.

"I think it's the same thing that ran Byron's van off the road," Dakota finished.

Once again, Lucy was at the mercy of her memories. *That awful night . . . Byron's face . . . that dark shape caught in the headlights . . .* Only this time it was as if pieces of a puzzle were slowly connecting in her brain.

"It—he—knew exactly what he was doing." Dakota's mouth tightened into a grim line. "He could have killed me in that very first second, but he didn't. He could have done it without any struggle at all, but instead he was like . . . like a cat playing with a mouse. I think he left me alive on purpose. I think he *wanted* me to tell you."

"*I know so much about you, Lucy . . .*"

And even though Dakota was talking, it was that *other* voice Lucy was hearing now—that dangerous, whispering, nightmare voice, smooth and sated with blood.

"I think he knew who I was," Dakota said.

So much about you, Lucy . . . who you see . . . who you spend time with . . ."

For the first time, Dakota actually shuddered. "And there's . . . something else."

Something I don't want to listen to, Lucy thought. *Something I don't want to know.* Every instinct went on instant alert, even as she tried to stay strong and calm for Dakota.

"At first," her friend began, "I was sure it was an animal. The way it attacked me—those sounds it was making, the claws and teeth and fur. But then . . . I saw his face."

Dakota's own face went paler. Her eyes misted with tears, though she made a valiant effort to hold them back.

"It was so quick, Lucy. So quick, and I didn't expect it at all. But when he let me go and started to leave—just for *one second*—he stopped and looked back at me. And I saw him through the snow."

No, Dakota . . . please . . . I don't want to hear this.

"It looked like Byron," Dakota whispered. "So much like Byron . . . I had to remind myself that he's dead."

22

The girls sat without speaking.

Sat and held on to each other, as though, between the two of them, they might somehow conjure up superhuman strength and supernatural powers.

And answers, Lucy thought bitterly. *Answers to impossible things.*

For it had been only last night when she'd seen someone with Byron's face peering at her from the hospital window. Just like before at the bookshop . . . someone with Byron's face . . .

Someone . . . or something . . .

The gruesome details of Dakota's attack played over and over in her mind. Without warning, she flashed back to the mysterious journal and a series of cryptic lines she'd once been able to translate: *during daylight . . .*

handsome young man . . . transform . . . wolf or large black dog . . .

"When it happened, it was like a dream." Dakota's strained voice finally broke the silence. "I was aware of certain things. I mean, I could see and hear certain things, but at the same time, I was sort of . . ."

"Terrified?" Lucy made a weak attempt at humor, but Dakota sounded only more grave.

"No. No, that's the thing—I *wasn't* terrified. And not just because I didn't have time to be. It was more like feeling . . . a kind of awe." She paused, as if thinking. "I know that sounds crazy—but even when I was being attacked, there was something so *powerful* about him. So *beautiful* about him . . ."

Lucy's heart clenched in her chest. *Yes, Dakota. Yes, I know those feelings well.*

"Sorry." Dakota rolled her eyes. "They've got me on lots of drugs. This could be just the drugs talking. My drugs having a philosophical conversation with you."

"I . . . I don't think it's your drugs."

"No?" Giving a deep sigh, Dakota leveled a stare at her. "Then it must be Jared."

Lucy felt blindsided. She stared back at Dakota, not even able to answer.

"The one who attacked me, I mean," Dakota went on. "It must be Jared. Even though," she added gently, "you don't want to believe it."

The hospital room . . . Dakota's face . . . everything swam in a sea of tears. "I helped him," Lucy choked. "I believed him. Do you know how completely stupid I feel?"

"Don't. He's clever, and he used your own kindness against you. How could you have known?"

"I *should* have known. I should have known *better.*"

The time we spent together . . . things we talked about . . . the way it felt when he touched me . . .

Lucy forced the memories away. It was her own fault she'd gotten involved—*way* too involved. She'd welcomed Jared into her world with wide-open arms, and that was exactly what he'd counted on.

"I've lured you, and you've followed. I've lied and pretended, even as you've taken me in and befriended me . . ."

"So who is he really, I wonder?" Dakota

wasn't looking at Lucy anymore; she was staring up at the ceiling.

"You mean, besides the one who's been stalking me?"

"If he's not Byron's brother, then maybe he's the one who killed Katherine."

Lucy's jaw dropped. "What did you say?"

"It was just a thought. Whoever he is, I still think he's sending you a message. A warning. Telling you he can do whatever he wants, showing how much control he has over everything. *Especially* you."

Lucy found herself stalling. More than anything she longed to tell Dakota about being lured to the blood bank last night, about Jared and his threats—but she couldn't expose her friend to more danger.

Hasn't Dakota already been through enough on your account?

"Don't you dare try to save me," Dakota said.

Startled, Lucy met her friend's leveled accusing gaze.

"Listen to me, Lucy Dennison—I know that stubborn look on your face, and don't you dare try to protect me. This—whatever he is—has it coming, and I'll be damned if I'm going to miss out on it."

"He might kill you next time," Lucy answered, before she even thought.

But Dakota wasn't fazed. "Then he'll have to die trying."

"For God's sake, listen to us. Talking like all this is normal."

"Well, it's kind of normal for *you*. But don't worry . . . I'm getting used to it."

"I don't even know what's happening. Or *why* it's happening. Or—"

"The thing is, it doesn't matter," Dakota returned quietly. "Maybe you're not supposed to understand. Maybe you're *never* supposed to understand. I mean, isn't that life? Finding yourself right in the middle of things you can't figure out, and wondering if you ever will? The truth is, it's happening, and it's happening now, and *that's* what we have to accept. So instead of wishing it would go away, we have to start where we are and do something about it. We can't let ourselves be victims. Especially not *his* victims."

Dakota stopped talking. As she studied Lucy's face, a frown line settled between her brows.

"What aren't you telling me? And don't even try to deny it."

"It's . . ." Lucy's brain grabbed the first thing it could find. "I'm worried about Gran."

"What about Gran?"

"She was worse this morning, and no one seems to know why."

"Is she in the hospital?"

"No. Nicholas thought she'd be happier at home. He's paying for a full-time nurse."

Dakota was looking more lost by the minute. "Nicholas? Who's Nicholas?"

"Jared. The *second* Jared, though, not the first."

"How could I have missed so much in just two days?"

"You'd be amazed."

"At this point in time, probably not."

"Look." Lucy stood up and motioned toward the door. "You really need to rest, and I should get back to check on Gran."

"Are you afraid that what's wrong with her has something to do with Jared?"

Again Lucy hesitated. As she glanced reluctantly at Dakota, she saw the sudden knowing in her friend's eyes.

"So I'm not the only one he's after." Dakota seemed to accept this without surprise. "And of course you won't be able to warn anyone else, because they probably won't be very receptive to the idea of being stalked by some man-beast-werewolf thing."

"Man-beast-werewolf thing?"

"Lucy, I was there. I know what I saw."

"But you make it sound . . ."

"Real?" Shrugging her shoulders, Dakota frowned. "We've already established the fact that he's real. Now we have to figure out how to get rid of him."

"But—"

"The *reason* he's here doesn't matter, Lucy. Trying to figure out all those whys is a waste of time; that won't get us anywhere. It's not about giving up, you know. It's about accepting and moving on."

"Will you please—"

"Although I guess he's not actually a man-beast-werewolf." Dakota frowned harder, considering this. "I mean, didn't he tell you the night of the accident that there wasn't a name for what he is?"

"How in the world did you remember that?"

"Because it's been bugging me. Ever since you first told me about it, I've been trying to figure it out. I've looked in the library, and I've gone through tons of books at the shop."

"You are totally unbelievable."

"The thing is, I didn't find anything new or particularly different. Just your typical vampires and werewolves and zombies . . . all the usual monsters and demons. Oh, and all of their derivatives, of course." Dakota paused, looking irritated. She carefully fingered the stitches on her forehead. "So then I started wondering, suppose this is something no one's ever heard of before? A *new breed* of something that nobody knows about? Except maybe it's not even *new*. Maybe it's incredibly ancient and it's been around forever—only it's just never been documented."

Goose bumps rose on Lucy's skin. She gave Dakota a tense smile.

"I think," Lucy said slowly, "I might have the documentation you need."

23

"A secret journal," Dakota said almost reverently. "And you're absolutely sure you can't read it now? Not *any* of it?"

"Believe me, I've tried. I've even gone over the same things I translated before. Nothing seems to work."

"Maybe it's something really simple— something so obvious, you're not seeing it. Just some little difference between then and now."

Lucy sat there looking dejected.

Her resolve to keep silent had finally crumbled, and for the last half hour, she'd been reviewing everything that had happened since the night of the ice storm, since the last time she and Dakota had talked. She'd tried to recall every event, every detail.

But she'd purposely left one out.

She wasn't going to mention the appointment she had tonight. Her appointment with Jared at the Wetherly mausoleum.

"Come in secret, and come alone . . ."

Just thinking about it brought her to the edge of panic. Once again she wished she could tell the whole truth.

But if Jared finds out . . .

She couldn't bear to consider the consequences—that another person she cared about might become Jared's next victim. *And as for Angela . . .*

God only knew what he'd already done to Angela. And though a part of Lucy couldn't help fearing the worst, she refused to give up hope—hope that Angela might still come home.

So she'd told Dakota as much as she dared. And the whole time she'd felt like some bad actor in a bad play, trying to pretend she didn't have to confront Jared tonight. Trying to pretend that she and Dakota might somehow be able to end all this madness.

She felt pretty sure she'd been convincing, that Dakota hadn't seen through her facade. In fact, her friend had listened attentively, never interrupting and totally nonplussed by each one of Lucy's fantastic accounts.

Until Lucy mentioned the journal.

"And to think it was there all that time." Dakota seemed particularly amazed by this fact. "Do you know how many times I've been in that room? How many times I've dusted that old mantel? And sat right where you did, in that very same fireplace?"

Lucy's shrug was apologetic.

"All those times I was so close to it . . . and I never even suspected." Dakota sighed. "Not once."

"It was wedged back behind some bricks. *Nobody* would have suspected it."

"You're missing my point." Dakota's tone was faintly chiding.

"Which is?"

"*You're* the one it revealed itself to."

"Revealed itself? I fell and broke the mantel, and the book fell out."

"But anyone could have fallen. Anyone could have knocked those bricks loose. There's no telling how long that book's been there in that very spot, waiting for someone to discover it.

But *you* discovered it. It was waiting for *you*."

Uncomfortable with the subject matter now, Lucy got up and walked to the window. The truth was, she *had* felt as if the book were waiting for her. No matter how much she tried to deny it, she *had* felt a connection when she'd first translated the text—and she *hadn't* wanted anyone else to share it. Besides that initial thrill of discovery, there'd been something so much more intense—as if somehow those desperately scrawled words had *spoken* to her. Spoken to her and touched her in a deep and long-forgotten place. A place where words weren't even needed.

Lucy roused herself from her thoughts and focused on the dreary morning landscape beyond the glass. Why did she feel so sad all of a sudden, and regretful, and disappointed in herself?

I wish I hadn't told Dakota about the journal.

Startled by her own admission, Lucy instantly felt ashamed. Of *course* she should have told Dakota—it was absolutely the right thing to do. *So why do I wish I'd kept quiet? That I'd kept the journal my very own, very special secret?*

"I shouldn't have taken the book," she said quickly, guiltily, turning back to her friend.

Dakota was gazing at her with perfect calm. "Undead? Did the journal really say *undead?*"

"I should just tell your dad about the book and give it back."

"Did it really say, *My son . . . the most powerful of the undead?*"

"Oh, for heaven's sake, Dakota. Do you think I'd make something like this up?"

"Well." Dakota sounded resigned. "At least we know what we're dealing with."

"We do?"

"And no, you're *not* telling my dad about the journal, and neither am I. Besides, it wasn't meant for him. He's had the building for years and years, and that mantel never broke."

Dakota shut her eyes for a second, then opened them again, her expression curious.

"Maybe that book is your weapon, Lucy. Maybe all the things you're supposed to know, and all the answers you're supposed to find, are right there in that journal."

"Wonderful. Right in front of my nose, and I can't read a single word."

"Listen, you're the one Jared wants. In fact, he wants you so much, you've become his obsession. And obsession makes a person weak."

In spite of the warm room, Lucy shivered. Dakota's expression grew pensive as she continued to think out loud.

"And not having his obsession fulfilled makes him powerless."

"How can you say that?" Lucy argued. "The more I resist him, the angrier he gets. And the angrier he gets, the more damage he does, the more people he hurts."

"And the more careless he acts. And the more mistakes he makes. That's human nature."

"I thought we already established that he's *not* human. Or . . . only *part* human. Or . . ."

"What have I told you before? Just because you can't see something doesn't mean it's not real. We're surrounded all the time by things that aren't human. Some of them are good . . . and some of them are bad."

"Then could I trade mine in?" Lucy made a wry attempt at joking. "For one of the good ones?"

"Remember, *you're* your own power, Lucy. You're the only thing Jared wants, and because of that, *you're* the only way to destroy him."

"And just how am I supposed to do that?"

Sighing heavily, Dakota shook her head. "I could think much better about all this if I had my scarf on. I'm suffering severe separation anxiety without it."

"Oh my God—your scarf!"

"Actually, I'm considering offering a reward."

"Dakota, I'm so sorry!" Lucy blurted out.

"Thank you. It *was* very dear to my heart. I have some really good pictures of me wearing it. I thought I could make up some posters—"

"No! No, I mean, I can't believe I forgot to tell you this part! After Texas dropped it off for me, I lost it. I didn't mean to, but I just—I had it in my hands, but I didn't have a vision or anything, and with your message and all, I was scared and upset."

"*What* are you talking about?" Dakota's eyes had gone huge and bewildered.

"Your scarf," Lucy insisted. "It was such a good clue, too—I don't know how you managed to do it. I *knew* you wanted me to touch it, and maybe I'd be able to see who hurt you."

"Lucy, I don't even know where my scarf is. I

lost it when that thing—Jared—attacked me."

To Lucy's dismay, Dakota began pointing out some dark, swollen bruises around her face and neck. "See all these? He had my scarf wound so tight, I thought he'd choke my whole head off."

Speechless, Lucy turned away. She could still see that long, ridiculous rainbow scarf—its sparkles soaked in blood—and the blood stained note enclosed with it: MY GIFT TO YOU. Very slowly, she recounted the incident to Dakota, then faced the girl once again.

"It was a phone number," Dakota explained quietly. "My dad said that from now on he wants me to have a cell phone with me wherever I go. I asked Texas to give you my number."

The number. Of course. That scrap of paper I didn't think was important.

"Dakota, I didn't know. It was scribbled on this old, torn piece of paper . . . I thought it was trash."

"Never send a brother to do a moron's job. However, this *does* mean I was right."

"About what?"

"That Jared could have killed me but didn't. That he wanted you to know. And my scarf was just another way to send you his message."

"But think about it. That doesn't make sense."

"Damnit. I love that scarf. I'll probably never get it back now."

"If he knows I might be able to recognize him, just by handling your scarf—"

"I mean, even if I ever *do* get it back, it'll never be the same, will it? It'll have all his spitty man-beast-werewolf germs all over it."

"Dakota, listen to me!"

Dakota went silent. She looked at Lucy in total frustration.

"He wouldn't show me his face in the lab," Lucy reminded her. "So why would he risk me touching the very scarf that might identify him?"

"But he also told you he's had *many* faces. The Jared you've seen might not look at all like the *real* Jared. You know how shape-shifters are."

"Umm . . . enlighten me."

"Well, they're like werewolves. And vampires. They can change from human to wolf, or human to bat, or human to mist . . . basically, to just about anything they want." Dakota paused a moment, her brow furrowing in deep thought. "Maybe he doesn't *know* about your power.

Maybe he doesn't *know* you might be able to read the scarf. So he sent it to taunt you, and he felt safe about it."

"Then why take it back, if he feels so safe? And how could he know I'd go out to the parking lot when I did? And how could he possibly plan that I'd drop your scarf and make it convenient for him to take it back?"

Dakota regarded her calmly. "He . . . couldn't. It was more like an accident he took advantage of."

"Exactly."

"Lucy, are you saying what I *think* you're saying? That there are—"

"Two different people." Lucy gave a solemn nod. "One who sent your scarf . . . and one who stole it."

"So, you think whoever sent you my scarf was actually trying to *help* you?"

"Yes. What if they *wanted* Jared identified, but then Jared found out? And *that's* why he had to get the scarf back?"

"My God, Lucy . . ." Dakota sounded stunned. "That means there's someone else out there. Someone else who knows what's going on."

24

"You're your own power, Lucy."

All the way home, Lucy heard Dakota's words echoing over and over in her head. Dakota had sounded so sure of her . . . had seemed to have such faith in her.

But Lucy had felt powerful before, only to be knocked down. There'd been times she'd actually felt strong and certain and capable, only to be blindsided, overwhelmed, and crushed. And now she doubted herself. Doubted her abilities, her strength.

Not to mention my sanity.

As she approached Gran's house, a bizarre thought suddenly came to her. *Maybe I was the one who died that night of the accident. Maybe I died, and Byron lived, and all these crazy things going on are just part of my journey of being dead.*

What was it Nicholas had told her yesterday?

"They say when someone dies suddenly—or tragically—their spirit stays behind."

Maybe that's what's happening to me. Maybe I don't really know I'm dead, that's why I'm still hanging around.

Just part of the journey of being dead. And maybe even being in hell.

Wonder what Matt would say about that *theory?*

It occurred to her then that she still hadn't heard from Matt, that he hadn't returned her phone call from the night before. *Not that I'm his only problem*, she reminded herself guiltily. He probably had lots of obligations today, even though school wasn't one of them. Maybe Father Paul had forgotten to tell him she'd called. Or maybe whatever situation had called him away last night still demanded him this morning. At any rate, his Jeep wasn't parked out front.

But no other cars were either, Lucy noticed. Except for the rented Land Rover.

That's weird. She'd specifically heard Nicholas call the doctor right before she'd left to see Dakota. Thelma should be here now, at the very least. And where was that private-duty nurse who was supposed to come today?

Lucy was shivering as she let herself inside. Afraid of what condition she'd find Gran in. Afraid of her own thoughts. Afraid of what she had to face at midnight.

Maybe there's still time.

Maybe there's still time to figure something out.

She closed the door softly behind her, ears straining through the silence. It was a heavy, expectant silence that permeated the whole house, and Lucy didn't like the way it felt. As she tiptoed down the hall, she could see through the partly open door of Gran's room, just a narrow tableau of Gran nestled among her lacy pillows, and of Nicholas sitting in a chair beside the bed, his head lowered in his hands.

Again Lucy's heart ached for him.

For him and for herself.

And for Byron.

More than anything right now, she wanted to go into that room and hold tight to Gran. Beg Gran to get well, to hang on, to stay here with all the people who loved and needed her so much.

Yet despite her intense longing, something

held her back. This was a time for Nicholas and his grandmother—a private, special time—and one she shouldn't be a part of. Nicholas seemed too preoccupied at the moment even to notice her presence, so Lucy made a quick escape to her room and locked herself in.

After shedding her jacket, the first thing she did was pull the journal from its hiding place in the closet. Then she sat cross-legged on the bed and carefully began leafing through the pages.

If only she could read them again! If only she could dig deep into their secrets! For Lucy felt—just as Dakota had—that there were answers hidden within these emotionally penned words, information that would come to serve her well.

She racked her brain, trying to recall what she'd discovered in them before. The phrases she'd been able to translate—the feelings she'd had, uncovering someone else's thoughts in some long-ago time . . .

Male, she recalled clearly, convinced. A strong, masculine hand had written these pages—*a strong and gentle and merciless hand. The sense of an enchanted fairy tale. Strong, beautiful letters . . .*

sensitivity . . . but also fear . . . resignation . . .

Lucy concentrated harder. Something else had seemed so important to her at the time . . .

Yes! Time is running out . . . and someone must know the truth . . .

She could almost see them now—those strange foreign words translating to English in her mind as she'd found herself in the midst of a dark and disturbing theme . . .

. . . during daylight . . .

. . . handsome young man . . .

. . . transform . . .

. . . wolf or large black dog . . .

And there'd been that drawing, of course. Even as she recalled her shock at seeing it, she flipped to the exact page so she could inspect it again.

The sketch of an angel with no face, an angel cradling a rotten skull beneath its great, soft wings . . .

Just like the angels guarding each corner of Byron's mausoleum.

The mausoleum where she would go tonight.

Lucy closed her eyes and drew a deep breath.

The most dramatic words of the journal had been the last ones she'd been able to decipher.

MY SON . . .

MOST POWERFUL OF THE UNDEAD.

And since then, her ability to translate the journal had mysteriously vanished. With no warning, and with no explanation.

Yet still a feeling of reverence remained.

A definite connection.

An overpowering sense of destiny.

Frustrated, Lucy toyed with the chain around her neck. She pulled the medallion from inside her shirt and rubbed it absentmindedly against her chin, trying even harder to concentrate. *What am I doing wrong? Why can't I read this thing?*

"Maybe it's something really simple," Dakota had said, *"something so obvious, you're not seeing it . . . some little difference between then and now . . ."*

She had to figure it out. If there really were answers here that could save her, she was quickly running out of time. *Maybe if I close my eyes. Turn off the lights. Sit in some other position. Go back to the bookstore. Or maybe there has to be an ice storm outside, jut like the night I found this book.*

But then she felt it.

Suddenly—surprisingly—it was happening again, her hand stiffening as though she'd been shocked, her fingers skimming over one page of the journal, her mind transcribing an unknown language into words and phrases of chilling implications.

"Oh God . . ."

Trembling violently, she shifted her attention from her rapidly moving fingertips to the translations spinning faster and faster through her head.

The mark he inflicts . . .vanishes within twenty-four hours . . .

. . . disguises himself however best serves his needs . . .

Lucy's eyes widened; her heart began to race. Page after page . . . darker and darker revelations . . . as her fascination quickly gave way to horror.

. . . unscathed by mortal wounds . . .

. . . only killed by One of his own kind . . .

. . . ageless battle . . .

. . . dagger of our ancestors . . .

. . . royal bloodline . . .

. . . soul of his chosen bride . . .

. . . by eleven and quarter last . . .

. . . every one hundred years on the anniversary of Transformation . . .

"Jared," she whispered.

The room began to tilt—the book slid from her lap. As Lucy collapsed on the bed, the walls seemed to cave in, as a succession of vivid memories assailed her from every side.

"I am familiar to you . . . you've seen many of my faces . . . I want all of you . . . I've lured you . . . lied and pretended . . . stroked your hair, tasted your skin, kissed you where no one's ever kissed you before . . ."

"No . . ."

"Do you deny the connection we have . . . the ache so deep inside you, no one can fill it but me . . ."

"No! It's not true!"

"I am your death . . . your life—you are my destiny . . ."

Lucy grabbed her head in her hands, trying to obliterate him from her mind—*the sound of his voice, sight of his face, touch of his hands, warmth of his lips, gaping hole in his side, burned tattoo, screaming tortures—unscathed—unscathed by mortal wounds—*

"That part of me flowing through your veins . . . you've become something else . . . only your own kind can accept and understand . . ."

"No! It's not happening! *I'm not changing!*"

"Not just your body that aches for me, Lucy . . ."

"Oh God, please no!"

"It's your soul."

With a desperate cry, Lucy lunged off the bed and grabbed her cell phone. *Dakota!* She had to call Dakota! But Dakota was at the hospital, and she'd forgotten to get the number while she was there, and the telephone book was on the desk in the living room.

But she forgot about the living room as soon as she opened her door, as soon as she saw Nicholas standing there, with Matt standing just behind him.

She knew from their faces.

Before she even worked up the courage to ask, she could tell from Matt's sympathetic expression, and the sad, shocked look in Nicholas's eyes.

But still she shook her head.

Still she shook her head and stumbled backward into the wall, even as Matt reached out slowly for her arms.

"Lucy—"

"No. I don't believe you."

"I'm so sorry, Lucy. Gran's dead."

25

"She went peacefully, Lucy. Sometime in her sleep. She didn't suffer."

Matt was right beside her, yet his voice came from a long way off.

"We have to be thankful for that," he added gently.

But Lucy could only stare, her eyes going from Matt to Nicholas and back again.

"I just saw her," she insisted. "I just saw Gran, and she was fine."

"She wasn't fine. We all knew that—her doctor knew that. Even he wasn't surprised when I called him earlier. There was nothing anyone could do except make her comfortable. Gran's held on for so long—she was tired, Lucy. Her poor body just gave out."

"But . . ." Lucy's voice faded helplessly as

Matt reached out and patted her shoulder.

"I think maybe she was waiting to see Nicholas. You know how Gran was. Maybe some part of her *knew*—maybe some part of her was just hanging on for his homecoming."

Nicholas. Lucy had completely forgotten about Nicholas. Traveling all this way. Clinging to all those hopes. And now this. No family . . . no memories . . .

Nothing.

"I'm so sorry," she whispered to him now. He looked stricken and confused, his face tight with grief. For one fleeting instant, Lucy could almost glimpse the child he once had been, the defensive, dark-eyed child who had never been loved . . .

"I'm sorry," she said again, though Nicholas didn't answer. Her mind couldn't seem to process what was happening . . . this unexpected finality . . . this whole concept of death.

Again. Death again . . . and again . . .

"I just saw her." Why did she keep saying that to Matt? Why couldn't she keep quiet? "I just saw her, and you weren't here."

Now it was Matt who glanced toward Nicholas. "I . . . was here."

"No. No, you weren't. I just . . ." Lucy realized now that Matt was dressed entirely in black, except for the white of his collar. His priest's clothes, his official and somber clothes, his presiding-at-death clothes. She turned toward Gran's bedroom, but the door was shut.

"Lucy," Matt said patiently, "I was here. I gave her last rites. I was holding her hand."

But of course that made perfect sense, Lucy told herself. Gran's door hadn't been all the way open. What she'd witnessed from the hall had been Nicholas's grief—Matt must have been standing on the other side of Gran's bed where Lucy couldn't see.

"Where's your car?" she asked now.

Matt looked slightly taken aback. He raised an eyebrow and nodded politely in the general direction of the living room.

"Why don't we all sit down," he suggested.

"I . . ." For the first time Nicholas seemed to rouse from his stupor. A muscle clenched in his jaw, as though emotions he wasn't used to dealing with were struggling to come out. "I don't even know what to do," he told Matt. "Who to notify."

Matt's smile was so kind that Lucy had to look away. "Let me handle the details. Don't worry about any of that now."

"I don't know why this is so hard. This shouldn't be so hard."

"Nicholas . . . she was your grandmother."

"Damnit, I didn't even know her!"

Before Matt could respond, Nicholas angrily pushed past him. A second later the front door opened, then slammed with a vengeance.

Lucy stood there, eyes lowered to the floor. She felt embarrassed about questioning Matt, guilty for suspecting Nicholas; she felt overwhelmed with grief.

"Should you go after him?" she finally whispered.

"Not now. I think he needs some time."

"I don't understand. Gran was fine just a couple days ago. And I was looking forward to being here with her. I never thought . . ."

"Come on, Lucy. Please sit down."

"Could I . . . could I just see her first?"

Matt's frown was troubled. "In a minute, I

promise. But right now, you're shaking like a leaf." Touching her lightly on the back, he steered her to the kitchen. "Did you know that God created hot chocolate especially for times like these?"

Lucy sat at the kitchen table, feeling as if nothing in the whole world mattered right this minute except for Gran. Phoning Dakota . . . the frightening messages in the journal . . . even her approaching rendezvous with Jared—for the moment, all of that was forgotten.

"And in answer to your first question," Matt picked up as though they'd never been interrupted, "I happened to be with Mrs. Dempsey when I got the page about Gran. Leaving the Jeep for an oil change. So Mrs. Dempsey—not wanting to interfere—immediately brought me over and dropped me off."

Lucy felt even more ashamed. "Sorry."

"No offense taken," he said quietly.

"I just . . . wish I'd known, that's all. I wish I could have been with her."

Matt, spooning cocoa mix into two oversized mugs, glanced back at her over his shoulder. "Lucy, I didn't know you were here. I swear. Why didn't you say something when you came in?"

Well . . . that's fair. "I could see Nicholas in Gran's room, and Gran looked like she was resting. And . . . it seemed, you know . . . kind of private between them. I didn't want to interrupt."

"If my services hadn't been requested, I wouldn't have wanted to be there either. Because of that private moment you're talking about. I know you're disappointed, but the truth is, you gave both of them a very special gift."

Lucy didn't feel at all generous. She stared down at the tablecloth and began tracing patterns on it with her finger.

"Matt, do you ever wish you'd been something else?"

"Well, for a while I did want to be God when I grew up. Till my mom told me there wasn't likely to be an opening anytime in the future."

"I'm serious."

"So am I. Everyone—especially Sister Benedict, who taught me catechism—was extremely relieved when I outgrew that particular phase of my life."

"What do you do when you get tired of people's problems?"

"I don't usually get tired of people's problems, because I don't usually hang on to people's problems. I prefer turning them over to a higher power."

"So you never . . . you know . . . worry?"

"I worry about you."

Lucy's head came up. Water was running from the faucet, but Matt had paused, one hand still outstretched, holding the kettle. After a long moment he looked at her, and his voice softened even more.

"I worry that you're vulnerable. And lost. And that you hurt so much."

Surprised and touched by these unexpected words, Lucy's eyes misted with tears. "Then why don't you just turn me over to that higher power of yours?"

"I have," Matt whispered.

Abruptly, he busied himself at the kitchen counter again, while Lucy crossed her arms on the tabletop and sadly rested one cheek against them.

Oh, Gran. I can't believe it. I can't believe you're

gone so soon. I never even got to tell you good-bye. I never got to tell you so many things . . .

"You know," Matt said gently, placing a steaming mug of cocoa down in front of her, "there's no need for you to move back to Irene's, if that's what you're afraid of. Even if Nicholas decided to leave, I'm sure I could talk Mrs. Dempsey into staying with you for a while."

"Just what I need—a babysitter." Lucy might have felt indignant if she wasn't so unhappy. "No, I can't stay. It's not the same with Gran gone and Nicholas here. I wouldn't be comfortable with that."

"Lucy—"

"Dakota told me before that I could stay with her family. Maybe the offer's still open."

"I'm sure it is." Pondering this a second, Matt made a mild attempt at humor. "God help them, poor unsuspecting people that they are."

But Lucy couldn't even smile. "Who's going to come for Gran?"

"I told you I'd take care of it. I just think I should wait till Nicholas gets back. In case he wants to . . ."

"Go with her? Do you think he'd even care about that?"

"I think right now he's still in shock. It could be that he has some special requests . . . or needs . . . about Gran that he hasn't even thought of yet. I don't wanna rush anything. Once some things are . . . done," Matt explained delicately, "they can't always be *undone*."

Lucy closed her eyes. She couldn't think about Gran being dead or what might happen to Gran afterward. It made her think of Katherine. It made her want to cry and never stop.

"It's okay," Matt comforted, and Lucy opened her eyes. She felt his hand on the back of her head, a light, hesitant touch, stroking her hair. "It's okay to cry."

Her body shook with sobs, though she made no sound. *Gran! Gran, what went wrong? I promised I wouldn't let anything happen to you, and I wasn't even here when you died!*

She'd let Gran down. She'd let Byron down. Because of her, Angela was gone, and Dakota had been attacked, and Byron was dead, and Jared was still out there—*because of me. All because of me!*

"Here," Matt whispered. "I'm here . . ."

And dreamlike, Lucy was out of her chair, and they were standing there together, face-to-face. She felt Matt's arms go around her, coaxing her close, his shirt damp beneath her cheeks, his chin firm against her forehead, the strong, calm beating of his heart.

"It's not your fault, Lucy. Please stop thinking that any of this is your fault."

And yet he knew the depths of her conscience, just as he'd known so many times before. Because that was what priests were so good at, she reminded herself—reading consciences, soothing hurts, dissolving guilts and absolving sins. Priests were safe and mortally divine; they understood your heart and still forgave you for what was hidden inside.

"Everything's wrong," she wept. "Nothing will ever be right again."

"Shh . . . that's not true."

"Everyone I care about gets hurt."

"You care about me, don't you? And look, I'm not hurt."

"You don't count."

"No? Now I *am* hurt."

229

Despite the circumstances, she finally managed a laugh. She heard Matt laugh, too—felt it vibrate deep in his chest. Slowly, he drew back from her and smiled into her eyes. And Lucy, returning his gaze, brushed her hand across his brow and down along his cheek.

Matt's smile faded.

She touched his lips gently with her fingers . . .

Felt the faintest whisper of a kiss upon her fingertips . . .

Broken heart . . . broken soul . . . broken life . . .

"You were in love once," she murmured. "But she died . . . no . . . was killed. And it nearly destroyed you."

He crushed her hard against him, even as her own arms slipped around his waist. She could feel him trembling . . . trembling so violently . . . so helplessly . . . holding her as though their bodies were one, holding her as though he'd never let her go.

He mumbled something against her hair, but she couldn't make out what it was.

His voice made a choking sound, as though he might be crying.

From a distant place, she heard a door slam.

There were footsteps in the house, and they were coming toward the kitchen.

Lucy immediately broke free, not even stopping to look at Matt, just turning and bolting down the hall.

She ran straight to Gran's bedroom and let herself in, then she locked the door behind her.

26

Lucy was breathless and shaking.

Shaking as hard as Matt had been shaking . . . shaking even more.

She could still feel his lips beneath her fingers, the ghost of a kiss against her skin.

His chest . . . his heartbeat . . . his sudden desperation . . .

She remembered what had happened in his office that day at school, how she'd managed to convince herself it was nothing more than an accident. But this . . .

As though every place he'd touched her had left a mark and a memory—warm . . . poignant . . . sad—and stirred unexpected emotions deep within her—pleasure . . . excitement . . .

Oh God . . . what have we done?

Guilt crashed down on her. *What happened,*

Matt? What happened in there? Why hadn't she pulled away or tried to stop it?

Why hadn't *he*?

How could she ever face him again? Lucy wondered now. Not to mention the fact that whenever Matt looked at her from now on, she'd most certainly be a reminder of something he'd have to atone for, some sinful blot on his soul.

Yet even as her thoughts flew in every direction, Lucy's eyes were fixed forward, focused on the bed that held Gran's body.

Someone had drawn the covers completely up over Gran's face. As Lucy moved closer, she couldn't stop staring at that shrouded figure lying so silent and so still. She paused beside the bed and, without warning, felt an icy stab of fear beneath her grief.

She reached for the covers, then stopped.

Maybe she shouldn't. Maybe it was better to remember Gran the way she'd most loved seeing her, nestled among the white lace pillows, wearing that sweet and kindly smile.

Swallowing hard, Lucy touched the top edge of the blanket. What if Gran were still alive? What if she turned down the covers and it was all just a horrible mistake, and Gran was reaching out for her hand?

Lucy almost lost her nerve.

She braced herself, took a deep breath, and began to uncover the body.

Oh God!

Stifling a scream, she jumped back from the bed. Gran was *staring* at her—*watching* her—holding Lucy in a wide, dark, eternal stare.

Lucy's heart lodged in her throat. She tried to choke it down, tried to make herself shut Gran's eyes, but all she could do was stand there in complete horror.

She wasn't sure how long she was frozen there, how long before she was finally able to move again. But at last she forced herself to touch Gran's cheek.

I'm so sorry, Gran . . . so sorry . . .

Lucy wished there was something she could do. No matter if it seemed small and insignificant now, or even if the gesture came too late—just some final thing she could do for Gran. She noticed the untidy condition of Gran's nightgown and bed jacket. Not a priority to either Matt or Nicholas in the tragedy of the moment—but at least Lucy could give Gran some dignity here at the very last.

Very carefully she began rearranging Gran's clothes—straightening, tucking, positioning.

Until suddenly she saw something she hadn't seen before.

It was wedged between the bottom sheet and Gran's body, practically hidden beneath Gran's left hip. And it would have been impossible to notice without turning the covers down as far as Lucy just had.

It was a piece of chalk.

A very short, very worn piece of chalk.

The kind that Gran always wrote with . . . on the slate that had disappeared.

Lucy's heart quickened. Of course there were a lot of perfectly rational reasons that the chalk could have ended up here. Something just as simple as Gran dropping it.

Yet something told Lucy this *wasn't* the reason.

And as she went to the other side of the bed to retrieve the chalk, she saw something else that stopped her in her tracks.

In the process of shifting all the covers, she'd exposed the left side of Gran's bed—a section of the old-fashioned frame that supported the mattress. And scrawled there upon the wood was a jumble of wide, white marks, as though a childish hand had been fingerpainting.

Except that it wasn't paint, Lucy realized.

It was chalk.

You did this, didn't you, Gran?

Frowning, she squatted down to examine the strange pattern. The marks didn't appear to be words—in fact, they didn't make any sense to her at all.

Until she began tracing her fingertip over the scribbles, squinting at them from several different angles.

And you wrote these upside down.

And it struck Lucy in that instant how impossible the endeavor must have been—how painful, how frustrating, how utterly time-consuming—for Gran to contort her body in order to reach this particular spot. In order for Gran to lean over and determinedly slash the chalk again and again against the side of the bed . . .

Where nobody would see what you were trying to say.

But I can see it, Gran.

Lucy could see it now with perfect clarity.

Even before she stood up, and stared at each word, and read them upside down.

FREE BYRON.

27

Byron . . .

Lucy's mind went blank.

The discovery was a shock—but even more shocking was the total ambiguity of those two words.

Free Byron.

What could it possibly mean?

All she knew for sure was that Gran had written the message—and had gone to great pains to do so. Gran had written them where they wouldn't easily be seen. And Lucy had an overwhelming premonition that the words were intended as a warning.

But to whom?

One of Gran's caretakers? Matt? Nicholas? *Me?*

The more Lucy considered it, the more she

concluded that Gran's message *must* be meant for her. No one else here had the sort of connection to Byron that she had—and it wouldn't be the first time she'd felt Gran trying to communicate something to her.

Oh, Gran, if only you could tell me what this means!

It made no sense to Lucy, no sense at all.

But it will, and very soon. Be patient.

Lucy started, her eyes going nervously around the room. If she hadn't known better, she would have *sworn* just then that a wary whisper had come from Gran's cold, dead lips.

Not exactly sure why, she ran her hand over the messsage on the bed frame. She rubbed at it till all the letters had been wiped completely clean.

Our secret, Gran. Just yours and mine.

Her heart raced faster as she straightened the side of Gran's nightgown, the sheets, and the blankets. Then she went back to the opposite side of the bed and drew the last of the covers tenderly over Gran's shoulders. Even at the mercy of that wide-eyed stare, she simply couldn't bring herself to cover Gran's face again.

"Lucy?"

There was a low voice, a soft knock at the door. Lucy hesitated, then reluctantly asked who it was.

"It's Nicholas."

"What do you want?"

He seemed uncomfortable disturbing her. "Are you . . . can I come in?"

"Where's Matt?"

"Outside. They're here for my grandmother's body."

"I . . ." Lucy's mind raced feverishly. "Could you just give me one more minute alone?"

"They really need to get in there and take her."

"Please. Just one more minute, I promise. Please."

"Just . . . don't make this harder."

Was Nicholas crying? His voice sounded deeper—almost gruff—yet there was a certain amount of detachment in it, too. Lucy felt an immediate rush of protectiveness toward Gran. There was something so insensitive and impersonal about this cherished woman whom Byron had loved so much being hauled out by strangers and a grandson she'd never known.

But Gran would be with Byron now.

If Dakota and Matt were to be believed, there really *was* a spirit, there really *was* something beyond, and Lucy *wanted* so *desperately* to believe.

For the sake of her mother . . . for Gran . . .

"For Byron's sake . . ."

Jared's words haunted her now, just as they'd haunted her since she'd first found him. She shut them determinedly from her mind and focused once more on Gran.

"Thank you, Gran," Lucy whispered. "Thank you for letting me know you . . . even if it was just for a little while."

Swallowing tears, she took a step back from the bed . . .

And felt a bony hand clamp hard around her wrist.

Lucy's scream cut off in her throat. As she looked down in horror, she could see Gran's body lying stiff and straight beneath the covers . . . Gran's eyes dark and round staring up at the ceiling . . .

And Gran's fingers holding her—holding her so tight that Lucy couldn't get loose, couldn't get away, couldn't even move, as the images, one by one, began stabbing relentlessly through her brain.

Rain—pounding rain—cemetery—open grave—face of a dead girl—blood of a dead girl—hand of a dead girl reaching for Lucy—

"Katherine!" Lucy cried.

School—classroom at school—the back of Byron's head. I know it's Byron—green necklace on the floor—blackout, screams and murder and where am I?—bathroom stall, I'm sick in the bathroom stall, but there's a hand, a gentle hand on my shoulder, calming me, comforting me. "The first time's always the worst . . ."

"The first time," Lucy murmured. Her head was pounding, echoing, pain shooting out of her temples—white hot pain—pictures flashing on and on.

Same day at school—someone touching me in the hallway. It's you, Gran, isn't it—you!—in the hallway, in the bathroom—trying to give me strength even then . . .

"You knew, Gran . . . you knew right from the very beginning . . ."

Van going off a road—flames, fire, bloodred moon swallowed in smoke . . .

"Don't," Lucy begged. "Don't make me watch this!"

But she was fading now, her whole body like a thin white vapor, misting away in the air, insubstantial as dust . . .

Yet still here in this very same room.

Though something was drastically different . . .

She was standing as a ghost might stand, watching as a ghost might watch—undetected, unincluded, unseen—while Gran lay in bed, very much alive, one frail hand resting upon the bowed head of a beautiful young woman.

Katherine . . . it's Katherine . . .

But a sobbing Katherine, a heartbroken Katherine . . .

A terrified Katherine.

"He's going to kill me, Gran—I know it! And there's nothing I can do to stop him!"

Katherine's voice was muffled, choked with tears.

"How can this be happening, Gran? I don't even know how to explain it, how to make you understand! I don't even know how to describe him—there's no name for what he is!"

Gran's fingers moved ever so slightly. As though

trying to stroke Katherine's hair . . . as though trying to comfort her. But Katherine would not be comforted.

"I know that you and I've always believed in things no one else can see. But this is a living nightmare—this is hell, and this is real, and there's no other way I can get out of it!"

Katherine nestled closer to her grandmother, and her tears continued to flow.

"They can run as a pack, or they can run alone. They can change their shapes in daylight or darkness; it doesn't matter. Mostly when I've seen them at night, they seem like wolves, but not quite wolves—or strange, wild dogs with horrible faces. But they can just as easily be fog . . . or shadows . . . or . . ."

A noise sounded at the window. Katherine tensed and jumped to her feet, an expression of sheer panic on her face. She extinguished the light by Gran's bed. She stood in the dark, her breathing rapid and shallow, her whole body trembling with fear.

"Wind," she whispered at last. "Sometimes they can be nothing more than wind . . ."

For an eternity, she paused. She listened. She drew a ragged breath.

"They stalk; they're swift and merciless. They can't exactly read minds, but they can sense things other animals can't sense, from miles and miles away. They have the power to heal their own wounds, and they look just as they did when their own human lives were taken, when they became the things they are now. Transformation, they call it. The Moment of Transformation."

Her arms locked tightly over her chest. With a strangely hypnotic rhythm, she began to rock . . . back and forth . . . back and forth.

"They can leave invisible marks on their prey, or they can rip them to pieces. They drink human blood and eat human flesh—and once they've taken enough of their victim, they can actually look like that victim, too, whenever they choose. And it doesn't have to happen all at once. Sometimes they'd rather play with their victims—for days . . . or weeks . . . or months—till they finally grow tired of the Game. Or until he tells them to stop."

Katherine's words were spilling out, but never above that strangled whisper. Her expression was haunted. Her eyes were hollow.

"He's their ruler, Gran. Their pack leader. Their alpha and their king—and he's been their ruler for hundreds of years. Descended from the original bloodline. And the only one allowed to take souls."

She was crying again. Those deep, desperate sobs of hopelessness and despair.

"Killing gives them power. Each time they take a human life, they get stronger. But to take a soul . . ."

A dark, mocking smile twisted Katherine's lips. A harsh laugh sounded in her throat.

"A soul is worth a century, Gran. Without it, he grows weaker. He can take anyone he pleases, force anyone he pleases, but every hundred years—on the anniversary of his Transformation—he must *have a bride. One special bride, favored above all others. And do you want to know the irony? She has to commit her life to him* willingly. *She has to surrender her soul to him—*freely!—*even though she'll never be free again."*

As a low murmur escaped Gran's lips, Katherine knelt quickly beside the bed, clutching Gran's hands in her own.

"Listen to me, Gran, I don't have much time. I'm the one he's chosen, and he'll find me wherever I go. And now that I've escaped, he'll track me down, and he'll kill me. But the truth is, I want *him to. Can you understand that? And can you forgive me? I'd* rather *be dead than to be with him; I'd rather die than be* one *of them. But I took something of his—something*

very old and very sacred. It explains everything about him—about them—*and I hid it in a secret place."*

Leaning forward, Katherine gently kissed her grandmother's forehead.

"I won't tell you where. Because he'll know if I do—he'll know if you're trying to protect me. He'll see it in the slightest expression on your face or in your eyes . . . he'll be able to smell *that you're lying. No . . . you'll be much safer this way, not knowing. But I* will *tell Byron when I see him. Only Byron. And he'll know the place I mean."*

With a sweet smile, Katherine gently stroked her grandmother's silvery hair.

"I love you so much, Gran. I know Byron's already on his way to the cemetery to meet me, but I had to come and see you one last time. I had to tell you all this myself, even though you probably already knew most of it. We always had that special connection, you and I . . ."

Gasping, Lucy came back to herself.

Her head felt light, and her body felt weightless. Except for Gran, she was all alone in the room.

No one was holding her hand.

She could see now that both of Gran's arms were beneath the covers, folded exactly as Lucy had left them. Nothing was disturbed; nothing seemed the least bit out of place.

Katherine had hidden the journal!

Deeply shaken, Lucy sagged back against the wall. She was ice cold, but her nerves were tingling as though an electric surge had gone through them. The room was thick with silence. She was almost suffocating in it.

It was Katherine! Katherine *was the one who had hidden the journal in the bookstore! And she died before she could ever tell Byron where it was!*

Lucy tried hard to collect her thoughts. That *had* to be it, she reasoned. After what she'd just witnessed—after what she'd just heard—what other explanation *could* there be?

A knock sounded at the bedroom door, startling her.

"Lucy?" Matt called softly. "We need to take Gran now. Please let me in."

She wanted to stop them but knew she couldn't. She could feel every emotion welling up inside her, spilling over in tears. "You . . . you'll be careful with her?"

"Of course," Matt promised. "There's no reason for you to have to see this, Lucy. Just leave everything the way it is. I'll get Mrs. Dempsey to help me, and we'll take care of it."

Lucy didn't answer. Instead she leaned over and, as Katherine had done, kissed Gran tenderly on the forehead.

"Thank you, Gran," she whispered. "Thank you."

Then, with the greatest reverence, she slid one hand beneath the covers and lightly touched Gran's fingers.

But there was nothing now.

Only silence.

28

"Dakota," Lucy said urgently, "did Katherine ever go to your dad's bookstore?"

The voice on the other end of the line sounded sleepy and slow. "Is that you, Lucy? What's going on?"

"Did you ever see her there? Please try to remember!"

"Well, yeah. I mean, I never actually saw her there, but I know she went. Pretty often, too."

"You're positive?"

"She always went after the store closed for the night. My dad knew how shy she was and how people treated her, so he told her where he kept an extra key. He let her borrow books, too, instead of paying for them. He knew she and Byron didn't have much money, with Gran's medical expenses and all."

"Dakota, for God's sake, why didn't you tell me this before?"

"Should I have?" The grogginess gave way to confusion. "Is it important?"

I think Katherine's the one who hid that journal in the fireplace. And I think it all ties in with why she was killed."

"Are you sure? How do you know that?"

"Dakota, Gran died today. Right after I got back from seeing you."

For a moment there was absolute quiet. Lucy could picture her friend's face—the sorrow and sympathy—and even over the phone, she could feel Dakota's pain.

"I'm so sorry, Lucy. I know it's a blessing, with her being sick for so long. But I also know how much she meant to you."

A blessing . . . Why did people always call it a blessing when someone you loved was taken away, and you were left behind?

Lucy firmly shut the irony from her mind. "She gave me a vision. I really *believe* Gran gave me a vision."

"But . . ."

"I'm not sure how. Maybe it was just the last

of her strength, the last of her powers, and she wanted me to share them. Or maybe . . ." Lucy closed her eyes, remembering the hand that had reached out and grabbed her—the hand that hadn't been there when she'd come back to full consciousness. "Maybe I just imagined it or . . . dreamed it. The important thing is, I *saw* it. And I saw Katherine alive, probably just minutes before she was killed. And no matter *how* I saw it, I know it's *real*."

"Gran must have known all along about your connection to Katherine. She must have known Katherine passed her powers on to you."

"Dakota, there's something else. After I saw you, I took out the journal again. And I *read* it."

"How? I mean, that's brilliant—but *how*? Did you figure out what made it happen this time?"

"Maybe you're my good-luck charm?"

"That's not it. I wasn't even with you the night you found it in the shop. Keep thinking, Lucy—you'll figure it out." Dakota groaned softly as though shifting positions. "So what did the journal say?"

"That's the good part. Well . . . if you can call it good."

"What would *you* call it?"

"I guess," Lucy said quietly, "I'd call it true."

Another silence passed, this one even longer than before. Lucy's hand was sweating on the receiver, and she realized her knees had gone weak.

"Lucy, please tell me."

Finding her voice at last, Lucy tried to stay analytical. "Some of the things in the journal—and some of the things in my vision of Katherine—were exactly the same. And all those things Byron told me about how much Katherine suffered? I don't think he knew even the half of it."

"Oh God . . ."

"Does the phrase 'eleven and quarter last' mean anything to you?"

"I don't think so; I've never heard it before. Why?"

"Dakota, I think I know now why Jared's after me." Despite her attempts at calm, Lucy's voice began to shake. "I think I'm supposed to take Katherine's place."

"Place?" Dakota sounded more bewildered than ever. "Place at what?"

"I don't think I should talk about it over the phone."

"Then come over here! Come over here right now!"

"I can't. I've got to try to figure out more of this. If I can just translate the journal again—if I can just find something out before midnight—"

Horrified, Lucy broke off. She'd put her hand over her mouth, but it was already too late.

"Midnight?" Dakota echoed. "What about midnight?"

"Nothing."

"Don't say nothing. It's not nothing—it's *midnight*. What does that mean?"

"I told you, it doesn't mean anything. I'm stressed. I'm not thinking straight. I don't even know why I said it."

"What are you going to do? Lucy? I can tell by your voice, it sounds like something dangerous."

"I promise I'll call you later. When I find out about Gran's funeral."

"Don't you hang up on—"

But Lucy had already clicked off.

Forgive me, Dakota. You'll understand someday and thank me. I hope.

Sighing heavily, Lucy stuffed her cell phone back in her pocket. She hadn't been able to watch Gran's body being carried away, so she'd left the house immediately, taking the journal with her. She'd walked to a nearby convenience store and browsed disinterestedly through the magazine rack—a momentary respite from the bitter cold outside. And then, still too nervous to go home, she'd bought a large cup of stale coffee, which she hadn't been able to drink. The vision of Gran and Katherine kept playing over and over in her mind . . . and the hidden message on the bed frame: FREE BYRON. She'd paced and fidgeted, and she'd finally called Dakota. But now, feeling fairly certain it was safe to go home again, she headed back.

There must be more answers in the journal . . . there must *be something else I can use!*

The house had changed dramatically; Lucy felt it the very second she stepped through the door. The unnatural quiet, the eerie cold, the desolate emptiness, a hollow shell without a spirit. It made her uneasy, and it made her afraid. And though she told herself over and over again that everything was fine, that all these feelings were perfectly normal in the wake of death, she still made certain all the doors and windows were secure, and she locked the door of her room.

Once more she sat down on the bed. Opened the journal to the place where she'd left off. Rested her fingers delicately upon the page, upon the words. Closed her eyes and tried to concentrate.

Nothing at first.

Nothing for so long that she grew restless.

Tapping her fingers impatiently, she turned pages at random, trying to find a spot that would come alive to her. Only this time, instead of leafing forward, she went back . . . and little by little, she began to feel words and phrases taking form in her mind.

Words and phrases she recognized—words and phrases she'd read before.

. . . *only killed by One of his own kind* . . .

. . . *ageless battle* . . .

. . . *dagger of our ancestors* . . .

And then one word—different from all the rest—became suddenly clear to her.

Written in a shaky hand.

Spattered with blood, but softened and faded from the shedding of many tears.

BROTHERS.

Lucy's fingers froze. She stared down at the page before her and tried to calm her breathing. *Don't rush . . . don't analyze . . . just focus . . . focus . . .*

BROTHERS.

Brothers loved by the writer of this book . . . brothers adored and cherished . . . but disappointments, sorrows, hearts broken beyond repair . . .

Lucy ran her tongue slowly over her lips. She was sweating, but her skin was like ice. Her body braced for whatever might come, and she pressed her fingers even more firmly against the letters.

Brothers . . .

Emotions strong wild tragic fatal—

Dagger—dagger of our ancestors—blade plunging again again again—twisting—slashing—burning like fire—burning in fire!—ropes around wrists, sleek naked body writhing in blood—blistering, roasting black, melting from bones—"God help me! Have mercy!"*—sobs screams shrieks ignored by the* *rage, attacked by the rage, punished and tortured forever . . .*

Only One . . .

Can only be killed by One of his own kind . . .

Lucy couldn't bear it anymore. The agony—the anguish—was so crushing that her shaky fingers slid to the bottom of the page, where they instantly connected with another flow of sensations.

Sweet night—leaves stars moonlight patterns—shadows swift on silent feet—dark desires deep as open wounds—wind flowing like blood streaming like blood hot wild fountains and rivers of blood—screams from secret places, screams that no one hears, pleasure pain and begging screams of terror and surrender . . .

Burning . . .

Burning lungs burning skin burning eyes . . .

Burning like the moon, red just like the moon, burning eyes burning lips burning souls . . .

She couldn't let go of the page.

As though her fingers were stuck there, held by some connection she was powerless to break.

Her body jolted with the impact of each new image—each new emotion. Her heart pounded as if it would explode. Her blood was spurting through her veins. . . .

"Jared!" she cried.

The book slid from her lap.

It toppled over the side of the bed and landed facedown on the floor.

Jared.

Lucy stared at the crumbled bits of paper . . . the chips of brittle leather . . . the aura of dust settling softly around the journal.

Jared is in these pages. . . . Jared has handled these pages. . . .

For Lucy knew this vision well—had seen it and felt it before, in the cold shadows of the Wetherly mausoleum.

The very first time Jared had touched her.

29

One hour till midnight.

Lucy sat on her bed in the dark, watching the clock on the nightstand. The torturous creeping of the hands, counting off the seconds . . . the minutes . . .

Counting off my fate.

She'd had to take a break from the journal. She'd been so distraught after this last session that she'd hidden it back in the closet and collapsed onto her bed.

She'd lain there, weak and exhausted. Trying to find clues in the visions she'd had— trying at the same time to forget them. She understood now why Katherine had nearly gone mad. No human being could *possibly* endure vision after vision of such gruesome brutality. Visions like these changed people.

Visions like these destroyed people.

Katherine had met a savage end, but hopefully had at last found peace.

Will I die like that? In the cemetery, like Katherine? With my throat slit, like Katherine? And relieved that it's all finally over, like Katherine?

Lucy considered staying right where she was. Just simply not showing up at the mausoleum at midnight. Maybe nothing would happen, anyway. Maybe it was all just a bluff. Maybe Jared was just testing her to see if she was intimidated enough to obey him. What would happen if she had an excuse? *Sorry, my car was stolen. Sorry, I had to study. Sorry, I overslept.*

But then she thought of Dakota.

Dakota attacked on that country road, lying in the hospital, bruised and battered because of me.

And Angela. One slim, desperate chance that Angela might still be alive, pinning all her last hopes on me.

Lucy got up and dressed in warm clothes. It was useless to try to figure out what would happen tonight, so how could she even prepare herself? Even though she'd had visions and read parts of the journal, how could she possibly predict what Jared might do? What Jared might have planned for her?

Every hundred years . . . must *choose a bride . . . she has to come* willingly *. . . surrender her soul . . . though she'll never be free again . . .*

An icy shudder gnawed through to her bones, a fog of unreality.

Katherine didn't want to believe it either.

But it's real.

And it's happening.

And it's happening to me.

What was it Dakota had told her? Lucy tried to remember as she pulled on boots and an extra sweatshirt.

"The truth is, it's happening, *and it's happening* now, *and* that's *what we have to accept. So instead of wishing it would go away, we have to start right where we are and do something about it. We can't let ourselves be victims. Especially* not *his* victims."

"You're absolutely right, Dakota," Lucy murmured. "I just wish I knew what that something is that I'm supposed to be doing."

She'd have to walk, of course. She couldn't ask Matt or even Nicholas for a ride, and she couldn't very well call a cab. *"Come in secret, and come alone."* She'd had to look up directions to the cemetery, and it was a fairly long distance by foot. She'd need to leave now if she was going to get there on time. With any luck, she'd freeze to death on the way.

She pulled her door shut and stood there a moment, glancing sadly toward Gran's bedroom. She'd heard Nicholas and Matt come home earlier this evening, their voices low and serious as they talked at the kitchen table. Matt had knocked on her door once to ask if she was okay; she'd told him yes and that she just wanted to sleep. It had been after nine when Matt finally left and Nicholas climbed the stairs to his room. Since then there'd been no sounds from the second floor. Lucy suspected that, like herself, Nicholas was depressed and worn out.

She wondered what he'd do now. Most likely he'd have affairs to settle here first, but then he'd probably go back to where he'd come from. Go back and try to forget the family that had already been forgotten once.

Lucy wished she hadn't been so quick to judge him. She still remembered the look on his face right after Gran died. The grief and shock . . . that sense of disbelief. And the genuine distress he'd shown at the site of Byron's accident.

I know how you feel, Nicholas. How it feels to keep losing people you love. How it feels to keep getting hit with bad surprises. You learn to deal with them. Right or wrong, you learn to deal with them the very best you can.

Letting herself quietly out of the house, Lucy paused on the front walk to peer up at his window. No light shone from behind the curtains. No light showed at any window at all. Shivering, she turned and hurried on her way.

It seemed to take forever to get there. Snow gusted up and down the sidewalks, dimming the streetlights, bitterly cold. Lucy kept her head down and her feet moving, though the night threatened on every side, and heavy clouds blackened the moon.

Then suddenly she stopped.

And something stopped behind her.

She stood and she listened, knowing something listened back.

And when she finally began walking again, its soft, shuffling footsteps echoed her own.

Lucy broke into a run. She fled panic-stricken along the deserted street till she spotted some cars parked along the curb just ahead of her. Diving behind the closest one, she held her breath and waited.

The footsteps almost passed her by.

But then she heard them hesitate.

And then she heard nothing at all.

Blood pounded in her temples. Her heart threatened to explode.

"I know you're there," the voice said. "And I know what it means."

Lucy's whole body went limp. A sob burst from her throat.

"*Dakota!* What the *hell* are you doing?"

She could barely stagger to her feet. Gazing calmly back at her over the trunk of the car was the stitched and swollen face of her best friend.

"I know what it means," Dakota said solemnly. "*Eleven and quarter last*—I know what it means."

"Are you *insane?*" Lucy advanced on her furiously. "You scared the *life* out of me! What are you *doing* here!"

"Eleven is the month—*November*. And quarter last, means the *fourth quarter* of the moon."

Lucy's brain couldn't compute. She could only stand there in numb silence as Dakota leaned toward her and kept explaining.

"The last quarter moon in November, Lucy. The moon starts into its final quarter after midnight tonight."

Lucy's knees crumpled. She sat down hard upon the curb.

"No need to be so dramatic." Dakota sounded slightly annoyed. "You really didn't think I'd let you go alone, did you?"

30

"Dakota, you can't come."

"Why not?"

"How long have you been following me?"

"Since you left the house. You need to be more aware of your surroundings, Lucy. If I'd been a stalker, I could have grabbed you long before now."

"Go home!"

"I didn't come from home. I came from the hospital."

"Oh my God—what are you *thinking*! Look at you! And you have a sprained ankle. You can hardly walk!"

"Look, it's okay. I left a note on my bed."

"Saying what?"

"That I was bored, and I was going to take a walk around the hospital."

Groaning, Lucy buried her face in her hands.

"Look," Dakota sighed, easing down next to her, "they never come in to check on me till late. And I figure by the time they search the whole hospital—because they *definitely* won't want to tell my parents I've disappeared—I'll be back again. Like nothing happened. No problem."

"It is a problem. Look at you. And whose coat is that?"

Dakota surveyed the very oversized, very padded orange monstrosity billowing out around her. One lumpy sleeve covered one arm, the other sleeve flopped empty and loose over her sling, and the whole thing was buttoned over her hospital gown.

"I borrowed it," she said simply. "From the room across the hall."

"You look ridiculous."

"Yes. Like a runaway futon."

Lucy's laugh bordered on hysteria. Her eyes filled with tears.

"Dakota, you have to go back. It's dangerous for me if you're here. It's dangerous for *you* if you're here."

"I can't leave you," her friend answered softly. "I *won't* leave you."

"You don't understand how *serious* this is!"

"I understand that at one minute past midnight, all the strange and bizarre things that have been happening will all come together. And that they all center around you, just like they did around Katherine. And that, no matter what, I'm *not* letting him have you. I'm *not* letting you take Katherine's place."

"But . . . the only way Katherine got away from him was to die."

Neither girl said a word. As the wind blew colder around them, Lucy slipped one arm around Dakota's shoulders and pulled her close.

"Please. *Please*, go back to the hospital."

Without giving her friend a chance to respond, Lucy stood up. She'd already taken several steps when she heard Dakota following.

"He already knows I'm here," Dakota said.

Lucy spun to face her.

"You know it as well as I do," Dakota insisted. "As clever as he is, as instinctive as he is—he already knows I'm with you, and that I know what's going on."

Lucy shook her head, still trying not to cry. "He can't read minds," she whispered.

"But I'm sure he can smell friendship."

The two of them gazed at each other for a long time.

Then they took off again, side by side, toward the cemetery.

31

If ghosts could rise and zombies walk, Lucy thought to herself, *this would definitely be the perfect night and place for it.*

"It looks like a scene from a horror movie," Dakota whispered.

Pausing to gaze at the mausoleum, Lucy had to agree. In all the times she'd been here, she'd never seen the graveyard look so scary. It seemed older somehow, more sinister and forgotten. The headstones more tilted, the graves more sunken. And as snow and fog drifted among the statues and markers and crosses, it was as if restless, suffering spirits reached out to her for comfort.

"Wait here," Lucy said.

"But—"

"I'm sure you're right—he already knows

we're together. But at least let me go in alone."

It was the one shot she had at keeping Dakota safe, Lucy decided. She had no idea what would be waiting for her beyond those iron-gated doors—only that it was something inhuman, something she didn't know how to fight.

Something that could promise only fear and pain and death.

"You'll be close if I need you," she reminded Dakota again. "You can go for help."

But Dakota put a world of meaning into one squeeze of Lucy's hand. "*I'm* the help."

"I know. Love you."

"Love you, too. Good luck."

Without another word, Lucy began walking toward the mausoleum. Walking quickly before she could change her mind. Stumbling over the snowy, uneven ground, and thinking how sad it was that the last thing she might ever see in this world of life was this gloomy world of death.

The rusty gates were unlocked but unopened.

Lucy hesitated only a moment, then drew a deep breath and pushed them boldly aside. Raw, stale air swept over her; an icy breeze curled ominously around her legs. Squaring her shoulders, she lifted her chin in defiance and waited.

Waited in the awful, throbbing silence—a silence as loud as her heartbeat. Waited there in the darkness, beneath the cold, relentless scrutiny of a stare.

Oh yes, she could feel his eyes again—their wariness and cunning.

Just like last time, and the times before.

"I'm here." Extending both arms at her sides, Lucy turned in a slow, deliberate circle. Her forced and false bravado masked the terror she felt inside. "Aren't you going to show yourself?"

She could sense him moving. Slipping smoothly through the shadows as he watched her, hiding just out of reach, hiding much too close.

"Where's Angela?" Her voice rose, echoing hollowly back at her. "You said if I came—"

"I know what I said, Lucy."

The whisper came from nowhere . . . and everywhere.

It slithered up the damp walls of the tomb and through every nerve in Lucy's body.

"Then come out," she demanded. "And bring Angela with you."

A moment of silence passed. A moment that seemed an eternity, till the whisperer spoke again.

"I assure you, she's in a safe place."

"You said you'd let me see her."

"As far as I'm concerned, *anyone* may see her. She's free to go, whenever she wishes. But now . . . let's talk about Byron, shall we?"

"Byron . . ." She felt her heart falter, a sickening lurch of hope and despair. "What . . . what do you mean?"

"Do you want him back?"

It was said with a tone of immense satisfaction and superiority.

Lucy felt his eyes glide over her. "Jared, why are you doing this? Please . . . what do you want me to say?"

"I want you to answer the question." A pause, and the hint of a smile. "I said, do . . . you . . . want . . . him . . . back?"

But Lucy couldn't answer. She felt warm breath upon her cheek, and an icy ripple in the air, and the shadows seemed to lengthen along the wall where Byron was interred.

"These are not difficult choices, Lucy. Either yes, or no."

The whisper was cruel and taunting, yet Lucy began walking toward it.

"Should I refresh your memory?" he asked her. "I distinctly recall you mentioning that you'd give *anything* to have Byron back. Hmmm . . . or was it that you'd give anything just to *see* him again?"

As Lucy kept inching forward, a laugh sounded deep in his throat. A laugh that quickly turned impatient.

"Well, no matter. The result is the same, at any rate. So please make up your mind, Lucy. *Do* you want Byron back again? To warm those cold places inside you?"

A tiny flame suddenly flared against the wall. And as Lucy's eyes struggled to focus on the flickering candle, she also saw the scene spread out before her.

The bottom crypt was open.

The stone slab that once had sealed it now lay in jagged pieces; the coffin—or what was left of it—had been smashed to splinters.

There was no Byron.

No body.

Only dust and soot, and bits of charre
bones, and burned black ashes, scattered thickl
over the floor . . .

"What a pity," the voice sighed. "It looks a
though he's out for the evening."

"*God—no!*"

"But I can give him back to you, Lucy. Al
you have to do is give yourself to *me*."

Lucy turned and bolted.

"Dakota! *Run!*"

She didn't hear an answer, and she didn't se
her friend. And as she finally reached Dakota'
hiding place, she was horrified to find i
deserted.

"*Dakota! Where are you?*"

The thing leaped out at her from the trees.

Sent her sprawling backward across a grave
even as she kicked and fought with all he
strength, even as it pinned her effortlessly to th
ground.

Through her panic, Lucy saw a human face
One that was all too familiar.

Jared gazed down at her, breathing hard, hi

hair whipped wildly in the wind. She could feel the firm length of his body, the ripples of sinewy muscle, his awesome power held tightly in check.

His amber eyes glowed with a strange light.

A feral light . . . hypnotic . . . keen with intelligence and wisdom. A wisdom, Lucy realized, far beyond that of any mortal being.

"Where's the book, Lucy?" he demanded. "I need that book . . ."

His words broke off as he pitched forward. Lucy saw the heavy tree branch behind him, descending in slow motion as Dakota tried valiantly to strike another blow. But this time the branch missed its mark, and, as Dakota stumbled, her makeshift weapon slipped from her hand.

Jared was on his feet in an instant.

A low, gutteral sound came from his throat.

As he whirled toward Dakota, Lucy scrambled for the branch and staggered up, swinging at him ferociously.

She heard the sickening thud of wood against bone, the crack of Jared's skull as he fell against a headstone and lay still.

For an endless moment the two girls stood frozen in place. They stared at each other without speaking, till Dakota finally broke eye contact and took a step back.

She pointed to the front of her lumpy coat. Her voice was thin and shaky.

"If it weren't for this broken arm, I think I could've taken him."

32

They laughed then, so they wouldn't cry.

Breathless, sobbing laughs as they held on to each other and stumbled from the cemetery.

And then true panic set in.

"You know it won't last," Lucy warned. "You know he'll be up again—he'll be after us."

"I know."

"He might even be up now. Already coming after us now."

"I know."

Lucy could feel Dakota weakening, the girl's injured body trembling with cold and pain.

"Dakota, you've got to get back to the hospital."

"I'm not going anywhere without you."

"You *have* to. You and I both know it. You're no match for Jared in your condition. You can barely stand up as it is."

"I'm just tired. I feel so strange . . . dizzy."

"Please. Do this for me, Dakota. *Please*."

"He was so fast, I didn't even see him. I didn't even hear him coming. He was just there. All of a sudden—just *there*."

"So do you recognize him? Was he the one who attacked you?"

"I think so. I'm pretty sure. Like I said, I only saw his face for a second. But . . . my God, Lucy . . . he looks so much like Byron."

Lucy's heart gave a lurch. "He's not Byron."

"What happened in the mausoleum?" Dakota asked now. And then, noting Lucy's expression, her tone went flat. "He didn't bring Angela, did he? I knew it."

The flashback nearly sent Lucy reeling. She closed her eyes to force it away . . . grabbed her throat to force back a scream.

"Lucy?" Dakota coaxed gently.

Lucy stopped in her tracks, giving Dakota a numb stare. How could she explain to Dakota what had happened? No words could describe the macabre scene she'd just witnessed . . . the cruel taunts she'd been forced to endure.

Her lips formed the name again—*Byron*—but

it came out a moan. She felt Dakota's arms go around her...felt Dakota's quiet strength and resolve. *And horror . . . Dakota's horror . . .* As though at some level Dakota sensed how shocking the experience had been.

"He said to keep away," Lucy whispered now.

"Jared said that? To keep away from him?"

"No. In my dream." Lucy took a deep breath. "Byron said, *'Keep away . . . there's no one in this place.'*"

"I don't understand—what are you trying to tell me?"

"Jared said—he said he'd bring Byron back." Lucy was gasping, trying to breathe. "That he'd bring Byron back, if I'd—"

"No!" Dakota hugged her tighter. "You can't listen to Jared. You can't believe *anything* Jared tells you."

"But Byron *wasn't* there. The crypt was empty."

"It was dark. You were scared and confused— it could have been any one of those crypts."

"No, I'm sure it was Byron's. I saw it myself."

"Don't you understand? You saw what Jared *wanted* you to see. He's a liar and a manipulator.

He's the *worst* kind of predator. He doesn't just prey on people when they're alone in the dark. He preys on their darkest emotions, too."

But how much easier it would be to die quickly, Lucy found herself thinking. *Die fast and have it over, rather than suffer a slow, agonizing death of darkness. Wandering in darkness . . . drowning in darkness . . . being consumed day after day by darkness.*

"Come on," Lucy said hoarsely, pulling free. "We can't stay here. We need to go somewhere safe."

"Then come to the hospital with me."

"No. It's safer for you if I don't."

"Look, he's not going to try anything with people around. And you can call Father Matt from there. He can give you a ride home."

There wasn't time to argue. What Dakota was saying made sense, but it wasn't just her friend's argument that finally convinced Lucy to go along with her. Dakota's strength was waning by the minute. Lucy shuddered to think what could happen if her friend walked the rest of the way alone.

The two of them started off again, jumping at

every sound. Each sigh of wind was Jared, each rustle of leaves was Jared—tracking them through the night, leaping at them from the shadows, attacking them without mercy. It took a long time to reach the hospital, and Lucy was frantic with worry over Dakota. If the poor girl didn't have some sort of relapse after all this, it would be a miracle.

The front doors of the hospital were locked at this hour; the only entrance was through the emergency room in back. It was a stroke of sheer luck that an ambulance arrived just as the girls cut through the parking lot—while the staff rushed out in a flurry of activity, Lucy and Dakota were able to slip in unseen. They parted ways at a service elevator. While Dakota rode up to her own floor, Lucy ducked into a bathroom and propped herself wearily against the sink. Dakota was right—she'd have to call Matt for a ride home.

And just what are you planning to tell him?

She was still shaken by their previous encounter. Still able to feel his lips against her fingertips, still embarrassed to face him, though the incident seemed almost trivial now, compared with everything else. She stared at herself in the mirror. She could tell him she'd been so distraught over Gran's death that she'd needed to talk to Dakota in person. *Not really a lie.* And then—because he'd probably be furious about her going out alone at this hour—she'd be very remorseful and contrite. *Yes, Matt, I definitely did a stupid thing, so could you please come over here and pick me up?*

Yes, that's good. It should work.

But Lucy stood there, unable to move, unable to pull out her cell phone or make the call.

Because now that she was alone, her thoughts crashed down on her. Especially the thought that had loomed between her and Dakota all the way back to the hospital. The thought too horrible to say out loud. The question too horrible to ask.

For if Byron's crypt was truly empty . . .

Then where was Byron?

33

Busy. Her fourth busy signal.

Come on, Matt, get off the phone.

Lucy rechecked the number and punched it in again. When she still couldn't get through, she tried Matt's pager, but got no return call.

Please Matt—I really need you.

Frustrated, she dialed the rectory, expecting Father Paul's irritated voice to greet her. But this time, the phone simply rang. No human response. Not even the answering machine.

That's weird.

Pocketing her phone, Lucy left the bathroom and hurried to the hospital's rear exit. Things had gotten calm in the emergency room; only one nurse worked at the desk, too preoccupied to notice her.

What am I going to do?

There were no cabs running at this hour. And as she slipped out the door and surveyed the parking lot, she knew she could never walk home alone.

Not now.

Not through this night of cold and snowy darkness. This night so perfect for disappearances. For things to stalk and work their evil.

Lucy's heart twisted into an icy knot.

Eleven and quarter last . . .

Jared was probably watching her right this minute, filled with rage and a lust for revenge. Something would be happening to her very soon—he'd be making a clever move, making himself known.

And yet the night around her seemed strangely empty and quiet.

Too quiet.

Lucy peered up at the sky. Snow was falling more thickly than ever . . . a pure white curtain between her and the world of reality. From the corner of her eye, she glimpsed a distorted shape at the opposite end of the parking lot. It was coming toward her, and it took her several moments to realize it was a car. As she turned to go back in, the Jeep pulled up beside her and stopped.

"Get in the car," Matt said tightly. His face was pale and drawn; his jaw clenched. And beneath the cold severity of his tone, there was an unmistakable quiver.

"Matt," Lucy gulped, "I can explain—"

"Get in the car."

"But Matt, I—"

"Just do it, Lucy."

Surprised and hurt, Lucy climbed in beside him. Matt immediately began speaking into his cell phone.

"Nicholas, I found her. No, I don't have a clue." Shooting Lucy a withering glance, Matt added, "We're gonna have a little talk, and then I'll drop her off. Thanks. No problem."

The silence that followed was painful. As Matt tossed down his phone, Lucy slid low in her seat.

"Do you have any idea—Do you know how scared—" Matt could hardly get the words out. Lucy had never seen him so angry, yet at the same time she could sense how truly frightened he was.

"Just how do you think I feel," he began again, "when I get this call from Nicholas telling me you're not at the house. That he wakes up and goes downstairs, and the front door's standing wide open."

"It wasn't." Lucy made a feeble attempt to defend herself. "The door wasn't open; I locked it my—"

"He said it's happened before. He asked me if you sleepwalk!"

"No, I don't sleepwalk, and—"

"He's been worried sick. In fact, he was just about to call the police and report you missing. Thank God he called me first."

"But I tried to call, and—"

"We've both been driving around town looking for you. What the hell were you *thinking?*" Matt accelerated so fast that the Jeep skidded. Swearing under his breath, he got the wheels under control and headed for the street. "Can you even imagine what you put us through?"

Miserably, Lucy fumbled for her excuse. "Okay, I know I should have told someone I was going out—"

"No. Very wrong answer." Matt spoke slowly,

as though scolding a dim-witted child. "You shouldn't have gone out in the first place."

"I was upset! I went for a walk!"

"Oh. A walk. In spite of the fact that Pine Ridge is dangerous. In spite of the fact that I've warned you not to go out alone. And in spite of the fact that Nicholas is grieving over the death of his *only* family member, and he doesn't need any more *disasters* to deal with right now."

"Nicholas doesn't even know me," Lucy said, more harshly than she intended. "And excuse me, but I don't think my life or what I do is very important in the overall scheme of his universe."

"Well, it's important in *my* universe, and I've asked him to keep a close eye on you from now on."

"Matt! I can't believe you did that!"

"Bad things can happen to you out here! I don't want you ending up just another helpless statistic!"

"I'm not helpless."

"Don't you know it could happen *this* quick— no warning! You wouldn't even know what hit—"

"I'm *not* helpless!" Lucy snapped at him. "And stop yelling at me!"

Another lengthy silence fell between them. As Matt gripped harder on the steering wheel, his voice grew husky.

"Don't do it again, Lucy. Please."

Lucy stared at him. His eyes were intent on the street ahead, his shoulders rigid with tension.

"Matt . . ."

"So many bad things . . ." For a moment he seemed lost in thought. Then he cleared his throat, his tone softening. "You can't do what I do and not see all those bad things, Lucy. They can happen anytime. To anyone. That's all I'm saying."

A range of emotions swept through her. She paused, then murmured, "I did try to call you."

"You did?" His glance was surprised. "When?"

"Just a little while ago."

"Try sooner next time. *Before* I bring out the search parties."

"I called the rectory, too, but the machine wasn't on."

"The machine's *always* on. Unless it's filled up

again, and Father Paul forgot to clear it. Which actually happens more regularly than people know."

He reached to adjust the windshield wipers. He held out one hand to the heating vent, splaying his fingers to absorb the warmth. As Lucy watched him, she suddenly wished she could touch that hand, so she quickly glanced away.

"I'm sorry, Matt," she whispered, but she kept her focus on the window now, on the night beyond, on the shadows beyond that, and the secrets beyond that . . .

I know you're there, Jared. I can feel you.

"I'm not helpless," she murmured again, then heard Matt chuckle softly.

"Are we talking about anything in particular?"

"Everything in particular." And then, before he could respond, she added, "Are priests divinely protected?"

"You mean, like do we have some sort of God-bubble around us?"

"I'm serious."

"Okay. My theory is, we're *all* divinely protected when we have faith."

"Faith in what?" Lucy turned to look at him.

He shrugged his shoulders and gave a mysterious smile.

"So that's it?" She sighed. "That's pretty simple."

"But not always easy."

His attention went back to the windshield. As he turned onto a familiar side street, Lucy frowned and sat up straight.

"What are we doing here?"

"Sorry," Matt said, pulling up to the curb. "I just have to make a quick stop—make sure things are okay."

"How come?" Rubbing the frost from her window, Lucy peered out at the old church. It rose darkly beyond the snowfall, looking for all the world like some overgrown mausoleum. In spite of the car's warm interior, Lucy couldn't suppress a shiver.

"Sheriff Stark paged me earlier." Shoving open his door, Matt jumped lightly out onto the pavement. "He said he was patrolling and thought he saw a light through one of those windows."

"He thinks someone broke in? Then shouldn't he be here with you?"

"He said when he couldn't get in, he walked around the building—but he didn't see the light anymore, and nothing else seemed suspicious. He just wanted me to know."

Could Jared still be here? Lucy wondered. Still living in the cellar? Or roaming through the empty church at night, making his plans? There were probably dozens of places to hide in there that no one even knew about.

Another shiver went through her. She opened her door and scrambled out. "Wait, Matt—I'm going with you."

"You bet you are. No way am I leaving you out here by yourself."

He was walking ahead of her, and Lucy hurried to catch up. She could feel her heartbeat quickening as the two of them neared the front steps, as Matt thrust his key into the lock.

A blast of dank air washed over them. That same odor she remembered so well, though it seemed even stronger tonight . . . like ditch water, too long stagnant.

The door closed with a thud; a vast tomb of darkness swallowed them whole. As Lucy waited for Matt to find the lights, she realized she was holding her breath.

"Wonderful," Matt muttered, feeling along the wall beside her. "Still no power. I just love these ice storms."

Don't go in there.

Lucy stiffened, her heart kicking in fear. She reached out to grope for his arm.

"Matt . . . do you smell something?"

"You mean mold, mildew, or dead rats? I think I've gotten immune to all of it."

"No. Something else." Squeezing his arm tighter, she was totally oblivious to his wince of pain.

"Ouch. Okay, I believe you. You're not helpless."

"Matt . . ."

"How am I supposed to see anything without lights?" he grumbled. "Why don't I ever remember to bring a flashlight when I come here? I should know better."

Don't go in there!

But Matt's back was to her now, as he continued flicking light switches at one side of the door. And as Lucy stared straight ahead through the blackness, she could feel icy ripples of fear up her spine.

"Matt . . ." Her whisper sounded hollow in the dark. "If the electricity's out . . . then what's that light over there?"

She felt him turn.

Felt him move close beside her, felt the slow, wary stiffening of his shoulders.

"What the . . ." But the rest of Matt's words trailed away as his eyes focused with hers toward the front of the church.

The altar was glowing.

Glowing and flickering red.

Bloodred shadows spilling onto the floor, clawing their way up the walls and ceiling, throbbing and pulsing like something alive . . .

"Candles?"

Lucy heard the question, but she had no idea who'd spoken. *Me? Matt?* She couldn't even seem to move her lips.

"Someone's been lighting candles." Matt's voice, she was sure of it. He sounded relieved and even a little embarrassed. "No one's been trying to vandalize this place. Whoever was here just wanted to pray for somebody."

She could feel him relax, the tension draining from his muscles as he started forward. Immediately she tried to hold him back.

"Matt, let's just go."

But if he heard, he gave no sign. Slipping from her grasp, he began walking slowly along the side aisle.

"Matt, please!"

Lucy followed after him. She could hear the frantic sound of her breathing, the wind cutting through every crevice of the church. Her pulse pounded loud in her temples. Mice scurried beneath the floorboards, and the flames on the altar hissed and sighed.

She clamped her hands over her ears, but the noises grew louder. *No, make them stop!* Bats' wings fluttering in the belfry. Rust peeling from cracked church bells. Wood rotting slowly around her. Stones crumbling to dust. And from somewhere close—very, very close—that subtle, much more hidden sound. That soft, low, rumbling sound.

Like a breath rattling deep in a throat . . .

Or a growl . . .

Lucy's hair lifted at the back of her neck. She

glanced around wildly, but the darkness had thickened like smoke. The only things she could see were those flickering pinpoints of bright red light . . . far, far, far ahead of her . . . gleaming and glittering on the altar.

"That sound, Matt," Lucy cried out. "Did you hear it?"

There was a thud and a scrape. Matt's feet tripping and balancing again. "I don't hear anything."

"Listen!"

"Lucy, you're creeping me out. It's just the wind."

"No, it's not!"

Don't go any farther! Go back!

"The thing I don't get," Matt was still grumbling, more to himself than to her, "is why anyone would come in here to light candles when this place isn't even used anymore. I mean, why wouldn't they just go to the other church?"

"Matt, don't go up there!"

"And as much as I respect their faith and their prayers, I can't just leave these candles burning. This place could go up like kindling."

"No!"

"Yes, Lucy, it really could. I can't take that chance."

Lucy's heart pumped out of control. Matt had already reached the steps and was starting his short climb to the altar. In a burst of sheer panic, she ran.

"Matt!"

She heard his strangled cry, saw him stumble backward as though his legs had suddenly given out. She saw his arm lift in a feeble attempt to wave her back, but she pushed past him and starred down in horror at the scene before them.

The body didn't look human.

Surrounded by candlelight, it lay on its back, fleshless hands folded in prayer, a mockery of peaceful repose. The head was practically severed. Both legs had been chewed to bone, and one foot was missing. It seemed the only things holding the remains together at all were shreds of blackened skin, and a few tattered strips of moldering fabric.

Squeaking in protest, a horde of rats backed off from their meal in progress, then skittered off beyond the shadows.

Bile rose into Lucy's throat. The stench of rotting flesh flooded through her, making her gag.

And suddenly, she thought the body must still be alive, because it was *moving*—in the bloodred glow of the candles, she could see it *moving* and *breathing* and struggling to sit up.

"Holy Christ," Matt choked.

Lucy gazed at the putrid mask of the girl's face, at the holes where the girl's eyes had once been, at the chopped-off strands of the girl's jet-black hair, so hauntingly familiar despite the tangled mats of dirt and twigs and soggy leaves.

And she realized then that what was moving were the maggots.

The thousands and thousands of maggots squirming inside Angela's chest, hungrily devouring her heart.

34

"Lucy," Matt said softly. "Come away."

She hadn't even realized that she'd screamed, that she'd whirled around and buried her face against him. Or that his arms were tight around her, keeping her close and on her feet, even as he tried to lead her off in the opposite direction.

"Lucy . . ."

But she couldn't stop sobbing, couldn't stop the violent shaking that wracked her body with terror and with shock.

"Oh, Matt, it's Angela!"

"Angela?" Matt looked stunned. "What are you talking about?"

"I know it is—I *know* it!"

"Come on, let's get out of here. I'm taking you home."

"No, I can't leave her!"

"Lucy, I am *not* going to let you stay—"

"We have to call the police!"

"I will, I promise. But first—"

"Look at her!" *Jared said he'd let me see her! But not like this! I never thought he meant like this!*

"You don't know for sure this is Angela." Despite his best efforts at calm, Matt seemed more shaken than Lucy had ever seen him. "How could you possibly tell? This could be anybody. God only knows how long it'll take to identify the body."

"Where's she been all this time? Where's he been hiding her? How long did he keep her alive?"

Yet even as Lucy struggled to look back at the altar, Matt was still forcing her down the aisle.

"Lucy, come on! There's nothing you can do."

"Please don't make me leave her!"

For one brief second, she wavered between hysteria and total collapse. They were at the doors now, and Matt was rubbing her icy hands, trying to warm them between his own, and Lucy stared at him through a numb haze of detachment. *Oh, Angela, what did he do to you? What did you go through before you finally died?*

"Wait for me here," Matt said firmly. "Right *here*, understand? And don't go outside. I'll be back in a minute."

"What are you going to do?"

"Make sure she's at peace."

And *of course*, Lucy realized, watching him walk back again, his dark silhouette moving solicitously among the shadows on the altar, his hands smoothly forming the sign of the cross. *He's freeing Angela's soul . . . freeing Angela of all those bad things . . .* And even though Lucy was too far away to hear his prayers, it was as if each reverent whisper of absolution echoed softly from the old church walls and wept inside her heart.

She barely managed to get outside before her legs gave out. Huddled on her knees in the snow, she wrapped her arms around herself and began to rock slowly back and forth.

Angela!

A whirlwind of images swept through her brain—Angela's face, Angela's defiance, Angela's longing to escape and desperate need to be loved. Lucy crumpled onto her side, knees drawn up to her chest, and the sounds coming from her mouth were primal sounds, animal sounds.

Maybe Matt's right—maybe that's not Angela on the altar. There's hardly anything left of the body. It could be anyone! Another victim like Wanda Carver! Some cold, hungry homeless girl who thought the church would be a refuge! Anyone! Anyone else but Angela!

But Lucy knew better.

All the hopes she'd had, the *false* hopes she'd had—wanting to believe what Jared had told her, doing what Jared had demanded, holding on to that last thread of hope—and for nothing! *Nothing!* Just one more victory for Jared. One more reminder of his absolute power and control.

And one more reason for me to hate him.

One more reason to want him destroyed.

Though her sobs had quieted, Lucy was still so overcome with grief and rage, she didn't hear Matt calling, didn't even realize he was there again until he eased down beside her in the snow.

"Whoever she is," he murmured, "she's in a better place now. May God have mercy on her soul."

But Lucy's tone was bitter. "Whoever left her like this didn't have any mercy."

Matt glanced away, but not before Lucy saw the expression on his face. He looked older somehow, and weary, and immeasurably sad.

"Lucy . . ." Matt seemed to choose his words carefully. "Whoever did this will ultimately be judged and held accountable. And—"

"Please. No spiritual lectures. Killers get away with killing all the time. So don't go on about justice."

"You know the justice I mean. A higher justice. One that's fair. And true."

Tears rose up again in the back of Lucy's throat. "I wish I could believe that."

"Well . . . you believe *me*, don't you?"

In spite of herself, Lucy managed a reluctant nod. "Yes. I believe you."

For a second he smiled at her, though it seemed to Lucy that his sadness had deepened into pain.

"We need to go," he said quietly.

"What are we going to do, Matt? We can't just leave Angela here."

Matt coaxed her up from the ground, steadying her as she took several faltering steps.

"How can I tell Irene? What am I going to say to her?"

"Shh . . . you're not gonna say anything to anybody. I told you before, we don't *know* this is Angela. And if it is . . ."

"It *is*! I'm positive!"

"*If* it is," Matt consoled her, "you won't have to break the news to your aunt. That's for the authorities to handle. I don't want you even thinking about it. Understood?"

Again Lucy's nod was halfhearted at best. Like a robot, she planted one foot stiffly in front of the other as Matt led her back to the Jeep.

"Where are we going?" she asked him. "Aren't you going to call the police?"

"After I take you back to the house."

"But—"

"Listen to me. If the police find out you were here, they'll want to question you. And you're not up to it, Lucy—you've been through too much already."

"So what are you saying?"

Matt helped her into the passenger side, then fastened the seat belt around her. "I'm saying that you were never here tonight. I came to the church alone, after I dropped you off at Gran's house."

"And how much penance will *that* lie cost you?"

"Look. Do you wanna be dragged through all the red tape or not?"

Slowly she shook her head.

"And leaving you out of it's not hurting anyone, is it?"

"Well . . . no."

Matt rolled his eyes heavenward and hastily crossed himself. "Then it's not a lie. It's a fib." And then, as if trying to convince himself, he mumbled, "There's a very big difference."

"Won't they notice my footprints in the church? And in the snow?"

"Let me worry about that."

As Matt slammed her door, Lucy couldn't help looking back at the church. She longed to put as much distance as possible between herself and Angela's grisly remains; she longed to stay behind and keep vigil at Angela's side. The horror was overwhelming. The *not knowing* what Angela had been through, the *imagining* what Angela had been through. Lucy felt so sick she could hardly hold herself up. When Matt finally stopped in front of Gran's house, she slumped there, unable to move.

"I want you to get some sleep." Matt's voice sounded far away, though he was sitting right next to her. "And absolutely *no going anywhere* by yourself—understood? As soon as I hear something definite, I'll let you know. And if it's Angela . . ."

"I know it's her; I've told you a hundred times it's her. Why do you keep saying it's not?"

"If it *is* Angela," he insisted again patiently, "then you'll hear it from me, and no one else."

"I don't have to hear it from you. I already know."

"You don't know anything, remember? Because you never went to the church with me tonight."

For a long while neither of them spoke. Then, on a sudden impulse, Lucy reached over and touched his hand.

"I really do believe you, Matt. And . . . and I trust you."

She sensed his hesitation. And then his eyes met hers.

"I know you do," he whispered.

Something in his tone pierced through her. As Lucy held his gaze, it was as if a whole range of raw emotions struggled across his face in the flicker of a heartbeat. She began to lean toward him. She could feel his muscles tensing, the racing of his pulse, the sudden surge of warmth through his body. And beneath the lingering smells of dank church air and bitter cold, she breathed in the scents of communion wafers and confessionals, countless hands clasped and comforted, tears and fears and hopes and regrets—his *regrets*—*regrets and suffering and passion and longing—all* his!—*all struggling, all weeping within his soul. . . .*

Lucy realized she was trembling. Even as she freed her hand from his and rested it upon his cheek . . . smoothed the tousled hair from his brow . . . traced the sensuous outline of his mouth . . .

"Lucy . . ."

Their bodies came together, cautiously at first, then urgently, insistently, her arms around his neck, her face between his hands, the heat of their kisses on lips and flushed, bare skin, desperate and tender, no place but this, no time but this, no world but this one, safe and sacred and sweet, and *I never want to leave this, here where I trust, here where I believe, here where there's hope.*

"Stop . . . Lucy . . . we have to stop . . ."

Yet even as Matt spoke, his arms went around her, pressing her to his chest.

"It's my fault," she said softly, trying not to cry. "I don't know what I was thinking, please—"

"It's not your fault. It was never your fault. Not now . . . not before. Not any of it."

"Oh God, I'm so sorry. You're such a friend to me—more than you could ever know—and this is so wrong. I never meant to ruin it."

"You haven't ruined it; how can you even say that? There's no way you could ever ruin it." Clutching her tighter, he buried his face in her hair. "Please forgive me, Lucy."

It seemed an eternity that they held each other. And when Matt finally pulled away, Lucy felt the darkness again, and the bitter cold.

She couldn't even look at him as they walked to the porch. Scarcely heard his casual explanations when Nicholas met them at the door. And when Matt hurried back to the Jeep, she couldn't watch him drive away. She went straight to her room and collapsed on the bed, the last twenty-four hours caving in on her, burying her alive.

At some point Nicholas spoke to her from the hallway. He asked if there was anything she needed; he sounded reticent but genuinely concerned. And though Lucy was touched by his awkward attempt at kindness, it made her only feel worse.

I know that ache of losing people you love . . . I should be comforting him.

But she didn't have the strength right now. Not even the strength to answer him, as he gave up and left her alone.

A cold numbness crept over her. She was far beyond fear and panic. Sleep was impossible, and so was salvation; she lay there wide-eyed, staring at the shadows on the ceiling, not even bothering to turn down the covers or turn on the lamp.

Jared will find me.

Jared will win.

Just as he won with Angela . . . abandoning her . . . leaving her alone in an abandoned place.

Oh yes, the message Jared had left was cold and utterly clear.

And Lucy knew it was meant only for her.

35

It was the nightmare that woke her.

Lucy bolted upright in bed, her heart pounding wildly. She was still in her shoes, still wearing her clothes and jacket, with no memory at all of having gone to sleep.

But the dream was still fresh in her mind.

Those lingering images of shadows crouched around her, long and low to the floor, circling her with calculated patience, on stealthy, silent feet . . .

And someone calling her name . . . someone trying to . . . what? Warn her?

A dream so real that she dove beneath the covers and hid, paralyzed with fear, half expecting at any moment for something to leap from the darkness and drag her away.

It took a long time for her to relax—even

longer to convince herself it had been only a nightmare, after all. That there were no lurking shadows, no monsters under the bed. That the house was locked up tight, and Nicholas was asleep upstairs, everything peaceful, and she had escaped all the bad things.

But you know better, you know you'll never escape, and Jared was right, escape is just an illusion.

Something moved outside her bedroom door.

The creak of a floorboard . . . a whisper of air . . .

"Nicholas? Is that you?"

Very slowly, Lucy forced herself to sit up. Her heart was squeezing so tight, she could barely speak.

"Nicholas?"

But it wasn't his voice that answered. Rather a soft meow, and then a purr, that echoed unnaturally loud through the silence.

"Cinder!" Lucy sighed in relief. "God, you scared me to death!"

Hurrying to the door, she opened it and peered out into the hallway. The cat was nowhere to be seen, though Lucy thought she heard it cry again, more muffled than before.

She caught a quick, subtle movement from the corner of her eye. Startled, she turned in the direction of Gran's bedroom.

The door was still shut. From beneath it, the glow of Gran's night-light still shone softly along the floor. Cautiously, Lucy approached the room and turned the doorknob. As the door began to inch open, she could almost swear that another floorboard creaked . . . that a shadow flickered briefly along one wall. She imagined something sliding out of sight beneath the bed.

Come on, get a grip. Find Cinder and let her sleep with you.

Perhaps, like all of them, Cinder was feeling Gran's absence. Mourning the loss of her, still needing to be close. But this room felt so cold and so empty. More empty than Lucy had ever imagined it could—such a hollow, empty promise of finality.

She wished she could cry, but no more tears would come. She wished she'd said more, done more, while Gran was alive . . . and that made her think of her mother.

Lucy reached out and touched the head-board.

Everything had been done, as Matt had promised. The linens had been stripped, leaving nothing but a bare mattress and the faint imprint of a small, frail body. The curtains, not quite drawn, let in a haze of snow-gray light. There was a pillowcase on the floor, Lucy noticed, that must have fallen accidentally when the rest of the sheets and blankets were removed.

She bent to pick it up.

She stroked the smooth fabric and the delicate lace trim, her thoughts so focused on Gran that she didn't notice the gradual quickening of her pulse or the throbbing of her temples.

Not till she put up a hand to wipe the sweat from her brow.

Not till she suddenly felt sick to her stomach, her breath coming in short, sharp gasps.

Her other hand holding the pillowcase began to tighten and clench, until her knuckles went white and her fingers ached from the strain.

A pillow.

Lucy caught the sudden flash in her brain and frowned at the single image.

A pillow?

Yes, this *pillow, stuffed inside* this *pillowcase* . . .

Growing dizzier by the second, she tried to let go of the pillowcase, tried to drop it back onto the floor, but it was stuck to her hand . . .

Pillow—large soft wonderful pillow ruffles of lace coming closer—sweet dreams pillow—nightmare pillow—deadly pillow—blocking out the light, shutting out the air, closer closer—heavy on my face wrapped around my face, harsh ragged breathing strangled whimpers garbled cries for help.

"Oh God . . ."

Eyes forced closed, nose pressed flat, sucking fabric, mouth stuffed with ruffles and lace . . .

Lucy couldn't breathe. Wrestling fiercely with the pillowcase, her eyes bulged from their sockets, her throat began to wheeze, her lungs threatened to burst wide open. *This is what you saw, Gran—this pillow,* your *pillow, this is what you saw in those last few seconds before you died* . . .

Those horrible last few seconds, lying there helpless and terrified . . .

While someone smothered the life out of you.

With a cry, Lucy flung the pillowcase away. It fluttered into the corner like a wounded bird as she turned and stumbled from the room.

Jared!

Lucy could barely see the walls around her, the floor beneath her feet—all she could see was Jared's face and Jared's eyes, all she could hear were his evil, whispered promises to hurt the people she cared about.

All the people she cared about!

But *Gran!* Somehow, Gran's death was the very worst of all. Ill and defenseless, unable to scream or cry, never a threat to anyone—yet fully able to see her attacker and the way her life would end . . .

Lucy thought of how Gran must have panicked.

She stopped at the foot of the staircase and leaned against the wall, trying to shut out the awful silence of Gran's struggles.

Did you try to call for help, Gran? Did you wonder why nobody came?

The images sickened her. Had it happened during the night? Early morning? And had Lucy slept right through it? Not suspecting, not waking up, not able to stop Gran's murder!

"Nicholas?" she tried to yell, but her voice

was shaking so badly, she knew he couldn't possibly have heard. Gazing up the stairs, she saw that his door was open, but the room beyond was dark. Should she even tell him about Gran? Would he believe her? And if he did, what purpose would it serve, anyway?

It would only hurt him and bring him more heartbreak. It would only mean more unanswered questions. More problems, more suspicions, more danger for everyone.

Lucy hugged herself tightly, chilled to the bone. She took a step back and nearly slipped and fell.

Slipped?

Puzzled, she lifted one foot from the floor. The bottom was definitely wet, and it seemed to be coated with something sticky. She felt along the wall for a light switch, flicked it on, and immediately gagged on a scream.

The floor was covered in blood.

The soles of her shoes were dark red.

As Lucy frantically turned on more lights, she could see still more blood, pools of blood, where something had been dragged down the stairs from Nicholas's bedroom . . . and here along the floor . . . and off into the kitchen.

"Nicholas!"

But Lucy knew he wasn't here. Even before she saw the back door standing open . . . and the bloody trail leading out into the night.

36

"*Nicholas!*

A blast of frigid air struck her as she ran from the house, but Lucy didn't feel it. Didn't feel the wind tearing at her clothes, the snow burning into her skin.

"Nicholas! Where are you?"

But Nicholas couldn't answer, and she was alone.

The light was murky at best. A starless, snow-filled sky, blanketed with fog. The night held its breath around her. The wind clawed but made no sound.

How long had Nicholas been gone?

Surely not long, not with his blood still wet upon the floor.

She could see the flattened path along the ground, the wide swath of darkened snow leading off into the trees behind the house.

Maybe he was still alive.

Maybe she could still find him.

And then what? What will you do?

For Lucy realized now that Jared had been here all along. Prowling through the halls . . . luring her into Gran's room . . . smiling at her horror as she'd discovered the pillowcase. And Jared had been watching while she slept, standing at her bedside, caressing her with nightmares.

Had Nicholas tried to warn her? Had *his* been the cry that awakened her from her dream, even as he'd struggled for his own life?

"Nicholas Wetherly . . . perhaps you could ask him to be your protector . . ."

Jared's words mocked her, filling her with rage.

"Surely you realize he has no power against me. And by trying to protect you, he could very easily get himself killed."

And that's exactly what happened, isn't it, Jared?

She remembered how angry she'd been when Matt had asked Nicholas to look out for her. But Nicholas had kept his promise to Matt . . . and now Jared was keeping his promise to her.

The rage she was feeling slowly began to shift. As though it were being replaced by something much more powerful, something hot and sharp and lethal, and far beyond her control.

No one could ever protect her from Jared. No one could ever change the course of her destiny. Enough blood had been spilled; enough people had suffered.

If Nicholas's life could still be bargained for, she was the only one who could do it.

So I'm the one you want, Jared?

Then I'm the one you'll get.

Tilting her face into the wind, Lucy sniffed the frozen air and tried to concentrate. The scent of blood was sharp against the snow. It hung in the back of her throat like rusty metal, and, after choking it down, she narrowed her eyes and stared off through the trees.

All the neighboring houses were dark. There were sheds and garages and backyards, driveways and fences. So many shapes beyond the snow, and so many places to hide.

Nicholas hadn't been hidden out here.

As Lucy's senses cautiously probed the night, she knew he wasn't even close by.

But something else was.

And as the low growl sounded behind her, she understood its meaning at once: *Don't turn around. Stay in place, and keep distance between us.*

Lucy whirled to face it, and immediately wished she hadn't.

The thing was crouched beside the house. Its head was lowered and its lips drawn back in a snarl. A wolf, yet not a wolf. Some unknown and ungodly breed of dog—some hideous mutation. Its long, sleek body was low to the ground, and snow clung to its thick, black fur. While Lucy watched in horror, it began moving in a tense circle, pacing back and forth beneath a first-floor window . . .

Gran's window.

Lucy heard the soft puffs of air as it snuffled at the windowsill . . . the impatient scratching of its claws . . . its plaintive whines of distress. And then without warning, it raised its head, its muzzle silhouetted against the windowpane.

The howl it gave was unearthly. A cry of unbearable anguish.

An animal cry . . . a human cry . . .

"No," Lucy murmured. "God . . . no . . ."

As the creature turned to confront her once more, their eyes met and held. *Familiar eyes,* she thought wildly—large and soulful, deep and black as midnight . . . *I know those eyes.*

"Byron!" she screamed.

But the thing had gone.

Right in front of her it simply vanished, leaving nothing but empty shadows.

37

Only a matter of hours now.

A few short hours, and Lucy would be his.

Can you feel it, my beloved? The slow, steady ticking of mortal time? The end of your life as you know it? The beginning of something perfect and eternal?

The anticipation was almost more than he could bear.

He closed his eyes and remembered the last time he had touched her, the last time he had gazed upon her face. He imagined all the things that he would do to her, things that would bind her to him forever.

He would take her home, of course.

To his birthplace and the country of his ancestors.

To the darkness and isolation of his own private world.

Where no one would find her or rescue her, and where no one would hear her screams.

They always screamed at first.

Begged for mercy, prayed to die.

But panic was a passing thing, and as all the others before her had done, Lucy would learn compliance. Repentance. Submission and acceptance.

And oh, how she would love him.

Just thinking of it made him ache and burn.

"Lucy," he moaned now, softly, then turned at the sound of approaching footsteps.

Familiar footsteps. Traveling the familiar pathway to his lair.

And as the door opened, and his visitor came in, he waited expectantly for the news.

"It's done," the visitor said. "Everything is ready."

"Byron is waiting?"

"In the mausoleum, just as you instructed."

"And the girl, Lucy's friend? You have her as well?"

"Yes. I took her from the elevator. She never even made it back to her room."

"Excellent. Deftly handled, as always."

"Did you doubt me?"

He leveled a look at the visitor. His voice was smooth, like silk. "Only that you've seemed a bit . . . melancholy of late. Not your usual amusing self."

"My job always amuses me."

"But I see no smile tonight. Do I sense some hesitation? A change of heart, perhaps?"

"You know me better than that."

"Yes . . ." he murmured. "Of all the people in the world, you are the one I know best." He stared out his window at the snow. A frown settled across his brow. "Do you remember when we were children together?"

The visitor's laugh was humorless. "Were we *ever* children?"

"Once upon a very long lifetime ago."

A moment, almost wistful, hung between them. And then slowly faded away.

"It's hard to remember days of childish innocence and reckless play. But I do remember your father." The visitor thought back. "I remember how much he indulged us. I remember how much he loved you. The plans he had for you. The pride he felt for . . ."

"My brother?"

"You're wrong. He was proud of you both. His greatest hope was that the two of you would someday rule side by side. And keep the pack together."

"And then his favoritism split us apart."

The visitor paused. His voice was gentle, but firm. "You were the one who chose a different path. You were the one who broke away and preferred to rule on your own."

"And look what I've accomplished. My followers are strong. They show me loyalty and devotion."

"That's not loyalty. That's fear."

"And their numbers continue to grow."

"Only so long as you don't hunt them down and kill them."

"Ah. Finally. A touch of your incomparable wit." His dark eyes darkened even more. "But you know I kill only out of necessity."

"The necessity of entertaining yourself."

"I must *destroy* those who *threaten* my legacy."

"Then you destroy legions. Your offspring— and your brother's—span the centuries. And you and I are both fully aware that *any* offspring from the royal bloodline is a threat to your legacy."

As an ironic smile curled his lips, he conceded with a nod. "Yes . . . only those of the royal bloodline may rule. And only One of my own kind can destroy me."

"And so Byron is already your sworn enemy. Through no fault—and no knowledge—of his own."

"I cannot risk either possibility."

"I don't think you need to worry. You've been quite successful through the years at eliminating potential threats."

"And this is why our relationship has stood the test of time." His tone was faintly mocking. "Only *you* would have the courage to insult me to my face. You . . . my oldest friend."

"Your only friend."

"I concur. So you accuse me of being an ineffective ruler?"

"On the contrary, you're a *very* effective ruler. Terror is a powerful motivation."

"As you've taught me. And taught me well."

"And as you never tire of reminding me."

Turning at last from the window, he regarded

the visitor with a deep and thoughtful stare. "Is this *regret* I'm hearing?"

"Immortality is a long, long time. There's no shame in doing things differently."

He watched the visitor glance away, heard the weariness of centuries in a sigh.

"Why must you continue this age-old battle?" the visitor asked him. "Why must you destroy your brother? Why must any more blood be shed?"

"Because he has hurt me in the past. He has *wounded* me in the past—in my body and in my heart!"

"And you have paid him back. Let it end here."

"It will never end between him and me. It will never end until one of us is dead."

"You had compassion once. When you were a boy. That is something else I remember."

"And you did *not*. That is what *I* remember. And now . . . it is too late for both of us."

A heavy silence fell between them. Lowering his head, the visitor gazed at the floor.

"You have Lucy's best friend. You've taken all her family. She believes Byron is dead. How do you think she'll feel when she discovers the truth?"

"The truth about Byron? Or the truth about you?"

He watched as the visitor's shoulders tightened, as the visitor's face grew pale. And he felt that smug sense of accomplishment that always came when he was cruel. He relished in it. It was a stimulant like no other—and the best defense of all. When one was deliberately cruel, one kept other feelings—*vulnerable* feelings—at bay.

"I think," he said now, going back to the question, "that Lucy will feel desperate enough to do *anything* that will save them."

"And then . . . will you keep your word to her?"

"What do *you* think?"

His visitor was leaving now. He escorted him to the door as a longtime friend and perfect host should do, and he kept his voice casual, conversational.

"A curious thing I've noticed recently," he said.

"And what's that?"

"You're not wearing your medallion."

The visitor gave a shrug. Smoothed the front of a black button-down shirt. Lightly fingered a white collar. Offered a bland smile. "Too risky, wouldn't you say? It doesn't quite go with the uniform."

"Of course. You're right. A very clever move on your part. Obviously, I'd never have thought to take care of that particular detail."

"Don't I always take care of everything?"

"Everything. And more."

"Well, I should go."

"Yes, preceding me, as usual. To prepare the way and make my paths righteous and straight."

"I'll see you at the mausoleum."

"Yes, you will." Pausing, he added, "Oh, and one more thing."

"Yes?"

"It would break my heart if I ever found that a friend had betrayed me. Or even *thought* of betraying me. For I'd have no choice then but to take my revenge."

There was no reaction, nothing said.

And then the visitor looked full into his eyes. "You always have a choice."

The door opened and shut on a flurry of snow. The room sank into quiet.

But even after his visitor had gone, he stood there with a reproachful smile on his face. And in the lonely silence, his whisper was loud and harsh.

"Revenge is the *only* choice. You, of all people, should know that, Matthew."

38

Free Byron . . .

Numb with shock and disbelief, Lucy began stumbling through the snow. This couldn't be happening, couldn't be real—she'd *known* Byron, *loved* him, *grieved* for him. He'd been honest with her about who he was—he'd *died* that night in the accident!

Free Byron . . .

She realized she was following him. His special scent still warmed the air around her, as though he'd just held her in his arms. Yet there was something else she noticed—something wild and feral. The strong smell of musk. The odor of a fresh kill.

"Oh God . . . Byron!"

"It's too late for Byron," Jared said.

He was upon her in an instant. Caught

completely by surprise, Lucy tried to fight, but she was no match for his strength. Jared grabbed her from behind and pulled her back against his chest.

"It's *not* too late!" Lucy cried. "I don't believe it—I *won't* believe it!"

"How much do you love Byron?" Jared's lips whispered in her ear. "And what are you willing to do?"

"I'll do anything. *Anything!*"

"Then, drink."

Drawing her tighter against him, he pressed the underside of his wrist to her mouth. She felt the two tiny openings in his skin. She felt the warm blood ooze between her lips.

At first she struggled, choking violently, but Jared's grip was merciless, and she couldn't turn her head. Lucy had no choice but to swallow. His blood flowed smoothly over her tongue and down the back of her throat.

She suddenly realized she wasn't cold anymore.

That her head had cleared, and she felt strong.

And yet Jared was still holding her up, urging her to take even more.

"Drink," he whispered. "For Byron's sake."

Her heart began to pound, her veins to burn. Her heartbeat was *his* heartbeat, and her blood was on fire. The night descended with dizzying speed, leaving her breathless, and she moaned in pain and pleasure.

She didn't even realize now that Jared had released her. Or that he'd wound her long hair around his hand, and eased her head back to expose her neck.

There was only one quick puncture, one hot sting.

And then the whole world spun away.

But I am *the world . . . part of everything . . . all living, all dead, and totally free . . . all that I'll ever need . . .*

She was running. She didn't know where she was, or where she was going, but there was no fear, no confusion, no need for maps or directions. Her feet scarcely touched the ground. Her spirit soared, exhilarated. She was lighter than air—she *was* the air—the air and the wind, flowing effortlessly through the dark, endless night.

A thousand sounds reached out to her—

flowers sleeping deep in the earth, leaves dying, pinecones dropping from pine trees miles away.

She could hear the snow falling. She could taste fog on the tip of her tongue. She could see field mice trembling in their nests; she could smell the fresh approach of dawn. Her clothes felt confining, like sandpaper against her skin.

It was the stench of death that finally stopped her.

The stench of graveyards and human remains.

The wet, stagnant stink of corpses in rotting coffins, and earth like brine, salted with centuries of tears.

Catching her breath, Lucy stood and surveyed her surroundings. Jared was nowhere to be seen, but the Wetherly mausoleum was directly ahead of her, and its rusty gates were open.

Where was Byron?

And what had become of Nicholas?

She ran her tongue over her lips. A trace of blood still lingered there, and she slowly licked it away. Her stomach clenched at the taste. Her nerves were tingling, her senses on high alert.

No need to hide now, Jared. No more secrets between us . . .

Her throat still ached from his bite. Her head was throbbing. The rush she'd experienced only seconds ago was beginning to fade, leaving her thoughts muddled and confused. On trembling legs, she walked toward the mausoleum, noting at once the trail of blood on the steps and through the doorway.

Lucy stopped, overcome with terror.

More terrified than she'd ever been in her life.

"You're your own power, Lucy."

Dakota's words came back to her, giving her strength. She slipped through the gates and paused just inside the threshold.

She knew at once that she wasn't alone. That there was something—someone—no, *more* than one presence!—waiting for her here. Quietly observing her. She felt someone hidden among the heavy gloom and candlelight and long-forgotten crypts.

She heard a quiet footstep . . . a muffled moan of pain.

And then that silky whisper she'd come to know so well . . .

"Lucy, do come in. We've been expecting you."

Her chest was tightening, her heart about to explode. She willed herself to move, but she was frozen.

His voice spoke again, impatient this time. "Come. You don't want to be late for your own wedding. It's bad luck—"

"No, Lucy, *run!*" The sudden scream cut him off—a scream Lucy recognized at once, though it was quickly silenced.

"Dakota!"

Lucy was moving now, forward through the flickering shadows, and she could hear Dakota trying to yell, trying to struggle. She could see Dakota lying on the floor across the room.

He was standing over her.

His back was partly turned to Lucy, and he was bent forward, his tongue tasting Dakota's throat.

"Let her go!" Lucy cried.

But Jared paid no attention, and Dakota was in no condition to fight. Without another thought, Lucy hurled herself at him, trying to wrestle him away—and at the same time, she felt someone grab her from behind and pull her off.

She clutched Jared's sleeve and held on.

There was a sharp sound of ripping fabric as she felt herself being yanked backward—as Jared's sleeve came off in her hand. And in that heart-stopping instant, Lucy saw something else. Jared's tattoo of a snake . . . and a sword . . . *no, not exactly a sword . . .*

Oh my God!

A complete tattoo, she suddenly realized—even as she felt herself trapped in a strong embrace, even as she fought to get free—*no puckered skin, no ridges of melted flesh, just smooth skin and a perfectly clear design . . . a snake with its tail in its mouth, coiled around a long, ornate dagger . . .*

*Not Jared's tattoo—*not Jared!

Even as the tearing sleeve knocked him sideways, as his teeth grazed Dakota's neck, as he smoothly caught his balance and turned his face to Lucy—

And it was *one* face, and it was *many* faces—all changing and converging in an instant, features twisting and rearranging as she watched in fascinated horror.

Demon faces and innocent ones—a homeless man with festering sores—swirling mist—wind and fog—a shadowy figure with a blindfold, the pale sharp features of a man delivering a headstone . . .

The face of a beast—wolf-dog-human—glowing eyes and thick black fur, and *Byron!*—*yes*, there was *Byron*, too!— *Angela—Katherine—Wanda Carver—Dakota—Gran* . . .

Me!

Oh God—me!

Lucy stared at him in horror, and his features settled into one distinct face, and as he gazed back at her, a faint, familiar fragrance filled the mausoleum.

A cloying sweetness.

A delicate, intoxicating perfume.

"Very tasty." Nicholas smiled. "But not as sweet as you."

39

Someone was still holding her.

She was vaguely aware of a tight embrace, of someone pinning her arms behind her back.

Dakota wasn't moving. Lucy could see a thin trickle of blood down the side of Dakota's neck, and the girl's face was paler than ever.

"Let her go!" Lucy demanded. "She has nothing to do with any of this! There's no reason for her to be here!"

But Nicholas was standing up now, regarding Lucy with calm intensity, adjusting his rumpled clothes.

"On the contrary, there is a *very* good reason for her being here," he said. "And if you promise to behave yourself, I'll have you released."

"Where's Byron? Where's Jared?"

"Jared . . . hmmm . . ." Nicholas took a

moment, pretending to think. "I'm afraid Jared wasn't invited to our little celebration tonight. But if he attempts to crash the party, we're quite ready for him. And as for your precious Byron . . ."

Chills crept up her spine. Just from the way Nicholas was speaking . . . just from the way Nicholas was looking at her.

"Your precious Byron? Why, he's right over there. Surely you didn't think I'd exclude *him* from our guest list?"

Lucy looked where Nicholas pointed. As a strangled cry caught in her throat, she twisted fiercely in the grasp that held her.

"*You* did this, didn't you! You bastard! *You* did this to him!"

"Now, now, calm yourself. It's all a matter of . . . shall we say . . . selective breeding."

But Lucy couldn't take her eyes from the thing in the corner. The hideous creature she'd seen earlier beneath Gran's window now chained helplessly to the wall. And though it quickly averted its eyes from her stare, Lucy saw the sorrow and humiliation gleaming from the depths of its midnight eyes.

"Let me go!" Again she tried to struggle; again the arms tightened around her. "Let me go to him!"

"There's nothing you can do for Byron now, Lucy. He's trapped between two worlds. Trapped by the legacy of his very own bloodline. So very tragic." Nicholas gave a deep sigh. "It happens occasionally. Not often . . . but occasionally. When the Transformation is unexpectedly interrupted. And never quite reaches completion."

"You can't leave him like this!"

"No? Well then, perhaps there *is* something you can do for him, after all."

"What have you done with Jared?"

Nicholas made eye contact with the person who held her. As though some secret signal had been given, she suddenly found herself free.

"I believe you two know each other," Nicholas added, even as Lucy whirled to face her captor. "Say hello, Matthew."

The words came through a fog. Lucy heard them, but they seemed to have no meaning. Time stopped, and she felt detached, and this reality was someone else's nightmare . . .

"Oh, forgive me. It's *Father* Matthew." Nicholas quickly corrected himself. "How could I forget? Our pious priest and saviour of souls?"

But still the words were beyond her, even as she stared up into Matt's face. He wore no expression, and his warm, blue eyes were strangely cold.

"Did you know," Nicholas went on conversationally, "that in our very first lifetimes together, Matthew was chief torturer and executioner of my enemies?"

Lucy could feel tears flooding her throat . . . brimming in her eyes . . . scalding down her cheeks.

"I don't believe you."

"Oh, indeed, it's quite true. Matthew was my closest friend . . . my most *trusted* friend, actually. I could always depend on him to carry out my orders. And he's always been exceptionally good at . . . shall we say . . . the fine art of persuasion?"

For a brief moment, Lucy's vision blurred. Her mind reeled backward as if in a vivid dream, and she heard Matt's voice in her memories . . .

"When it comes to the art of persuasion, being a priest has definite advantages. . . ."

"You're lying." Voice trembling, Lucy shook her head and stood her ground. "Matt would never do anything like that."

"But I assure you, he has. Would you care to hear specific dates, times, and descriptions? Matthew has an exceptional memory. And he loves his work."

But Lucy was already backing away from Matt . . . from the frightening chill in his eyes. Eyes that continued to follow her, but without caring . . . without mercy . . . *without Matt.*

Numbly, she braced herself against a wall. The room was shifting in and out of shadow, and the air in the mausoleum had gone oppressively stale. Dreamlike, she watched Nicholas lift something from his side and hold it out toward the nearest candle.

The object he was holding flashed scarlet and silver as he turned it slowly in his hand.

A knife.

A long-bladed knife, honed razor-sharp to perfection . . . its sturdy handle encrusted with jewels, glimmering in the flickering light.

In a kind of fascination, she kept watching as he ran one finger along the edge of the blade. As blood oozed onto the knife. As he ran his tongue over it, licking it clean.

I know this knife.

Startled, Lucy felt another memory begin to stir.

I know this knife! I've seen it before!

Her eyes shifted immediately to the tattoo on Nicholas's arm. The knife with the serpent coiled around it . . . the tattoo so similar to Jared's . . . *the mysterious words from the journal!*

. . . only killed by One of his own kind . . .

. . . ageless battle . . .

. . . dagger of our ancestors . . .

Not a knife, Lucy realized now. *A dagger! The dagger I saw in my vision.*

Dagger . . . dagger of our ancestors . . . blade plunging again again again—twisting—slashing—burning like fire—burning in fire!—ropes around wrists, sleek naked body writhing in blood—blistering, roasting black, melting from bones—"God help me! Have mercy!"*—sobs screams shrieks ignored by the rage, attacked by the rage, punished and tortured forever . . .*

Only One . . .

Can only be killed by One of his own kind . . .

Lucy's head was spinning. She tried to think, to calm her frantic breathing, as another image jolted her.

Jared sleeping in the cellar of the church, and how she'd trailed her fingertips over his scars—*a bolt of rage, a hatred so intense—deeper and much more gruesome—something stabbed the flesh, twisted—cut the flesh, slashed with relentless force—Jared tortured—both scars from the same merciless hand.*

"You know, Lucy," Nicholas's pensive tone pulled her back again. "Matthew has such a deft hand. A sense of knowing just how far to go . . . how to make life linger in the worst possible way."

Oh, Matt, no . . . Matt, how could you . . . ?

She was vaguely aware of Nicholas coming toward her now. Of Nicholas stopping just inches from where she stood.

"We're fortunate to have Matthew, you and I. In fact, consider him my wedding gift to you. Think of him as your own personal . . . bodyguard."

Another chill worked its way up her spine.

But this time when she glanced at Matt, something seemed to glitter in those deep, blue eyes. His body was rigid. His face like stone.

"I can *trust* Matthew with such a personal matter, Lucy. Because he knows you belong to *me*. And *only* me."

"I don't belong to *anyone!*"

"Ah, but you want to. Oh, how *desperately* you want to belong to someone . . ."

A burning shiver replaced her chill. Nicholas was leaning into her, and against her, and murmuring in her ear.

"With me, you'll live forever. You'll have powers you never dreamed of . . . every wish you could ever want. You'll never grow old, and you'll never hurt, and you'll never be lonely again. Of all my brides, you shall be the one most treasured. And I will love you through eternity."

His voice was hypnotic. As Lucy tried to resist its spell, she felt his lips on the side of her neck, sending wave after wave of delicious sensations all the way through her.

"I know what you are," she said angrily. "I know all about you."

"Then know this. The fate of those you love rests on your decision."

Lucy's heart was pounding. With every deliberate touch of his lips, her blood flowed hotter and hotter.

"Even now," he confessed to her, "your friend Dakota lies languishing. One more bite . . . one more feeding . . . and she'll be diagnosed with a rare—and virtually unknown—blood disease. No doctor will know the origin, or how to treat it; the blood that contaminated her will never be found. And, unfortunately . . . there *is* no cure for this fast and fatal infection."

"Stop it!"

Tears ran down Lucy's cheeks. She sensed a movement from the corner of her eye, and heard Matt's voice beside them.

"Nicholas, think of what you're doing. Her willingness is compromised—she'll only end up destroying you."

"Keep out of this, Matthew." Nicholas's tone was hard. "I wouldn't advise your interference."

The points of his teeth skimmed delicately over her skin, feather-soft and needle-sharp. His hands moved swiftly, his touch as light as air.

"You'll save Dakota?" Lucy pleaded with him. "You'll save Byron?"

"I give you my word."

His kiss burned as Jared's had burned, only the pain was much worse, much deeper. With a sharp cry, she clutched at him, shuddering in fear and anticipation. His lips moved slowly down to her throat.

"Tell me that you want me, Lucy."

She was sobbing now, trying to choke out the words. "I . . . I want you."

A terrible howling cut through the darkness. Snarls and frantic barking as the creature—once Byron—now lunged from the end of its chain.

"Shut him up!" Nicholas snapped to Matt. "Or I'll put him down."

"No!" Lucy begged. "Please don't hurt him!"

"Take care of it, Matthew!"

There was a dull thud. A sharp cry, as the howling abruptly ended. Lucy was frantic.

"What did you do! What did you do to Byron?"

"Your choice, Lucy. Matthew can leave him blissfully unconscious . . . or put him blissfully into eternal sleep."

"I'll do anything you want!"

"Then give yourself to me."

Trembling, she prayed for some escape, some miracle, but there was nowhere to go. His arms were locked around her, forcing her to the floor. He nuzzled the sensitive hollow of her throat.

"Freely," he whispered. "Willingly. Give me your heart, Lucy . . . and your soul."

The pain was becoming unbearable; she couldn't catch her breath. He took his time. He tasted her need and despair.

"Yes, Lucy . . . that's right. See how easy it is . . . ?"

Let go . . . all I have to do is let go . . . it will all be over soon . . . over at last . . .

She struggled to resist him, to destroy him— she yearned to be one with him, and to live forever.

"Oh God," she wept, hating him, holding him.

"Love me, Lucy. Do it now."

40

She could feel his ageless strength and perfection a warrior's body, a knight, a king. He ripped the medallion from her neck. He caught both her hands and pinned them above her head.

"I want you to watch this, Matthew." Nicholas's voice flowed like black satin. "This kiss of immortality."

"No," Lucy whimpered. But over Nicholas's shoulder, she could see Matt standing close by, could see his pitiless eyes, intent on their every move.

Nicholas ran his tongue slowly up the side of her neck. "See how she hovers so delicately between this world and the next? This beautiful soul of hers, this broken heart of hers, just begging to be free?"

Matt said nothing. As Lucy twisted her head away, Nicholas gave a soft laugh.

"My kiss will free her, Matthew. My blood will flow with hers for all time. And witnessing Lucy's Transformation will be your punishment for falling in love with her."

His voice went suddenly cold; his grip tightened on Lucy's hands. Gasping in fear, she watched his dark, dead eyes flick from Matt's face to her own.

"Your job was to win Lucy's trust," Nicholas said calmly. "Report her every confidence to me. Know her movements day and night, and guard her with your life."

Matt! Had she screamed out loud or only in her head? She was biting so hard on her lip, and Nicholas was leaning over her, and she could taste blood—*his? mine?*—salty and sweet and sickening, on her lips and down the back of her throat. Her eyes squeezed shut, then opened again, and Matt was still there, still silent, still watching.

His eyes were more blue than she ever remembered.

Gleaming with tears through the candlelight.

Matt . . .

"Nicholas—" Matt began, but Nicholas cut him off with a mocking laugh.

"You touched her, Matthew. You kissed her. And you gave her *this*."

With scarcely an effort, Nicholas threw the medallion. It clattered across the floor and landed at Matt's feet.

"Did you think I wouldn't know? Just as you thought I wouldn't discover who summoned Jared here? Or who left that scarf for Lucy to find?"

Again that laugh, deep in his throat. A subtle shift of his body. A caress . . . like warm liquid.

"You gave Lucy your medallion," Nicholas went on. "Knowing that with it, she might be able to decipher our family history. And thus . . . once again you hoped to warn her."

Of course. *Of course!* Why hadn't she realized it? That every time she'd translated the journal, she'd been wearing Matt's medallion . . .

The medallion with the mysterious design . . .

"Someone gave me this a long time ago . . . it's helped me through some pretty rough times . . . it's an ancient holy symbol . . . I hope it'll be special to you."

As Matt's words drifted back to her, Lucy finally figured it out. The design on the medallion—the design imprinted on both Jared's and Nicholas's arms . . .

"I should kill you for this, Matthew," Nicholas went on calmly. "But this is a far worse—and painful—punishment. Don't you agree?"

With a defenseless moan, Lucy struggled beneath him. Matt's face was growing hazy, yet she could still see his eyes—those deep, blue eyes she recognized so well now—*Matt's* eyes gazing straight into hers—the guilt and shame and suffering, the hurt and regret—all reflected there in Matt's loving eyes.

"*Don't!*" Matt shouted.

Lucy saw his quick movement, but Nicholas sensed it sooner. Even as Matt reached them, Nicholas was already pulling away from her, with blood on his lips.

Lucy hadn't even felt the bite.

But she did hear the shock in Nicholas's voice, as his smile instantly froze in place.

"Jared," he hissed.

As though Matt were no more than a shadow, Nicholas threw him aside. Lucy heard the sickening thud of Matt's body hitting the wall, but it was this sudden change in Nicholas that terrified her even more. The look in his eyes as he glared down at her—not lustful any longer, but filled with wrath and loathing.

"Oh, clever girl. *Very clever girl.*"

"What?" Lucy cried. "I don't know what you're talking about!"

"His taste flows through you." Nicholas slammed her hard against the floor, hands above her head. "His vengeance is in your blood."

The impact of the floor had left her stunned. Her head was pounding—her arms felt twisted from their sockets.

"What sort of bargain did he make?" Nicholas demanded.

But Lucy could barely move. "No . . . no bargain—"

"*Liar!*" This time Lucy heard the crack of her skull against stone. The world blackened and spun around her.

"Let her go!" Matt's voice came from the other side of the room, as he struggled to his feet. "Her blood's been tainted far too much— she's of no use to you now."

It was as if Matt had never spoken. Nicholas's grip was ruthless—and unforgiving.

"We could have made this so easy, my love."

"Oh God . . . please . . ."

"And your friends might even have lived."

"No!"

His bite this time was vicious. It came swiftly, brutally, and Lucy shrieked in pain. In less than one heartbeat, she felt her skin being ripped, her flesh being torn, blood spurting from her throat. But Nicholas didn't drink. Furiously, he smeared Lucy's blood over her own face, on her lips and her neck, and through her hair.

Everything was fading. As if she were floating above herself . . . and the darkness was floating around her . . . and she and the darkness were one. She heard a muffled cry, a faraway scuffle of footsteps.

She saw a glimmer of jewels in the candlelight.

"Stand off, Matthew!" Nicholas's voice trembled with rage. "Or watch Lucy die."

There was a razor-sharp chill against her breast . . . a slow glide of steel across her heart . . .

"Let her go," Matt warned. "Or I'll kill you myself."

"You were the one behind this. Giving her to Jared, instead of *me*! *Sacrificing* Lucy for your own selfishness—"

"*Not* for myself—for *her*! I want her to *live*! I want her to be happy."

"She'll *never* be happy! I'll make her life a living hell! *And* yours!"

"Do you honestly think hell could be any worse than this?"

She sensed Matt moving closer. Nicholas tensing. A blade slicing cold through her skin . . . blood oozing hot from her chest . . .

"Well then, Matthew." Nicholas sounded pleased. "Since you long so badly for Lucy's heart . . . let me just give it to you."

41

Oh my God . . . I'm dying . . . he's cutting out my heart.

There was no pain. Lucy felt only a slight pressure trailing along her skin. From the furthest edges of consciousness, she sensed what was happening, yet was powerless to stop it.

I must be bleeding. Getting weaker. Soon I'll go to sleep, and be at peace.

As in a dream, Matt's voice drifted out to her, soft and sad.

"I have nothing to lose now, Nicholas. So understand this—I *will* kill you."

"You?" Nicholas's tone was mocking. "Granted, I can only be killed by One of my own kind. But braver and stronger men than you have done their best throughout my lifetimes. And all of them met very gruesome ends."

"This lifetime will be different."

"Only for you, I fear."

But before Matt could answer, another voice spoke unexpectedly from the darkness. "If there is to be a battle tonight, that battle will be mine."

It came from the shadowed doorway of the mausoleum, and Lucy knew she should recognize it . . . knew she'd been close to it before . . .

"Jared." For the second time, that name hung bitter on Nicholas's lips. And as Lucy moaned, Jared's reply echoed calmly through the gloom.

"Fair trade," he said. "My life for Lucy's."

"*No* trade. Lucy's life is nearly over anyway. Where's the sport in that?"

"Let Matthew take her out of here. Then you and I shall decide the future, once and for all."

An expectant silence filled the room. The pressure on her chest began to ease.

"You have the dagger," Jared reminded him. "A definite advantage."

"Ah, yes. The one and only weapon that can strike the fatal blow."

"And isn't this what you've been wanting?

The chance to finally settle things between us? To face your own flesh and blood?"

"I've taken enough of your flesh and blood throughout the centuries. I'd think by now you'd be tired of all that suffering."

"I *am* tired, Nicholas. That's the whole point. I'm tired of these endless plots and conspiracies. I'm tired of the hatred that divides us. I want it to end. I'm tired, and I want it to be over. One way or the other."

Once more, a long, deep silence. Lucy could feel the tension in the air, the wariness and suspicion and hostility.

"You're in love with her," Nicholas said at last. "You're in love with Lucy."

Jared's voice softened. "We have an agreement, then, you and I. A battle to the finish."

"With pleasure."

"Matthew," Jared instructed, "take Lucy to a safe place."

Again Lucy sensed movement. She was being wrapped in something warm, something that smelled of comfort and reassurance. Matt's arms around her, lifting her from the floor.

Matt's shoulder beneath her cheek . . . Matt's lips against her hair . . .

Matt's sharp, sudden gasp.

His choke of agony and surprise.

Something warm spraying over her face, and the world falling around her, turning upside down . . .

"Matt!"

A rush of horror surged through her—a rush of truth and inescapable doom—rushing stronger than adrenaline, flooding her with a cold and cruel certainty.

Matt's grip had loosened, though he was still holding her. His movements were clumsy and awkward, though he still carried her in his arms. His shoulders slumped; his expression went dazed. And as he staggered determinedly toward Jared, he began weaving from side to side, with strange sounds coming from his throat.

Wheezing . . .

Gurgling . . .

Jared was watching them, but not moving. Like a statue of bleached stone, his eyes were wide, his mouth open in shock.

With a strangled cry, Matt stumbled and pitched forward. Only this time, Lucy felt him slip away.

"*Matt! No!*"

"One down," Nicholas hissed. "One to go."

And suddenly Jared was running toward her, and Lucy could hear the echo of Nicholas's laughter from every rotting tomb, and Matt was crumpling slowly to the floor.

"Take her," Matt pleaded, but the words turned to liquid in his throat . . . those thick, bubbling sounds in his throat. "Jared . . . take Lucy—"

"What's *wrong*!" Lucy screamed. "*Do* something!"

She could see Matt crawling, dragging himself between her and Nicholas, even as Jared snatched her away. Matt couldn't seem to lift his head. Each anguished breath grew more frantic, more faint, and something wet oozed out beneath his face across the stones.

"*Please*, Jared! *Help him!*"

But there wasn't time. Nicholas was already standing over Matt, his temper calm now, and eerily composed. His eyes were narrowed, his expression bland. He gazed down at his only friend with an almost detached curiosity.

And then Lucy saw his lips begin to quiver . . . the quick glint of tears in his eyes . . .

He slammed his boot down on the back of Matt's skull.

The soft explosion of brain and bone was far worse than the screams echoing in her mind— the shattering of her memories, the crushing of her hopes, the breaking of her heart. She didn't remember Jared carrying her, or finding herself alone in the doorway of the mausoleum. Her next conscious awareness was of the fierce battle being played out before her.

Like a terrible nightmare, there was no sense of reality.

No sense of logic . . . no sense of time.

It happened too fast, and it moved in slow motion.

Those tall, dark silhouettes, so much alike, wrestling among the shadows. Sworn enemies in a fight to the finish—bound by blood and ageless codes of honor. Their shouts of rage and regret. Their centuries like yesterdays, all bitterness and blame, brutality and betrayals.

Furious and fearless and far too late for forgetting.

As Lucy watched them, it was suddenly as though she were watching herself. Her own desperate struggle for what might have been in the past—for what could be in the future.

Standing there in that doorway between life and death . . . on that tenuous threshold of two different worlds . . . Lucy made her decision.

Without a word, she began moving painfully toward Jared.

It's not too late—I can *still* stand with him! I can still help him win!

But before she could reach him, something flashed through the dark and caught the candlelight. *A dagger?* Lucy froze and held her breath, every sense on edge, every muscle taut.

She heard a cry, and she knew it was Jared's. Her soul shrank with terror, yet she forced herself to keep going.

"Jared!"

"Run, Lucy! You're not safe here!"

"I'll never be safe anywhere until he's *dead*!"

Resolve gave her courage; resolve drove her on. She could see Jared struggling to his feet, slipping in blood, his clothes saturated with it, his body torn from a dozen savage wounds.

Just like the first day I met him . . . the day he came into my life . . .

Except for the dagger, she realized.

The dagger she glimpsed just briefly now, clenched flat against his palm, with its blade hidden up inside his sleeve.

Nicholas was hunting for it.

He was turned away from Jared, and his eyes probed every corner, every crypt, every inch of blackness, before finally coming to rest on her.

And then he smiled. A cold, smug smile of victory.

"You're right, Lucy. You'll never be safe from me. For I plan on living a very long and endless life."

In less than a heartbeat, he grabbed her and pulled her against him. She never saw him move, and he never noticed the shadow stir behind him.

And when Lucy pushed—just one quick, violent shove—Nicholas didn't even have time to feel surprise.

There was a gleam of silver.

A glimmer of priceless jewels.

The cold swish of steel through darkness.

And then the hideous cry—the ungodly shriek of tortured souls and twisted hearts and sins neither felt nor forgiven.

Dying into the silence . . .

Snuffing out the candles, one by one.

42

"Jared?"

"Yes, Lucy, I'm here."

"Is he..."

Jared's voice broke. "I never wanted it to end this way."

Her arms went around him, pulling him close. *And this isn't what I expected,* Lucy realized—*I didn't think I'd feel sad. Not after all I've been through, not after all the things Nicholas has done...*

Yet now, as she and Jared held tight to each other, she felt a strange and disturbing emptiness.

Here in the quiet, in the shadows, that sense of unreality came flooding back again. As though none of this had ever happened. As if these last terrifying weeks of her life had been nothing more than a dream.

"But *you're* real," she whispered to Jared at last.

Without warning, a faint breeze drifted through the mausoleum. A hint of fresh air and clean snow . . . the promise of a new dawn. It seemed to clear away the stench of death, flickering the candles to life again and pushing back the darkness.

She felt the beating of Jared's heart, in time with her own; she felt the slow, easy mingling of their blood. And she suddenly remembered that Dakota was here . . . and Byron . . . and . . .

"*Matt!* Oh God, Jared, we've got to help him! We've got to get you and Dakota to a doctor—"

"Dakota will recover, Lucy. And I don't need a doctor . . . only time to rest."

"But what about—"

She broke off abruptly at the sight of Nicholas on the floor beside them. Those lusterless eyes staring up at her . . . those pitiless features in such calm repose. After so many lifetimes of evil, the cruel lines had finally faded from his forehead and around his mouth, leaving him with an expression that was almost vulnerable. In spite of herself, Lucy choked back tears. She forced herself to look away.

"I want to see Matt," she whispered.

"Lucy . . ."

"There might still be something we can do!"

"You know there's not. You know that."

But Lucy wouldn't listen. She could see where Matt had fallen, and before Jared could stop her, she walked over to the familiar figure lying facedown on the stones.

"Oh, Matt . . ."

The dark, wet stain had widened around him—had soaked his clothes and hair, had pooled beneath his head.

"Lucy, please don't."

But she was already cradling Matt in her arms, turning Matt's face to the light.

His throat had been cut from ear to ear.

Slashed so deeply that his head was nearly severed.

"Matt . . ."

She held him, and she rocked him . . . stroking his pale, white cheeks . . . smoothing the clotted hair from his brow. His face was at peace, his eyes eternally blue. And as her kiss warmed his ice-cold lips for just an instant, she could almost imagine he smiled.

"I'll take care of him, Lucy."

"Take care of him?" Her tone was doubtful, though not unkind. "Matt was one of your very worst enemies."

"Matthew chose to be your protector. And I have no more enemies. I'll take care of him for you. I promise."

He offered Lucy his hand. After several long moments, she lowered Matt gently to his resting place and allowed Jared to help her up.

"So what happens now?" Lucy asked him.

Yet even before he could answer, a thousand emotions flooded through her—ripping at her heart—making her sick and lonely and afraid. Afraid of the truth. Afraid because she already knew.

Jared turned away from her. "We go back to our lives."

"Our lives?" Lucy couldn't decide whether to laugh or to cry. "*This* has been my life since I came to Pine Ridge! *All this* has been my life! And now Gran's gone, and my mother's gone, and Irene and Angela and—"

She broke off, overcome again with the reality of her situation. She could feel Jared watching her, could feel his raw determination to keep distance between them.

"Dakota's a good friend, Lucy. She needs you. And you need her."

"And Byron?"

Jared seemed to be carefully choosing his words. "Byron's one of us. A descendant of the Wetherly royal bloodline. He needs to be with his own kind. To complete his Transformation, to live as he's meant to live, just as other Wetherlys have done for hundreds of years."

A painful lump formed in her throat. Lucy tried hard to choke it down.

"Will . . . Byron remember me?"

Reluctantly, Jared came toward her. He cupped her face in his hands, solemnly searching her eyes.

"Byron will remember you. We never forget the ones we've loved . . . no matter the miles or the centuries."

A brittle silence fell between them. It was Lucy who finally broke it.

"Let me come with you, Jared."

"Lucy—"

"Please! After all we've been through—"

"After all we've been through, how can you even say that to me?" Turning abruptly, Jared began to pace. Back and forth among the shadows, impatient now, and angry. "We belong in two different places, you and I. We belong in two different *worlds*!"

"But I'm *part* of your world, don't you see? I'm part of *you*! Nicholas said it himself—that your blood flows through my veins—"

"As does his!" Genuinely frustrated, Jared ran a hand back through his hair. "Lucy, this . . . consummation . . . is a *sacrifice*. A sacrifice no mortal is ever prepared to make—or should ever be *expected* to make! Your life would never be the same. *You* would never be the same."

"But I'm *already* not the same! When Nicholas said it, I didn't want to believe him—except now I know he was right! There *are* changes in me—things I'm noticing more and more each day! I can sense things no one else can even see, I'm aware of things before they even happen. Smells and tastes and feelings and instincts I never had before. Because of Nicholas! Because of Katherine and Byron and—"

"Living as one of us is a lot more than being

able to sniff your way home." Jared's lips twisted, a wry attempt at humor. "It takes time to develop your powers . . . and even more time to perfect them."

"You mean lifetimes."

"Yes. *Many* lifetimes."

"Then what's going to happen to me? If I'm *part* of both worlds, but *between* them?"

"Oh Lucy, you're young and naïve. You don't know anything about our world—and very little about this one. How can you possibly choose—*wisely*—if you haven't even experienced your life *here* yet?"

"I know that I love your goodness," she answered without hesitation. "And Byron's goodness. And that if you hadn't shared your blood with me tonight, I probably wouldn't be alive right now. Because your goodness gave me the strength to fight Nicholas."

"It's not goodness, Lucy—can't you finally see that in spite of everything else? We're the outcasts of time—we're souls beyond redemption. We do what we need to do in order to survive. It has nothing to do with good or evil—it's simply our nature."

Jared's voice was trembling. He gazed down at the dagger still clutched in his hand. He dragged it slowly, purposefully, across his thigh, wiping off the last of Nicholas's blood.

"I want you to have a good life." He spoke so softly, she could barely hear. "I want you to be happy. I want you—"

He stopped. A muscle clenched in his jaw.

"I want you to be loved. Even though I . . . oh God, how I wanted to be the one to love you."

Lucy flung herself into his arms. Holding him as if she'd never let him go—his fevered kisses and moan of desire, the desperate crush of his embrace—

"Jared, please—please take me—"

"You have no idea what you're asking."

"I know exactly what I'm asking. I know exactly what I want."

And she was floating . . . floating . . . lost in his passion and need for her . . . safe in her love for him . . . breathless . . . joyous . . . his lips caressing her . . . tasting her skin . . . her bruises . . . her hurts . . . her tears . . .

"But you never know exactly what you have," Jared whispered, "with a shape-shifter."

His body pressed tighter. His eyes fixed on hers.

Amber eyes, Lucy thought dreamily, gazing back at him. *I remember . . . Jared had amber eyes . . .*

Not like these eyes staring back at her . . .

Eyes of many colors and timeless shades . . . swirling and fading . . . glowing sharp and waning sad—*ocean blue green and gold endless midnight black* . . .

"Jared?"

And a faraway haze of confusion . . . a helpless haze of confusion . . .

"This is what you wanted, Lucy."

"Jared . . . wait . . ."

"And you trust me, don't you?"

"Yes . . . yes . . . but . . ."

"That's right . . . come with me . . ."

His voice flowed over her like silk . . . over her and through her . . . sweet like perfume . . . warm like blood . . .

As he tilted her head . . .

And smoothed back her hair . . .

And sank his teeth in her throat.